SIX
TRUTHS
AND A
LIE

ALSO BY REAM SHUKAIRY

The Next New Syrian Girl

SIX TRUTHS AND A LIE

REAM SHUKAIRY

LITTLE, BROWN AND COMPANY
New York   Boston

Little, Brown and Company
Hachette Book Group
1290 Avenue of the Americas, New York, NY 10104
Visit us at LBYR.com

First Edition: March 2024

Little, Brown and Company is a division of Hachette Book Group, Inc. The Little, Brown name and logo are trademarks of Hachette Book Group, Inc.

Little, Brown and Company books may be purchased in bulk for business, educational, or promotional use. For information, please contact your local bookseller or the Hachette Book Group Special Markets Department at special.markets@hbgusa.com.

Library of Congress Cataloging-in-Publication Data
Names: Shukairy, Ream, author.
Title: Six truths and a lie / Ream Shukairy.
Description: First edition. | New York : Little, Brown and Company, 2024. | Audience: Ages 12–18. | Summary: Told in their separate voices, six Muslim teens are falsely accused of an alleged attack on a Los Angeles beach and must trust or turn their backs on each other to prove their innocence.
Identifiers: LCCN 2023006661 | ISBN 9780316564595 (hardcover) | ISBN 9780316564618 (ebook)
Subjects: CYAC: Muslims—Fiction. | Prejudices—Fiction. | Explosions—Fiction. | Secrets—Fiction. | Los Angeles (Calif.)—Fiction. | Mystery and detective stories. | LCGFT: Detective and mystery fiction. | Novels.
Classification: LCC PZ7.1.S51797 Si 2024 | DDC [Fic]—dc23
LC record available at https://lccn.loc.gov/2023006661

ISBNs: 978-0-316-56459-5 (hardcover), 978-0-316-56461-8 (ebook)

Printed in the United States of America

LSC-C

Printing 1, 2024

To Bushra and Tessniem,
and to the boldness of our sisterhood

PROLOGUE

Unbelievable is an antonym of itself. So suspend disbelief for a sec.

Your younger sister taking the last cookie is unbelievable. Spilling coffee in the car is unbelievable. Often, what we call unbelievable is too believable.

Unbelievable was Samia getting stuck in traffic on the 10 along with everyone else running late for their Independence Day parties.

Unbelievable was the Fuel Tank Low light on Abdullahi's Civic, which he wished was a 1967 Chevy.

Unbelievable was Nasreen arriving too early to the bonfire because she had to respect her parents' curfew.

Unbelievable was Qays flouncing around the beach shirtless, flaunting his muscles in the late-afternoon sun.

Unbelievable was Muzhda twiddling her thumbs, pretending not to take a peek at the boys.

Unbelievable was Zamzam having to chaperone her little brother at this ridiculous bonfire.

None of that, in actuality, was unbelievable.

Unbelievable was a war on an idea.

Unbelievable was a terrorist attack that wasn't.

Unbelievable was a cop shooting a teenage boy for holding a cell phone.

Unbelievable was six strangers ending a bitterly ironic Fourth of July in holding cells.

For those six, *unbelievable* ceased to exist in their lexicon. The Independence Day Six could be saved by the truth, but only if they managed to get others to believe it. Believing is seeing, and sometimes justice chooses not to see. Sometimes the circles in the Venn diagram of truth and justice fail to overlap.

In a way, the truth has come to be an antonym of itself.

For the Six, the truth and the lie—what is believed and what is not—made no difference.

Samia. Nasreen. Qays. Muzhda. Abdullahi. Zamzam.

Believe them.

CHAPTER 1

NASREEN

MONARCH BEACH WAS CROWNED LOS ANGELES COUNTY'S safest beach three years in a row.

That was what Nasreen told her parents to gain a whopping fifteen-minute extension to her curfew, ringing in at the ever-desirable 10:00 PM.

Though she was thrilled with the extension at first, arriving at the beach quickly fizzled her excitement. The MSA's Inter–High School Independence Day Bonfire Spectacular wouldn't get going until around the time she'd have to head home. Her parents stood by their curfew even though she explained to them that this was a Muslim event for Muslims, hosted by several Muslim Students Associations. Repeating the word *Muslim* that many times should've confirmed her safety to her mama and baba, yet it didn't get her any more leeway.

She trudged away from the boardwalk and over to the sand, sunshine blending into orange as the sun drew farther away from the earth. The chilly night breeze from the months of May and June lingered into these first days of July. She held her elbows tighter and kicked herself for not bringing a jacket despite her mama's reminder.

As she approached the bonfire pits, she stopped near a boy with an impressive beard for a high schooler and a tank top that flashed a big *USA* in neon red and blue. He glanced up, cocking his eyebrow at her.

"Here to help set up?" the boy asked, hoisting a bright blue cooler onto a foldable table like it weighed nothing. Though twice her height, he looked her age, and his parents likely also came from one of the nooks and crannies of South Asia. "Hey, don't I know you?"

Nasreen shook her head in disbelief. Or perhaps belief.

She was certain he hadn't seen her around; no one here had ever seen her except maybe in passing at one of the mosques in the city. She definitely wasn't on a setup committee, nor a cleanup one, nor a planning one. Nasreen was a spectator, spectating, but more specifically waiting for someone to arrive for a conversation that had to be had. She'd delayed it long enough, and now she couldn't keep living with the discomfort of her secrets. Secrets made her irritable and want to throw up. And the more this boy watched her, the more her temper shortened and her stomach gurgled. Perhaps that was just her hunger because she hadn't been able to eat all day. Or it was anxiety about how she would find her way out of the hole she'd dug herself into. She usually had a knack for hiding away at the first sign of trouble, but this time was different. This time she'd created the trouble, and confronting it—or rather her—made her feel hot and itchy.

Just try to enjoy the festivities for a little while.

The boy emptied the cooler, full of an egregious amount of halal hot dogs, onto the table. "Are you from Monarch Beach High?"

He was hell-bent on conversation.

Nasreen pushed her black-rimmed glasses up along the bridge of her nose like she always did when she was nervous. She was never good at talking to boys.

"No," she replied, though she recognized some of the faces of Monarch Beach High School from the masjid. "I go to Saint Modesta High."

"Oooh, drip." He raised his fist to his mouth and looked like he'd just eaten a spoonful of cayenne pepper. "Are you, like, the only Muslim there?"

That's the first time I've heard that one, thought Nasreen. The lack of originality was precisely why she didn't bother with boys. She rolled her eyes in response.

"Here, you can help with the dogs," he offered, but Nasreen made no move to help. He paused, tongs in one hand and a bag of coal in the other. "Or, um, you can help at the Huntington pit next door, or the Valley pit to our left. Sorry, Saint Modesta didn't cut it for our bonfire this year. Not enough representation over there, if you know what I mean."

Nasreen covered her smirk with her hand. Saint Modesta High School was a private Catholic school with a high acceptance rate to Ivy League schools. For all her sixteen years, including the choice of her high school, Nasreen's parents had prepped her for Ivy League greatness. Or perhaps pretentiousness.

All it did for Nasreen was make her the token Muslim Desi girl in any of the friend groups that she was invited into at school. Eventually, she decided that sometimes it was better to be alone.

"I thought this bonfire was about bringing the schools together, not dividing us," Nasreen said.

He snorted. "You'll catch my drift once everyone else shows up."

As Nasreen traveled between the groups, hot-dog boy's comment started making sense.

There were three pits. The farthest north was Huntington High School's firepit, and going south were Monarch Beach, then Valley. An invisible wall separated the groups. The prefix *inter-* in the title of the event didn't require that the schools mixed, so they didn't. Excluding the students assigned to various committees, Nasreen was the only one who breached the invisible borders.

She skirted around the pits, starting with Valley, where they had Maria Cookies instead of graham crackers, then tiptoeing around MB, where there were too many coolers to count and students were wildly overdressed for the beach, and finally arriving at Huntington's pit, where the students lounged on blankets and kept it laid-back. Not a cocktail party like MB and not a rave like Valley. Huntington's vibe was just chillin'.

For what felt like a full day but was only fifteen minutes, Nasreen searched the beach like a fish out of water. Her stomach growled, and she picked at her nails relentlessly.

"Hey, Saint Modesta!"

Nasreen shut her eyes, searching for patience under her eyelids. It was the first boy, from MB. The boy with the hot dogs. He dropped off a cooler, spreading the wealth of the more affluent students of MB. The social-class cues hadn't gone unnoticed.

Nasreen flashed him a look. Perhaps a snarl at the nickname. "What is it?"

He quirked his brows. "You're making your rounds. I knew you were cut out for a committee."

That was the problem. Nasreen knew she fit the mold of committee member because she was consistently on one or two committees year-round. She wanted to loosen up for one night, to stop calculating the appropriate participation in high school events needed to avoid the title of high school outcast.

"Sup, Choudhry."

Nasreen and hot-dog boy both turned their heads at the last name, but no one meant to call her. No one here even knew her, not yet at least. Turning back, he smirked at her. "Hope we're not cousins."

Nasreen really didn't need this Choudhry chatting her up. She slipped away and continued her search, arching her neck to get a glimpse of hijabis' faces as the wind whipped up their scarves. But however many times she circled, her someone didn't show up. Another quarter of an hour passed, and Nasreen's heart raced. Did she let something slip in her messages? Had she already been caught?

The sun was properly setting now, and the oranges melted into the pinks into the purples into the light blues. Though the colors deepened and darkened into the night, there was plenty of light left in the day.

Sunset dared to last forever.

"Heads up!"

Nasreen glanced in the direction of the warning. A football

7

whacked full force against the side of her head. A sound like her glasses cracking foreboded a sharp pain from behind her ear where the temple tip pressed into her tender skin. Luckily, her glasses were indestructible, as proven by all the cracks, snaps, and whacks they'd taken.

"My bad."

As her head began to throb, the boy grabbed the ball and ran back over to his friends. She had a few choice words that she didn't use. Nasreen's teachers and classmates described her as having monk-like patience. In any case, it wasn't the fault of the kid who didn't catch the overthrown ball, but the dude who threw it. Nasreen stared at the shirtless guy, who snickered with his other topless buddies beside the MB pit. For all Nasreen's patience, she had a practiced glare that spoke volumes. The shirtless guy maintained his no-apology stance, not even providing a polite bow of the head to her. He gave her a cocky shrug from his ten yards away. For a second, she wished she could punch him right in his glistening white pecs, but she willed that thought away.

"You okay?" Somehow Choudhry found her again. He followed her glare. "Don't worry about Qays. He's cool. Last year he took our school all the way to the soccer CIF state championship and—"

"I'm gonna stop you there," she said as she looked away from the arrogant so-called high school star named Qays and promptly erased his name from her memory. "He's just another terrorist to me."

Choudhry choked on laughter. "Should we unpack that?"

"No," Nasreen scoffed. "Don't act like you and your friends don't call each other terrorists on a daily basis."

Every Muslim teenager called their friends terrorists at one time or another. It was ownership of a slur reappropriated as a joke. And the cycle of rebranding continued. At least, that was what Nasreen told herself.

Choudhry accepted this with a shrug.

"I'm going for a walk," Nasreen said finally. "If I don't come back before my curfew, don't bother telling my parents. I'll just never go back home."

He knit his brows, though his smile appreciated the quip. "How would I know your parents?"

"Cousins, remember, Choudhry?"

He flashed her an easy grin, and she wondered if she came across as abrasive as she felt inside. So many years of being the only Pakistani American in her classes had made her exceptional at hiding the brash side of herself so that she could be warm and approachable. But on the inside she felt coarse and cold. When she was with others who looked like her, she unraveled into the harshest parts of her.

Precious seconds ticked by as Nasreen walked north, past the pits, to the lavish beach homes that dotted the cliffside.

Maybe this bonfire would be a total mistake. Nasreen was trying to set things right, but everything could blow up in her face. Nasreen hoped that her plans weren't all for nothing, because despite acting the model student, she had one or two secrets of her own.

Looking back at the pits, she knew without a doubt that she wasn't the only one.

CHAPTER 2

Q~AYS~

HIGH SCHOOLERS IN AND AROUND LA REGARDED QAYS AS a specimen of raw yet sculpted beauty.

Qays knew this. Light brown hair preened into curls with a fade: the trademarked Arab fuckboi hairstyle. Soccer, weight lifting, and hookah: the patented Arab fuckboi hobbies. A killer smile and charming stubble interrupted by his strongly hooked nose: courtesy of his Levantine roots, which, some might argue, was where Arab fuckbois originated.

No one minded Qays's burly nose, not even him. Humans found absolute perfection unnerving anyway. Qays's nose set him apart, and he embraced it. His indifference toward it made him more alluring, and he knew that too.

He was also aware that he wasn't obligated to apologize to the girl with the glasses who had been standing in the line of his throw. As high school royalty, he didn't need to adhere to social niceties, and so he didn't.

Qays always did what he wanted, and anything he didn't want, he did only if it needed to be done. He didn't care much for what others expected of him, but he was the high school soccer phenomenon with the 4.4 GPA, the soon-to-be senior with express interest from Stanford men's soccer and a scholarship on the table, so he never fell short of expectations. Rather, he dabbled in the sport of exceeding them.

It wasn't that Qays needed Stanford with all the schools and soccer programs scrambling to get on *his* wait list, but the added interest never hurt.

Qays loved added interest.

Like the girls. So many girls. He heard their giggles as he passed, smelled the lingering vanilla scent every time he turned corners. But no matter how many girls lined up for him, no matter how much flirting came about naturally for him, he hadn't taken the step to really date any of them. Not yet anyway. His thoughts on that subject were still undetermined.

Omar, Qays's carbon copy in the acceptable best-friend kind of way, gestured to the collection of girls from MB, Valley, and Huntington spying him, disguising their smiles behind feathery fingers. "Your fan club keeps growing. They're coming from all over."

Qays barked a laugh, catching the football one-handed. "What can I say? I have a wide range of influence."

"What happens when you curve all of them for Kelsey?"

Qays's mouth perked up with a naughty grin. "Who the hell is Kelsey?"

"There'll be a Kelsey," Omar said, shoving his friend.

But Qays didn't think there would be. For all his Adonis good looks, he knew Adonis came from Lebanon and was the son of a king of Syria, where Qays's grandparents lived after the Palestinian diaspora in the '60s. He'd be true to Adonis's roots, not pander to the white narrative just because it was easier.

He didn't remember these facts solely to bag the 5 on his AP Art History exam; he knew them because Qays committed his legacy to memory. His Arab blood ran thick.

"Yo, what time is it?" Omar asked the boys. The sun, like everything in LA, was moving fast.

"Blunt o'clock," Qays muttered, taking the cue. Omar passed him the soccer ball this time, and Qays walked closer to the squad of spectators.

He turned up his charm, from where it rested at medium all the way to high. Flicking the soccer ball up and juggling it, he hit it with some around the worlds and crossovers, toe bounces and knee catches in between for fun. He gathered admiration from his growing audience, dazzling with 360 turns and hamstring catches and hops. He kept his head down, not because he needed to concentrate for these simple tricks but because it made him look like he was doing this for his enjoyment alone. *Yeah, right.*

When he finished, he gave an exaggerated bow for the applause as his excuse to survey the crowd. His eyes landed on one girl, and he was immediately drawn to her.

She stood aside from the others, overlooked, inconsequential. Everything about her demeanor whispered *lackluster*. She was slight in stature despite her height and willowy frame. If Qays hadn't thought she was vaguely familiar, he might not have seen her at all.

He stalked over, the collective whispers not nearly as amusing as the grunts and huffs around him. Because Qays had chosen, and she should not have been his type.

"Hey, don't I know you?" he asked, sneaking a peek at her. Girls liked confident, shy boys, and he was practiced in being this contradiction.

She nodded almost imperceptibly. After several attempts to clear her voice, she managed, "You tutored me last year."

"Oh, right!" He snapped his fingers and locked eyes with her, tugging at his memories. "I remember you." Though Qays's charm was on its highest level, he wasn't lying. Last year, his AP English teacher asked them to choose between doing a semester-long research project or tutoring English language learners at an after-school program at Valley High. Of course, Qays had chosen to tutor students over hours of research and writing a fifteen-page report. So for the first semester of his junior year, he spent evenings helping students write essays about the most obscure things, from their favorite meals to their worst experiences. And since most of the students were refugees, the stories were pretty heavy.

"You do?" she asked, her tone hopeful.

Qays felt like he did, but it had been a while and he couldn't help but be a flirt. "Of course. But just for fun, remind me your name."

"I'm Muzhda," she said, her mouth relaxing into a smile. Qays's chest squeezed, and he felt himself smile against his will. He was surprised he hadn't remembered her quicker. She had distinct, artfully drawn brows that eased away from each other, and her parted lips revealed the slight gap between her two front teeth. Her scarf swept around her gaunt face, allowing peeks at her soft brown hair. Her face was carved and chiseled in the most unexpected places. *Beautifully*, Qays thought; she had the unique face of a model who wasn't necessarily pretty, but whose stark features transformed gracefully as the eyes grew accustomed. She was beautiful.

He recalled he'd noticed her charms when he first sat with her over an essay about her first pet. Time went quickly for Qays; people passed him like the pages of a book flipping in the wind. But her smile brought her back to him all at once.

Beauty wasn't a monolith. Qays had the good looks that littered Instagram. Muzhda had the editorial allure of *Vogue*.

He'd made a mistake. He usually picked out strangers whom no one noticed. From afar, Muzhda in a plain black dress cinched at her waist was unmemorable. But face-to-face, the ruby-gem belt around her waist ricocheted light, and a part of her glittered like lightning.

Qays noted how her eyelashes were so long they touched the hood of her eyes.

"This is awkward." Muzhda giggled, and her copper skin flushed. "I guess you don't remember me."

He regretted choosing Muzhda now, but he couldn't take it back. *It'll be fine*, he thought. *This is routine.*

Qays recuperated. "No, no, I promise I remember you. I just wanted to see if you could do a favor for me." He glanced down. Glanced up. Bit his lip.

The red on Muzhda's cheeks matched her belt. Qays knew she'd blush just like that—he was a fuckboi, after all—but he didn't expect his own cheeks to feel warm too. By the end of the first semester last year, he'd started to look forward to tutoring Muzhda, and it seemed his body hadn't forgotten those feelings, even if his mind had.

"A favor?" Muzhda shook her shoulders, maybe in a shudder, maybe in an am-I-awake moment.

He shrugged. "You seem trustworthy." *And a good deal enamored.*

She squinted at him, eyes searching. "MB's soccer star asking a favor from a Valley girl?"

Qays frowned at the unfortunate nickname for female students at Valley. The traditional Valley Girl came from affluent suburbs and was nothing like the Valley girls of Valley High, the skid row of LA high schools. Usually Qays wouldn't think twice about it, but hearing it from Muzhda made him uncomfortable.

The world was full of contradictions. Like Qays's draw to Muzhda. Yet here he was, so captivated that it puzzled him.

She leaned close, and he got a whiff of rose. Not the vanilla he'd expected.

"I assume the favor involves danger." Muzhda's voice rumbled.

Qays searched for his voice.

"Or crime?"

He swallowed hard.

She leaned away and waved a hand around her. "Because there are plenty of MB girls here to do your bedding—I mean bidding." She roared with laughter.

Qays fought his perplexity and wondered how he'd put her out of his mind so easily last year. "What can I say? You fit the job description perfectly."

"Not sure if you're being racist or classist."

Qays flashed a celebrity smile. "Neither. I wouldn't ask you to do anything I wouldn't do myself."

Muzhda's eyes, which he noted were an ancient shade of hazel, narrowed. "Then why not do it yourself? Sorry, the Valley/MB crossover doesn't compute for me," she said with a lift of her chin. "Not when you're adding that to the Afghan/Arab mix and the jock/nobody mix. Something's up."

"Nothing's up."

"I'm not an idiot, Qays."

He *had* made a mistake. His errand runners were always submissive, eager-to-please, already-in-love-with-him strangers. He excelled at picking them out of a crowd. But Muzhda was none of those.

He was flummoxed, in more ways than one. Not since the seventh grade had a stranger had this much control over his primal senses. And he felt foolish that in trying to find the demurest girl, he'd stumbled upon a girl who was more than a pretty face vying for his attention. If this were *The Bachelor*, he would need only one rose, and he would hand it right over to her if she said his name one more time.

These feelings were fast and foreign to him. But he couldn't back out now. He needed to fully commit. His boys' night depended on it.

"Can't I just be chatting you up?" he asked, deepening his voice. "Reconnecting with one of my students?"

"Sounds unlikely."

"Say I thought you were the prettiest girl here."

"I'd call you a liar."

"But you are the prettiest girl here." And not a word of that was a lie. His heart even skipped a beat. *The traitor.*

She blushed. "Save it for the others."

"Don't act like you weren't watching me from the moment I arrived."

"I specialize in long-distance cute-boy observation, but I'm not trying to go to second base like some of us." She cocked an eyebrow at him.

He placed his hand over his bare chest, right over his heart, and Muzhda's gaze shamelessly followed it. "Are you calling me a player?"

She bit her lip to suppress a smile. "I hear the rumors."

Qays grinned. He was enjoying himself too much, a big no-no with errand runners. He didn't deny the rumors, though that was all that they were. He watched her, forgetting himself.

Muzhda swayed under his stare. "So, about that favor?"

"Oh, that." Qays didn't want her to go. He was starting to think the errand wasn't worth it anymore. A part of him didn't mind bantering with Muzhda all night by the fire, but Omar and his other friends were waiting on him. So he went for it. "There's a package in locker 208 by the bathrooms. Do you think you could get it for me?"

Muzhda pouted slightly, and it did a number on Qays's imagination. "That's it?"

"That's it."

"What's in the package?" she asked.

"It's best you don't know," he replied.

"It's safe?"

"As much as it is legal."

They exchanged grins.

Muzhda acted coy. "Then why can't you get it yourself?"

He spread his arms out like *Christ the Redeemer*. "Wouldn't want to taint that soccer-star image."

She smirked. "Because your image is such a white sheet."

"My parents think so."

Muzhda rolled her eyes and slipped something off her wrist. She dropped it into Qays's open palm.

"What's this?" he asked, passing it between his hands. It was a plain bracelet, beads alternating black and red, just like her outfit. Circular white beads spelled out MUZHDA, finished off with a heart-shaped gem.

"Wear it," she ordered.

Qays hesitated.

"I'm not stupid," she explained. "I'm not getting your mystery, maybe dangerous, quasi-legal package if you don't have the courage to wear a bracelet with my name on it."

Qays could only smirk to hide his jaw dropping.

"Think of it as collateral," she added.

"For you or me?"

"Both."

He wore the bracelet, and she smiled, her eyes bright. At least Qays knew she enjoyed his company just as much as he did hers.

She turned to hide her smile, inching away slowly. "I'll go get your package, and we'll make the swap."

"It's 11-31-07."

"Your birthday?" Her eyes sparkled.

"November only has thirty days."

Muzhda stuck her tongue out at him, and Qays felt like his brain melted out of his ears a little.

He recomposed himself. "It's the combination."

Muzhda faced him as she walked backward toward the Valley pit, toward the pier and the lockers. "Locker 208, 11-31-07. See you in a bit, Qays Sharif."

Qays watched her black silhouette fade into the night, slipping away from him. He looked around at the others, shyly wondering if they'd just witnessed her like he had, but everyone was looking up at the sky with bubbling anticipation. Innocently unsuspecting of what would come for them with the first fireworks.

CHAPTER 3

SAMIA

IF HER TRIANGLE-SHAPED, YELLOW-TINTED SUNGLASSES crafted with a tangle of metal wiring made any statement at all, it was that Samia lived for the aesthetic.

She hopped out of the still-dripping-wet Taycan. Samia's parents didn't understand why the car wash charged their cards every time she went out with their car, but she couldn't stop. A pearl-white car is only a car straight out of the car-wash tunnel. Anything more than a thin layer of dust made it look like a dirty toy, which totally soiled Samia's look.

Throwing the long end of her amber jersey hijab to one side, she pressed her lips together to smooth out her lip gloss. With delicate fingers she gave her eyelashes a little boost. She straightened the pearl hair clip attached to her scarf and adjusted her glasses low on her nose because the sun had already set. Light lingered in the air, but not for much longer, and Samia cursed the traffic on the 10 for making her late.

"Whoa there." A voice crept up behind her.

She jumped. Grimy beach parking lots were not the place for surprise visits. As soon as she turned, her heart rate sank back down. "Oh, it's just you."

Abdullahi shut the door to his new Civic, which gave off a middle-class vibe Samia hoped she'd never have to endure. "You're late too?" he asked.

"I'm never on time," Samia answered. Her makeup didn't do itself; neither did hems on her bell-bottoms. If Samia's conscience blocked her from making her parents pay for every expensive clothing item on her wish list, she'd make impeccable knockoffs of them.

Abdullahi sighed. "I didn't think I'd be here again." Though they weren't technically walking together, Samia paced herself with him, feeling safer now that he was within earshot. She'd known Abdullahi since kindergarten; they went to the same schools and shared the same classes all the way until biology class at Huntington High last year. They'd probably end up in a few classes together in their junior year too.

"To the annual bonfire?" Samia didn't follow. "Literally every kid we know comes to this. You don't even need to go to MSA. But this is the place to be on July fourth."

"I thought I'd outgrow it. Move on to other things. New things. Different things. Maybe by next year."

Samia pulled out her phone because Abdullahi was getting existential. Nostalgic for a life he wasn't yet living. He was always careful with his EMT-in-training hands and appeared collected with his EMT temperament and passion to help others. She could never pinpoint whatever profound word it was that described Abdullahi. Practical, philosophical, deep. Samia was many things, mostly vain, always busy with the trending page, but never, ever deep. Depth almost always ruined her aesthetic.

"There's usually something new at these bonfires," she said lightheartedly. "Someone new to meet, something new to try."

"It all blurs together to me." Abdullahi sounded wistful.

"A good time is a good time," she added. "Who cares if it's all a blur?"

Abdullahi smiled. He had never taken anything too seriously when they were younger, and it seemed he hadn't changed. "Life is just like scrolling through a feed. One highlight after another."

Samia pretended to bristle at his sarcasm. "I'm almost offended."

"I didn't think you could be."

"And you'd be right."

"In any case, I'm sorry," he said. She rolled her eyes at the apology. In the past, she'd known Abdullahi to be so nice and sweet that other people took advantage of his empathy. But then they'd grown apart, and she'd stopped being preoccupied with others. Especially those who had trouble prioritizing themselves.

"In any case," she mimicked, "you haven't changed one bit."

He stuffed his hands into his pockets shyly. It reminded her so much of when he'd sat next to her in the first grade at Saturday school writing the Arabic letters and words for her on her classwork when the teacher's back was turned. Or the boy who'd run the fastest to the lunch line to buy her the most popular snacks before they ran out. He was someone who always jumped to be the helper, while she was always the one who needed help. At some point, being around someone so good exhausted her.

When she looked at him again, the shadow of a mustache and the sharper angles of his features transformed his face. Suddenly, he felt like a stranger to her. It had been years since their friendship fizzled out, years since there were more similarities than differences between them.

Now Samia wanted to be anywhere that she had a chance of having a good time and capturing the perfect shots. Her parents were first generation; they were born and raised in California, so they weren't strict. And her grandparents, half of them from Lebanon and half of them from Syria, were too old to be anything but loving, even if they were too blunt for her parents' taste. After high school, she would chase the influencer lifestyle to any social media platform. Her life was meant to be glitter and gold, and she'd do anything to achieve that. To her, *self-made* meant nothing if it didn't make enough money, and *gold digger* was an insult only if marrying money was wrong. Since money bought her gorgeous, shiny, very real things, it couldn't be wrong. Still, she could see how Abdullahi was noble for all his romantic ideals and morals, but she could never be like him.

Her phone dinged.

Most of Samia's groups, messages, and apps were muted. The ding was a big deal. It meant someone she cared about had messaged her. Someone she hadn't muted.

"Where are you going?" Abdullahi's voice faded as Samia tilted forty-five degrees, toward the cliffs.

23

"Meeting someone," she called back. Then with a wink, "Don't be a stranger."

He said something else then, but she didn't hear him. Abdullahi was always saying something and nothing at the same time, so Samia opted not to bother. When she tossed her head back, he was already gone.

The air chilled, lifting the fringe of her jacket up, whipping it behind her to the sound of waves that constituted the soundtrack of Samia's life. The ocean had been with her since day one. It defined who she was: an LA girl, a sun-kissed hijabi babe, a fashion aficionado with a pair of sunglasses for every mood. Samia adapted with trends; like the ocean, she changed with every tide.

And like the ocean, other secrets lurked beneath the surface.

CHAPTER 4

MUZHDA

MUZHDA WASN'T DRESSED FOR TREKKING DOWN THE beach, but she was never going to say no to Monarch Beach High's Qays Sharif.

Over her years of dutiful observation, Muzhda had discovered two things: that jocks were snotty sleazebags and that the only snotty sleazebag who was a pleasure on both the eyes as well as the heart was Qays.

And I'm attracted to snotty sleazebags, Muzhda thought miserably, because the breeze had turned into wind, and that wind was cold.

But she'd do it again and again and again if it meant seeing her bracelet on Qays's wrist. If it meant she'd have another chance to banter-flirt with him when she got back. Ever since he'd stopped tutoring her, he'd never looked at her again, even though she attended his games, celebrated his Ws, admired his loud personality at inter–high school events, and lived for his rare appearances at the local masjid. She went to Valley and he went to Monarch Beach; their paths rarely crossed unless she deliberately placed herself in his line of sight. When he'd approached her earlier, it'd felt like fate bringing them back together. He had been a good tutor to her before, reading her work and editing it with thoughtful attention, but today he was different. She was confident she wasn't the only one who'd felt the sparks.

The pier's lights brightened as she approached the south side of Monarch Beach. A crowd stood at its gates, since the pier was closed for Monarch Beach's 31st Annual Fireworks Show. The beachgoers either made their way to higher ground by the street or rushed to the shore for an unblocked view of the night sky. As the start time approached, parents hoisted their toddlers onto their shoulders and teens prepped their phones for their social media posts. Muzhda might not make it back in time to watch the first firework burst into the sky beside Qays.

Her heart fluttered, and she blushed furiously. She was already imagining a relationship with him. *There I go again, getting ahead of myself,* she thought giddily.

Miraculously, the bathrooms were deserted. She stopped, a little spooked. Only a quarter of the streetlamps by the bathrooms and lockers functioned to their full capacity. MB was swanky. She would expect this of a Valley beach, if it had a beach, but it was a neglected neighborhood adjacent to the superfluous beach city.

Muzhda sidestepped the sticky stains that led out of the stalls. Looping around the bathroom toward the lockers, she tried to brush off the eeriness that tightened her shoulders. She looked out at the lit bonfires dotting the coastline. She didn't want to think about how she'd find her way back carrying Qays's package of God knows what.

She held her elbows, bracing herself. *Qays wouldn't make me do anything dangerous,* she told herself. She'd felt comfortable sharing her mistakes, those misspelled words and run-on sentences, with him at the Tutor Center. Even though she'd been living in America since she was a little kid and spoke English perfectly, her writing always lacked. Every English teacher she'd ever had insisted that she get tutoring for her writing and reading. For years, it bothered her. Then she met Qays at the Tutor Center. She'd never seen a boy as handsome as him.

But she wasn't delusional. Qays was hot, and he wasn't the nicest kid, but he was thoughtful. She liked that he read her stories and didn't criticize what she wrote, no matter how dark, weird, or wild. He accepted them and commented only on the grammar or spelling or organization. He was one of the first people to make her feel like she wrote well. She could bet money he might even recall one or two of her stories. Like the ones he'd spent an extra-long time reading or the ones he'd chuckled at. It had thrilled her when he'd made the smallest comments about her stories. His kindness drew out with time.

A crash snapped her out of her thoughts, and she jumped. She whipped her head around to find the source of the sound, a car, a bike, anything, but found nothing. She was alone.

Shivers snaked up her back and down her arms. She shook the feeling that something was off. Her eyes traced the numbers along the rusty steel-blue lockers.

001, 002, 003.

Belatedly, Muzhda wondered if she'd placed too much trust

in Qays. Apparently enough to do reckless errands for him. She worried *reckless* had a cousin named *dangerous*.

She quickened her pace.

055, 056, 057.

She tried to ground herself in her task to stop her thoughts from carrying her to the darkest corners of her mind. Her fears easily took over anytime she felt the smallest bit of doubt. Could she forget how to get back to Qays? Could she return to the bonfire pits and not find anyone? Could there be someone lurking in the shadows around the corner?

She was being irrational, she told herself. After she retrieved the package, she would hurry back to the pits and watch the fireworks with Qays. At the end of the night, he'd forget to return her bracelet to her. Then he, the soccer star with everything and everyone at his fingertips, would find a way to get it back to her.

128, 129, 130.

Following the numbers down the row, Muzhda reached locker 208, where she inputted Qays's combination. Inside, a small package wrapped in a brown paper bag had been tossed into the back corner. A scent familiar to Valley High hallways and bathrooms punched her right in her nose. A loud *doom-doom* beat inside her ear.

Even high school soccer stars surrender to recreational methods to relieve their stress. But that didn't make carrying Qays's package any lighter. No, it added to the pressure.

Her hands trembled as she grabbed the package. She tried to think of the law, to remember if she could be in possession of this plant as a minor, but she didn't know. How would she if she'd never smoked it before?

Everything, including Muzhda, screamed *suspicious*. Her elbows and knees felt weak, and adrenaline ran through her veins on high. She heard a rustling and the pattering of footsteps coming closer, and her fingers held on to the package like a vise. She hid her head in the shadow of the locker door as a man speaking urgently into his cell phone ran behind her.

Sweat lined her skin, her hands clammy and her neck cold. She was in the wrong place, and it felt like it was getting closer to the wrong time. She felt it in her bones. Turning away from locker 208, she stopped thinking. She didn't want her rational brain to convince her that she was being irrational for her fears. She let her heart take full control. She ran.

Faster, faster, faster.

She rounded the corner, her heart carrying her feet farther than her eyes could see. Her heartbeat drilled holes in her ears. The image of her bracelet on Qays's wrist took over her spirit like something wild. The force of her fantasy becoming reality was strong.

Muzhda's foot caught midrun, and she felt her fantasy being ripped away as her speed launched her forward. The hope in her chest crumbled, and her arms splayed out like wings in front of her. The package went flying. She yelped as she crashed into the ground, a layer of sand on the concrete burrowing into her palms and her forearms. She winced, her skin erupting in a million tiny stings.

As she writhed on the ground, her body flailed against strings and metal. She grimaced, unable to locate what part of her was pulsing with pain. It came from everywhere. Her entire body felt like it had been torn into pieces from the hard fall. Jerking and twisting, she tried lifting herself, but something snapped under her weight, and her chin connected with the ground. Her jaw chomped down on itself, and sharp stabs reverberated up her cheekbones and down her neck. She couldn't find her voice. She wriggled as much as she could, but the wires, the buttons, and the metal she had tripped over tangled her. Tears stung her eyes as she realized she was trapped.

Heaving breaths and the sound of footsteps approaching froze her in place. Her pain was secondary to the thought that someone would find her, and she was completely vulnerable to whoever—or whatever—came next. She sent a prayer that someone was coming to help because if not, she wouldn't be able to defend herself. She felt like she was in a vise that was narrowing and there was nowhere for her to go or hide.

"Are you okay?" It was a deep voice, sympathetic and out of breath.

She tried to look up, but a fierce spasm in her neck screamed in protest. Her eyes felt like they were on fire, trying to communicate what her jaw refused to cooperate to reply.

"I was running, and I saw you fall....Do you need help?" he asked, his tone growing unbearably pitying.

Suddenly, two hands filled her vision. "I'm going to touch you, if that's okay." He hesitated; then his arms slipped under her.

Muzhda whimpered from the shock that racked her body as he tried to lift her. A strangled cry escaped her throat, her lips effectively stuck open by her rigid jaw. The stranger set her down again.

"This stuff shouldn't be here," he said. "We should call a grown-up."

Muzhda's insides twisted. Was he not an adult? She wanted a grown-up to fix this, to lighten the pain that came from everywhere.

30

"Your jaw might be dislocated," he added.

Then locate it, she wished she could say. But there was something more. Yes, her bones felt like sand and her blood like melted metal under her skin, but the vise was beginning to feel like a stone pressing down on her chest. She gasped for air.

"I don't have my phone." The boy's voice trembled with uncertainty. "Okay, here's the plan. I'm going to turn you."

Muzhda couldn't refuse. She was so focused on breathing through what felt like a tiny straw connecting the air outside to her lungs. Ever so slowly, he nudged her body until she flipped off the wires and metal equipment. None of the glimpses of tablet screens and grids of buttons made any sense to her. But that was the least of her worries. She needed to breathe. The night sky stretched above her. A pair of kind eyes that weren't Qays's found hers. Muzhda garbled sounds, failing to form any coherent words.

He knelt beside her, making sure to keep himself where she could see him. Muzhda hadn't noticed she was crying until her neck became slick with her tears.

How did the night turn into this in just a few minutes?

"You're going to be okay." His movements were precise and cautious, one arm scooping up her legs and the other under her torso. "Ready? On the count of three, I'll lift you. One, two—"

The sound of tires screeching squealed in the parking lot, steps above them. Car doors slammed. Muzhda strained her eyes to see anything other than the sky, but her neck didn't budge.

Click.

The boy's head snapped up at the loud sound. His soft eyes turned to stone. Muzhda's chest folded in on itself, the vise tightly shielding her heart.

"Oh no."

His voice broke, and the vise fully compressed. The tiny straw that was helping her breathe vanished. There was no air.

"I'm going to lift you, and then I'm going to run." His words were ice. "You'll have to follow me, okay?"

No, she wanted to scream. Her voice tore at her throat, clawing to tell him *I can't run* and *Please, please help me*, but only tortured sounds escaped.

Click.

Without another word, the boy's arms tensed beneath her, and shards of pain shot through her body as it heaved upright. When she opened her eyes, he'd already turned, ready to run. Muzhda willed her foot to move, but she instantly crumbled forward. Her jaw snapped shut as the bones locked back in place. Her face was on fire.

I'm sorry. She wished she'd heard the boy apologize as he left her there, but her mind conjured up Qays's voice. In reality, the boy yelled something as he ran, but his words didn't hold meaning to her.

As quickly as he'd appeared, the boy left her field of vision, deserting her to the black expanse of sky. A loud crack and pop shattered her eardrums, summoning all the fear from the depths of her gut up her neck. She caught her breath violently, fear like knives driving up her throat. A deep hole grew in her chest, and every hope, dream, and fear poured out.

"Don't leave me!" she cried.

The sky above her exploded in stars.

CHAPTER 5

ZAMZAM

ZAMZAM SAT ALONE AS SHE LOOKED OUT AT THE HORIZON, her face glowing from the scattered lights bursting in the sky. She counted to ten, then down to one, then back up to ten. This was her current coping mechanism to deal with the wide range of emotions that ravaged through her at any given moment.

She watched the random individual fireworks that went off along the beach before the official show. With every firework, Jamal was more and more dead. At least he would be after Zamzam killed him for forcing her to come to this event.

Zamzam was meticulous with her time. She had planners and backup schedules in addition to the detailed Calendar app on her phone. She planned out her life to the second; everything she did had a greater purpose, played a role in the bigger plan. When anything got in the way of her schedule, like this bonfire, she had to count or hum or read to bide the time until her irritation settled and she felt like herself again.

One day she planned to write—with astonishing detail in her fifty-year-plan notebook—a memoir called *The Curse of the Type A Virgo.*

School, track, homework. Summer readings and tutoring sessions for the SATs. Hospital volunteering to bolster her medical-school apps, even though medical school was over four years away. But Zamzam was determined. She would do anything, *everything*, to get that title.

Doctor.

This bonfire was *extra*, and not like the *extra* in *extracurricular*, which benefited her and fit into her plans. Nor was it the time she penciled in for rest between work, volunteering, studying, and errands.

If it weren't for her younger brother, Jamal, Zamzam could be sitting at home, curled up with her grumpy Scottish fold, X, who loved her despite her unreasonable schedule.

She was Zamzam Thompson, and schools would be finding reasons not to accept her, so she had to do everything in her power to make her applications seamless, faultless. She couldn't give anyone a reason not to say yes.

She was also the Zamzam Thompson who would trade her pinkie toe not to chaperone her little brother on his hangouts. He wasn't even a student at Valley yet; his first day was still a month and a half away.

"Zamzam!" Jamal called her name. The *zam*s in her name rhymed less with *ham* and more with *hem*, though not exactly like either.

Zamzam sat up straighter on the cheetah-print lawn chair that she had discovered and colonized at the earliest opportunity. Jamal waved at her and gestured to his friends, who had started to swagger-walk away from the Valley pit. Compared with his friends, Jamal had yet to fill out his teenage body, but they, like the other Valley kids, were all a richness of shades, more so than the faces at the Huntington pit, and nothing at all like the MB pit. Coincidentally, that was the pit that had become the epicenter of the event, and the pit Jamal and his friends were walking toward.

Jamal had done right. Like Momma had ordered before they left: *Don't breathe a breath without your sister knowing it.*

Zamzam grumbled to herself but freed the cheetah-print lawn chair of her ass. She followed her brother and his friends at a safe distance. As she walked past the Valley pit, the faces all blurred together. Maybe that girl took AP Chem with her, that boy might do track with her, but no one really had a name attached. Her schoolmates were just a means to an end, lab partners she needed to get the A, and she had no intention of remembering them. Even the track team suited her perfectly. It was an individual sport, free of unnecessary relationships.

Zamzam was a realist, and if the life she wanted required diligence and discipline, she'd suffer them. They weren't all that bad once she got used to them.

But that diligence she lived by didn't matter. Because when the world wanted to derail her, the world did what it wished without consent.

At least Jamal still asked for permission.

Zamzam observed her brother give daps to some MB goons,

and she couldn't help but smile at the ease with which her brother befriended people. He was likable in the way Zamzam used to be before she exchanged fun for responsibility. It hadn't been a conscious decision to make the switch. One day she became the eldest child in the house and carried the weight of the role for her mom and Jamal. If her younger brother could enjoy more of his youth because Zamzam sacrificed more of hers, at least she could find joy in seeing him so happily carefree.

A firework popped nearby, the sound echoing in her eardrum. She flinched, and when she opened her eyes, she couldn't see Jamal. "One, two, three ...," she murmured to herself, taking a breath as a pale chest blocked her vision. She craned her neck, but the bodies only packed closer together, squeezing her between selfies and TikTok recordings.

"Excuse me." Zamzam squirmed, pulling her yellow-and-fuchsia-print shawl tighter on her shoulders, covering her bare neck.

The crowd thickened like honey. Zamzam stepped around a coterie of band geeks, then halted by a gang of frat-boys-to-be.

The pale-chested jock, muscles and sparse chest hair abounding, body-slammed into her. "Oof," she heaved, her body hurtling backward.

Frowning, she leaped back up to him just as a clique of hijabi models nearly trampled over her. She spun around, half hunting for Jamal and half awaiting an apology.

But the jock was kneeling, hands working fast over a long cylindrical firework. His frat brothers goofed around about him, hollering and cackling.

Zamzam chucked her counting coping mechanism out the

window; it wasn't doing it for her anyway. She marched up to him, arms crossed and ready for confrontation.

"You knocked me over," she said with a fiery glare.

He tilted his head up to take a better look at her. "Did I?" he asked, his words fading into a chuckle. "I didn't see you."

She tapped a finger on her forearm. He didn't seem to notice her impatience. He called to his friend, who was dribbling a soccer ball. "Omar, you have a lighter?"

"Excuse me!" Zamzam couldn't rein in her tone.

He glanced at her again. "Oh, sorry, do *you* have a lighter?"

His soccer-ball friend, Omar, threw a lighter at him, which he caught one-handed. Steadying the enormous firework with his left hand, he pressed down on the release and brought it close to his face, illuminating his nose, the only part of him that looked as if the sculptor had run out of time and couldn't chisel out.

Zamzam scoffed, regretting she'd come to get an apology at all.

The jock flicked his gaze up at her. "I'd step back if I were you."

Zamzam wouldn't. The firework wobbled every time he spoke; he hadn't set it deep enough into the sand. Scratch that. He shouldn't be trying to set it into the loose sand. If he lit it and released, someone was going to get hurt. She had to tell him.

"Unbelievable," she started.

The jock pulled the plastic strap off the fuse with his braceleted hand. In another swift motion, he lit it, jumping back as the sparks sputtered into his face, cursing to himself.

Her eyes widened. "You—"

The firework wobbled. Once, twice.

As the fuse of the firework shortened, Zamzam's heart began

to race; she felt the blood pumping hard in her neck. The firework curved up wildly from its unstable base.

Zamzam froze in place. No matter which direction she moved, the probability of getting pinned by this dumb jock's pyrotechnics was the same. He must have done the same math as she did, because the panic contorting his face mirrored her own.

"Shit!"

The snaking firework hissed at them, convulsing from the igniting saltpeter. Zamzam thought to run or duck or dodge yet did nothing but radiate panic.

What came next happened within a span of minutes that felt like they lasted hours. The firework's high-pitched screeching made time zoom as it nose-dived back toward the beach.

Zamzam braced herself and stepped backward. The film around her slowed again. Her heart felt like it beat at a dangerously low speed, every atom in her body drawing inward.

BANG!

The eruption of a thousand fireworks setting off simultaneously shook the earth. The sand quaked beneath her feet, and time resumed as Zamzam's reality broke. The world's balance tipped, hurling Zamzam around like she was a doll.

Kids collided and fell as they tried to run. Zamzam righted herself and came face-to-face with the jock who had lit the firework that began this mayhem.

A wave of warmth heated her back, and all at once, the jock's face lit up as if it were daylight, fires igniting in his eyes. Zamzam twisted her neck to see where a mushroom-top cloud of fire in the middle of the ocean ripped apart the black sky.

The earth jolted again, making her and the jock lose their balance. The sound of dozens of Hellcats revving their engines inside Zamzam's ears threatened to shatter her eardrums. She clamped down on either side of her head as the pressure pressed against her skull, threatening to burst out through her skin.

Kids sprinted away from the beach, horror pasted on their faces, but Zamzam's horror came from another place. Her mind could fear only what it knew, and it didn't comprehend explosions in the middle of the ocean where an oil rig should be. Zamzam's mind feared Momma's wrath.

Jamal.

Her brother's safety became her singular worry, her anchor to reality. While the kids fled the beach in a stampede, Zamzam ran in search of her brother.

Above her, the fireworks show commenced, a pretimed celebration coloring the sky.

Her stomach tightened at the sight of kids vomiting and hyperventilating around her. She dropped her eyes to the explosion over the water that was on fire, slowly burning the oil rig on the horizon. Farther along the coast, the pier was fractured to pieces.

"Jamal!" Zamzam's voice climbed up from alarm to terror.

She whipped back around to another pit, where people were helping one another up, where kids lay motionless, trampled.

Then there were police sirens.

Zamzam's tight stomach released all at once. She bent over, and her insides mutinied against her, pushing up their contents through her esophagus and out onto the sand.

A thigh struck the side of her head, and the backing of her hoop earring burrowed into the crook of her neck.

"Fuck!"

Zamzam's spinning vision homed in on the jock from before. He skidded to a halt and wiped Zamzam's puke off his bare foot, uncensored disgust etched on his face.

"You!" she screamed. "This is your fault!"

His eyes lazily left his soiled foot to look her square in the face. "My fault?"

"I lost my brother," she cried, marching up to him and wiping her lower lip. "And it's because I was distracted by you!"

He grunted coolly, but then shuddered. His hands were shaking.

The sirens were even closer. Zamzam gagged.

He yelped. "Do not puke on me."

"Get away from me," she muttered, throwing her hands up protectively.

"Qays!"

Zamzam and the jock looked up at the fence between the elevated parking lot and the beach.

"Cops!" the kid warned.

That single word punched Zamzam in the gut, making it all the more difficult to breathe. A legion of cops in black uniforms scattered like ants onto the beach, heading straight to stop kids among the swarm of hijabs, beards, shades, and patterns. The officers converged onto them, clawing off scarves and hoodies, dropping teenagers' bodies right down to the ground with a baton to the back of the knees.

Zamzam's throat closed up as she watched the scene before her, police officers whose confusion eclipsed the kids' terror, making them act atrociously. This was something Zamzam understood. She had seen it happen before. Reality cemented itself.

The jock, who had just been called Qays, took hold of Zamzam's shoulders. She fought against him, but he held tight.

"Do you see anyone there?" he asked, voice pitched high, pointing down the beach in the direction of the shattered pier. "Is anyone coming?"

Senses heightened for the task at hand, Zamzam shoved Qays's chest. "I need to find my brother."

She wasn't an accessory to his crime, if committed, nor would she help the kid who made her lose Jamal. The cops were coming, advancing toward the shore quickly, and the closer the cops moved to them, the more they cut down kids, wielding their batons and Tasers like swords.

"You can't run," Qays said bitterly, eyes trained on the onslaught of uniformed officers.

Zamzam slowly closed her eyes, and Qays was forgotten. She listened, her ringing ears drowning out the sound of the cries, yearning for the sound of the ocean. Zamzam had lived her entire life by an ocean. The ocean spoke to her.

The ocean was an expanse of hope. Whenever she was at her lowest, when life beat her down and there were only ends in sight, she came to the ocean. Because when the light shined on the water like a cascading staircase up to the sun, it was impossible not to see it as a metaphor for her aspirations. Zamzam trusted the ocean.

She exhaled slowly. After years of living in her sparkling city by the water, distracted by glittery titles and school competition and older-sibling duties, the world slowed down just enough that she heard the ocean speak to her.

Run.

And like any girl who heard the ocean's words shake the marrow of her bones, shivering at the smoke and the shouts while the uniforms mowed down the beach, Zamzam listened to the water.

She took the boy by his braceleted wrist, and she ran.

CHAPTER 6

QAYS

"LAPD! GET DOWN ON THE GROUND!"

"Hands up in the air! Now! Now!"

Qays's body was inclined to cooperate, but his mind raced with all the reasons he shouldn't. If the vibes didn't lean toward Yawm Al-Qiyamah, he might've turned to the officer and explained. But Qays couldn't make sense of the fire in the ocean and was sweating with worry that Muzhda hadn't come back from the far side of the beach. There was little else he could do besides comply.

He threw up his free arm, resisting the girl's grip with the other. He huffed and grunted, trying to turn back to face the officers, but the girl was stronger than she looked. She dragged him toward the ocean, her printed shawl smacking his face as she ran.

"Why are you running?" he yelled over the commotion,

lumbering after her, hoping she'd come to her senses and let him go. "You can't keep running into the ocean."

She didn't respond. Instead, her eyes drilled into the fire in the middle of the ocean, the flames burning brighter, growing bigger as they approached the shore. Qays was supposed to be watching a fireworks show color the sky and an upside-down, crackled painting of the sparks on the water.

The fire, the wood from the pier scattering on the sand and digging into his heels, and the cops chasing them to the water's dead end—they didn't feel real. Though he could hear the explosion still ringing in his ears and feel the heat of the fire, he couldn't believe they were there. Explosions in the ocean didn't happen at Monarch Beach.

He shot a look to the Promenade, on the south side of the beach, and saw a lone figure running back toward the pits. His breath caught.

Muzhda.

Relief soothed the ringing in his ears. She would be fine, she could take care of herself despite the chaos, and this all would soon be over. Sometimes life got wrecked, but Qays always found a way to make it right again.

Dampness cooled the soles of Qays's feet. The girl's pace slowed as her breathing deepened. She groaned, releasing his wrist, then resting her hands on her head, which was wrapped in a half turban. She tilted her head back, her eyes brimming with tears.

"What is happening?" she cried.

Qays's brows furrowed in defiance of the panic in her voice.

Her question was obviously rhetorical. The explosion in the ocean would be explained away as a bad dream in no time.

The shouts behind them grew closer.

The girl shuddered, adjusting her shawl around her body.

As the tide drew in, the waves licked their toes.

Qays leaned closer to the girl, the second girl to alter the course of his night. He was an as-needed type of guy. This entire tragedy of a night was add-ons: a pier being blown to bits, an oil rig exploding into a ball of fire in the ocean, a hundred Muslim kids scattering like donkeys in the presence of a lion.

And the other catastrophes of the night: his heart fluttering around a girl he sent to do his dirty business, and another girl leading him away from the cops, tiptoeing closer and closer into the dark ocean.

Even for a fuckboi, he'd attracted more feminine attention than normal tonight.

She glanced over her shoulder at him. Lines marked her cheeks where tears washed away the grime on her skin. Her chin quivered. She stepped farther into the ocean.

The hair on the back of Qays's neck stood on end. "What are you doing?" His voice cracked.

"I don't know. I just know I can't go back that way." She shivered, glancing behind her.

He stepped closer, watching her feet carefully, coiling his muscles in case she made a move. "Come back," he coaxed her. He hated that he could hear a tremor in his voice.

She shook her head, eyes widening as they stared behind him.

Qays glanced back at the police. He didn't think his heart

could beat any faster. "They're just scared. We're all scared. It'll be over tomorrow morning."

Her mouth twisted. "Do you really think so?"

He opened his mouth for a response he didn't quite believe but didn't get a chance to reply.

"LAPD! Don't move!"

The girl flicked a wilted gaze at the water.

"Hands in the air!"

This time Qays didn't have a second thought. He complied immediately, but the girl took her time, tilting her body until her back was to the ocean. She stared at the beach and the human chaos created by the fire in the sea. A fog was creeping in, or maybe it was smoke, and it blurred the lines of what had started it all.

"It's over now," she murmured. Her face scrunched up as a sob escaped her lips. Her fear waded over to Qays, and his faux courage crumbled.

Frightened, his body went gelatinous.

A baton whacked against the back of his knees, and it stung in every bone in his legs. It swept the strength out from under him, and he dropped to his knees. Water splashed up against his face, and he righted his thoughts. He shouldn't be scared. He was just a kid. Yet the cops came toward them, converging on them like they needed containment rather than protection.

Strong hands clasped his arms, yanking them down and pinning him into a submission hold. Frustrated but helpless, he couldn't resist against the tactical boot, thick and heavy, thrusting into his shoulder blade, knocking the air out of his lungs. His face crashed into the damp sand, the impact of the fall threatening tears.

Qays hated the feeling of tears making their way to his eyes. If he cried, it made this real. Metal secured his wrists, clicking with a finality that infuriated him. The handcuffs dug into Muzhda's beaded bracelet.

Qays's anger flashed, and his eyes opened. The girl hadn't braced herself for the cops, and when they hit her locked knees, she jerked forward terribly. They slammed her body to the ground as she cried out. She lay parallel to him on the ground, and her brown eyes, wide with fear, locked onto his. An officer had his hand around her neck to keep her down and his knee secured on her back. Like Qays, she didn't resist. A wave washed onto the shore, soaking them, filling their open mouths with salty water. They gurgled and coughed as the wave receded.

"We'll be okay," he said to her without thinking. His voice sounded desperate, almost childish, and totally unlike him. He had to do something about it. He rose his voice at the officers. "You've made a mistake."

The knee against Qays's back flattened his chest until he couldn't breathe. A sob escaped the girl's throat. He bit down on his lip.

Then the officer began to read them their Miranda rights. Qays's hearing came and went like the waves.

"You are under arrest...."

Qays talked a big game but was always going to go to Stanford. No question about it.

"...used against you in a court of law...."

He liked to act coy, but he relished in the attention he got for the scholarship.

"...an attorney, one will be provided for you."

Qays liked to be chased after. His senior year would be dedicated to getting chased and then end with Stanford, his new stage to make it bigger than he already was.

The officer grunted into Qays's ear and lifted him off the ground at the same time the girl was brought to her feet. Two officers were placed on either side of him.

"We didn't do anything," Qays murmured. His chest stung with each breath.

They reached the pits and the wreckage before them. Food littered the sand, chairs and coolers were toppled over and broken, and abandoned shoes and clothes were strewn around. Firefighters attempted to put out a fire that spread around the Huntington pit. A tray of hot dogs remained burning, wafting the smell of charred meat at them. The girl bent over, vomiting what little stomach acid was left.

"Zamzam!"

The girl in the print shawl called Zamzam looked startled, and the officer tightened his grip and his attention on them both.

"Jamal?" Zamzam cried.

The boy, who intensely resembled her, hurtled down the stairs from the parking lot. An officer chased after him, but he was fast.

Jamal backed off when he saw the police, his face distraught like he was fourteen going on forty. "But—but she didn't do anything," he said, voice soft, scared.

"Listen, Jamal, now, *listen* to me," Zamzam said firmly, her voice stripped of the rawness Qays had heard in it before. "Go home. Do not go anywhere else. Do not do anything else. Tell Momma what happened, and we'll clear up the misunderstanding. *Nothing* will happen to me, I promise."

Qays almost believed her.

The officer led Jamal away, and he let her, mindful of where he placed his hands and how he moved.

The two burly officers on either side of Qays bumped him up the stairs to the parking lot. Caution tape and barricades had gone up, the crowd of kids pushed back for space. As they pushed him onward, Qays didn't drop his head. He'd never had any reason to lower his head in front of his peers, and he wasn't going to start now.

This will all be over in the morning, he thought. The sentence drummed against his skull.

The officers led Qays to the row of police that had formed between their cars and the ambulances and the crowd of kids. The row parted as they approached, giving them a path to pass through. A woman whose lifted chin made her seem extra important stepped in front of him, stopping the officers on either side of him.

"How did you get here?" she asked, almost to herself. She glanced at one of the officers. "Does he look like someone who'd get caught up in this?"

Qays wanted to agree, though he was sure if he did, he'd be leaning in to the minimal amount of privilege granted to him by his good looks and the fact that his face didn't scream *Arab*—it only mildly shouted it. He was ready to accept the fruits of his privilege,

49

even if just for the chance to explain away this misunderstanding, but the tension between the officers gave him no space to speak.

"He was on the run with her." The officer on Qays's left shrugged, gesturing to Zamzam. "And he doesn't look like he'd be totally innocent."

The woman narrowed her eyes at Qays. "Name?"

Qays's throat burned from ocean water. This was his ticket out. This was how the world righted itself and he could go back to his normal life. This would become an aberration in his past that he'd cope with in countless sessions of therapy, but in his past all the same.

"Qays Sharif," he said, his voice raspy and catching. He said his name with all its fullness, the deep ق in the back of his throat, the rich vowels, the delicate ر. All the parts that made his name Arab and all the ways he could decolonize it.

The woman surveyed him, her face deepening in thought. She looked back at the cop cars and shrugged. "Fine, take him in."

Qays could have screamed. The aberration persisted.

His eye caught on Omar and his friends, who watched in silence as he passed. Their eyes were glassy, grime and sand engraved so deeply in their skin, they would not be able to wash it off. None of them would be able to wash this night off. There was horror there, but Qays was immune to it because this night was a blip in the system. A series of mistakes and coincidences. That they were taking it so seriously was the only thing legitimizing the events. At least, that was what Qays told himself.

Because the alternative was this night and its consequences hardening into an ugly reality.

His friends watched him cross from the beach to the police cars like five-year-old kids observing a wild animal at the zoo for the first time.

Wonder, astonishment…and a little bit of fear. Except the fear was not little at all; it was growing bigger and bigger until it was all he could see.

No one else was in handcuffs. Cops were comforting some of them; paramedics came to the rescue of several injured and wailing. Stretchers lined up beside the police cars. These were kids who looked like him. Then why was he in cuffs and not them? What gave Omar a free ticket and not him?

The police-car door opened. Qays's feet froze solidly on the asphalt.

Due process. Bail.

If he stepped into this car, that was what awaited him. This felt wrong, incorrect, illogical. It was her fault, the girl in the print shawl, the girl named Zamzam who had taken his wrist and run. Qays tightened his jaw and clenched his fists behind his back. His bare chest flexed and bulged.

He could see the headlines.

Stanford hopeful taken into custody.

Monarch Beach's soccer legend arrested on a tragic Fourth of July.

The police officer inched him closer to the car. He pretended it was just another sleek Dodge with a poor choice of paint. The stodgier officer placed his hand on Qays's head and leaned him over, sloping his body onto the car, providing Qays with a view of his compatriots in steel.

First was Zamzam, but her face was tough now; gone were

51

the traces of the weakness she had before she saw Jamal. Weakness she had betrayed when she'd looked into the black ocean.

Next were two girls, shivering. One with running mascara, dressed in a deep yellow hijab and clothes that looked like they attached to a bungee cord. The other with cracked glasses and a stricken face peeking from behind a curtain of black hair.

Then there was a boy, shorter than Qays and sturdier than him. He was out of breath, a layer of sweat across his brow.

The five of them looked across the car tops at one another, a million questions swimming behind their glances.

They were all strangers until he saw the girl already sitting inside. His stomach dropped.

Muzhda's scarf was askew, and her was face colorless despite the parking-lot lights flooding in from the window. She pressed her lips together and stared back at him. Her eyebrows, so artfully drawn, furrowed. Her eyes shined with tears.

Somehow, she was more beautiful.

Qays opened his mouth to speak. He wanted to reach out to her, comfort her. Impossibly for Qays, to apologize to her. He felt as though there was so much to say, but a ball blocked the words from leaving his throat.

The officers tossed Qays into the back seat. They slammed the car door. A chorus of shutting doors followed.

Before, Qays had always seen his future ahead of him. His life consisted of so many free handouts for a guy like him that he could see at least four years into the future. *Success* was always at the end of it.

Now, all he could see in front of him was the back of the driver's seat headrest inside a cop car.

There were six of them. Qays, Zamzam, Muzhda, and the other three.

There was an explosion, maybe two. The oil rig in the ocean, the pier from the shore.

And Qays was in handcuffs, eyes to the driver's seat in front of him, and he couldn't see his future.

CHAPTER 7

ABDULLAHI

WITH HIS HANDS CUFFED IN FRONT OF HIM, HE SHUFFLED down the hallway of the police precinct, two officers trailing him. After booking, they took the others into custody, but the officers didn't take Abdullahi with them to the holding area. The police worked quickly, and it felt like the night was passing at two times the normal speed; the fast-forwarded static and high-pitched voices warbled in his ears.

Abdullahi followed Deputy Vega, keeping his elbows tight by his sides, trying his best to relax his shoulders. He attempted to let his mind wander away from the stressors, but the contacts in his eyes burned from the dryness of the sand, the bonfire smoke, the exhaustion. Every other blink, he squeezed his eyes shut to lubricate them. He wanted to rub them, moisten them with tears, but he didn't dare move or betray a single emotion.

Nonmenacing.

Menacing wouldn't even be in Abdullahi's vocabulary if he didn't need to know it to call himself its antonym. He collected vinyls and admired cars from the '60s. He would listen to Billy Joel's "Vienna" on repeat while driving up and down the 1. His favorite movie was *Hairspray*, specifically the one where John Travolta plays the mom.

Deputy Vega's ponytail bobbed as she walked. He focused on that, the way the low-grade lighting reflected up the tail, then traveled down it as they passed the antique light fixtures. The precinct was in old LA, vintage LA, Abdullahi's type of LA.

Deputy Vega passed a card through a reader above a knob, then punched numbers into a keypad on a door. It beeped and clanked open to a dimly lit room. It was more cluttered than a normal interrogation room, at least from what Abdullahi knew of interrogation rooms on television.

"Have a seat," Deputy Vega instructed. "Feet apart, hands flat on the table. Officer Keith will adjust your cuffs to the table. No sudden movements as he approaches. Got it?"

Deputy Vega had a suave air about her; no fine lines yet, so she was young and ambitious. She wore a thick layer of foundation, so her face had no color and no shadows, just one even layer of tan liquid. Before she turned away, she smiled with her mouth, but her eyes didn't change. They were wide and observant, even a tad bit sad. Abdullahi wondered where that empathy came from.

He stepped into the room and blinked hard. He maintained the act of seeming calm and collected, like he had been told to should he find himself in this situation. The worst thing to do was to overreact. Yes, his hands trembled, and his mouth was dry from the constant swallowing, but he kept telling himself he'd be okay. He was the guy that guided spiders out of the house despite his phobia because he couldn't bring himself to kill them. Surely karma dealt in kindness and they'd soon realize they'd made a mistake.

The officers filed in after him. Officer Keith cuffed Abdullahi to the metal bar on the table.

"Don't think about getting up," he commanded. Abdullahi's gaze dropped. He wouldn't have dared.

Officer Keith stationed himself against the wall behind Abdullahi, the other officer at the door.

Abdullahi hadn't gotten a look at them before, but the wide one-way mirror reflected the room, offering a good view. The officers were fit. Not the stereotypical doughnut-eating, coffee-loving cops. Not small-town cops, not LA models or actors with a law-enforcement side gig. Full-fledged gym-rat, buzz-cut cops.

And they were white.

Abdullahi's pulse stabbed at his neck, straining his muscles, stiffening his jaw. A moment ago, he hadn't been sweating so profusely. Maybe Deputy Vega's Latina presence had lent him some false comfort.

In the mirror-window, Abdullahi got a good look at what the night had done to him. His twists were sandy, his skin ashy. His blinking was out of order: fast, harsh, erratic. His clothes, jeans and an oversize faded shirt, sleeves to elbows, hem over crotch, were dirty in more places than they were clean.

He looked like every other kid at the beach. Confused and terrified. But to the police, he'd looked guilty enough to bring in.

After a while, the door opened, and a man in plain clothes walked in. *The boss*, he guessed. Abdullahi blinked his eyes hard.

From this point on, an investigation would unravel, the web could be spun any way, the headlines could be pitched however, and the truth could be molded into whatever.

I won't need to be guilty to be found guilty.

Files smacked the table, skidding across Abdullahi's vision. Sinewy fingers adjusted them perpendicular to him, then rested on either side of the files. Straight and neat and narrow.

"I'm Detective Pennella," the man said. "With your cooperation, we'll get through this quickly. I'd like to get to the others before the night is over."

"I'm first?" Abdullahi whispered accidentally. He knew better than to speak. He didn't even know if his family had been notified. Since he'd arrived at the station, he'd known nothing about what was happening outside.

"Yup, you're number one. Going alphabetically, shall we say?"

Abdullahi didn't think *we* was a thing to Detective Pennella, but he didn't argue. He was the one in cuffs, and the detective had all the power.

They hashed out the normal information, if any of it could be called normal.

"State your name for the record."

"Spell that for me."

"Louder."

"Place of birth for the record."

"Date of birth for the record."

"Oh, you're a Capricorn," Pennella mused. "My wife'll give me the full rundown on that later."

Detective Pennella didn't wear a ring on his finger. It sounded like a weak attempt at small talk.

He smiled at Abdullahi, and his mouth could have had molars for every tooth from how huge and square his teeth were. He was handsome like most people in LA were, with a hefty dose of synthetic enhancements.

"Okay, looks like we got the right kid," Pennella said mostly to himself and the recorder. "Do you want some water?"

Abdullahi shook his head no.

"Verbal responses from now on," Pennella ordered.

"No."

"Thank you," Pennella added. Abdullahi glanced up at him, and Pennella's smile was gone; his jaw bulged ever so slightly, though he flicked through the files, seeming disinterested. "No, thank you."

Abdullahi breathed out. Their relationship was beginning to code itself. He resigned to it. "No, thank you."

"Good." Pennella's smile was back on. "Now let's start at the beginning. The more you cooperate, the faster this will all be over. You're not in any real trouble right now, Abdul, but let's see how long that lasts."

Abdullahi hadn't said he could be called Abdul. It wasn't his nickname, not even his Starbucks name. He blinked twice, his eyes scorching. He boiled his courage, thickening it until he could speak up to button-down Pennella despite the pecking order.

"What about my rights?" Abdullahi asked, voice brittle.

Pennella stopped sifting through the files. Seconds passed. "Ah yes, smart kid, Abdul."

He read him his rights. Officially.

That gave Abdullahi some ammunition. "What if I don't want

to answer questions without my lawyer? I'm underage. Don't I need my parent in here with me?"

Pennella sighed, laying the files on the table. "You didn't list a parent on your file. And this person? Fatima Talib? Who is she?"

"My older sister," Abdullahi answered. "She's in college. She's an adult."

"But she's not your guardian," Pennella said dismissively. "Don't you have parents?"

He nodded.

"Verbal responses."

Abdullahi wanted to cry; maybe then his eyes wouldn't feel like soil in flesh sockets. He hadn't listed his parents, because he didn't want to worry them unnecessarily, but it seemed too late for that.

"Yes."

Pennella's expression flattened. "Then we'll contact them." He leaned forward, index finger jamming into the table. "But fair warning, Abdul, this is not your standard investigation. Right now, unless one of you sets the story straight, we're in new territory. Where protocol isn't protocol anymore."

"Where the Bill of Rights isn't the Bill of Rights anymore," Abdullahi completed. His throat narrowed as he said it, but he had to say it. He couldn't make sense of what had happened on the beach any more than this detective could. He'd been running along the sandy beach when the ground shifted and the sky exploded into a great fire. If anything, he was the only one who had known something was wrong before it happened.

Pennella's lips twitched, and he glanced at the recorder.

Abdullahi did, too, and he wondered when the red light had switched off. Pennella clicked a button, and the red light turned back on.

"We didn't find anything on you," Pennella said. "You don't have a cell phone?"

"I left it off in my car," Abdullahi said. He often didn't have his phone on him, because he couldn't keep up with all the texts and social media. He preferred speaking on the phone to texting and would rather have a Nokia flip phone and an iPod for music, like he'd seen in old movies.

"Ah, your car?"

"I drove to the beach."

"Then where are your car keys?"

"They were in my pocket." He wanted to stop talking, he really did, but he was terrible at saying no to people and even worse at ignoring them. "They must've fallen out when I ran."

"And why were you running from the bathrooms?"

"The cops were there, man." Abdullahi would curse if he were the type of kid who cursed. "I was scared, so I ran."

"You weren't at the event with the other kids. It was just you and the girl."

Abdullahi's stomach reacted to the mention of the girl. His stomach acid burned, and he felt it crawl up his esophagus. He forced himself to swallow to remain composed in front of the detective and on record. For now, he couldn't think too hard about the girl he'd seen on the beach. How she'd so desperately needed help and how he'd failed her. If karma indeed dealt in kindness, then Abdullahi must be in this predicament because he'd left her.

Pennella placed a photo in front of Abdullahi, but Abdullahi did not look down. If he did, he wouldn't be able to control his body.

"Do you know her?" Pennella asked, leaning forward.

"I don't," Abdullahi answered. "I was trying to help her up when the cops showed up, and I ran." He left it at that. He needed a lawyer. He needed time to think. Abdullahi enjoyed spending time alone for self-reflection, journaling in his Notes app, dabbling in poetry when he felt more sentimental than usual, but he worried what thought prison he'd put himself in, given what he'd done tonight.

Or what I didn't. His stomach flipped, and he refocused his energy on the prickling in his eyes.

"Why were you there in the first place?" Pennella persisted. "Why weren't you with the other kids?"

"I was in the bathroom," he said, his voice strained.

Detective Pennella clicked the recorder. The red light went out. His gaze moved to behind Abdullahi.

Officer Keith moved then, uncuffing Abdullahi from the table and leading him from the room. Abdullahi's parents would be notified, and hell would be raised. The investigation that wasn't an investigation would continue. Except this wasn't a maze of thin webs. The web of this investigation was as thick as lace, stitching thicker and larger, until eventually, it would become obvious what exactly was going on.

CHAPTER 8

SAMIA

THE OFFICERS CLEARED THE BOOKING AREA OF MOST STAFF and vacated the holding area for Samia and the other kids arrested with her. As if they were the criminal VIPs.

She stared down at her tasseled sandals, teardrops falling onto her pedicured feet and white-polished toenails. Her palms were cut up and caked with dried blood, and her jeans were ripped, but not for the fashion. Her fake eyelashes clumped together, drooping with the extra weight.

This could not be her life. She was a hijabi Insta-model, brushed up and photoshopped. Her social media was proof of her bright life; her sunshiny personality exuded off the screen. She was not this sorry person, crying because of one night gone terribly wrong. She rubbed her foundation and mascara tears away.

The holding area gave her a first-class view of the precinct.

Samia could see most of the cubicles and desks, and if she stood in the left corner and poked her nose through the bars, she could see a sliver of the reception area.

Eventually, the holding-cell door opened, and Officer Lyle Keith—the cute one—pushed Abdullahi into the holding area. He uncuffed him and ordered him to the other side of the area. "Away from the girls," he warned.

The precinct was small. It had only one holding area, and it, too, was cramped. It held Samia and Abdullahi and the other girls, Nasreen and Zamzam.

Samia rushed to sit beside him, leaving the other two girls, who hadn't shed a single tear, on the left side of the cell.

To hell with their self-righteous feminism, thought Samia. It was feminist to cry. Tears were genderless, and she wasn't about to avoid emotions in the name of phony strength. No, no way.

She fired her questions at Abdullahi. "What did they ask you? What did you tell them? Oh, this is bad, isn't it? Did they tell you about what that was at the beach?"

Abdullahi shook his head slowly. There was something more off about him than the others. Sure, they were all equally scared, but the cloud of doom hung especially low on him.

Samia's desperation snapped. "Well, then did you tell them we don't have a clue about what happened either? They grabbed us by mistake. Out of all those other kids on the beach, why did this have to happen to us? You and I have the cleanest records in the county!"

One of the girls scoffed. Samia thought she knew which one.

"What?" Zamzam started at Samia's glare. "Do you think you two are the only ones here by coincidence?"

Samia narrowed her eyes at her. "I'm not the one you should be worried about. At least we know each other. I have someone to vouch for me. No one here can say that about you." She returned her attention to Abdullahi. "They must've said something about what happened at the beach. How—how did it all just go up like that?"

He placed his elbows on his knees and his head in his hands, doubling over as the lines in his face deepened with worry. Samia wanted to comfort him but kept her hands to herself. She wasn't sure how she could.

"Where did that other boy go?" Zamzam asked carefully. "I—" She swallowed hard and pulled at her half turtleneck. "He was arrested beside me."

Samia's head snapped up. "Qays?"

"Is that his name?"

"Like you don't know," Samia said disbelievingly.

Zamzam set her jaw. "How would I know him? Or rather how do *you* know him?"

"Everyone knows Qays Sharif."

Abdullahi absentmindedly nodded in agreement.

"Not me," Zamzam said.

"And not me," Nasreen added, peering through her broken glasses. They must have made her world look like kaleidoscope hell.

Samia snorted. "Well, that isn't saying much. You don't know anyone."

Nasreen breathed haggardly. Her frame shook, but she didn't shy away from Samia's stare.

Zamzam raised a brow at them. "You two keep staring at each

other, and I'll start thinking there's something going on between you two."

Samia and Nasreen glanced away, then back at each other.

"As if," Samia said quickly, then pointed her eyes away. Nasreen might as well be a stranger to her. Tonight was the first time they'd met. "I've just never seen her around, so I assumed she wasn't in our high school loop."

"Our loop?"

"Monarch Beach, Valley, Huntington."

"If her theory is correct, then where do you go?" Zamzam asked Nasreen, eyes narrowing.

Something in the holding cell shifted. Maybe it was Zamzam's tone, or the way Nasreen glanced at Samia as if to ask for help, but Samia's defenses turned their attention to the other people in the cell with her.

Samia stood up abruptly. "I didn't know we were interrogating each other now."

Zamzam flashed her a wild look. "Defend her again, and you're both officially on my suspect list."

Energy rushed to Samia's head as she advanced toward Zamzam. "Back off." Before she could process her actions, her finger jammed into Zamzam's shoulder.

Zamzam stared in disbelief at where she'd been touched. She stepped up to Samia defensively. "Square up."

"Bring it."

"Guys...," Nasreen started.

In what could be described only as jinn possession, Samia launched herself at Zamzam, shoving her first. Zamzam went for Samia's hijab. They latched onto each other, their nails like claws and teeth. Samia was taller, but Zamzam was stronger and pushed Samia until her back was against the cell. With Zamzam's forearm against her throat, Samia swatted at Zamzam, smacking her in the nose. Their shoes squeaked against the linoleum floor, the sounds of their scuffle smothering the air like hot wind on a humid day.

"Guys, please stop before someone sees us," Abdullahi pleaded. He looked outside the cell nervously.

"Enough."

The two girls sprang apart at the loud, demanding voice. Outside the cell, a few papers ruffled, and an officer stood from his desk. "Zamzam Thompson and Samia Al-Samra, sit apart!" the officer commanded.

Zamzam wiped her nose, which at some point had started to bleed. Everything was sticky, Zamzam's blood on Samia's clothes and the melted glue on her eyelashes seeping into the crevices, cementing her eyes shut.

Abdullahi paced the cell. He cocked his head at Zamzam; cupped his chin in his hand as he observed Nasreen, who was obviously pretending to be less scared than she looked; and then plopped back down next to Samia.

"They must be holding Qays with any others they arrested," Abdullahi guessed. He masked his voice well, sounding stable and dependable. Sounding like Abdullahi. The boy who picked her for his team so she wouldn't be last, even though she was dreadful at sports. He fixated on the center of the holding area, at the drainage hole covered with a mesh screen. "Listen, I'm not sure what happened tonight. The detective didn't debrief me or anything back there. This is serious. It's real. Whatever the crimes are, we are their only leads."

Samia leaned her head back against the wall. She reached up, extracting her fake lashes and forcing herself to feel the sting of every lash ripping off her eye line.

Abdullahi continued despite Samia's wishing he'd stop. "We don't know anything, but they don't have much more information other than us. They do have a common goal, though."

"To find the person responsible," Nasreen finished.

"Exactly." He blinked extra hard. "I don't think we should use our time in here fighting with each other when we can be making things right by getting to the truth."

Samia grunted. "You trust these strangers? You really think Mister-Perfect-Soccer-Douche-Stoner Qays Sharif had nothing to do with it?"

Zamzam clicked her tongue. "The fact that this dude is known as Mister-Perfect-Soccer-Douche-Stoner is proof enough he's probably too dumb to do anything like what we saw. He had a stupid firework he could barely light. That's probably all they have on him."

A quiet descended among them, holding the screams from the beach, the warmth of the explosion on their faces, the rush of terror like an infection ravaging through the crowds, the injured bodies struggling to make it off the beach. Samia paled at the thought that some people weren't just injured tonight.

"That—" Nasreen began, before the words lodged in her throat. She tried again. "That was terrifying."

Samia's body tensed at the images of the beach in chaos plastered in her mind.

Abdullahi rubbed a hand down his face. He looked at Samia. "And you think Qays did *that*? You were at the same beach as

I was, right? That kind of destruction? You think any of us are capable of something like that? We're *kids*."

Samia harrumphed. She hated to admit she was wrong, but she regrettably agreed with him.

"We need to protect our necks," Nasreen said. "They're clearly ready to come after us."

"We can't go around saying random stuff that'll get us in trouble," Abdullahi said, voice shaking. This was unfortunate for Samia because she thrived off saying the wildest things to get reactions out of people. "They hadn't even called my parents before questioning me. I doubt that's legal. I don't think they're doing any of this by the book, so all we can do now is expect to be in this for the long haul. And right now, we only have each other."

Zamzam adjusted her turban scarf, which Samia had knocked sideways. "He's right," she agreed. "We're in this mess for real. Might as well work together."

Samia's stomach flipped. If working together meant honesty, she needed a rain check. If *she* had one or two secrets she'd rather not share, no doubt the others—with secrets of their own— would be less than forthcoming.

Abdullahi shuddered, and it infected the rest of them. Terror, it appeared, was contagious.

An officer passed by, announcing their parents had been called and that no more interrogations would continue. Tomorrow, it would begin again. Samia could breathe in the tiny moment of relief that gave her.

Abdullahi stretched on the ground; then Zamzam lay across a bench, tucking her knees into her chest and facing the wall.

Nasreen hid her face with her hair and leaned herself against the wall, but her body remained rigid. Samia paced the cell a while longer.

The holding cell was timeless. It might've been midnight, but it could've been dawn; they might've been sixteen-year-olds, but they could have also aged fifty years in that single night.

Samia spread her legs on the remaining bench, and her knees creaked. She hadn't been mistakenly taken into custody for some stupid prank on a macabre summer night. This, the prison bars, the police, the explosions, they were all real.

And she wasn't sad or worried about it. She was very, very afraid.

THE LOS ANGELES JOURNAL

TERRORIST ATTACK DEVASTATES LA BEACH

Dozens of casualties at deadly Independence Day celebration

LOS ANGELES—Carnage and destruction sweep Monarch Beach as oil rig *Bonnie* and Monarch Beach Pier are suspected targets of a terrorist attack. Crowds of Americans commemorating their freedom with Independence Day festivities were victimized in the assault. Over a dozen are estimated to be injured, and two have reportedly been killed.

Monarch Beach, a quaint beach in North Los Angeles and the county's safest beach three years in a row, became ground zero for the first major attack against the United States of America since 9/11. At approximately 9:01 PM on the Fourth of July, an unknown organization currently under police investigation is suspected to have bombed *Bonnie* off the coast of the beach. A minute later, a second explosion tore apart Monarch Beach Pier, fracturing the pier to pieces and slaying a security officer. Los Angeles County, with aid from the federal government, is acting quickly to contain the sizable oil spill resulting from the attack.

Bonnie, a federal oil rig, operates under PetroMile, the leader in the petroleum industry, which has refused to comment. The LAPD have several suspects in custody. However, they have yet to conduct press briefings, suggesting international interference and motives, likely from the Middle East, and have deferred reporters indefinitely. Large gatherings of Muslims at Monarch Beach suggest evidence to the theory.

◆

CHAPTER 9

NASREEN

NASREEN WAS CALLED INTO THE INTERROGATION ROOM bright and early on the fifth of July, the first day her nightmare didn't end after waking up.

This Detective Pennella character exuded hubris. Or perhaps outright vanity.

Nasreen placed her index fingernail under her other nails, excavating the dirt that had crammed under there the night before. She did so without looking and despite her quaking hands. The dirt fell into her lap in clumps.

"You are very interesting," Pennella began as his eyes glazed over the files in front of him so quickly, there was no way he was reading a single word on them. She doubted they could have collected that much paper's worth of data on her or any of the others in so little time. Unless the data collection had started before.

Even then, Nasreen hadn't done anything of substance in her life to warrant that much data. She lived her life like a retiree, she had a self-imposed early bedtime, she gardened in her spare time, and *risk* was a foreign concept to her. The only way he could've collected all of that was if he'd dialed into her pet snake's brain and downloaded their conversations. She didn't talk to anyone as much and as honestly as she spoke with Carrots. Well, Carrots and one other person.

"It seems you aren't a member of the organizations that gathered at the beach last night?" he asked.

Nasreen remained silent.

"Come on, Ms. Choudhry," Pennella groused. "I'm on your side. I'm here to help. After this, you might be able to see your parents. It's not right to keep you here if you haven't done anything. Let's clear this mess up, and you can be on your way. How does that sound?"

Like the absolute worst, Nasreen thought bitterly. *You haven't even told me what it is that I haven't done.*

His furrowing eyebrows softened his face, and if she hadn't been prepared for it, Nasreen might have betrayed her oath of silence. His crumbly expression had a talent for making others want to be on his side.

It was either his confidence or his birthright. One was more legitimate than the other, but neither existed in Pennella without its counterpart.

"Let's start with the facts," Pennella suggested.

The only fact Nasreen knew was that Pennella's chestnut hair made his plum dress shirt easier on the eyes. She pulled her most distrusting expression over her face, and the mood shifted. With every second, Nasreen became less cooperative and Pennella grew more agitated.

He cleared his throat. "Why don't you start at the beginning? Tell me a little about yourself. Your family, your school."

Nasreen pressed her lips together. Counted five seconds. Five seconds was how long her teachers at Saint Modesta were required to wait to see if the students had any questions after asking, "Any questions?"

At the count of five, Pennella moved on. "Or you can start with last night."

Nasreen reckoned detectives should wait longer than teachers before abandoning their previous prompt.

Pennella sighed. "Like what time did you get to the beach? Why aren't you a part of their organizations?"

"Organizations?" She sucked in a breath. "You mean the MSA?"

His quirked lips betrayed a hint of a smile. It *was* his birthright. "Yes, tell me about the MSA," he said.

"MSA is an acronym for the Muslim Students Association, a club for students who share an interest in Islam," Nasreen defined.

"A religious organization."

"I said a club for students who are interested in Islam. They don't have to be Muslim to join."

"Yet most of them are," Pennella said. "And you aren't a part of these organizations because..."

"You're the detective." Her voice trembled. She tried to muster the confidence she'd honed by being the only Brown person in most of her classes, but that confidence was hard to cultivate and, on a night like this, even harder to harness.

"That I am." Pennella smiled. Nasreen had to give it to him: He seemed a bit dim, but at least he wasn't cruel. He sifted through the papers again, and Nasreen nearly cried. "It says here you go to Saint Modesta, the number one private Catholic school in LA County. They treat you okay there?"

Nasreen wouldn't look at him, revulsion taking root in the back of her throat. Nasreen's parents really loved sending her to places that took the number one slot on lists. She pushed the dirt out from under her pinkie fingernail.

Pennella huffed the question away. "I'm guessing Saint Modesta High School doesn't have an MSA. So sounds like you had no reason to be at the beach. These religious organizations—"

"*Clubs*," she whispered under her breath.

"—were having their annual event. So the others had reason to be at Monarch Beach. You did not. Unless I'm missing something?"

Pennella was smug as hell, though his implication was weak.

"I don't think I was the only nonstudent at their schools' MSA event," Nasreen said.

"Ah yes," Pennella agreed. "But you are the only one who was found cliffside, far, far away from the pits, loitering dangerously close to trespassing. You *and* Samia."

Nasreen flinched at the name. She could feel every bit of the dirt on her skin. She wanted to shed her skin, like Carrots did every month, and discard the night's memories that were imprinted on it.

A fire in the middle of the ocean, a plume of smoke, and a thousand pieces of wood blasted across the beach. She had been standing in perfect view of it. But she had fallen on the right side of the law. Whether she had trespassed wasn't the question. They didn't cuff her to a table for trespassing. For all the tragedy of errors, Nasreen knew she was, in ways that didn't concern the detective, in the wrong.

"All I ask is that you give me your full story. Unedited," he requested.

For cops like Pennella, when the investigation was bigger than they could handle, it was easier to provide the story than to uncover it. Especially when there were so many options before him. He could be the writer in this work of fiction.

"And I can," she desperately agreed, leaning herself all the way forward. "But I need a lawyer first."

Pennella's scowl quickly softened into a disappointed frown. Nasreen clenched her jaw and tried to relax back into her chair, but her body was rigid. She felt that Pennella wouldn't answer her if she pulled even an inch away.

My life is over. The thought slipped through her defenses, and it broke her composure, but she pushed on to keep some control of the situation. "It's a new day," she murmured. "Don't I get a phone call? You said you'd like to help, Detective. In any way that you can."

Detective Pennella looked dejected. "I'll take you back to holding and see if we can arrange a way for your parents to see you."

Nasreen shuddered. Not at the detective and the loose threads he was chasing, but at the image of her mama and baba showing up to bail her out.

Because Nasreen was innocent, of some things more than others. She'd rather stay in the holding cell than explain to her parents why she was all the way by the cliffs with a girl neither of her parents knew.

The standing officer led her back out of the interrogation room and to holding. The gate clanked shut, and she stumbled onto the bench, light-headed. The others were all weary-eyed, seemingly having lost ten pounds each after the rough night.

"Did you do it?" It was Samia who asked.

Ask for your parents. Don't tell them anything. That's what they'd agreed to.

Samia blinked at her with her mascara-flaked almond eyes.

Nasreen sat and immediately caved into herself, and whatever false conviction had kept her upright in the interrogation room left her body. Exhaustion nestled into every crevice of her body, the fear she'd felt in the room hitting her belatedly. She tried to respond to Samia, but the idea of opening her mouth made her want to sleep for three whole days. Her stomach growled, and the sound of it made her cry.

None of them paid her any mind; they had all taken turns crying, some more loudly than others, and it was Nasreen's turn to mourn restful nights and peace of mind. She had never felt so hopeless, but these weren't just feelings; her body was having a reaction to the change. She would have to find a way to save herself from this, no matter what.

When she had the strength to look up, Zamzam and Abdul-lahi were gazing off into the four-foot distance and Samia was stress-biting her dry lips.

If these strangers were in the same situation as she was, then they were supposed to be her allies. Nasreen eyed the two other girls. Was she supposed to feel some sort of sisterhood with them? Some kind of trauma bond?

Each of them would desert the others at the earliest opportunity to get out.

Or perhaps, only Nasreen felt that way.

Which might be the greatest point of all.

It was surprisingly easy to convince herself of this in this state. Like her parents always said, there might be only one open spot for people like them, and Nasreen better do her damn best to make sure she got it. Sure, it was a solitary life, but she was used to it. It was why she preferred snakes to cats or dogs, because they were misunderstood, solitary creatures.

The doors to the front of the police station opened; Nasreen was well acquainted with the sound after a full night at the station. The three others sat up. Zamzam ran to the corner of the cell with the best view, her eyesight the least compromised of the four.

"Is it our parents?" Samia asked hopefully.

Abdullahi's shoulders slumped. "I don't think so. It's some white lady in a suit."

"They can't do this," Zamzam said aloud, mostly to herself, which she did quite a lot. "We're kids. We need our parents. We have a right to counsel."

"Eh," Abdullahi grunted.

Nasreen's throat felt like sandpaper.

"Shh, shh," Samia said at the silence, her arm flailing behind her. "Detective Penne is in the reception area."

Detective Penne was what Samia called Pennella. She could joke about him because she hadn't sat down with him and crapped her pants yet.

"He's saying hi to her," Samia narrated. "She looks *so* fancy. And *really* old. Those years suntanning in Cancún were *not* the move, Debra."

The older woman probably wasn't a Debra.

Nasreen hated that Samia had cried all night and then cracked jokes about Detective Pennella all morning while Zamzam emanated enough anti-Samia energy for the entire precinct. Samia seemed to be able to make herself immune to anything with her backlog of coping mechanisms: bad puns and fashion, among others.

Or perhaps, Nasreen hated that Samia felt secure enough in herself to act however, no matter how many dirty looks Zamzam cast at her.

"Damn it!" Samia screamed in a hushed voice. "She's coming!"

Samia twirled wildly, then dashed into the opposite corner of the cell as if there were anywhere to hide here.

The clicking of heels grew louder and louder while the keyboard tapping and chatter dwindled until they completely stopped.

Detective Penne, in his ugly plum shirt—

No, Detective *Pennella*, in his ugly plum shirt, approached the outside of the cell. Abdullahi, Zamzam, and Nasreen recoiled. Samia stepped closer to him.

One of these things is not like the other.

Pennella gestured to them. "Here they are, Mrs. Favreau."

The heels clicked against the linoleum twice, and she stepped into their view. She had her black hair tucked into a bun, her Mallen streak sweeping across the front. Her navy skirt suit had a peplumed blazer, and she wore pearl earrings with a matching necklace.

Nasreen thought her clothes must not have been why Samia called her fancy. There was something in her face, in the way her fine lines wrinkled over chiseled bones to make her look both ancient and majestic. The way the blue of her eyes pierced through the four of them, intensified by her crow's-feet, made Nasreen feel both like a roach beneath her foot and a diamond all at once.

This woman was no Detective Penne.

"Ah, my friends," Mrs. Favreau said, straight-faced. Her voice was throaty, with a 20 percent elderly intonation that didn't make her seem like she'd book a cruise, but like she owned a cruise liner and could crush her competition with her pinkie.

This woman would wreak havoc on a middle-aged couple being audited for a few hundred dollars.

"There are others?" she asked to the side without breaking eye contact.

Pennella replied in the affirmative. "We repurposed another room for holding. This group is younger, juveniles technically."

Her eyes brightened. "We're dealing with some adults?"

"Nearly there. Age seventeen."

"Ah. I'd like to start there, if you don't mind."

They spoke as if Nasreen and the others didn't have ears.

"Not at all," Pennella said. His voice was tensed like this woman had power over him. "We'll debrief you inside. This way, Mrs. Favreau."

"Oh, please," she cooed as she gazed into each of their eyes, one by one, lingering as if reading into them. "Call me Kandi."

Kandi Favreau and Detective Pennella walked away, a trail of officers and other men in suits following them.

A tightness clawed itself into Nasreen's chest. It had been

wavering in her throat for hours, but it finally found a home, nestling like a parasite deep in her thoracic cavity.

"*Fuuuck*," Samia cursed. "What is this? Investigation Pantry?"

It was quiet, and Nasreen could imagine Zamzam's eye roll, but then Abdullahi let out a low chuckle. He sniffed and nipped it in the bud. Zamzam laughed through her nose, a series of puffs for medium-mild funny. Like the second pepper option on a menu's spicy meter.

"This isn't funny," Nasreen grouched. She cut a miserable look at Samia, who had the audacity to look pleased with herself.

"Sorry for trying to lighten the mood. Go back to your end-of-the-world sulking," Samia said. Her hijab was tied differently, both ends over her shoulders; her jeans were cuffed; and her shirt was cinched. Had she repurposed her clothing to create the illusion of a new outfit for the new day?

Unbelievable.

"Is this a joke to you?" Nasreen demanded. "Is it just content for your next Insta post? Get a grip, Samia."

She scoffed. "You talk like you don't have an alibi."

The tightness in Nasreen's chest—Gustavo, she'd decided to name it—dug its talons deeper around her heart.

"I don't," Nasreen said.

Samia's eyes were half-open, lids heavy. She drummed her acrylic nails on the bench. "Well, I'm not stressing because I do."

"Who were you meeting at the beach?" Abdullahi asked her. "After we saw each other in the parking lot we went in opposite directions, but the cops picked us out."

Samia sighed. "I was meeting someone I met online. An online friend."

"Why are you being so ominous? Was it like a date?" Abdullahi asked.

Nasreen's breath caught in her throat.

"Something like that." Samia was very still, her voice flat.

"With who?" Abdullahi pressed on. When he was met with silence, he added, "I mean, if we can tell them who we were with, then we can get alibis. If more people start coming forward, then they can't corner us into a version of the night that's not true."

As they listened to him, the girls turned toward him in the center of the cell. Nasreen felt strangely drawn to the steadiness of his voice.

"Look, I'll even go first," he said eagerly. Or perhaps manically. "I went to the bathroom, and then I saw a girl on the ground and tried helping her up. No, I did help her up, but she was really messed up. Then the cops came, and I had to run, so I don't know what happened to her." His voice cracked. "The detective tried showing me her picture in there, so maybe that's not helpful because they already have her as a person of interest. But there, that's everything on me."

Nasreen didn't think Abdullahi was lying, but she also didn't feel like he'd given the full truth.

After a pause, Zamzam said, "I was with that stoner jock they arrested. The one you called Qays, so I'm no help either."

Zamzam and Abdullahi looked at Samia and Nasreen. Both girls busied themselves, Samia with the knots in her hijab and Nasreen with cleaning her cracked glasses.

Zamzam tsked. "If you two aren't the most sus—"

"They arrested Nasreen and me together," Samia bit out. "That's all." Misunderstanding settled across the cell, and Nasreen wanted to scream. Samia rolled her eyes because she had that luxury. Like she'd said before, she hadn't done anything wrong. Only Nasreen had.

"If all of us were with each other," Zamzam reasoned, "then our stories mean nothing. They make us look like we're accomplices."

"They didn't arrest us at random," Abdullahi muttered. They were strangers, but with the wrong narrator, they could seem like so much more than that.

"Fuck," Samia whispered. "We're fucked!"

And perhaps they were.

CHAPTER 10

QAYS

TWENTY-SEVEN.

Twenty-seven beads on the bracelet Muzhda gave Qays.

Ten red, ten black, six letters, one heart.

Clear string, tidy knot.

Rigid against the floor, Qays let his eyes roam over the beads until there were two of them, then four, then six, and his eyes were perpetually crossed.

No windows. No sound. No air.

Just Qays, alone, in a room for days that could have been months. With the rate at which his bladder filled, it had been neither. Still, he could count the beads only so many more times.

Twenty-seven beads. Ten red, ten black, six letters, one heart.

It had been too long since someone smiled at him. He needed it. Craved the attention like a drug.

Muzhda's smile hadn't been intoxicating, though. It had been magic. If he could see her smile once every day, it would satisfy his daily quota until the next morning, when she could smile again.

Twenty-seven beads. Ten red, ten black, six letters, one heart.

Qays's eardrums coddled the subtlest noise from the other side of the door. His heart raced, and he sat up, his neck spasming out of its cramped position. He turned toward the door, which was finally opening.

Everything ached. His body stubbornly rejected movement as his arms were cuffed and officers transported him down a hall, placing him in a metal chair. Smudges caked over his vision from the abrupt overload of sensory stimuli he got moving from that dark room to this interrogation suite.

Twenty-seven beads. Ten red, ten black, six letters, one heart.

When his vision caught up with him, a knockoff Ryan Reynolds and a black-haired Helen Mirren stared back at him. Qays tried to straighten up despite the pain that shot down his back. He'd need some PT before the new season.

"How's it going, bud?" the man started off. Qays didn't know if he was *bud* or if there was a dog in his blotted peripheral vision. All he could think was *Twenty-seven beads, ten red, ten black, six letters, and one heart.* The man continued, "Detective Micky Pennella here with Agent Kandi Favreau. It is thirteen thirty-two, July fifth…."

Twenty-seven beads. Ten red, ten black, six letters, one heart. One night, half a day.

"Now for some housekeeping," the detective added.

Qays answered all the detective's mundane questions. Or at least he thought he did. Everything was one big smudge. The questions the detective asked: *Why were you there, whom were you with, what did you do, when did you arrive, where were you when it all went to shit, how did it all go to shit?* Qays gave them his timeline and his location on the beach, offered all that he knew, but he left a hole right in the center. The hole that grew around Muzhda.

He didn't talk about her, because, well, his brain was a flurry of her strange, silly, somber stories and flashes of moments when they'd accidentally brushed hands during tutoring sessions. They were never this significant, yet they were suddenly all he could think about. He was having trouble convincing himself that she was just a girl he'd barely known whose smile's spell he'd only just fallen under.

Muzhda.

Twenty-seven beads. Ten red, ten black, six letters, one heart. One night, half a day, and no smiles.

He needed a smile. He needed the chalky coating on the inside of his mouth to go away. He needed his skin to feel less like crust and more like a balloon. He was Qays Sharif, and he always knew what he needed and none of this was it. He hoped after every meaningless question that it had been the last one.

There was a lull in the onslaught of questions. A quiet descending on a beach in the cold winter, a silence despite the ferocious wind and the devastating waves.

The female agent cleared her throat.

Favreau, her name was, Qays thought inversely.

"The gravity of the situation is quite severe, as you must have the foresight to see for yourself," she said with polished fragility. Qays knew because he was practiced in the art of manipulation. He'd gotten to where he was by using others.

Muzhda.

Twenty-seven beads. Ten red, ten black, six letters, one heart. One night, half a day, no smiles. A gallon of regret.

Favreau continued, "And we just want to have all the facts. We thank you for your cooperation, Mr. Sharif."

But…

"But," she continued, as he'd predicted, "we have a few more questions before we can send you back."

"Back?" Qays croaked. *To that smileless room?*

Favreau's lines deepened with faux concern. "Only until we're confirmed for another facility that is better equipped for the circumstances. We'll get you into more appropriate confinement in no time."

Qays's ears short-circuited. *Confinement.* Qays had answered their questions to the best of his ability; his part in this play was over. He should be allowed an exit.

Favreau tapped the end of her pen on the table. "When was the last time you left the country?"

Twenty-seven beads. Ten red, ten black, six letters, one heart. One night, half a day, no smiles. A gallon of regret and a damning question.

The detective was sitting back, his housekeeping questions long over. Favreau had the big guns, and the guns said *Muslim*, *Arab*, and *terrorist* on them.

Qays could place a soccer ball into the upper right corner, two centimeters shy of the post. He could hit that shot ten times in a row, eyes closed. He was sharp when he was awake, when his brain wasn't one huge fog. He'd let them drag him far enough in this interrogation before coming to his senses. And there were others, like Zamzam, with their own stories and lives he might have put in jeopardy. And while the hole around Muzhda widened, he wanted to build a fence around it. He wanted to protect her.

"Mr. Sharif?"

Qays set his dry lips in a tight line. "I want a lawyer."

Favreau's mouth twitched; her eyes dared him to say it again. "It says here you arrived four days ago to LAX from Tel Aviv. How long did you spend there? Where did you go in Israel?"

A nerve in Qays's head burst. "I went to Palestine." His voice was like steel.

"I see," she chirped, satisfied. "That'll be all for now. Thank you for your cooperation."

She pushed away from the table, and the detective glanced up at her, flustered. He began to gather his things as Favreau sized Qays up one last time before heading for the door.

Qays's heart beat a thousand times per second. His confusion played on his emotions, and he blurted, "Is Muzhda okay?"

Favreau's hand froze on the doorknob.

"Muzhda Ahmad?" The detective butchered her name, brows furrowing.

Yes, Muzhda. Muzhda Ahmad.

"She's—"

"That'll be all, Detective Pennella," Favreau bit out, her eyes sharp.

Just as the officers had lobbed him into the interrogation suite, they delivered Qays to his smileless closet.

Maybe he'd said too much without thinking to the woman with the big guns, the woman with a plan behind her eyes as deep and intricate as the wrinkles on her face. It hadn't been his intention; he couldn't remember a single word he had shared in that small room, nor whether or not he'd told them about Zamzam, but he knew he'd kept Muzhda out of it.

He lay in the same corner, placed his neck at an angle for continued discomfort, and looped his arm around to stare at his bracelet. Like a crustacean coiling back into its crusty, sandy shell, Qays curled in on himself.

She's okay, Qays imagined the detective saying.

Twenty-seven beads, he counted.

Ten red, ten black, six letters, one heart.

One night, half a day, no smiles. A gallon of regret and a damning question.

A starry life and the storm that would destroy it.

CHAPTER 11

MUZHDA

OVER THE NEXT WEEK, THE OUTSIDE OF THE PRECINCT became a war zone. The parking lot divided like the nation.

One side red with rage, self-diagnosed with injury, claiming an attack where it hurt them most: right in their freedom.

The other lifted banners of the Independence Day Six, their faces in a row, digitized and starkly shadowed, their names bold beneath their faces.

Nasreen, glasses framing her narrow-set eyes, drawn pensive and guarded. Her dark hair whipped around her like a flame.

Abdullahi's face flashed across the banners wide-eyed and soulful. Fresh lineup, square jaw, a face open like a book to others because his heart was three times the size of a normal person's. His trust too true.

Samia with red lipstick, filled eyebrows arched, and a prominent beauty mark on her left cheekbone. Even her avatar glittered.

Zamzam with a colorful print scarf, the colors contrasting with the rich tone of her skin. Plump lips slightly open, her chin lifted in anticipated defiance. Her eyes set firmly on a challenge.

Qays, striking like the striker he was, his curls like a lion's mane. His expression full of the gratification of an outstretched hand that's always receiving.

Then Muzhda herself, cream hijab floating around her gaunt face like a cloud, hazel eyes accentuated with gold turned up to the sky. Her picture popped up across the sea of humans, more than the others.

She felt like she was watching the crowds from above.

Muzhda recognized more than one of the faces—the boy Abdullahi looked familiar—but in her state, she couldn't exactly recall why.

The banners with their faces poked at the air. The chanting carried over to her, their names on defense against the hateful words of the others.

Civil rights.

Terrorists.

American.

Immigrants.

One word came from both sides of the fence, though its meaning couldn't have been more different.

Freedom.

The doors to the precinct opened. The crowds quieted, then picked up in an uproar as bodies stampeded toward the sheriff.

Out the side door, uniformed officers ushered the Independence Day Six into three black Range Rovers. The first two cars drove off with their passengers. The third was idle.

Muzhda waited. She watched the side door, her energy dwindling. Then LA, the city of sun and angels, began to cry. Raindrops bled down the windows. Those with the Six stood their ground, while the others ran for cover. LA, the city of sun and angels, fractured.

The car door opened.

Qays flew sideways into the back seat, his hair dripping wet.

Her bracelet sat there on his wrist, where it always belonged. Her heart could flutter.

He righted himself as best he could without proper use of his arms. The doors were bolted; the vehicle wasn't a standard automobile but specially made for its purpose. It was strange they weren't in police cars. Almost as strange as the wires and electronics she had tripped over at the beach the day that felt like decades ago.

Qays grunted, his neck unnaturally crooked and his posture shot. The engine purred. As they drove past the crowds, faces of reporters who had been duped by the sheriff's press conference hoax slammed against the window.

Through her lens, the world was an oil painting touched by drops of water, dispersing from solubility into a dozen directions, each explosion of color bleeding into its neighbors. The faces outside melted from anger into horror by an effortless act of God.

Rain.

Qays's body fell over as though he fainted, leaning on her shoulder. He sat up, wincing at his outstretched neck, then slumped back into himself. Eventually, he tilted his head toward her until she could see his face.

His beautiful face was gruff from patchy stubble, his threaded eyebrows slowly growing back in. Naturally, her eyes dropped to his lips, which were grotesquely chapped.

But still kissable, she forced herself to think in a moment where uncertainty and fear leaked into every pore of their existence.

He jumped at the sight of her. "Muzhda?"

"Qays."

He was suddenly very awake, dark circles and crusty corners aside. Muzhda wondered what she must look like. Surely nothing like the angelic Muzhda on the banners outside. If this Qays was the trampled version of the boy on his banner, the thrilling boy with everything at his fingertips, then what was she?

"But—but—but how?" he croaked, his voice hoarse. "Where are they taking us?"

"What will they do with us?" added Muzhda in a whisper.

Qays dropped his head.

The rain bled deeper.

Muzhda wished she could reach out her hand and comfort him. No matter what happened next, at least she had loved a boy while she was free. For her, what she felt when she saw Qays before their world went to hell had been love, albeit a young fool's love, but it had counted.

"You're wearing my bracelet," she murmured. It contrasted with his skin and was infinitesimal beneath the cuffs, but it was there. The final syllable of her name and the heart showed clearly. The sight would have delighted the butterflies in her stomach. But they didn't flutter.

She wondered what had shifted. A change of heart made her guarded. What would've happened if she hadn't gone down the beach like he'd asked her? Would she be here?

Maybe the butterflies didn't flutter because her resolute love for Qays was soiled now. Soiled by the night that took everything from her.

Qays groaned as he lifted his gaze to meet hers. His eyes, once so bright, dulled at the edges. "Can I keep it?"

Muzhda was surprised he'd want it. Maybe she had left a deeper impression than she thought. Maybe it wasn't just the butterflies that had fluttered during those tutoring sessions.

She swore the sun peeked through the patchy rain clouds. The vise was fused over her heart after the Fourth, but what she had felt before her world ended could still count for a moment. She wanted it to count for Qays.

So she said, "Always."

CHAPTER 12

ZAMZAM

ZAMZAM THREW OUT LOGIC, REASON, AND RATIONALITY. There was no sense in pretending her life was a painting in the era of realism. Her life fast-forwarded through the pretty brushstrokes of the impressionist era and came to a full stop in surrealism. Her world was a variety of disproportional geometric shapes that didn't resemble anything she could recognize.

Coarse fingers gripped Zamzam's head and yanked down hard, tucking her head into her neck as they escorted her from the black vehicle that was all harsh lines. She stared down as the black tarmac became white floors. Her flip-flops looked more tattered against the high sheen of this new building.

Ahead of her, the heels of the officers who were dragging Abdullahi took a hard right, while Zamzam's took a hard left. She threw a glance behind her, a flood of fear sweeping over her chest. Abdullahi might have been a stranger, but his downturned eyes had become familiar over the last week. If anything, in this foreign, surrealist world about her, those strangers had become constants.

For days they didn't get answers. And they tried. She'd asked Detective Penne (the nickname had caught on) countless times why they weren't allowed to see their parents or speak to attorneys, but no dice. The guy simply replied, "It's above my pay grade, sweetie."

She'd let the *sweetie* part slide because he looked as spooked as they were.

She'd asked every officer in earshot, and they'd stared at her like she was underwater. Sound didn't seem to travel through the change in mediums, Zamzam's medium being common sense. She didn't get to ask Kandi Favreau, either, because, for some reason above everyone's pay grade, Kandi Favreau didn't want to see her.

The officer jerked Zamzam's head up and made her face a white door, too close to it to glance around and get her bearings. Goose bumps activated across her flesh as Samia's sniffling from beside her intensified.

Shut up, Samia, Zamzam thought miserably. That girl was losing her damn mind, from cracking hysterically awful puns to her nightly breakdowns. Sure, Zamzam wanted to be a doctor to help people, but Samia might have been the exception to that altruistic notion.

The door buzzed loudly to open, and Zamzam winced. She, Nasreen, and Samia stood against a wall and in a line marked by nearby drains. This room didn't need a surrealist twist; it was already an impossible place for her to exist in. Every possible scenario she'd imagined boiled down to this. She was at an unknown location, at the mercy of officers holding weapons; the only thing protecting her was the thin layer of fabric her clothes provided.

Zamzam's life was like a pendulum clock, and the night at the beach had screwed up the precise swing that kept her in time. She needed to set the pendulum swing back in the right time, but the more time that passed on this broken pendulum clock, the more her life was derailing further from what it was meant to be.

Zamzam wanted to tell Jamal that she'd correct all of this. She'd tell him she wouldn't leave them like her older brother had. Yazeed had been the dependable one, until he wasn't. Until his absence left the gaping hole in her life that made her too numb to carry on. He had been the one who was successful and smart and did all the right things before Zamzam had to take his place. Because Yazeed had graduated salutatorian and decided, when he left home for college, he didn't need his family anymore.

Zamzam needed to graduate valedictorian because she despised the hole left by her older brother, and she needed to succeed more than him *while* sticking by her family to seal the gaping hole forever.

Yazeed's abandonment was a strong motivator. School, home, and work were all that mattered. She didn't even glance at anything else.

Except for that bonfire, when all-American-boy Qays fired a firework in the wrong direction and the world broke. She was now a human firework herself, misfiring into this combustible shitstorm.

"Strip," the officer ordered as the three girls were uncuffed.

Zamzam glanced around at the female-only officers on standby. Three of them had guns, large ones, prepped and held in tense, ready-to-fire arms. All they needed was to release the safety, aim, and shoot.

Samia didn't fight back a harrowing sob. She could be an actor with the way her cries targeted the weaknesses in Zamzam's defenses.

Still, Zamzam held herself, solidifying her frown. She had to be strong for Jamal and Momma.

"Strip!" the officer barked at them once again.

But Jamal and Momma weren't here. She didn't have to put on a brave face for them. Her eyes and nose stung. She was good at holding on for her family. Their small unit had fractured before, had become even smaller than it already was, first with her parents' divorce, then with her older brother leaving them for his own selfish reasons.

Nasreen whimpered and slipped off her shoes first. Samia joined her, sobs breaking like a bird's screeching. The two girls began to strip off their clothes, which had begun to smell of onions and rot, extracting them like a stubborn layer of extra skin. Their hands trembled. Clothes were protection used to cover vulnerabilities, insecurities, one's self. Removing their clothes scrubbed the girls down to their cores. They chose what to do with their bodies; they were theirs and theirs alone. Forcing them to strip stole away the liberty they had over that choice.

Zamzam felt her cheeks become wet. Involuntary tears streamed down her face. She didn't need to be strong for Samia and Nasreen. Some part of her that she'd never recognized before envied how the other girls could let go. And now finally, just like them, she was coming undone.

"All. Of. You," the officer enunciated, pointing her baton at Zamzam.

Samia dropped her jeans to her ankles. Then she projectile vomited straight ahead of her, and her body heaved forward with such force, her knees struck the ground hard. Zamzam could hear Nasreen gagging.

An officer grumbled a slew of curses. "Hurry up and strip so we can get the water started and clean this shit up."

Zamzam's body shook violently as she shamelessly released her cries. She'd cried only half as dramatically when she and Momma had realized Yazeed wasn't coming back.

The pendulum swung too fast, too slow, too out of time. Zamzam stuck to the plan, but following a straight path didn't mean she would be complacent. She needed to reset the swing.

"I want a lawyer," Zamzam murmured. Her voice found its footing. *"I want a lawyer."*

"Follow orders," the officer snapped. "Once you're neutralized, we'll get the next orders."

Zamzam wiped at the tears on her cheeks with trembling hands. "No one's told me why I'm here. I'm not a criminal. If I'm a suspect, fine, but I deserve the proper procedures. I'm an American citizen. I have rights."

The officer huffed loudly. "This is a matter of national security. We're preparing you for questioning."

National security?

Zamzam shook her head in disbelief. "I didn't do—"

The officer slammed her baton against a pole; the shower room clattered and echoed. Samia cowered, her bare shoulders shuddering. "No talking!" the officer shouted. "The orders are to strip. You'll get your answers after you're neutralized."

But she couldn't. If she stripped, she would be giving up her freedom to decide for herself. She would be admitting she belonged here, that this was what she deserved, and that she had done something, anything, to deserve this. If she stripped, she'd be relinquishing the first part of herself to a hungry system that wanted to swallow her up.

The officer didn't even let Zamzam blink. She took two long strides toward her, took a fistful of Zamzam's scarf, and unwrapped it, shoving her head about until it came undone. Zamzam staggered away, pulling her arms to her chest, as the officer lifted her baton and drove it down onto her shoulder. She yelped, collapsing to the ground, pain shooting down to her elbow and stinging the tips of her fingers.

"Strip. *Now.*"

"Please," Samia begged her. She looked at Zamzam from between the matted reddish-brown curls that covered the top half of her blotchy face.

Zamzam groaned, failing to hold her body up on all fours. With her eyes fixed on the shoelace on the officer's boot, she used the arm that wasn't shaking with pain to push herself up.

She came eye to eye with the woman who had dropped her to her knees. She would keep dropping her until Zamzam gave in.

But she couldn't give in. For Momma and Jamal, she couldn't.

Zamzam was practical, logical. The one time she wasn't, she listened to the ocean, and she ran.

Item by item, layer by layer, Zamzam peeled her clothes away, making her less, diluting her until she was no one, as naked and unprotected as when she came into the world. Except then, she had had Momma to hold her, and now she had no one.

After forcing a drained Samia to her feet, the officers ordered the girls to turn around. Water hissed behind them, and then the volume cranked up until Niagara Falls was in the room with them. The water shot at their backs, their bodies pressure washed like the side of a building. Zamzam felt the freezing water etch scratches into her skin that would leave invisible scars she'd have for the rest of her life.

They rotated as they were told, lifted their arms above their heads as the water hosed them down. Samia wailed. Nasreen quaked, her cries loud enough to be heard over the roaring water pressure. But Zamzam fought her logical nature. Her nose stung, and her eyes burned with tears screaming to be let out. *Strong, responsible, dependable* were what made up Zamzam. She had become comfortable with those adjectives, yet now, with her face wet with tears, they felt like false promises. Words that promised her, if she lived by them, she would never be where she was now.

And with the other girls, she cried.

CHAPTER 13

KANDI FAVREAU'S CELL PHONE WAS A NOOSE. WHEN SHE took a call, knots tightened around the names that came off her lips, and by the time the call ended at least one person was gallows bound.

Detective Micky Pennella barged into Favreau's room during a phone call, and she raised one delicate finger. His expression smarted, and when she raised her other four fingers, he stopped in his tracks.

"Yes, schedule a meeting with the executives," she said. "They can rest assured we're working toward a common goal." She rushed to end the call, turning to Pennella as she did. "Show me what you got."

He strode forward, extending a portfolio to her. "My team delineated the suspects' coordinates. Also, Stewart sent in the extensive ID profiles for each suspect in custody as well as those who were killed in the attack to determine motives. You were right." At the clear and obvious, she snorted. Pennella continued, more diffidently, "Three of them had traveled outside the country in the last year."

Favreau's feathers ruffled at that. She had known that would be the case all along.

"Does the media know?" asked Favreau.

"They're keeping a tight lid on it," Pennella answered, like a good puppy dog handing his owner the newspaper.

Favreau's mouth stretched into a thin line. Her eyes pored over the files in her hand, the map of Monarch Beach against the wall, the Xs over the rig and the pier, the pictures of each of her suspects placed in various locations. There were six of them, scattered up and down the beach in pairs, a puzzle entreating her to complete it. Every puzzle was a facsimile of the last; humans weren't innovative enough to create a new puzzle for Favreau to solve. The best puzzle solvers were the puzzle makers. They were the ones who could dissect a puzzle because they knew what components made up the larger picture. Favreau excelled at inventing puzzles.

"Then tell them to loosen the lid," Favreau muttered.

"Of cou—" Pennella blinked twice. "Excuse me?"

"Lefty loosey, Micky."

Pennella's diffidence puckered into unease, and he furrowed his brows. His self-esteem was flimsily patched up; it made her want to punch right through and make it fall apart.

"Is there a problem, Detective?" she postulated. "Of the information that we wish to keep from the public, the suspects' past itineraries are not included." She reached up to the map, her painted nail traveling the line in the Pacific Ocean that demarcated state waters. The oil rig was well within her sphere of influence. She was a federal agent, and the oil rig belonged to the federal government. Besides, PetroMile hadn't exactly refused to cooperate with her investigation. Quite the opposite, actually.

She was building a puzzle.

Pennella shook his head like a shaggy dog, but his hair, freshly set for the change in venue, was stiff. He wiped his hands on his pants. "I'm not sure I follow."

Favreau smiled at him, a waxy, doll-type smile that was misleadingly youthful. "You're a detective. Your job is to follow."

"Leads, yes," he added, sweating despite the cool air from the vents. "But this isn't what I was expecting—"

"A chance to work with the FBI?" she interrupted. "I'm surprised you're not more enthusiastic about the opportunity. This case will be huge. The media's already all over it, and I will make you the face of the investigation. When we solve this case, they'll have you to thank for making Americans feel safe again. I like to work behind the scenes. No need to credit me at all."

Kandi Favreau was a woman cable news called an expert. People went to her for her brains and partialities, not for her medals and awards. She was known by the people who needed her services, and unknown to everyone else. Her discretion made her powerful.

But this case was different. While it degraded her to ingratiate herself with this second-rate detective, to use him as her pawn, and to probe the minds of stupid but nonetheless murderous adolescents, the powers that be, money and politics, required her expertise. Sure, she felt like a preschool director, chasing four-year-olds streaking naked with knives while scolding their inadequate teacher. But Pennella and the kids weren't the reason she'd been called to this case. She excelled in cover-ups, and the gaping holes in this investigation required more than a sewing kit.

Her painted nail trailed up the map, to where the two girls, Nasreen and Samia, were found beside the beach homes. She let it fall, down to the bonfires and the sand, to the names Qays and Zamzam. Her nail dipped to Muzhda's location between the pier and the shopping promenade.

Her mind spun.

"You're young, Micky," she coaxed, "but I see the chief of police in your future."

Pennella looked dyspeptic. He wiped his brow with the back of his sleeve.

Her eyes flashed at him. "Tell them to loosen the lid, but barely. The media always sniffs out what it wants."

Pennella accepted the order, but she wouldn't call him eager. She raised a brow at him as her nail met Abdullahi, a question mark beside his location on the night of the attack.

"Do you really believe the kids? That Abdullahi Talib was just 'in the bathroom'?" she asked. She was testing him.

"That's what he said," Pennella said. "But I don't think it matters really. He told us he happened upon Muzhda at the site we identified was linked to the explosion."

"To the attack," Favreau corrected.

He rubbed the back of his neck. "Well, we're just speculating it was an attack. Regardless of what the media is saying, we don't have enough proof other than the six suspects. But as far as our investigation is concerned, it's an explosion until we can gather more information."

Favreau couldn't do her job if Pennella wasn't on the same page as she was. He didn't even seem to be reading from the same book. And the only books Favreau read were ones she wrote.

"We're in a crisis, Micky," she said. "It's a rookie mistake to downplay it. We have plenty of information to call it an attack. Do you think the judge would have approved them to be kept on remand if we didn't have enough plausible evidence that they're dangerous? We're not keeping them in custody because we want to test run the system on them. We're keeping them in custody because the courts believe they're too dangerous to be let out on bail. Until this changes, we do the work."

"But the courts only think they're dangerous because we're building a case that says they are."

Favreau sighed, her breath heavy with impatience. "If these six aren't dangerous, then who is? Who takes the blame for this catastrophe if not them?"

Pennella frowned, glancing at the files in front of him. "I'm not sure I follow."

Favreau tapped a file. "For one, Qays Sharif gave us a lot to work with. He recently visited Palestinian territories. There's our connection to international anti-American groups. We have that firework he lit up. We can use it as a diversion or connect it to the explosions. Muzhda is easy; she was found at the origin of the signals to blow up the rig. It's only a matter of time before Abdullahi admits he was with her. Zamzam was found with Qays. And these two girls, Samia Al-Samra and Nasreen Choudhry," she drawled as she pointed to the Xs marking their location, "they're our biggest mystery. They're disconnected from the rest of the group and were found on the cliffs with great views of the oil rig. I'm sure they'll prove useful. We have the bare bones for this investigation. We have six kids without alibis and a catastrophe. We have a case."

"I—" Pennella hesitated, his mouth dry. He collected his notes and sat opposite the map; she could see her ideology wash through his mind. "I suppose Qays and Muzhda are also connected by the fingerprint samples on the package containing marijuana. And Abdullahi *was* found running from the site where Muzhda was found. And Zamzam was caught fleeing with Qays. Al-Samra, Choudhry, and Sharif all visited Muslim countries in—what's so amusing?"

Favreau couldn't help but chuckle. Pennella was young, which was why she insisted on calling him Micky, in addition to putting him in his place. He was trying so hard to make it make sense when it really didn't have to be all that difficult.

Her laughter died out.

"You have so much to learn." She opened her briefcase and passed him a thick binder branded with the White House seal. "That's your orientation. Read it tonight and you'll be up to speed. In the meantime, don't ask questions. Leave pulling together the details to me."

Silence descended as she returned to her map and her wall. Pennella turned page after page, too quickly to be reading, but quickly enough for the delectable assault of juicy secrets.

When Pennella spoke again, he sounded distressed. "How do

we know the remand will stand for much longer? The judge might have approved it because the country is scared. But what if they get out on bail and the investigation gets complicated?"

Favreau crossed her arms over her chest. She fought hard against the grin that pressed against her jaw.

"You worry too much, Micky," she started, hand lingering on Abdullahi's picture. "Monitor our suspects. Get creative—there's so much we can learn when they're in the right conditions and their desperation kicks in. Those who can be tried as adults should be heavily monitored. Separate them if necessary. Even if the younger ones get out on remand, the courts can easily be persuaded to keep the older ones on remand. But don't get comfortable. If it might help our case, let them mingle. See what they come up with. Let our suspects do the heavy lifting for us."

Finally, she could see Pennella's cogs turning. "An investigation is like a web," she continued, "and these six are our threads. We don't leave investigations like this without a face to the crime. We unravel until we get what we need. But if you pull at this string"—she plucked Abdullahi off the board—"versus this string"—she pulled Nasreen off with her other hand—"the unraveling looks quite different. We need to find the string that leads us to the result we want. That *all* of us want. If we need to be a little flexible with the law, so be it."

She gave a pointed look at the binder. "Read up, Micky."

CHAPTER 14

ABDULLAHI

KARMA WASN'T A CONCEPT THAT ABDULLAHI ACTUALLY believed in. Like zodiac signs or MBTI, it was a concept he learned so he could take a conversation turn with his peers at Huntington. But when he didn't have to pretend to be like others, karma and zodiac signs meant nothing to him. Abdullahi knew in Islam there were ways—like fasting or charity—to try to cover up a sin. Except he didn't know how many fasts or how much charity he needed to cover this one up.

For the first time in his life, he had insomnia. In the past, if he had any trouble falling asleep, he'd put on a Christmas movie, *Home Alone* being his go-to, and fall asleep to the wholesome holiday cheer from the '90s.

He was a '90s kid at heart, having been raised on all the things his older siblings grew up on. He was the youngest, a good ten years younger than the sibling closest to his age. By the time he came around, his parents were done parenting and his three older siblings became his parents. He had the best mix of parents: His mom and dad were sweet like grandparents; Amin, the oldest and his only brother, was his hero; and his sisters, Maryam and Fatima, were his protectors. Maryam was the strict one who enforced curfews to keep him safe from the dangerous world, and Fatima was the lenient one who covered up for him to shield him from Maryam's wrath, to let him live and fail and learn.

He felt he was the luckiest boy ever until now. Would his parents be able to handle the news? Would Amin be disappointed in him? Would Maryam chastise him? He knew Fatima would hug him and tell him it would be okay because it wasn't his fault, he couldn't have predicted, he wouldn't have known, he couldn't have caused what happened. That was why he'd told the police her name instead of his parents'. He needed her to make everything better. Maybe then he'd be able to sleep.

He shifted in the cell they kept him in at night. This was the cell he'd been placed in at the new location, his first night completely alone. When he was with the others, he had found comfort in being together. He'd gotten one or two hours of sleep, but in this freezing cell, he kept reliving that night, the details etched under his eyelids, and the only way not to see them was to keep his eyes open.

After an eternity, the door outside the cell opened. The officers got him up, secured handcuffs around his wrists again, and led him to a plain room with two benches, a table, and a chair, all fixed to the ground. The cell was for the nights, and this was the day room. He walked around in circles, ate tasteless food, and did the yoga poses he remembered from when he tagged along with Maryam and Fatima for their yoga phase.

After a few hours, the door opened with a clang, awakening Abdullahi from a silent daze. The officers shifted in the doorway and then abruptly shoved a boy in handcuffs into the room. They shut the door, leaving Abdullahi alone with this other boy. Abdullahi felt his brain physically contract and expand as it made sense of the new addition to his solitary space.

The boy spoke first, giving the day room its first exposure to speech. "You look wrecked."

"You should see yourself," Abdullahi said, his voice out of practice.

The boy introduced himself, walking over to one of the benches. Abdullahi tried to find the similarities between the boy in front of him and the picture of the other male suspect the police had shown him in one of the interrogation rooms. He had seen him in passing, but he was too preoccupied with what the officers would do with him to pay much attention. This Qays had lost the ample amount of muscle he'd had in the photo. His cheeks sagged, and his eyes were rimmed with dark circles. His curls were shapeless with frizz.

Abdullahi bet he looked just as disorderly.

Abdullahi introduced himself and glanced at the cameras in the corners of the room. He needed to speak with someone. The police might want them to discuss the Fourth so they could analyze for the inconsistencies or catch them exposing themselves. Abdullahi tread carefully.

"Do you know why they brought you in here?" Abdullahi asked.

Qays shook his head. "I don't know, but I want to go back."

Abdullahi thought of the cold cell, thought of what he might see if he closed his eyes, and was grateful he was here.

Abdullahi sat on the bench across from him. "What could possibly be better about sitting in a cell all alone?"

Qays looked up from his hands, his brows furrowed. A frown tugged at the corners of his mouth. His gaze fell back into his lap. "I don't understand."

Abdullahi thought he was in bad shape, and he was, but Qays emitted an aura of grief that surpassed his own. Abdullahi's siblings always said there wasn't anyone as positive as him. While he wasn't feeling optimistic in the least, he was leaps and bounds further along than Qays.

Qays cleared his throat. "Have you seen the others? What are they like?"

"Zamzam, Samia, and Nasreen?" Abdullahi shrugged. "Anytime they're in the same room as each other, they're ready to kill each other."

"And the other girl," Qays said, his eyes drooping. "Muzhda?"

Abdullahi's hands felt numb, and his chest tightened. *Muzhda.* "I don't know much about her."

"I do," Qays began, and Abdullahi wished Qays would stop talking. He glanced around at the cameras as Qays continued. "I used to be her writing tutor at Valley. She would tell the wildest stories. She used to write these stories that would put what it's like to be kids like us perfectly into words."

Abdullahi didn't want to know about Muzhda before the Fourth.

Guilt burned like acid in his throat.

What would our lives have looked like if I hadn't run that night?

Qays lifted his head, and it hurt Abdullahi to look him in the eye. "Anyway. What are the others saying? Are any of them suspicious?"

"As suspicious as you and me."

Qays's expression turned bleak. "That doesn't make me feel any better."

Abdullahi's heart sank. He agreed. If they were as guilty as Abdullahi felt and Qays looked, then they were properly screwed.

The door opened then, cutting their conversation short. As they led him back to his cell, Abdullahi knew he was in for another sleepless night.

CHAPTER 15

QAYS

QAYS THOUGHT BACK TO MUZHDA'S POISED SMILE ON THE beach. It was both relaxed and nervous, steady and uncertain.

But her smile was long gone. In the cell they'd transferred them to, Muzhda became a girl who only cried.

From the moment he saw her, Qays thought she wasn't like other girls, but he was wrong. Like other girls, she cried nonstop from the unending stress. Like other girls, she blubbered through the tears and snot. Like other girls, her puffy face was so wet it reflected light like the ocean did the sun.

And like other girls, she was still so beautiful through it all.

They were in holding, somewhere dark with one window above them and the cell. They were separated by bars, the new holding area split in two, one side for him and the other for her. To Qays's relief, he wasn't alone, but that meant Muzhda had to suffer along with him.

Ever since the detective had returned for an update, Muzhda hadn't stopped crying. The detective said Qays might be able to see his family if he cooperated with their process, that they voided their right to bail because of the severity of the crime, that they could hold him in a high-security facility because he would be tried as an adult. And because he could be tried as an adult, he wasn't kept with Abdullahi and the others, who were younger.

Apparently, Qays was too dangerous. It was a word that followed him all the way from his parents' homeland. A Palestinian girl playing with her cat on her roof or a Palestinian boy lighting a firework. *So very dangerous.*

He stretched his lean limbs in the beige issued uniform that they'd given him. On his way out of the room where he'd been forced to strip, he'd seen officers bring in the other three girls. He'd been transported back to the Fourth when he saw Zamzam, still dressed in her clothes from that night. Her eyes, wide with fear, snapped him out of the daze he'd been in. He didn't want to mirror her fear; instead he wanted to model strength for her, and for Muzhda right now. After all, he was used to being team captain.

He resumed his internal pep talks. Qays told himself that his parents would get him the best lawyers and clear this up and that he'd be back to his normal life in no time.

Muzhda sniveled, her long brown hair shaking with her shoulders. Some girls were part-time hijabis, like Qays's older sister. It meant she wore it sometimes, when she felt comfortable or confident enough to wear it out in public. Maybe Muzhda was a part-time hijabi too.

"Look, this situation sucks for sure," Qays said, feeling much more Qays than he had since the bonfire, "but you need to stop crying. It's not doing any good for either of us."

She sniffed, and her hands wiped her face again. He couldn't see her face anymore; he had gotten only glimpses of it since they brought her in with him.

"Not everything has to have a purpose," she replied in a fragile voice. Qays sincerely doubted that. "I'm coping," she added.

"So am I," he said back. "I'm coping by trying to figure out why they'd put me here in the first place. We're not high-security prisoners. We haven't gone to court. We get bail. We get phone calls and attorneys."

Muzhda's sob fell into her lap, and she folded onto herself even more. He wanted to reject it. Irritation ripped through him.

"For real, you've got to stop."

"I—I can't."

"Sure you can." Qays leaned back until he was lying on the thin blanket over the bench that was his bed. "Start with regulating your breathing. Breathe in, breathe out." He demonstrated the motion with his hands.

"Oh my God," she scoffed through her sniffles. "You're full of shit."

"Excuse me?" Qays propped himself up on his elbows, a mocking laugh rising in his throat but getting choked off by his confusion.

"I said you're full of shit, Qays," she repeated.

Qays's eyes bore into the back of her head. It swayed with every nasally word from her trembling voice. His cool composure cracked. He switched to asshole mode. "You looked pretty in love with this pile of shit a week ago."

"Regrettably," she said.

116

"It's not your fault. I'm every girl's weakness."

"My ass."

"No." Qays grinned. "It was *my* ass."

"Are we really bantering right now?" she snapped weakly. "Is this a joke to you?"

"It's not that big of a deal," he said. He hoped.

She scoffed. "To *you*. I wonder why you feel like it's not that big of a deal."

Qays stared at the two knobs that were her knees. He waited. If his older sister had taught him anything, it was that with the way Muzhda's inflection rose and didn't dip at the end of her sentence, she already had a theory. It killed him that she withheld it from him.

"Take a guess."

"For the same reason you probably thought you could charm me forever," she continued. "But what the hell, Qays? You and your friends wanted to get high but couldn't be caught getting the weed before the fact. Why did I have to pick up your stash? I bet you'd throw me under the bus as soon as you get the chance. That is if you haven't done that already. In your perfect world, you're untouchable. And you'll do anything to protect your repu- tation. Homecoming king this fall, Yale the next."

Qays's pride was bolstered by her near-accurate prediction, but then seized when he realized he didn't remember what he'd told the detective that first night when he was scared shitless. He regained some composure. "We're all in the same boat. Wrong place, wrong time, taken in by mistake. It'll get fixed. Trust."

"Was I in the wrong place?" Her voice thickened with emo- tion. "Or was I in the right place, but then I listened to you,

117

walked away from my friends and safety to the wrong place, where they found me and picked me up with a bag of weed? All because of you."

Qays's breathing slowed.

"Did it occur to you that this might be your fault?" she asked. "Does that matter at all to you, or are you only thinking of how to save yourself?"

Qays tried to fight against the implication, but her words didn't spark any cognitive dissonance. He persisted in his indifference. "Like you said, homecoming king in the fall, Stanford the next."

"And as a minor, the *Stanford* soccer star can't be caught getting his weed, but he can be caught high?"

She waited for his answer. Qays hated feeling like he owed her an explanation, so he got it over with.

"Being high isn't illegal."

"Excuse me?"

"Being in possession of weed is illegal as a minor. But once I'm high, no one would know."

"Stanford wouldn't like their young star being in possession of marijuana as a minor."

She was right, of course. But Qays brushed off the truth with a laugh. "To be honest, I'm more scared of my parents. Besides, how would they know? Technically you're the one who had it, and they don't know any better."

The more he spoke, the more trouble he had convincing himself that he hadn't been wrong to send her down the beach on the Fourth.

She let out a cry disguised as a laugh. "I really thought that douchebags were my type because of you. At least I can say this has cured me of my irrational feelings."

Qays frowned. He could admit that he was not at his best, but they'd had good days. Days when her stories transported him and they discovered all the ways they were similar. But even on his worst days, he needed to be liked. It didn't have to be in a good way; he was okay with being liked because he was an asshole, because he had the ability to be liked regardless. It kept him moving forward, and he hated looking back.

The only thing he hated more than looking back was looking inward at himself.

So outward and forward he went. His issued blanket came in two parts, a light inner fabric and a thicker parchment-like material. He separated them with effort, the sound of ripping fabric slashing the stale air. With the light inner fabric in hand, he crossed his cell. Standing above her, even with the bars between them, he could see how her shoulders shook.

"What is it? Go away. I don't want you to look at me."

Qays folded the blanket. Twice, three times, four, until it was a long thin rectangle.

"Here," he said, offering it to her through the bars. "Wear it if it makes you feel better."

She glanced up at him; her hazel eyes, flecked with slivers of gold, were enveloped in a bloodshot crimson.

His breath caught. His eyes fell to her hands, which he imagined draped around his neck. Qays shook his head. It was not the time to hit on a girl, nor the time for those kinds of daydreams.

Muzhda threw the fabric over her hair and tossed the longer end over her right shoulder. She stood up, wiping her face of her tears for the final time. Her expression shifted; she was more determined, more settled, more the Muzhda from the night at the beach. Qays could see that was what she'd needed, that even though it was just a scarf, it meant something so much greater to her than he could understand. With a hijab on, she leveled up.

"Thank you," she murmured. "But I still don't forgive you."

Qays exhaled. He wanted to reach out, to tuck the loose strands of hair into the makeshift hijab, but he didn't. His eyes traveled to his bare wrist. When they'd taken his clothes, they'd also taken away her bracelet.

"I don't remember ever apologizing," he said back, because he was Qays after all. No matter how much Muzhda's eyes flummoxed him.

Then they turned away from each other, walking to either ends of their divided holding cells, their north and south poles untouching. After a long while, long enough for Qays to subconsciously trace Muzhda's name on the bed at least two hundred times, she spoke again. "What did you tell them?"

"The truth," he replied.

"Are you sure?" Judgment filled her voice, judgment he deserved.

Qays's finger paused on the z of her name. No, he wasn't. He said a version of the story that Qays—the scared, worried-for-his-future Qays—had wanted to believe was true. A version he couldn't recall anymore. He felt like a kid who was asked about something he'd lied about and was caught so easily by grown-ups. He glanced back at Muzhda.

The redness had subsided, but her face was still bloated and bleak. Her eyes were small and narrow, her entire face puckered. She looked...disappointed.

No one had ever looked at him like that. And he didn't want anyone else to. His parents didn't know he smoked argeelah at hookah lounges, let alone weed. Admissions would care that he was a minor in possession of a controversial substance. Qays played offense. His defense always needed work. He realized he was overexposed only when it was too late. He would have to either play catch-up or come clean. Neither of these was his strength, but he had to protect himself and his future.

Lost in his thoughts, he didn't realize he was staring in her direction. Muzhda glanced at him before tucking herself in for the night. She stuck her tongue out at him and turned away to sleep.

And he couldn't help but smile.

CHAPTER 16

SAMIA

SAMIA WANTED HER HIJAB BACK. OR *ANY* FABRIC THAT could act as a scarf. A damn towel would suffice. Then she'd be a real "towel head." Fucking racists.

She yelled and cried and banged on the walls to get a state-issued scarf like the hideous beige clothes they'd given her. If she wasn't going to get her due process, she'd give their hearing some due losses.

Eventually, her voice wore out. Whatever was left was damaged. Still, she banged on the door and cried out for the officer.

She was in a room because it was daytime, and in the daytime room it was more likely the officers answered her. In the cell, at night, she was all alone, watched by the officers through a screen.

"Samia," called Abdullahi. The police or the FBI or whoever was playing some game with them had placed her with Abdullahi today. One day she was in the daytime room with Zamzam, who had helped her try to berate the officers into giving them scarves, and the next with Nasreen, whom she did not talk to, period. It was obvious they were recording them, observing them like they were animals and waiting to see who would bite first.

"Samia," he repeated. "Give it a rest."

She pressed her back against the door, sliding down. "I can't," she croaked. "I feel naked."

She had gotten used to not wearing a hijab around Abdullahi. At first, she felt insecure, but then she made him out to be like her brother, and he did his best to give her privacy. That made it a little bearable, but it went only so far. She still felt like a huge part of her was missing. Her hijab, in its wonderful variations on her social media pages, was her armor.

Samia's phone was probably popping with social media notifications. Well-wishers, haters, never-gonna-makers, and even the ammo suitors and haram police were probably reaching out to her as if they had had a single honest connection with her instead of eyeing her daily posts with envy or lust.

Samia didn't feel anything for those people. She had felt something real with only one person in her DMs, and now just the thought of speaking with them made her want to barf. She felt betrayed, and she didn't forget easily.

"How much longer is this going to last, Abdullahi?" asked Samia in her creaky voice. "What if we just told them everything, all of us on the same day?"

Abdullahi grimaced. "Without a lawyer? That's a death sentence."

"But I did nothing wrong," she rasped.

"I don't think that's—"

The door opened, and Samia slid across the floor to make space. Two male officers stepped in, and Samia looked away, just like how babies covered their eyes thinking it made them invisible.

"You." One officer pointed at her. "Let's go."

"I want a scarf," she requested with her grated voice.

The officer huffed. He gestured to his friend, some overcomplicated gesture only the two of them could understand. The other officer left, and upon his return he had a white one-piece tube scarf. He threw it at Samia, and she caught it.

"This?" She spread it out with the tips of her fingers like it was coated in poison.

The officer breathed his onion breath at her. "We'll be back in a minute."

Samia glared at it like it was the cauliflower on a vegetable tray.

"Don't complain about that," warned Abdullahi. He knew her too well. "You sacrificed your larynx for that scarf."

Pouting, she slipped it on anyway, ignoring the fashion crimes she was committing with the egg scarf.

"You look like you," Abdullahi said, finally fixing his gaze on her. He snorted. "Sort of."

She bet she did, no matter how heinous the style was. Regardless, she'd won. She was finally not without her body armor. She hoped she'd be able to get her revenge on them for making her be without it for so long.

"What do you think I should tell them?" she asked Abdullahi.

Abdullahi sighed, turning his stubbly face away from her. "I can't speak for you."

"But I want your advice." She did. Abdullahi was wise beyond his years. *Mature* didn't quite describe him, and *wise* didn't sound as serious and boring as maturity.

"My advice?" he repeated. "My advice is that they're gonna pit us against each other in there. They already have, setting us up in different pairs every day. If they wanted us to speak the truth, they'd keep us separate, keep the truth unblemished."

"You watch too many true-crime documentaries," she said.

"Do I look like someone who watches true crime?" he asked, brow raised.

Samia watched quite a bit of true crime, so she knew Abdullahi was not the type to watch. He'd get too anxious. Besides, she couldn't call on a single bit of knowledge she'd learned from her shows and podcasts, and if Abdullahi sounded like he knew what he was talking about, he must not be a fan.

Abdullahi crossed his arms over his chest. "It just feels like they want us to corroborate our stories so they can see all the hiccups when we say it back. When they ask for your side of that night, I don't know what's better, a lie, a truth, or a lawyer."

"How can you be so sure they don't just want this to blow over?" Samia's eyes widened at her own choice of words, and Abdullahi flinched. She groaned. "What? We can't use the word *blow* without freaking? This isn't the 2000s."

Abdullahi looked away. His aura shifted; it wasn't the usual mysterious, old-timey air around him. When he looked at her, he seemed spooked. "Nothing will ever be the same."

She wanted to latch on to his words, but in that moment, he looked more lost than she felt.

"I don't think you should trust me or anyone," he murmured. "We're all wrestling with our demons."

"You don't have any demons," she insisted. In her life, Abdullahi was consistently good.

His brows knit with hurt or stress or a concoction of both. Samia thought it looked unnatural on him. He rubbed his face, but the struggle on it went nowhere. "I gave you my advice. Take it or leave it."

Samia neither took it nor left it. His words simply loomed.

Samia couldn't believe the FBI was in front of her scrolling through her Insta page, @muslimsnatched.

It was a masterful juxtaposition of textures and colors, themes and filters, a sprinkling of sunshine in every picture, and even the black-and-white ones from her trip to New York City radiated rays of luxury. She was proud of her work, and she hoped the Kandi woman at least appreciated the artistry. She skimmed over Samia's favorite post: her lying in all leather, stilettos poking out of a gold bathtub at a Beverly Hills estate that she'd scammed a real estate agent into showing her just to get the shot.

@muslimsnatched's life was star-studded (she scoped out celebrities for hours at Westfield and Rodeo for the gram) and first-class (she always paid extra for the likes). Samia and average were oil and water; they did not mix. Yet she was in a drab room wearing a tubular egg scarf with arguably the worst-dressed plainclothes officers. Both facts would have been equally unbelievable before this summer and should have been the least of her worries. But it was either tube-scarf internal commentary or doom, and the former helped with self-preservation.

Detective Penne clicked a Destroy Samia's Life button, and when he searched her handle in front of her, the screen read *No results found*.

No, no, no, no, no, Samia thought. Her social media was her escape. It was her break from reality, an edited, handpicked reel of the prettiest moments, to distract from the ugly truths. She'd been a thousand short of a million followers, and they took it away from her just like that. Wasn't there some intellectual property law she could sue the FBI over?

She realized this should have been the least of her worries in her current situation. But nothing felt as concrete and real to her as the internet did.

"We understand this was your life," Detective Penne said, "and believe me, it can be restored once our investigation is over. We've only disabled it for your safety. We know you didn't do this, Miss Al-Samra."

"What is *this*, exactly?"

Kandi spoke. "The United States of America was victim of a terrorist attack on July fourth at Monarch Beach, where you and your friends were gathered. An oil rig, *Bonnie*, was bombed, as well as the Monarch Beach Pier. There were several casualties. We have reason to believe it was one or more of the suspects who are in our custody. You are all under investigation for terrorism and murder. Currently, you're not a suspect in the murder case; you were nowhere near the scene of that crime. You are a suspect in an act of terror. So the sooner we get to the bottom of this, the better for you and your life."

Act of terror. Samia wanted to laugh at that, but her body betrayed her and shuddered. She knew exactly what to do to protect herself from fear. She placed a filter on Kandi's words; she heard them through rose-infused eardrums. The FBI was obviously stereotyping and profiling them. Soon enough, they'd realize that, in their panic, they were chasing their own tails trying to find someone to blame. Because the only thing terrorizing was the No Results Found page on Detective Penne's laptop. @muslimsnatched. Samia's on-screen life. Her everything. Gone.

She wanted it back up and running. If she wasn't online every day, every hour, every minute, then she'd be forgotten. The internet was fast-paced, brutal. If she didn't occupy the spot for Muslim fashion and lifestyle, if she wasn't posting daily, if she wasn't making every thirteen-year-old girl want to be her, they'd find another hijabi babe and want to be them instead.

"Tell us what happened that night," Detective Penne urged.

Samia opened her mouth, lips eager to spill. *A lie, a truth, or a lawyer,* Abdullahi had said. The truth about the Fourth, though it was embarrassing, wasn't on Samia. If it helped to clear her name and get her out of here, she could give him the truth.

Samia cleared her chafed throat. "I assume you went through my DMs."

Detective Penne's face brightened while Kandi's remained stoic.

"I'd been DMing this person for a couple months," she rasped. "Their handle is @mus_SM."

Kandi pulled up a file and rested her gold-rimmed spectacles on her straight nose. Detective Penne searched the username on the laptop for reference. The handle popped up; the profile picture was of a shirtless guy at the beach, his back to the camera. Only a handful of followers. No posts like always.

"Like the DMs between us said," Samia continued, "we were finally meeting at the beach. We had been talking so long. His name was Faris. He was older than me, a senior. He liked all the things I liked, and he thought I was pretty, but he wasn't a sleaze-bag like all the other guys in my DMs. I liked him, but whatever. I wasn't head over heels or something."

A lie, a truth, and a lawyer. Samia could have a bite of it all. She liked Faris. A lot. To the point where she ignored the red flags, like the zero posts and the lack of followers. He was sweet, Samia was lonely, and she wanted to feel taken so she could shut down the dozens of thirst DMs with more dignity and assurance. No matter how she portrayed herself, she didn't enjoy feeling like an object in a picture all the time. Faris was the only person who made her feel like more.

"Anyway, we kept DMing. I'm sure you can pull them up." Yeah, Samia blushed a little. Thinking about the FBI reading through her flirty texts made her cringe, but she was sixteen and thriving. Samia waved her hand in the air. "I guess you could say we mutually agreed we should meet at the bonfire. I was a little late. I got to the beach at, like, eight fifteen, eight twenty. I went toward the cliffs. I didn't say hi to my friends, because they would've never let me out of their sight if I saw them first. I went straight to meet Faris."

She omitted the part where she saw Abdullahi in the parking lot. It seemed a necessary detail to leave out.

"And this Faris," Detective Penne began, leaning forward with interest, "what happened to him when the first bomb hit?

Assuming he was your virtual boyfriend, would he really run off without you?"

Samia flattened her clammy hands on the table. This was the first time the FBI had been so direct with their words. *The first bomb? Was there a bomb?* Samia highly doubted it; otherwise the FBI was wasting a lot of resources interrogating her about a silly story with Faris.

Hearing the severity of what might've happened at the beach on the Fourth actually relieved Samia a bit. All she had to do was tell her story; the FBI would realize they were dealing with someone whose greatest crime was wearing double denim of different shades, and they'd move on.

She chewed the inside of her cheek until she tasted blood. She had cried a lot over the past few days, partly out of sadness and fear, and partly from anger. When she mixed those together, the product was embarrassment, and embarrassment hurt more than the rest.

"Faris catfished me," she admitted. Her chest felt like it would burst.

"Cat what?" Kandi asked, peering at Detective Penne, who translated.

Kandi rolled her eyes. "So this not-Faris person, can you ID them for the alibi?"

Samia swallowed, scorching her throat. Her eyes darted. She shrugged.

Kandi's hands sprang into action; a light behind her eyes flashed. She laid five pictures out in front of Samia. There were the three who had been in custody with her. Zamzam, Abdullahi, Nasreen. The fourth was the all-American, sought-after heartthrob, Qays Sharif. The fifth, the outsider, the one Samia didn't know, was a willowy girl with amber eyes and an editorial face.

"Is that person here?" Kandi asked.

Samia nodded again, and Kandi drummed her fingers on the table like her eagerness needed some sort of escape.

The Faris feelings blossomed and popped. There was no Faris. Samia had been duped, but it was better to be duped than to be not-Faris, truthfully believing that Samia's feelings wouldn't vanish as soon as she knew he was a lie. Because Faris was sweet and caring and always commented on her photo composition and lighting and not her body or what most guys think of when they see a girl. Faris felt too good to be true, and it turned out she was right, because Faris was a lie.

A lie, a truth, and a lawyer was a lot more complicated than Abdullahi probably meant it to be. But then again, Abdullahi was always meaning something more than what Samia thought. And she could've gotten it all wrong. She figured she'd spoken way too much already to have gotten it right.

"Could you point them out for us?" Kandi pressed.

Samia raised her eyes to Kandi's. "If I do, can I see my family? Will you let me speak with a lawyer?"

"Of course," Kandi said curtly. "Our thanks for your cooperation."

A lie, a truth, and a lawyer.

Samia's hand came down over Nasreen's photo.

CHAPTER 17

NASREEN

IT HAD BEEN EIGHT DAYS SINCE NASREEN DID NOT WAKE UP from her nightmare.

She'd had her rendezvous with Detective Pennella and Agent Kandi Favreau. Nasreen emulated Carrots slithering into the corner of his cage, attempting to camouflage into the environment so they'd overlook her. That first night she'd had a random streak of courage, but it would only hurt her in the long run. So she acted like she would at Saint Modesta, and it had the same effect it did in her classrooms. The adults in the room were polite to her; they didn't ask any hard questions.

Earlier that morning, an officer delivered her backup glasses from home to her, so she could at least see the broken world without the added cracks. Her insides recoiled every time she imagined her mama and baba bringing them to the police precinct or this dungeon building. Her mama with her gray streaks, dropping them off, or her baba with his tucked in, short-sleeved paisley button-downs, looking troubled. Or perhaps devastated.

Most likely ashamed.

She didn't say much of anything to Pennella or Favreau. Nasreen had wandered away from the bonfires because she'd needed some air. Yes, there was a lot of air because they were at the beach, but there was no room to breathe at the pits. The kids were judging her for being from Saint Modesta, or so Nasreen assumed, as if she was any more stuck-up than the prick who'd thrown the football at her. The prick named Qays Sharif, whose name she learned when Pennella and Favreau placed his picture in front of her, along with the other four. Then they asked her to blame one of them.

Well, not *exactly*. They'd said, "The others have started to point fingers. Get ahead, Ms. Choudhry."

So she'd gotten ahead. But not for Pennella or Favreau or the FBI or justice or patriotism, but for her own reasons. For her mama and baba and her family's reputation.

Out of the five pictures, she picked the only person she'd known before this fiasco ever started. The only person that could say something to wreak havoc on the Choudhry name. At least, in the eyes of her mama and baba.

She chose Samia.

Anyway, it made sense. Nasreen had fallen over the rocks by the cliffs trying to scale the fence to private property. They knew that because they'd shown her the tape. There she had been on a private home's CCTV, her wobbly legs swinging over the white fence, then the weight of her body tipping her back onto the state beach.

The officers returned Nasreen to one of the day rooms, but it wasn't the room with Zamzam. Every time it was different, and this time it was her turn with Samia. Nasreen sat as far away from her as possible.

Samia pounced. "What did you tell them?"

"I didn't have to tell them anything," Nasreen said. "They already had me on tape."

"They have you on tape?" Samia's eyes bugged out of her head like a dragonfly's. It didn't help that her white scarf made her head especially bulbous.

"On CCTV because I tried to jump the fence."

Samia laughed through her nose. "Why did you try to jump the fence?"

Nasreen stared back at Samia. There was no need to answer that question. Samia knew why.

"They said I'd get a lawyer soon," Samia said.

"Me too."

Silence passed between them. With Abdullahi, the quiet was calming; with Zamzam it was manageable. With Samia, the silence filled Nasreen's lungs. She was deep underwater, and there was no surface to kick herself up to. The pressure just rose, rose, rose.

"It's fucking freezing in here," Samia finally said, and the pressure broke.

Nasreen sucked in the thick air. The two girls crossed their arms, and Nasreen rubbed along her forearms for warmth.

Samia sloped her body in Nasreen's direction. "Who'd you pick?"

Nasreen glued her eyes to the wall. "I don't know what you mean."

"Don't bullshit me. They've got to be asking all of us," snapped Samia.

Nasreen sighed louder than she'd meant to. She had to take in whatever air she could before the silence returned.

Samia scowled. "Damn, you did me dirty."

"Like you didn't choose me too?" Nasreen bit back.

Samia turned away from her. "As if you aren't guilty."

"I'm not."

"Then why'd you run? Why'd you jump the fence?"

Samia's words jerked Nasreen back to the Fourth, and it gave her whiplash. "I didn't."

Samia's gaze flattened.

Nasreen retracted her statement. "I ran because you attacked me."

"Verbally."

Nasreen scoffed discreetly. "It looked like you were ready to hit me."

"*Verbally*," Samia enunciated. "You're not the victim."

Nasreen's cheeks flushed. "I'm not the victim." She tasted the words on her lips. The police called them suspects; she'd started to believe it. But she was wrongfully suspected, which meant she was, in fact, a victim. Even if Samia felt she was the only victim among them.

"You're the victim," Nasreen said absentmindedly. She hadn't intended to hurt Samia, and they had gotten caught up in something much bigger than either of them.

Samia obscured her face from Nasreen's view. "I chose you in there," she began, voice low, "because I wouldn't be here if it wasn't for you."

Nasreen felt numb. She bet it was haram to sell her soul for some miracle that would erase Samia's memory, to bury whatever happened at the cliffs forever with no chance of ever digging it back up.

"I guess we're even, then," Nasreen said.

They stared at each other, Samia's glare dripping with venom as Nasreen's frown filled with desperation.

Samia rolled her eyes away from Nasreen and huffed to herself. "Abdullahi was right. They're pitting us against each other."

"They should've done their research," murmured Nasreen. "We were never on the same side to begin with." Attending Saint Modesta made Nasreen an outcast but also an objective observer. Though she'd been at the bonfire for only an hour, their school divisions were deep, highlighting their differences based on their social classes, their backgrounds, and their cultures. Their survival instincts tempted them to blame one another to save themselves.

Getting out was Nasreen's priority. For her mama and baba. And maybe something more that she wasn't ready to open her heart to. If she had the chance again, she'd pick Samia over and over to exonerate herself.

It was all too convenient, this pointing of fingers. What Pennella and Favreau knew and what they didn't.

A lull in their conversation amplified every detail. The cameras in the corner, the little patch in the ceiling that must be a microphone, the officers shuffling in the periphery.

After a while Samia sighed. "They mentioned a bomb in there. If they're investigating something huge, don't you think they'd let us leave if we just explained our stupid reason for being there?"

Nasreen's heart rate skyrocketed. "No," she blurted. She took a deep breath. "We shouldn't say anything until we get lawyers."

"What's the big deal? We're just kids. It was an honest mistake. At least for me."

"It's not your secret to share." Nasreen's voice cut through the air. Her head spun with the consequences. It might've been Samia's honest mistake, but it wasn't Nasreen's. Honest, maybe, but a mistake it was not.

Turning her body away from Nasreen, Samia murmured, "I only chose you because I know you didn't do what they're accusing us of. Even if they looked into you, they'd find nothing. Can you say the same?"

Nasreen held her breath. She wished her reasons were unselfish. She hardened her heart again, that part of her that she rarely softened, and didn't respond. She was used to being alone in a fight. She had to think of how she could deny the truth in Samia's story of the Fourth.

At the silence, Samia tsked, clicking her tongue to exit from the conversation one final time, leaving Nasreen alone with her thoughts. Her head filled with fears of what it had meant to meet Samia at the beach. To lead her to the edge of the coast and reveal herself.

CHAPTER 18

ABDULLAHI

EVERY DAY ADDED CREASES AROUND ABDULLAHI'S SLEEP-less eyes. He nodded off in the day room, leaning into the sense of security he got around Zamzam. His neck fell forward, and he jolted awake. Zamzam was staring at him.

Abdullahi had already taken turns in the day room with everyone. Nasreen was oddly quiet, and Samia badgered him like an annoying sister, but Zamzam was different. He didn't feel compelled to speak with Nasreen, and he rather hoped he and Samia would talk less, but he'd never spoken with Zamzam alone. He wanted to.

They studied each other in silence.

Zamzam had the same tube scarf as Samia, but she wrapped it around her hair like a turban instead of the egg situation Samia was dealing with. Her teeth chattered from the chill. At night in his cell, it was so hot, his sweat stuck him to the synthetic mattress lining. In the day room, the AC froze fingertips and obliterated appetites.

They were exhausted.

Zamzam cleared her throat, and Abdullahi realized they were watching each other like it was hour eight of bingeing Netflix: lids heavy and eyes empty.

"I picked Qays, FYI," Zamzam said.

He let out a coiled breath. While he depended on Samia not to implicate him, he couldn't speak for Nasreen or Zamzam. Pennella and Favreau had asked Abdullahi to suggest one of them, too, but he insisted on getting a lawyer first. They didn't get a peep out of him. Abdullahi loved words like *courteous* and *chivalrous* and *loyal*, not just because of their meanings, but because they sounded so beautiful. He wanted to be able to use them to describe himself.

So while Abdullahi was grateful she hadn't chosen him, a ton of weight fell on his chest to think of that broken kid, Qays, being blamed.

"Did you know him?" Abdullahi asked, unable to mask his disappointment.

She shrugged. "No. But I wouldn't be here if it wasn't for him, so ..."

Abdullahi's brows furrowed. "But you could've opted out like me. You didn't have to blame someone who you didn't believe was guilty."

"Some say stupidity is a crime," she mused.

"I heard he's a Stanford shoo-in."

"Stupidity comes in all shapes and IQ levels."

Abdullahi frowned. "I don't know if that's fair."

"Fair," Zamzam repeated, her mahogany-brown eyes narrowing. She seemed insistent on rejecting the guilt that so freely ate away at him. Guilt was a parasite, and Abdullahi was all flesh, whereas Zamzam had reinforced herself with iron.

"I can't tell if you're a clown or just soft," he heard Zamzam whisper.

Abdullahi flushed. When they'd given him photos and asked him to incriminate one of them, he could have chosen *her*. She wouldn't know any better. But he couldn't. It felt deceitful to suggest she was involved in the explosion. She'd been so far from the pits and tangled in a web of wires and equipment. He didn't have enough evidence, and if he accused Muzhda of anything, they'd easily rope him in with her.

"Sorry." Zamzam apologized with a sigh. "I didn't mean that you were a clown."

"What did you mean?"

"Maybe naive?" Zamzam didn't say it like an insult, and it didn't insult him. He was naive, if seeing the best in everyone was naivete.

"But don't you see this is a witch hunt?" she asked. "One of us is their fake witch, and they're trying to figure out how to convince the majority of the public witches still exist. I'm just trying to survive."

Abdullahi heard a bit of bitterness in her voice. Maybe he could persuade her to do the right thing. "We shouldn't give in to their lies, though. I don't think any of us are guilty of that explosion."

Of other things, maybe, but not that.

"How do we know Qays didn't do the same as me?"

"Have you seen Qays yet?" he asked her.

"Not yet," she answered. "Maybe they don't want us speaking."

"I don't think Qays is thinking about who to blame. He looked unwell."

Zamzam's laugh was short and bitter. "We're all unwell."

Abdullahi didn't push back. Because, despite how ridiculous everything was, he was a little in awe of Zamzam. She was beautiful, with her seamless dark skin, high cheekbones, and two-toned lips, and she was sharp, glittering like a polished knife in the sunlight. He was a hopeless romantic, quietly waiting for the person whom he'd want to know more. He felt something pricking at his heart. Abdullahi wore his emotions on his sleeve and smack-dab in the middle of his forehead. Zamzam was layered, and it intrigued him.

She turned to him. "Don't you think we adjusted too quickly? We accepted our fate hella quick."

He shrugged. "We all know we're easy targets. I don't know about you, but I'm always on guard. When they finally pick on me, whether it's the cops or a teacher or whoever, I'm thinking, it was about time. Now I can restart the timer for the next time. Right?"

Zamzam grimaced. "I guess. I mean, you and I live that life. But maybe Samia and Nasreen didn't. And they already had their breakdowns and moved on from them too."

He dragged his finger along the bridge of his nose. Last he saw her, Samia was demanding things from the cops left and right, somewhat successfully, and Nasreen was quietly cruising.

Then he registered it. The speculation edging into Zamzam's voice.

"What, you think they had something to do with that night?" Abdullahi completed her conjecture.

"Something's not adding up."

Abdullahi agreed.

"They must be hiding something from us," Zamzam added. "And they didn't think to clue us in."

"Can you blame them?" he asked. "They have officers watching us all the time."

Zamzam's eyes shot at him. "Why are you defending them? I get that Samia is your friend, but why are you acting like you owe Nasreen or me your loyalty?"

Loyalty. He liked the way that word sounded. His romanticizing brain pined for the rare values of the harsh world. "I think it's the right thing to do."

"How chivalrous of you."

Abdullahi smiled. For the first time, he didn't feel tired. He felt good. He missed feeling good. Maybe of all the words Abdullahi loved, *good* was the best. A single syllable that encompassed all he strived for.

He was tired of talking about all the bad things that happened to them. "What will you do when you're out of here?" he asked her.

Zamzam began listing. "I'm enrolling in an SAT prep course, I'm gonna zoom through the summer work for all my AP classes, and I'm gonna run every morning so I'm not out of condition for track. Maybe start volunteering at a hospital or start a medical-assistant training program." She paused, and Abdullahi swore he saw her eyes wet. "What about you?"

Abdullahi didn't need time to think. "I'm going to fall asleep watching all the *Home Alone* and *Back to the Future* movies. I'm watching everything John Travolta has ever been in. I'm gonna finally start saving up for a 1967 Chevy Impala. I'm gonna let myself fall in love."

Zamzam blinked at him. "That sounds nice," she said. "Maybe one day, when I'm a doctor and my family can manage without me, I'll come find you and you can drive me in your Impala and show me some of those movies. I think you could teach a course in how to relax."

Abdullahi thought he'd like that, but he also wondered if he'd ever be able to truly let go of the Fourth.

Zamzam looked away, and a silence filled the room. It didn't last long. "That other girl, what was her name?"

The exhaustion returned to him full force. Talking to Zamzam had distracted him, even if for just a moment. "Muzhda." Abdullahi's heart felt heavy as he pronounced it with the ʒ rather than the *z* sound.

Zamzam raised her eyebrows slightly. "Yeah, her. She's the only one on the list I didn't recognize. You know her?"

"No," he responded at lightning speed, then bit his lip. He held his breath. He didn't know Muzhda. He knew her face, and only when he was in the room with Pennella and Favreau did he put a name to it. And seeing her made him feel like his stomach was an erupting volcano. His hands shook like the Parkinson's patients he'd sometimes seen when he rode along in the ambulances during EMT training. He'd had to flatten his palms on the table to not give away his emotions.

"You *do* know her," Zamzam concluded. She'd been reading him the whole time, and Abdullahi was too distracted by her to

143

realize it. He'd let his guard down despite his acknowledgment of the FBI surveillance. That somehow bothered him less than Zamzam's blatant observation of him.

"I don't." He gave her a half-truth. "I think I saw her at the bonfire. It brought me back to that night—that's all."

Zamzam sighed, and it sounded like she got the last word without actual words. The suspicion in her gaze and her body language exuded from her, touching the oxygen in the air and fermenting into doubt.

Doubt. Not to be mistaken for *reasonable* doubt. Doubt was the haze that clouded the web, the fog that threatened to make anyone who walked into it get lost. With low visibility, fingers begin to aim every which way, with no care for misdirection.

Reasonable doubt was different. It was the bad taste in your mouth after telling half-truths; it was the one missing piece of the thousand-piece puzzle; it was the leftover gear after the car's already been assembled. Without that bad taste, that missing piece, or that extra gear, without reasonable doubt, it would be over for Abdullahi. If Zamzam was prepared to blame others to save herself, to create any reasonable doubt, why couldn't Abdullahi do the same?

He could blame Muzhda, the girl he recognized in the pictures, and a girl whom he didn't really know. Besides his better judgment and his general concern for humanity, Muzhda wasn't special. Her life and his life didn't have to be connected, not unless the Fourth defined him.

But this investigation didn't define him. He was cars from the '60s and the smell of coconuts and vanilla. This investigation was all cop cars and the lingering scent of epoxy.

So if he did blame Muzhda, he'd have his own chance to get

off scot-free, even if it was a small, better-than-nothing chance. Zamzam did the same when she implicated Qays.

But after all he'd already done, how could he do that to Muzhda?

Abdullahi tried to see it from Zamzam's perspective. Maybe she wasn't being unfair. Maybe all she was asking was for Abdullahi to play the game before his goodwill got him into even more trouble.

CHAPTER 19

QAYS

"FAMILY VISITS."

Qays shot up off his bench at just shy of the speed of light. The pain lashed at his neck so quick he didn't get a chance to flinch. He stood at the door of his cell, trying to keep his cool, but his legs were coiling, ready to sprint, his energy three steps ahead of him. His mind was already with his mom, his dad, his sister, and his little brother.

Qays was a midfielder. He was the playmaker, the innovator on the field. He loved learning tactics to plan and execute plays, and so while Muzhda gave him the silent treatment, he made hundreds of plans, each one ending with him at Stanford and this summer behind him.

The other common thread in all his plans was making peace with Muzhda.

Muzhda, who hadn't moved an inch when the officers came in.

Earlier that morning, they'd announced they would finally be able to see their parents. From what Qays had pieced together, the DA was under a lot of pressure to rush them to trial. These things took time, and either a lot of time had passed, or time was passing in a vacuum, every minute an eternity. He'd seen Detective Pennella and Favreau only once since the night after the incident. And of the others, Qays had been allowed to see the boy named Abdullahi once. He'd been in holding with Muzhda since then, surveilled. He figured that was why he could be in a cell connected to Muzhda's, when prisoners were typically separated by gender.

Prisoners. He and Muzhda weren't prisoners yet; they hadn't been tried.

"You have ten minutes with one family member," the officer told him. "No touching. Hands on the table at all times."

He wasn't a criminal, and he was sick of being treated like one. He glimpsed his reflection in the mirror, and though he appeared normal, albeit paler than usual, his agitation and anger bubbled inside him like radiation, burning him from under his skin.

"When I finally get my lawyer," Qays said under his breath, "you'll all be out of jobs."

The officer cackled. "This punk."

The word *punk* repeated in Qays's head until next thing he knew, he was faced with another door to a room whose contents were a mystery. Yes, it could be his parents, but it also could be a courtroom filled with an angry mob. In here, Qays's plans amounted to nothing.

But beyond the door wasn't a surprise all-supreme judge sentencing Qays to GTMO without a jury or trial. No, beyond the door was his father.

And Qays was glad for it. If it had been his mom, he would've broken down then and there and forgotten the no-touching rule; he would need his mom to hold him until the air in his lungs felt like a mercy and not a punishment anymore. With his dad, his tall and sturdy, bald and bearded father, Qays could keep on modeling his strength like he'd done ever since he was little.

But his dad looked tired now, his bulky muscles softer on the edges. His biceps didn't threaten to rip his T-shirt sleeves like they usually did. His face looked like it had been scrubbed over and over to remove the color usually there.

Qays didn't remember a time when his dad wasn't happy. He was a successful businessman, an immigrant to the United States at eighteen, where he lived the American dream to the fullest. He'd worked his ass off to open his olive-oil import business, which supplied hundreds of restaurants and brands. He owned a three-story home a minute's walk from the beach. He had a loving wife and three children with good grades and success written in their futures. Qays's sister, Dina, was in law school. Qays was going to find fame, whether in soccer or business, but preferably both. Qays's little brother, Muneer, was going to be a better soccer player than Qays could ever be once he passed the last clumsy leg of puberty.

Qays's father didn't have problems. Until now.

So, despite holding his head up high as he sat opposite his dad, the first thing out of his mouth after spreading his hands on the table for the officers to see was, "I'm sorry, Baba."

And yes, his voice cracked, and he wasn't proud of it. *Catch a break, Qays,* he thought, cringingly in the third person.

"Nothing to be sorry about," his baba said, his voice projecting louder than Qays was prepared for. "Keefak, baba? They're not bothering you, are they? I promise you I have the best lawyers working to get you out. Laa, I won't sleep until I do everything I can to get you out. No matter what they say, they can't treat you like a prisoner. I don't know what lies they told that ridiculous judge to keep you here."

"They won't let me leave?" Qays's insides screamed. "Don't you just post bail?"

His baba shook his head. "Not when they keep you on remand for some haki fadi about you being too dangerous. Don't worry. We'll sue them when this is all over, and then they'll see."

Qays fought back the tidal wave of emotions as he listened to his baba rehashing the only thoughts Qays had been having for days. He'd get the best lawyers. Qays knew that. He'd get out. Qays knew that. They'd make them pay in court; people would lose jobs over this. Qays *wished* for that. His baba would see that into existence.

As his baba continued to explain all the plans set in place, loads of weight from worries came off Qays's shoulders. He could take a break from those thoughts because his dad had it under control. Now Qays just wanted the pain in his neck to go away and to be free from the gnawing feelings surrounding Muzhda, but the ache didn't go away. He was beginning to think it didn't come from the cot he slept on, but from his muscles clumping up into a trillion tiny knots across his body, tightening a millimeter more every moment he didn't get forgiven by Muzhda. He tried to let go, of the plans and lawyer talk, to hear something real.

"How's Mama?" asked Qays, manually loosening the knots.

"She wanted to come," his baba said, eyes like Qays's, once

149

so bright but dimmed now. "But they only let one of us see you. And I don't know if she'd be able to keep it together if she saw you like this."

Qays's eyes strained; he physically fought the tears he didn't want to shed in front of his dad. It felt like an impossible feat to keep them at bay when he thought of his mom worrying about his meals, wondering if he was getting any sleep, praying he wasn't hurt.

He wanted to feel taken care of, but it was right of his baba to come instead of her.

Qays didn't want to face her until he was able to see his future again. But when he peeked at it, he saw only gray, when his future had always been a color bright and true and vibrant like his dad. The luxurious red of fame. The blinding white of promise. The comforting black of security.

"Qays?" He heard his baba peripherally. "Are you okay, baba?"

Qays's tight eyes filled with tears, but they weren't blue, just clear, allowing for the gray to filter through. There was *so much gray.*

Qays waded through it until he found something else to latch on to. "How's Dina? And Muneer?" he asked.

"They're worried about you. Muneer's coach suspended him from the team because people threatened the soccer club. Tab'aan, we're fighting back. They can't discriminate against us like that. And Dina is heading protests all over LA and talking to news outlets about how good of a kid you are. They should know your character. You're a good kid."

Qays bit his lip, hoping for the bright yellow color of shame, but still nothing. He dived deeper. "What about the others that were arrested that night?"

His baba sighed. "We're looking into them. But the investigation is a mess. It's covered up in places and split wide open in others because the police and the media are controlling everything. Someone leaked that they're trying to connect you with the murder because of some bogus fingernail samples on some marijuana—"

"What?" Qays interrupted, coils tightening. "No one said anything about murder."

"It's not important. It wasn't you," his baba replied. "They think I don't know my son."

Qays's eyes dropped to his hands. The veins in his forearms popped out in ridges despite his brain sending signals to relax. His father knew the Qays at home, the Qays on the soccer field, the Qays on the report cards, but he didn't know the Qays who got high with his friends on the Fourth of July.

"Did they tell you anything about me?" Qays asked.

His baba smirked. "They said you were messing around with a firework. They don't remember what it's like to be a kid?"

Qays gulped. "Nothing else?"

His expression darkened. "They're trying to connect you to some hashish with some girl." *Hashish* meant weed. "They think you're mhashish? They don't know how hard you work to take care of your body for soccer?"

Hanging his head, Qays didn't have a reply.

"It was one of the others trying to get you involved." His baba hesitated and lowered his voice. "If you know anything about them, tell me. I'll let the lawyers know."

Qays shook his head in disbelief, just as he had when Pennella lined up headshots of the other five in front of him on the interrogation table. They'd asked him the same thing, just with different words. *Do you recognize any of these people?* Favreau had asked. Qays had said yes. He'd pointed at Zamzam. He didn't point at Muzhda.

"None of the others did anything," Qays said.

His baba sighed again. "Ismaa', it's not going to be a happy ending for all of you. The media and law enforcement are convinced it's you six. We are going to try and save you from being one of the victims to this injustice."

All he heard was more gray words. It truly was Qays's most hated color.

"So we won't help the others?" Qays's voice was small, childlike. He could think only of how Muzhda was a suspect because of him. If he was a good kid, she was so much better.

"They'll get their lawyers. They'll fight it out in court. Each man for himself."

"And what if the only way to make me innocent is to make one of them look guilty? Even if they didn't make that explosion happen?"

His dad's eyes sloped down, their blue a somber, somber hue. "You know the Roman gladiators?" he asked.

Qays nodded.

"You're the modern-day gladiator, Qays. We have to fight for your life, no matter the costs. Trust me, nonprofits are scrambling to take the FBI to court over the way they dealt with this, but I'm four steps ahead. The Sharif family is always steps ahead of others. Four steps from now, we'll be in court trying to prove your innocence, not having the age-old discussion of whether this was constitutional. That conversation never ends in our favor. As Palestinians, few things do."

Though it made sense, Qays didn't want to accept it. Trampling over the other players, fouling others just to get a floppy shot for himself felt like the Qays thing to do, but it also made bile rise in his throat and his empty stomach flip.

It was a new feeling for him.

"Qays, are you listening?"

He hadn't been listening; he'd been stuck in too much gray.

His baba continued his legal spiel. "They say that you'll be tried as an adult because of all this empty talk about national security, but I won't accept it. Until you're tried in court, you should at least go out on bail. They can't keep you here...."

And on and on his dad went.

Eventually, the officer called time, figuratively blowing the whistle. Qays didn't comprehend how his body left his dad and returned to his cell, because everything was gray.

Gray, gray, gray.

"Looking blue, homecoming king."

The coils in Qays's neck unfurled the tiniest bit at Muzhda's soft voice. He met her gaze; she was facing him for the first time in days. The fabric he'd given her was draped lazily over her chestnut-brown hair.

"You're talking to me now?"

She shrugged. "You might have some news for me."

News? Plans? Plays? Qays's life was a rigged game. His baba had said as much. It was either take a major, life-threatening L or play dirty. Play dirty and let Muzhda and the others suffer the consequences.

"He didn't say much," Qays lied.

"Your dad?"

"Yeah."

"Must be nice," she said wistfully. At Qays's furrowed brows, she clarified, "To see your dad."

He shifted uncomfortably. "Did they not tell you when your family would visit?"

Muzhda's lips spread into a smudged smile Qays wished he could draw into completion. "My family isn't going to visit me," she said. "They can't offer me anything right now."

Qays couldn't read her. Was she happy they wouldn't come, or had the delirium set in for her? Was everything gray for her too?

She continued, "I was seven when my parents moved us to Los Angeles from Afghanistan. They waited until they came here and were settled before having my siblings so it wouldn't be messy. My little brothers and sisters are all citizens because they were born here, but I moved here as a kid. My parents never bothered to get their citizenship or renew their green cards. So they lived here undocumented and strung me along with them. I was completely undocumented until DACA. Do you know what that is?"

Qays nodded. He had some friends who were in America under that status. DACA recipients weren't citizens, and there was no path for them to become citizens, but they were in a program that allowed them to go to school or work. But if they committed a crime, let alone a pier-shattering felony, their status would be revoked. They'd become illegal aliens.

Two words that should never be linked together to describe a human being.

"So you know that means I'll get deported because of this," she said. "I don't remember Afghanistan much. Mostly just my family and the houses and the countryside. I went there once

154

when I was eleven, but it was such a headache to get approved for international travel because of my status that my parents didn't try again. This is the end of the line for me. Deportation to a country that was destroyed by the place I call home now. I can never go back because once US soldiers show up in your town, it's over. And I barely remember it. I speak Farsi because that's the only language we use at home, but it's not all of me. I love it, obviously, but it's different."

Qays felt like he'd read this story before.

"You know when you reset a device and it goes back to the default settings?" she asked.

He nodded.

"When I reset, my default is here. My default language is English. Sure, I can tell you one hundred and one Afghan dishes, but I can't describe how it makes me feel like I'm at *home* when I eat them in any language but English." Her lips melted into a sly smile. "I'm a living paradox. Without the paradoxical elements of myself, who am I?" She tsked. "And they won't even let me live my contradictions in peace."

Qays's heart lifted just like the corners of her lips. He knew that feeling all too well. To be two parts of a whole, never fully either.

When Qays was little, his parents went overboard teaching him and his siblings how to share. Qays's parents could afford two, three, four and more of everything, but they were adamant that Qays and his siblings ration what their parents gave them. There were extra bedrooms at home, but Qays had to share a room with Dina until she became a teenager, and then he shared one with Muneer. He had to split his ice cream sandwiches with

155

Muneer even though there were more in the freezer. When they got takeout, his dad dumped all the fries and side dishes onto a big plate for everyone to eat off of together. Maybe that last one was to teach personal portion control; Arab parents always had bewildering agendas.

Eventually, Qays got his own room, his own ice cream sandwich, and his own large order of fries. These firsts were all vivid moments in his memory. He remembered how they'd given him a gratifying sense of ownership. And yes, it had been extra of his parents to make them share everything, but if they hadn't done that, the feeling of finally having something belong to him alone would never have been so satisfying.

That ownership over his own serving of fries or that sense of belonging in his own room—Qays knew their value. It grew him into the person he was. And that was exactly what Muzhda stood at risk of losing. Despite not belonging in just one place, she lived in the comforts of the paradox they threatened to take from her.

And whose fault was that?

The question burst into a violent green color that made Qays feel sick to his stomach. He elected for the gray this time, choosing the haze of the unknown over the penetration of such accusatory thoughts.

"So you think your parents would give up on you?" Qays asked, exerting effort to sound placid.

She stood and paced her cell. She clenched and unclenched her fists, arching her back when she got to one end of her cell, and then stretching her arms at the other, stalling. Qays looked around at the officers who were stationed at the doors. They weren't outright watching them, but they could very much be listening.

Muzhda turned to him, frowning, with her hazel eyes glittering. "I hope so."

"You *hope* so?"

"This is too much trouble for them."

"No, no way." Qays couldn't accept it. "The money for an attorney, your DACA status, whatever it is, your family will figure it out. They'll take care of you."

"How can you say that so confidently?" she asked, her voice flat. "You barely know me."

"I just know your family wouldn't abandon you. They're your *family*."

She gave him that smudged smile of hers. "There it is. Your homecoming-king innocence."

"I'm not innocent."

"Got 'em." Muzhda laughed, and it sounded as satisfying as seeing chocolate melting in commercials. She looked at the officers and pointed at the black bulge in the ceiling that was most likely a camera. "I got his confession, guys. No need to thank me."

Qays tried to suppress his smile. "That wasn't a confession. That was denial."

"Potato, tomato." Muzhda tut-tutted.

They grinned at each other through the cell bars, which ceased to exist for a moment but then came crashing back down between them.

Something still didn't sit right with him. "You really think your parents would make you fend for yourself?"

Muzhda stepped as close as she could physically get to Qays in her cell. Her slender fingers wrapped around the iron. "Do you know why I like you?"

Qays's eyes dropped to her lips, and he forgot how to use his tongue to answer.

"Because you represent everything I've ever wanted. Your confidence, your humor, your conviction. I model those qualities after you. But some things I can't copy and paste into my personality. Your security, your freedom, your hope. I don't have the privilege of those things. I'll always be afraid that my status will be taken from me or my parents might be deported by ICE if they're found. And now that I'm here and we're on their radar, it's only a matter of time before they're found. Then where does that leave my siblings?"

Qays didn't realize that as she spoke, he'd walked up to her and held on to the bar she held, but just above her hand. Through the metal, they were touching.

"They're running?" Qays asked, his voice low.

Muzhda pressed her lips together but kept her head up high, never letting go of her confidence. Qays's confidence.

"I'm sure they're running. I'm sure they're chasing them," she said, pointing at the cameras in the room. "If it weren't for this mess I'm in, ICE wouldn't even care about my family. My parents are so good at being invisible that no one ever notices them."

Just like Muzhda, Qays thought. From afar, Muzhda had seemed insignificant, but when he'd approached her that night at the beach, she'd amazed him. She still did.

Her gaze held his before dropping off, consumed by unspoken thoughts. Muzhda sighed haggardly and laid her back onto her bench. Qays stared at her, his chest rising and falling with hers.

They were connected by a thousand strings that had sewn themselves between them long before the Fourth. Her confidence and wit originated from Qays's. Muzhda had admired Qays at those afternoon tutoring sessions and who knew how long before then. That would usually bolster Qays's ego, and he'd smirk and go about his day, sure in his ability to dazzle the world.

Even the Feds wanted to connect them through Qays's carelessness with a bag of weed that night on the beach.

The next thoughts that crossed his mind entered at an excruciatingly sluggish speed: Qays lived to be praised, but with Muzhda messing with the inner workings of his brain, he couldn't chase away the feeling that for all the admiration he'd collected, he didn't feel admirable at all.

CHAPTER 20

ZAMZAM

ZAMZAM REMEMBERED EARLY ONE MORNING, A MONTH after Yazeed had left them and stopped calling and five years after her parents' divorce, when she stumbled upon her mom praying in the living room. She remained at the mat after the Fajr prayer, and she could tell her mom had been crying. She wanted to sit beside her mom, to hold her hand, to allow herself to be her mom's comfort. Instead, a ball grew in Zamzam's throat, a ball of anger that burrowed into the hole left by Yazeed. She'd felt abandoned by her dad and her brother, but it was her mom's grief that broke her. Zamzam wouldn't be able to sit beside her on a prayer mat and hold her, but she could attempt to fulfill the roles they'd left. There would be no forgiveness for Yazeed or her dad. Not after what they did to them.

When it came to Jamal, the story went a little differently. No matter how many times Zamzam told her mom that Jamal was a good kid and he wasn't going to abandon them like their older brother did, Zamzam's mom was adamant: The Thompson family had a faulty Y chromosome. Something made them break house rules, leave home, and turn their backs on their loved ones.

Zamzam didn't want her mom seeing her like this, but there was no avoiding it.

Her mom, in one of her knit sweaters she wore even in July, looked out of place in the visitors' area. She ignored the no-touching rules and pulled her daughter into a tight embrace. Luckily, the officers were gracious enough to let them have a full second before breaking them apart.

Zamzam thought she needed that hug, but really, it felt slimy. She was self-sufficient Zamzam. Hugs made her want to crumble in her mom's arms and let the spite that drove her forward melt away.

Zamzam grounded herself. "Is Jamal okay?"

"He was shaken up," her mom answered. She broke another rule—which made Zamzam think there was some mutation in their X chromosome too—by reaching over the table to hold Zamzam's hand. "But I don't want you worrying about us. Save your strength."

Zamzam was supposed to be her mom's strength, but she nodded anyway, eyeing the guard and retracting her hand before he caught them. Zamzam always had to be alert because she walked a thin line, never, ever stepping off for fear the line was a beam and she'd fall off either side.

She heard the doors open behind her, and her heart beat faster against her chest. She watched the guard nervously, expecting him to take her back to the cell. She'd sat with her mom for only a few minutes, and she wasn't ready to go back. But the officers didn't remove her. They brought in three strangers instead, each of whom sat at different tables. The other suspects came in next, Nasreen first, shyly reuniting with a man who might be her father, then Samia, quite dramatically with hers, and finally Abdullahi, with a woman who looked too young to be his mom. The tension between him and the young woman was palpable, like it was unnatural for them not to embrace. Zamzam noticed that their faces were both pleasantly heart shaped and open to the world. Abdullahi's tired eyes filled with so much love as he looked at the young woman, Zamzam could feel it across the room. The woman said something to him, and he transformed. He stopped slumping, and his face filled with something as impossible as hope. While Zamzam's head was bowed in embarrassment, Abdullahi's head rose higher.

Before sitting, Abdullahi glanced her way and smiled. Yesterday, he'd looked like he'd aged, and now he looked like a little kid again. It made her jealous, how easily he let go.

Zamzam directed her next look pointedly between Samia and Nasreen. Abdullahi sat and looked away, but she knew he knew.

Her look said, *Watch them.*

"Chaos. It's chaos out there, Zamzam," her mother said. "There are protests in the streets. The public won't stand for it, and I think the protests are putting the right pressure on the situation. The governor is willing to step in if it'll help the public unrest. But he's also up for reelection, and he's too scared to do anything that'll anger too many people. They can't do this to you, Zamzam. You're supposed to be innocent until proven guilty.

There are nonprofit organizations who will have all their top lawyers challenge the decision and let us post bail for you. And there are protests across the country and a hundred lawsuits from advocacy organizations. Soon we'll be able to post bail and get you out of here while we prepare for trial." Her mom lowered her voice, her eyes widening. "They're *Feds*."

Zamzam bristled. "I know that, Momma."

Her mom continued in hushed tones, "I talked to one of the top lawyers in the state. Well, actually, he approached us. He said he'd represent you pro bono."

Zamzam squinted at the elated relief in her mom's voice. She trained her judgmental eyes on the ridges of her mother's braids beneath her hijab. "Why would he do that?" she asked.

"Lawyers can get a lot of publicity from these cases," her mom answered.

"But he has to have a reason, Momma. Is his firm a nonprofit or experienced in civil rights law? Did he pitch himself, or did you just accept him?"

Her mom raised a thin eyebrow at her daughter. "He came to me with an angle."

"An angle?"

Her mom swept the room with her unsettling gaze; it looked unnaturally bitter. "These other kids got you wrapped up in this mess, Zamzam. This never should've happened to you."

"It shouldn't have happened to me," Zamzam murmured, tasting the words on her tongue. That was exactly what she had been thinking and what she'd told Abdullahi too. Of all people, this never should've happened to her.

Her mom smile-frowned, and it messed with Zamzam's head. "You're the good kid," she told her.

At that, Zamzam had a second thought.

She glanced at Abdullahi, who must've sensed her eyes on him because he glanced her way too. His furrowed brows separated in relief as if he got Zamzam's next words through expedited ESP before she spoke them. "They're all good kids."

"Not like you."

Zamzam held Abdullahi's gaze. *Exactly*, she thought. *They're not like me.*

"Some of them might be better," Zamzam whispered.

Her mom shook her head. "Don't get attached, Zamzam. Those kids being charged might be our only way out."

"What?"

"That's what the lawyer said."

"But—" Her voice fell away. Her mom wasn't sounding like her mom anymore.

Isn't this what I wanted? Zamzam thought. *So why does it sound so bad coming from Momma?*

A chair screeched across the tile floor. Everyone's eyes shot up to the woman across from Abdullahi, who was staring straight at Zamzam.

"Is something wrong?" she called across the room at her.

Zamzam's skin erupted in gooseflesh. She pointed at herself. "Me?"

The young woman scowled. "Yeah, you. You've been looking at my brother and talking to your mom like you have something to say."

Zamzam's mom stood, too, looking like a tower of ice.

Zamzam didn't dare move. The officer's hand went straight to his waist belt, but he didn't move to stop them. Too late, Zamzam realized they wanted to see how this would play out. Why else did they coordinate the visits in this way?

"Don't speak to my daughter that way," her mom said in a steadier voice than Zamzam expected. "I should be the one questioning your brother. God knows what kinds of things he made Zamzam do that made her end up in here."

"My brother didn't do anything." Abdullahi's sister seethed.

"Please, calm down," Samia's father called out, astonishingly soft-spoken compared with his daughter.

Zamzam's mother scoffed. "You expect me to believe that? It's *always* the boys."

"Momma—"

"No, Zamzam, listen." Her mom's tone shut Zamzam up. She continued to fire at Abdullahi's sister, slandering Abdullahi even though she didn't know him. *No good, sloppy, reckless.* It sounded like she was describing Yazeed. Those words didn't describe either boy, but they must've made her mom feel better. Then her mom switched targets, addressing the room: "Come to think of it, Zamzam's the only one here with a real alibi."

The room tilted. Zamzam might have let it slip that she was with Qays when the oil rig exploded. But thinking back on that slipup, it might have done her more harm than good. Because if Qays could be made out to be guilty, then so would Zamzam.

Samia's father snorted. His brows slid over his eyes, and he looked like a villain. "You're going for the alibi with the other kid they have in custody?"

"Ever heard of partners in crime?" Abdullahi's sister challenged, her body tense as though protecting her cub.

"They probably both did it!" accused Nasreen's father, slamming his hands on the table as he stood up.

"My daughter would never!" Zamzam's mom snapped back.

As their family members stood up, their argument maturing into threats of lawsuits, the officers moved to bring the four teenagers back inside. In response, their family members returned their attention to calling out comforting words to them, even though those comforting words felt empty when they were faced with returning to their cells.

Out in the real world, Zamzam was sure there was plenty more time and space for arguments.

Abdullahi was right. The Feds wanted them to fight. The best way to break ties between people was to control the conditions, push them to their limits, and then let natural behavior do the rest. And the accusations that were being fired were incriminating, all the ammunition Favreau would need, straight on a platter.

For her freedom, Zamzam thought she could do what her mom was doing: toss the blame as far away from herself as possible and to hell with the others. But in the visitors' area, the noise around her had muted, Samia's father holding back Nasreen's, Zamzam's mom's and Abdullahi's sister's mouths open wide midyell. On their way back to their cells, Zamzam and the other kids exchanged looks. They barely knew one another, but she knew she couldn't stand behind an attorney in a brown suit spinning a timeline and a story that put Abdullahi in prison. Or Samia and Nasreen, either, though that thought brought considerably less guilt. She couldn't, not when she didn't know whether they did it. And as time passed, she was less and less confident that any of them had done anything.

She was logical, responsible, dependable Zamzam, and she wasn't so easily swayed.

Zamzam shuffled to the heavy gray door that led to her cell and waited for the officer to let her back inside.

THE LOS ANGELES JOURNAL

FOUR OF THE INDEPENDENCE DAY SIX FREE TO THREATEN LA STREETS

Monarch Beach terrorist attack suspects released on bail, court date set

LOS ANGELES—As the country mourns in the aftermath of the Fourth of July Monarch Beach terrorist attack, law enforcement has released on bail the four suspected minors of the Independence Day Six, those aged under 17.

Ashleigh Bloom, a longtime preschool teacher and the wife of security guard Jeremy Bloom, who was killed on impact in the pier explosion, was interviewed in the days leading up to their release. Still grieving the sudden loss of her husband, she shared, "[The Six] are dangers to society. We don't know which of them did it. . . . It could have been all six of them. My husband would still be here if it weren't for [them]. Not that I would be able to sleep without Jeremy beside me, but I won't be at peace knowing they're out there."

Members of the Independence Day Movement argued that the Six must be given their constitutional rights and brought to clear and unquestionable justice. They refused to comment on the American freedoms and liberties also under attack by the terrorist groups suspected to have blitzed Monarch Beach on July 4. They continue to lead riots in major US cities under claims of peaceful protest.

Following legal action against the federal government by the movement, Abdullahi Talib, Nasreen Choudhry, Samia Al-Samra, and Zamzam Thompson were released on bail set at unknown, varied amounts. Evidence against the suspects continues to be withheld by the FBI as the release of the court dates for the Six approaches. They remain under further investigation and high-security measures.

According to witnesses, Qays Sharif was seen in possession of explosives along the beach and had been seen speaking with Muzhda Ahmad minutes before firing an explosive. Ahmad, who entered the United States as an undocumented immigrant from Afghanistan, has been brought under further investigation. Sharif recently spent time overseas in Israel, where he visited family in Palestinian territories. He will be tried as an adult and was not released on bail at this time.

◆

CHAPTER 21

NASREEN

IT HAD BEEN FIFTEEN DAYS SINCE NASREEN'S NIGHTMARE did not end after waking up. Even though her parents scrounged up enough money with the help of the community to post her bail and she was waking up in her own bed, she woke feeling trapped. She was legally prohibited from leaving Los Angeles County, and though it was by no means a rest stop on Route 66, her home suffocated her in ways the cell hadn't. She'd stared at Carrots slithering in his glass cage, wondering how he lived in that confined space. Maybe despite all the love he received from her, he felt trapped too.

Since she'd left the facility, she'd been home. Her parents tried to get her to tell them about that night, but she couldn't say a word.

They discussed taking her to a therapist. For now, her lawyer would have to do.

Her mama nudged her. "Sit up, Nasreen."

She straightened her posture. Her lawyer, a Ms. Penelope Carson, was Dior-tier counsel, recommended by one of her baba's posh supervisors, and the Choudhrys never slouched in front of money. Ms. Carson's office was in one of the tall, shiny buildings with a view of the ocean, but Nasreen couldn't look out the window. It was the first time she'd left her house since being out of custody. She felt out of practice, and everything reminded her of the Fourth.

"Here we are," Ms. Carson started, flitting her red-manicured fingers across the files until they landed on Nasreen's. "We'll begin with prepping Nasreen for next week's interview with the FBI. Like I said over the phone, the DA's stance is aggressive. They're insinuating all sorts of connections between the six defendants, but the defendants most implicated are Qays Sharif, Muzhda Ahmad, and Abdullahi Talib. Qays Sharif appeared to have had an explosive device, and they connected him with Muzhda through some DNA samples on a package. Abdullahi found Muzhda, who was at the site where the explosion at the rig originated from. Zamzam was also seen running with Qays."

"What does this have to do with Nasreen?" her baba asked, agitated.

"Nasreen is a weak point in their prosecution. There's been an effort to conceal some information from the public by Petro-Mile, to protect their company from more harm after their oil rig exploded. It's been difficult to piece everything together. That's why I need to know everything about that night from her." Ms. Carson's gaze fell to Nasreen. Nasreen looked away.

"But they let us post bail," Nasreen's mama said, grasping for some hope. "Isn't that good news?"

Ms. Carson leaned back in her chair, her body angled slightly away from them. "Not necessarily," she said from the side of her mouth. "She's still a minor now, but releasing her on bail instead of detaining her while they set court dates suggests they might try to postpone the arraignment until Nasreen is closer to eighteen. That way they can try her as an adult."

Nasreen's mama tightened her grip on her daughter's hand. "Can they do that?"

Ms. Carson crossed one leg over another. "It's in the FBI's best interest if they think their prosecution could be successful. She'd be tried as an adult, so the duration of her sentence, if life, would fit the severity of an adult, not a lesser sentence reserved for juveniles."

"But that's two years away," Nasreen's mama murmured, dread thickening her tone. Her mama smoothed her sleek black-but-streaked-white hair, and her hand came away shaking. "Nasreen is expected to have to live with this for the next two years?"

Ms. Carson's gaze darted to Nasreen, whose face felt like a dulled sculpture, like the ones she had seen displayed at the Getty Museum. They never did strike her as beautiful; they were restored, yet they were grimy and blunted in all the important places. Somehow the other spectators didn't find it as difficult to imagine them as magnificent as they once were.

The brilliance of those sculptures lacked. Perhaps because Nasreen never felt like anything could be sufficient, that she would never be sufficient enough. Now Nasreen thought it was because after centuries and centuries, nothing could fix a broken sculpture, no matter how expert the restoration.

Nasreen felt like the night of the Fourth had been centuries ago, and the passed time had dulled her. The Fourth had taken a snapshot of who she was and preserved it, and every day she would just be a version of herself on the Fourth, and no amount of rehabilitation could make her any sharper. It wasn't the next two years for her; it was this moment stretching into forever.

"I'm sorry, Mrs. Choudhry," Ms. Carson said, her finger tapping against her glass desk. "I'm your legal counsel, so I have to give you an unedited briefing of what Nasreen is facing. My job is to defend her in that courtroom, and we can press charges to minimize how much this damages her future. Two years of fighting this out in court is considerably favorable to any sentence she could receive if the prosecution succeeds with the case they've put forth."

Her mama and baba nodded slowly, glancing at each other. They just wanted their daughter to be safe and with them. And sure, they had their daughter at their side, but she wasn't their same daughter from before.

Ms. Carson continued, "Right now, if we go in for a *voluntary* interview, Nasreen will appear cooperative compared to the others, who will respond to an interrogation summons."

It was all twisted; the gases in the air were turning liquid.

Ms. Carson clapped her bony hands together. "To prepare for the interview, I'd like to talk about that night now. No mics, no records, but I need to hear the *absolute* truth from you so that I can defend you. Currently, the evidence stacked against you is... substantial."

Nasreen didn't ask how. Maybe it was because of Samia or one of the others who'd testified against her. Fingers pointing, guns waving. No rules. No adults. A bunch of kids wielding accusations.

"What are they saying?" Her mama sniffled. Nasreen, whose hearing had blurred, wondered when her mother had started crying.

Ms. Carson paused. "I think it's best I speak with Nasreen privately. After we speak, I'll take any of your questions, but my time with your daughter is limited."

"I don't want to leave her," her mama said.

"I assure you, Mrs. Choudhry, it'll make things go much faster."

"We don't want faster." Her baba's jaw clenched. "We want to make sure our money is well spent. This is our daughter's life, and you aren't cheap."

Ms. Carson didn't blink. "I understand, but Nasreen might not be as open with her parents in the room."

"Our daughter doesn't keep secrets," her baba replied, and Nasreen's gut dropped. "There's nothing stopping her from being completely honest. Are you suggesting our daughter doesn't trust us?"

Nasreen felt her soul sink in her body.

"Of course not," Ms. Carson said, eyeing Nasreen, who watched the conversation unfold from inside a diving bell, like in that movie her French teacher at Saint Modesta had made them watch. Ms. Carson glared back at Nasreen's baba. "But she *is* a teenage girl. I only want her to be comfortable."

"And you think we don't make her comfortable?" Though he

kept his cool, Nasreen's baba was becoming increasingly agitated. She could tell by the way the muscles in his neck tightened. He stood then and continued: "Nasreen, let's go. I don't think Ms. Carson can represent Nasreen the way we want."

Her baba was already at the door, and her mama sighed shakily before following suit. "I'm sorry you feel that way," Ms. Carson said stoically, eyes fixed on Nasreen still sitting in the maroon suede armchair.

Nasreen didn't move, even when her baba called her name again. She knew very well, just like with her private-school education, that it was her father's money being spent and she was expected to follow. But she stared out from her diving bell at what her father perceived in Ms. Carson. White, Equinox member, Drybar regular. Ms. Carson had her prejudices and preferences, and she made no effort to hide them. Clearly, she thought Nasreen's story would change when her parents weren't around. Nasreen wasn't supposed to trust her parents; she was supposed to want to get away from them, as was the Muslim-girl stereotype.

But that was not why Nasreen kept her secrets close to her chest. She hid parts of herself because she wanted to protect them.

Ms. Carson wouldn't guess that Nasreen's mama regularly ignored her baba's suggestions because her baba rarely heard himself when he spoke; he just liked to exercise his tongue. Her baba had strict rules for her, but when Nasreen made mistakes or broke rules, he seldom gave her even a stern talking-to. And every summer, Nasreen and her parents drove up to Sequoia National Park, where they pitched tents between the redwoods, cooked meals together on a portable stove burner, and roasted halal marshmallows at a campfire, telling scary stories while trying to spot deer or bears wandering through their campsite in the dead of night.

And Nasreen loved every moment with them.

They were the image of a happy Pakistani American family, and Ms. Carson probably didn't know how to superimpose them onto the wholesome family TV shows she watched. And that was exactly what made Ms. Carson a formidable ally.

"No, Baba," Nasreen said, the diving bell buffering her defiance, "I think this is where we need to be."

Ms. Carson's mouth twitched upward, all smug. Nasreen hated it, so she continued, "Ms. Carson knows how they think. She has the same prejudices as the prosecution."

Ms. Carson raised a brow. "I don't."

"You do," Nasreen shot back. Her AP English teacher had taught her about something called implicit bias when they were reading Shakespeare's *Othello*. She'd explained that every comment and action could be more deeply analyzed if we took into consideration that Othello "the Moor" was not like all the other characters. There's the play *Othello*, analyzed without color, and then there's the play *Othello the Moor*, in which every character and Shakespeare's choices were driven by a bias none of them truly understood nor realized was rooted in them.

Basically, Othello got a lot of hate for being a Moor, but he was messed up, too, everyone a product of their twisted environment.

Nasreen pressed her glasses up with the back of her hand. She made herself comfortable in Ms. Carson's office armchair. She said, "You understand them, so I want you on my side."

Her baba glanced back at her, his hand on the doorknob. She could always melt his will when she chose to fight.

"And I want to speak with her privately," Nasreen added.

Nasreen's mama patted her husband on the shoulder, resigning as always when Nasreen decided to put in a final word, because they wanted her happy. They excused themselves.

Ms. Carson's eyes illuminated. "Let's get started?"

Nasreen cleared her throat, pushing through the thick walls of the diving bell. "But before we begin, do I have your word that everything I say stays between us?"

"Of course. You've got client confidentiality. Even from your parents."

"Okay." Nasreen shuddered as the truth rattled the inside of the diving bell. "Because I want to work with the others. Abdullahi, Samia, and Zamzam. I don't think any of them did it."

Ms. Carson walked slowly around her table and leaned against the edge closest to Nasreen. "I don't think that's a good idea," she started, looking down at her. "The others are in deeper than you. Samia might be the only one who doesn't have as much incriminating evidence against her like you. We need to look at the case objectively. I can't promise you that by helping you we can also help your friends."

"They're not my friends," Nasreen answered with a pang of longing.

Ms. Carson placed one of her oiled legs over the other and absently swayed the bright red soles of her Christian Louboutins. "Even better."

"But..." Nasreen swallowed her words.

But it feels wrong.

Ms. Carson pressed Nasreen until she told her everything, from the time she arrived, to everyone she met even in passing, to the MB hot-dog boy who shared her last name. It invigorated her that Ms. Carson was a total stranger. Nasreen divulged all the facts. Her feelings, the reasons for her actions, and the choices she'd made weren't facts yet. All she told her was what happened.

Months ago, Nasreen made a fake social media account. Uploaded a picture of her shirtless cousin as the profile picture. At first it was just for fun, an endless scrolling time suck. But then she happened upon Samia's sparkling page and shot her a private message about one of her posts, thinking it would go unread. Samia read it. Nasreen pretended to be this boy named Faris. They became friends. More than friends. Nasreen was happy in her lie.

Thankfully, Ms. Carson listened and never asked why.

Then, on a particularly dull day, Nasreen agreed to meet Samia in real life at the Fourth of July MSA event at the beach. Nasreen went with the intention of coming clean, about how she went too far and that she wanted to try to be friends.

She started at the pits. She observed the kids; she spoke with the boy named Choudhry. Shortly before nine o'clock, she walked alone to the houses, cliffside. Samia saw her and, at first, tried to create space. Maybe she didn't want some random girl walking up on her and Faris. That was when Nasreen introduced herself. She pulled open their DMs and explained who she was. Time slowed as the purple of the sky darkened into night.

The words coming out of her mouth were all wrong. Even to her own ears, Nasreen knew there was no right way of saying she'd lied to Samia for months about who she was. There was no timeline in which Samia was going to feel anything but betrayed.

Samia yelled at her and called her names as humiliation washed over her. Nasreen had gone to the beach to tell the truth; she came away with fear and regret.

When Nasreen couldn't take the yelling anymore, she tried to jump the fence onto the private beach to get away. When she was halfway over the fence, they heard the sound of the explosion and the windows of the cliffside houses shattering. Terrified, she fell back onto the rocks on the public beach, breaking her glasses.

"The houses' windows and doors were all shut that night, and they shattered after the explosion. I had nothing to do with it," Nasreen swore.

"And what about Samia?" Ms. Carson asked.

Nasreen shook her head, her cheeks reddening. It was embarrassing that a second person knew her secret.

"We were in a good position to see it happen," she began, "but it's not like we were masterminding an attack. I'd never even met Samia in person before that day."

"But you had communicated with her, and that complicates things." Ms. Carson pulled up a picture on her laptop of the Monarch Beach cliffside residences. "Could you point out where you two were?"

Nasreen pointed beside the Spanish-style home with a terracotta infinity pool, the second one from the fence, three stories like the others.

Ms. Carson gave a tiny smile as she clicked onto another file. There on the screen was the shattered window and another picture of the glass and bits of clay freckling the pool.

Nasreen sat up, a weight off her chest for the corroborating evidence. "Yes, that's it!" she exclaimed.

Ms. Carson's smile widened, but rather than being reassuring, it seemed unhinged. "I'll take a look at the footage they have in evidence. You see how this can go either way, Nasreen?" she asked, her smile wiped off now but her eyebrow arched as she scanned documents. "The only thing in the investigation that pulls you in with the others is some witness claiming that they heard something fire from one of these houses. But if we can prove that the windows shattered from the vibrations of the explosion with a time stamp, then Samia becomes your alibi, proof that you had nothing to do with this. If we can't do that, then they get to claim Samia as your accomplice in this conspiracy. It's very important that you tell me exactly what you told them."

So Nasreen told her all that she had said, anxiety climbing up her neck and cheeks and bursting as color. "But I don't know about Samia. She might have told them something different."

Ms. Carson groaned. "They really roped you all in by interrogating you without your attorneys present. Even if we get those interrogations thrown out, it's easy enough to find other evidence that proves whatever they want to prove. I'm going to see what I can find on Samia to see how we can push some of the limelight off you."

Nasreen started in her chair. "But Samia's innocent."

"Sure, dear, but let's hope she's even a fraction less innocent than you. I'm sure that's all we'll need. I'll also look into the others. That'll be all for today."

Nasreen stood up, feeling dismissed. She couldn't leave like this. "But…it's wrong to do that to them."

Ms. Carson placed a firm hand on Nasreen's shoulder. "It's not about right and wrong. It's about winning. With cases as severe as this, your sentences mature. Some of you might go to juvie for a year or two before being transferred to a prison, so we want to keep you from getting *life* in prison. Do you understand that?"

Nasreen dropped her head. Of course, she understood. She'd have to take any chance that Ms. Carson could get to spare herself that life, even if it meant betraying the others for it.

CHAPTER 22

QAYS

"SPICY NACHO."

"Salt and vinegar."

"Milan."

"Joshua Tree."

"New York style."

"DiGiorno."

"Soccer."

"Soccer," Muzhda agreed. Qays finally found common ground with her. He stood up, shifting the air in the drab day room, and pumped a fist in the air, grinning in glorious victory.

Muzhda's full mouth worked, fighting a smile. "Mint chocolate chip."

Aghast, Qays answered, "Rocky road."

Muzhda gaped at him. "Rocky road's got gelatin in it."

"Blow on it, say bismillah, and enjoy the marshmallow."

"You're a child," Muzhda shot back, surrendering to laughter.

High-security detainees. That was what they called them. They were in this investigation limbo, but it was fine with Qays because for thirty minutes every day, he was allowed into an enclosed recreational area with a few tables and benches, and he got to see Muzhda.

Muzhda with a smile that sparkled like diamonds, Muzhda with a blush like a shy California sunset. Muzhda, who loved salt-and-vinegar chips, musicals, DiGiorno pizza, and mint-chocolate-chip ice cream, and who was also the only other high-security detainee that Qays knew.

The investigation was widening around them, but in here, all that mattered was him and Muzhda. There was little Qays could do besides wait for his attorney to come to him with news. In the meantime, he tried to survive the gray. Talking to Muzhda helped with that.

She flicked invisible lint off her beige shirt and threw back stray hairs into her scarf. Qays had the inexplicable urge to push a strand behind her ear. It was hard to control these urges when they were in the day room. He snapped himself out of it.

Then Muzhda asked, "How about dogs?"

"Chocolate Lab."

"Chow chow."

"Fancy," Qays said approvingly.

She smiled, closing her eyes. "A girl could dream."

"Have you had one? A dog?"

"Kinda. It's one of my only memories from Afghanistan. We had a guard dog in my grandparents' yard. They said we couldn't name him, because he technically wasn't a pet. But he ate our scraps and played with us, so he was a pet by everything but name. So my cousins and I named him. He looked like a German shepherd, so we named him Jacques because I was six and my cousins were dumbasses who told me Jacques was a German name."

She giggled, and all the gray fell away. They weren't high-security detainees who weren't allowed to post bail; they were two teenagers on a hideously drab date to the day room. Not Qays's first choice, though it was infinitely better than them sitting in their cells. If they were out in the real world, Qays would have taken her out for dinner, but considering the circumstances, this would have to do.

"It's weird, you know, when I close my eyes like this, my memories of Jacques are so vivid. Sometimes I forget the way my grandpa sang to me or the smell of my grandma's cooking or my cousin Kamila's god-awful pigtails, but I can never forget that stupid dog." She chuckled to herself.

Muzhda's eyes flashed open; they found his in complete vulnerability. "Jacques was a guard dog who I played with even though my grandparents warned me against it. He wasn't domesticated; he didn't become my pet just because I'd given him a name." She sat on Qays's bench, keeping healthy high-security-detainee distance, whatever that meant. She offered her arm, then flipped it. Along the length of her forearm was a time-stretched oval-shaped scar, dark against her copper skin. "This happened one night when I was teasing him with a lamb's bone from dinner. His teeth went all the way to the bone."

Her breathing shallowed, and so did his. "After he bit me, my mom ran water from the yard pump over it. Every time the water washed away the blood, wallah, I could see the light pink flesh and the white bone underneath. Then the blood flooded over it again and again. My dad drove me down to the hospital, and the rest of the family followed in taxis.

"When I got home with an arm full of stitches and wrapped in gauze, Jacques was still sitting at the gate. Everyone was so distracted by me, they hadn't realized he followed us into the yard. I was sitting in the kitchen that overlooked the yard when my grandpa went outside at Maghrib time. They wanted to set up our dinner outside, and Jacques refused to go out of the yard and guard from the gate. There were kids running around, and my grandpa was probably scared. If a dog attacks someone in America, the vet puts them down immediately. I was six, and we were in Afghanistan, so I didn't know that. I thought Jacques would be given another chance. He was our guard dog, period. He didn't get retired or released from service."

She glanced at him, her face gaunt. "I think, maybe, I could have learned to love him again. He was just a dog. He didn't know any better." She paused. "I remember the next part the clearest. My grandpa was yelling, so much. Too much. Jacques was whining. I had to cover my ear with my good arm. My parents tried to move me away from the window. Then there was a gun in my grandpa's hands and a shot, and Jacques dropped dead."

Qays wasn't surprised; he'd known Muzhda knew how to tell a good story, and he'd been expecting that outcome. Yet in the way she recalled it, he felt like a ghost was passing through the room. His mouth dried; his stomach curled.

"I blamed my grandpa for killing him. I didn't think I could ever forgive him. Isn't that funny? That I thought I could forgive a dog, but not my grandfather?"

Qays cocked his head and shrugged. It sucked, sure, but it wasn't uncommon for people to be more compassionate toward animals than humans.

"I got over it eventually, but I can never forget it. I hate that that's my strongest memory."

Qays held her amber gaze in his. "It's because you loved him."

Muzhda gave a short and airy laugh, looking away. "I sure did. Why I love those that hurt me is beyond me."

Color sprouted on her cheeks as she stole a glance his way, and Qays's cheeks warmed too. Her stories were so real and pure and honest, all the things he craved, all the things he couldn't be.

Turning away, she squinted at the officer in the room, who slouched like he'd forgotten to drink his morning coffee. Scooting dangerously closer to Qays, she murmured, "Your fancy lawyer is coming today?"

Qays nodded as her breath on his neck sent electricity down his spine. He trained his eyes on her slender fingers gripping the bench.

"What will you tell him?" she whispered.

They were being watched, but the officer's eyes were half-open without caffeine to support his eyelids.

Qays shrugged.

"Will you tell him about me?" She looked up at him.

"What about you?" he asked back in confusion.

She pointed at his chest. "Milan." She pointed at herself. "Joshua Tree." Then back at him. "Attorney with a $100,000 retainer." To herself. "Public defender."

"What are you saying?"

She sighed, her eyes transforming wildly with desperation.

"What will you say about me? When they ask you about me, what will you tell them?"

"Nothing you wouldn't say yourself."

Her eyes glimmered in the shift of light. "They'll listen to you first and more and better. It matters what you'll say."

The officer perked up, his weary eyes locked dead on Qays. "Hey, you have a visitor."

They whisked him out of the day room and away from Muzhda. The color she brought with her left, the gray returned, and Qays still didn't have an answer.

His name was Steven Alsace. He was middle-aged and well groomed and resembled a saluki more than Qays thought a man possibly could.

Qays had read that salukis were originally bred in the Fertile Crescent, a place he'd learned about in seventh grade. The Fertile Crescent, aka Mesopotamia, was home to Sumer and Babylonia, the oldest known civilizations in the world.

When Qays was twelve, his teacher stretched a weeklong unit into a month of looking at an oblong green map that didn't look like it belonged on Earth. They spent weeks learning to label the Tigris and the Euphrates on a white sheet of paper delineated by thin black lines that didn't seem to quantify time and space. To the kids in his class and to him, Mesopotamia was from a fantasy world that humans called the land of the earliest written language and art.

He was AP Art History years old when he learned that Mesopotamia was modern-day Iraq, eastern Syria, and southeastern

Turkey. Yet at age twelve, when Qays read his seventh-grade world-history book cover to cover, the text never once mentioned the Middle East. History was written either purposely out of context or by authors who practiced convenient omission.

The Fertile Crescent was too nice a name for a land most people were conditioned to imagine as a backward desert.

All that to say Steven Alsace likely had French ancestors, but he sure as hell looked like a saluki from the Fertile Crescent.

Either way, the future was looking bleak for Qays and spiffy Steven Alsace. They were at an impasse.

Qays let his cuffs scrape the table. "Just tell them I don't know her."

"Favreau is trying to connect you kids on the basis that you were acting on behalf of an entity. A terrorist organization."

"Didn't they sweep our social media? I'm clean, I'm sure Muzhda's cleaner, that Zamzam girl is probably retired, and Samia's that airhead influencer. The other two are most likely more of the same. We're not connected to a terrorist group," Qays concluded.

"Noted," Alsace said, all snide. He appeared to ignore Qays's comment, just as he had all his other comments. "Favreau is capitalizing on any and all connections. You have a past history tutoring Muzhda, and the fingernail-swab samplings came back a match. Traces of marijuana were found under your nails and Muzhda's. It calls suspicion to the both of you."

"That's because I pressured her into getting my weed for me and my friends from the lockers. That's all. Other than that, we barely know each other."

"They seem to think your brief time together at Valley High

189

School could have been premeditation of this act. When they tie you to some terrorist organization—"

"Any specific organization take ownership yet?" Qays interrupted.

"No," Alsace said. "But that doesn't mean they won't."

"You can't just invent a Muslim terrorist group and frame six kids."

Alsace raised a single eyebrow. "Favreau specializes in cases like this. In 2009 she incarcerated a New York City cab driver on affiliations with Osama bin Laden because a racist patron left a nasty review online saying he looked like he lived in a bunker and had an Arabic last name. He was a Sikh and suffered from hepatitis B."

Translation: *Yes, Favreau could invent a terrorist group and frame six kids. And it's likely her goal.*

Qays scraped his cuffs on the table the other way. "I don't care. We find another angle. Muzhda didn't do anything. She and I are strangers."

Alsace doubled back. "They have you on possession of an illegal explosive."

"It was a firework, and I'm an idiot. Ask Zamzam—she was there when I lit it."

"Ms. Thompson could be working on her own version of the story, which will be very different from yours and very different from all the others."

"All versions disagree on everything, and none of them include the truth? I'm sure that'll lay things out nicely for Favreau."

"If the truth mattered, you would look more closely at

Muzhda's file instead of avoiding it altogether," Alsace said, exasperated. "Why protect her?"

In front of his eyes, Muzhda materialized like a memory of what felt like ages ago but had been less than an hour. Sitting beside him, asking him, *What will you say about me?*

Qays shook his head until Muzhda vanished from the room. There was something more there, but it hurt him too much to think about it.

"And there's the other thing about the marijuana," Alsace added.

Qays huffed. "I'm an idiot who gets high once a month with my friends."

"You're a minor, and they connected your package to Muzhda. Now whatever they have on her, they have on you, and vice versa. So she becomes our best escape route for your acquittal."

Qays pushed back. "I'm your client, aren't I? And I'm asking for another angle. One where Muzhda is covered but that still gets us results."

"We can't cover for her, Qays," Alsace replied, frowning. "They found her at the origin of the signal of the blast."

Qays's fist slammed the table, controlled and calculatedly unhinged. Alsace flinched into a scowl, cautiously eyeing the guards. "Then make her their blind spot," Qays bit out. "I didn't tell you everything about that night."

"Then enlighten me."

Qays inhaled deeply. To protect Muzhda, what other choice did he have? At the end of the day, someone had to take the fall so the rest of them could walk and so Qays could go back to running. Forward. Toward his bright future.

"After they arrested me, I looked down the beach for her," he whispered. "Everyone had run. There was no one standing by the lockers. The police had already moved in. But I did see someone. Running toward us."

"Did you see their face?"

He suppressed the urge to rub the back of his neck. "No."

"They already have Mr. Abdullahi Talib coming from that direction. If you had anything to do with him, that just means you have more of a connection to Muzhda."

Qays's brows furrowed. "Why, what does Abdullahi have to do with Muzhda?"

A buzzer sounded. Alsace collected his folders and laptop and put them into his briefcase. Before he could answer, the officers led Qays back inside. Not back to Muzhda. Back to the gray.

CHAPTER 23

ABDULLAHI

ABDULLAHI HAD THOUGHT HIS SISTER MARYAM'S REASSUR-ing words would cure him. But even now that he was out on bail and could seek the comfort of his siblings, who were doing all they could, his brain was heavy with fog. His insomnia sapped all the energy it took to be himself.

He had to do something. It broke him to see Maryam fight with Zamzam's mother and the other parents. If anything was going to give him a sense of purpose instead of endless dread, it might just be bringing them together.

He started with Zamzam.

Valley High School was in a part of Los Angeles that breathed. Its lungs were the street art and mismatched mom and pops and dank cuisine. Its counterpart was the LA in a girdle, with its primped and preened landscaping, gentrified shopping strips, and fusion cuisine that never drizzled more than a teaspoon of sauce.

The city was masterfully constructed, a Van Gogh painting of color pockets if the palette were made up of ethnicities and social classes. Years of experience of redlining on the East Coast and in the Midwest made it so the West Coast could be Van Gogh when the East was more of a Picasso. Online, he could probably find a school-district website with the image of the district borders, a jagged, Greece-shaped appendage. Monarch Beach had been completely eaten out of it, and the northern side, where Huntington's district resided, was also chewed out as if by worms.

Abdullahi found Zamzam easily. He knew exactly where to look and whom to ask because the LA landscape was predictable. Abdullahi attended the masjid a lot of Valley High School students went to because, in a county this large and with so many mosques to choose from, people could be picky. And sure enough, when he pulled up to it, a group of people were fundraising for the Six out front. Abdullahi wore sunglasses and a baseball cap to hide his hair and wasn't recognized. He didn't stick around once he got the information he needed to find Zamzam. He jumped back into the car, grateful the judge hadn't imposed restrictions on driving within the county, though the early curfews imposed on them made it hard to meet in secret after dark.

Abdullahi politely requested a meeting at the least conspicuous time of day, when it was too hot in July and the entire LA population had to be submerged in a body of water.

Zamzam shielded her face from the glare bouncing off the hood of Abdullahi's car as he rounded into a parking lot.

"This better be good." Zamzam turned on him as he bounced out of his car.

"Thanks for coming," he replied. Zamzam really was too enigmatic for Abdullahi's own good. She had a pull to her, a *Look at me, but don't look too hard, because you can't handle my shine* kind of vibe.

"It's just the two of us?"

"No." Abdullahi's eyes searched the streets. "The others should be here."

Samia's Taycan peeled into the lot then, and once the car stopped, she kept it idling, haphazardly intersecting the parking-spot lines on the ground. She jumped out, keeping her car door open and draping her arms over it. A half-in, half-out stance.

"What's up, Abdullahi?" she asked, barely giving a nod toward Zamzam. She was barefaced and paler than Abdullahi remembered her.

He scanned the lot. He'd purposely chosen the back lot of a market and restaurant plaza. The Korean market out front was closed for construction, and the soft-tofu and bulgogi BBQ restaurants were closed between lunch and dinner service. The back lot was never frequented by anyone, so the whole area was deserted save for a couple employees prepping for dinner. They were on the cusp of Huntington and Valley territory, and very far from Monarch Beach by LA traffic timing. No one would notice them here.

Abdullahi wrung his fingers. "Is Nasreen coming?"

Samia shrugged. "I don't know. I got the message to her that we'd be here, but she left me on read. I have a feeling she's not going to play friendly."

"Is that what this is about?" Zamzam interjected. "Playing friendly?"

Abdullahi evaded her question with one of his own. "Does anyone know what Nasreen's like?"

Zamzam crossed her arms. "We have lawyers for a reason. We shouldn't be here debriefing each other. We're not on the same side, and it's hella suspicious."

"Aren't we?" Abdullahi muttered. He could feel his shirt lining with sweat.

Samia snickered at Zamzam. "You clearly don't know Abdullahi."

"I don't know any of you," Zamzam shot back. "That's my point. I know it feels like the right thing to do is to play nice, but the only right thing is to get out of this without it ruining our lives."

Any more than it has, Abdullahi thought. Zamzam did make a good point.

"Relax, babe," Samia told her, then leaned heavily against her car. "Abdullahi doesn't have an agenda. He's just concerned."

"Well, thank God we have you for translating."

"You're welcome."

"Oh, shut up and turn off your engine. We don't need more air pollution because of you."

"My car's gas emission should be last on your list of worries."

"Guys." Abdullahi interrupted their banter. "We need Nasreen here."

Zamzam rolled her eyes. "Why? Who the hell cares? This is a waste of time. Why are we even risking meeting with each other?"

"You don't need to be so angry with him," Samia snapped.

"Guys."

"Are you his lawyer?"

Samia scoffed. "Someone's got to be."

"Is this a game to you?" Zamzam's eyes narrowed.

"Guys."

"It'll all blow over."

"Spoken like a true Huntie," Zamzam blurted. *Huntie* implied Samia was from Huntington, but it also implied she was a sheep among many other sheep. A basic, someone who followed trends thoughtlessly, eyes glazed over.

Fire blazed behind Samia's eyes. "You're such a bitch."

"Guys."

Zamzam threw her hands up and cut Abdullahi a look like he was partially to blame for Samia's existence. "I'm *done* here."

She started for the front lot toward the intersection. Abdullahi stared at Samia, hoping she could see how exhausted he was, how he was getting zero sleep while praying for a miracle. Samia dropped her head back and groaned.

Clicking off the engine, she chased after Zamzam, who was still in their line of sight. Reluctantly, the two girls returned to Abdullahi, Samia fighting a rash from having to apologize while Zamzam sported a smug smile.

Abdullahi clasped his clammy hands together. "Let's pretend for two seconds that we don't all have lawyers and the FBI isn't chasing after us, and that someone gives a damn about what's right and wrong. Can we do that?"

"Can you really think of anything else?" Samia snarked.

Zamzam agreed to level with him.

"Let's get our stories straight." Abdullahi extended the peace offering. "I know you've seen the video that's started circulating."

The three of them exchanged worried glances. The video had surfaced and gained internet traction quickly. It was a blurry video, only five seconds long, but it was undeniably Abdullahi running around the corner of the bathrooms at Monarch Beach, and two voices. First, Muzhda screaming, "Don't leave me!" followed by Abdullahi yelling, "It wasn't me!"

Abdullahi couldn't watch it; he'd only seen it by accident and then run to the bathroom to throw up. He couldn't hear her voice. It was already so vivid in his memory; he didn't need to make things worse with video and audio.

Their words from the video had become taglines for the protests that sprouted across the country. Even Abdullahi knew the video was going to make things messier than they already were, but Samia and Zamzam seemed unfazed.

Zamzam clicked her tongue impatiently. "I don't feel comfortable discussing without Nasreen present. God knows what she's telling her attorney about us."

Whipping out her phone, Samia clicked across her screen until she was sufficiently dissatisfied. "She left me on read again. But Nasreen doesn't matter."

"What do you mean she doesn't matter?" Zamzam demanded. "If she's not here, my story's off the table."

Samia's lashes fluttered. "Nasreen's a nonissue."

"You seem confident in that answer, considering you don't even *know* her. Unless?"

Samia's mouth hung open. "So what if I know Nasreen? I know Abdullahi too. I marginally know Qays because the entire world knows Qays. You and Muzhda being the outsiders is what's more suspicious."

"Is that because we're strangers or because we're from Valley?"

Samia lifted her eyebrows and her shoulders, an excruciatingly snide combination.

Zamzam cocked her head. "Are you ever not condescending?"

Samia's eyes lit like a fire. "*You're* calling *me* condescending?"

"Would someone listen to me!" Abdullahi interrupted, voice raised. His pits were soaked, and the sweat would begin to show through his faded pastel T-shirt any minute. "Don't you want to know where I was that night? If Zamzam was with Qays, and Samia was with Nasreen—"

Samia made a disapproving sound. "Allegedly."

"Does no one care where I was?" Abdullahi's voice hitched at the end. He needed to get the Fourth off his chest. He needed to explain why it felt like he didn't deserve the thoughtlessness of sleep. He needed to be thinking about the Fourth, about Muzhda's screams, about running from her, every second of every day until he didn't feel like it was all his fault.

"What does it matter?" Samia whisked away the doubts circulating around them. "They have that video of you now with that girl. You were with Muzhda, right?"

Abdullahi gulped. "I wasn't with her. I found her. She was lying across these devices and wires and—"

Samia pounced. "My lawyer said those devices were linked to the origin of the explosion. He said we should look into why they were there and whether or not Muzhda sent a signal that triggered the explosion, but everyone's glossing over it. There has to be a cover-up. Other than saying it's tied to Muzhda, they barely mention it." She stepped closer to him to whisper, "Everything surrounding Muzhda is shady as fuck."

Zamzam tsked. "You can't just blame the poor girl."

Abdullahi's hands shook. If he was going to ever be free of the insomnia that stemmed from leaving Muzhda at the beach, he was going to need to protect her. "No, I don't think she's guilty of anything. As surprised as I was to see her like that, she was more surprised. She looked trapped. *And* she was hurt."

"Maybe someone planted her there," Samia offered. "But who cares? No one here loses anything if Muzhda takes the blame."

"You'd do that to her? To her family?" Zamzam asked. She was visibly repulsed by Samia. She glanced at Abdullahi. "Let's take a vote. All in favor of Samia testifying against Muzhda first, say 'condescending bitch.'"

"I'm not saying anything everyone isn't thinking," Samia clapped back. "Fuck off."

"Gladly." And Zamzam beelined for the front lot again.

Samia sighed, likely at her own temperament. "Sorry, Abdullahi. I'll find a way to get Nasreen to come if you schedule another meetup, but make sure Zamzam comes too. I'll play nice. Well, nicer." She eyed Zamzam's diminishing figure, continuing, "I just don't see the point of acting all high and mighty. Anyone can see how the prosecution is going to play dirty. We might as well meet them where they're at."

"I can't say I agree," Abdullahi replied.

"Ugh, and now you're looking at me like I'm the Wicked Witch of the West."

"It's the Wicked Witch of the East, bro."

Samia rolled her eyes but couldn't help but smile at the reference. "Even your memes are old." She opened her car door. "I gotta go. I'm working on this prison editorial Instagram look-book, and it's almost ready to go live. Life must go on."

Then Samia was off to deflect using her backlog of wild ideas, and Abdullahi was stuck with his thoughts like he was every night, mentally constipated about that night. The girls didn't even flinch at Muzhda's name, but Abdullahi couldn't go a few minutes without remembering how she'd looked that night. Helpless. Alone. Trapped.

Rather than stand around, Abdullahi jumped into his car, and whether it was from the heat of LA, the fumes from the back doors of restaurants, or a plain lapse in judgment, he raced around the plaza and down the street and honked until Zamzam looked over at him. Her hijab whipped as her head turned, and she shifted her body, her arms resting on her hips.

He waved her down until she shuffled closer. She dipped her head into his window, peering at him with her deep brown eyes.

Zamzam was a firecracker, but her turbulence only attracted him closer.

Mustering up the courage, Abdullahi filled his chest with air. In his head, he searched the list of one-liners he'd heard in the oldies and perused the chivalrous acts from the knights that he'd read about and watched. He'd practiced the kind and dutiful, gentlemanly words, and yet face-to-face with Zamzam, he couldn't form those thoughtful phrases. Instead, he said the only words that untied his tongue.

"Need a ride?"

CHAPTER 24

ZAMZAM

ZAMZAM COULDN'T BELIEVE HER LIFE. SHE'D STRAYED SO far from her plan, the plan and her life didn't exist in the same universe.

She wasn't the kind of person who bickered or let people like Samia get under her skin every time she spoke to them. She wasn't the kind of person who caught rides home with a boy. It was so disorienting that she didn't recognize her reflection in Abdullahi's side-view mirror.

"Take a left here," she prompted, but Abdullahi made a U-turn.

"I want to go the long way if that's okay," he said, turning the AC low and dropping the windows as he turned right onto Pacific Coast Highway. It was a Saturday afternoon in July. The perfect beach day. Usually, PCH would be bumper-to-bumper, drivers dueling for a parking spot, but the beach wasn't the same since the Fourth.

Abdullahi was cruising at a smooth fifty-five, right at the speed limit. Zamzam's hand glided through the wind outside, and for a split second she was a girl being driven home by a cute boy. The split second ended. She retracted her hand and dropped it in her lap.

She waited to be dragged down by her responsibilities, which piled and piled, but the Fourth had put everything on pause. And every second she wasn't working toward a goal, she was falling more and more behind. How would she make up for the tutoring sessions or hours of volunteering she missed? Every hour wasted reduced her chances of achieving her dream. It should fill her with dread that the title she so desired would never precede her name: *Doctor Zamzam Thompson.* Yet sitting in the passenger seat beside Abdullahi, instead of dread, she felt unconscionable calm.

Her eyes swept the dashboard and center console. She gasped as she picked up a program badge from the center tray. In the picture Abdullahi had a fresh cut and no stubble; he looked years younger, though the issue date was only months ago. She asked tepidly, "You're an EMT in training?"

"Was," he replied. "Huntington offers a two-year program to get certified, but I had to suspend it because of this. Maybe I can continue once this is over, but I doubt it."

She smiled at the boyish Abdullahi on the card. It felt strange, like the corners of her mouth cracking. But smiling kept the dread at bay. "Why do you want to be an EMT?" she asked.

Abdullahi breathed in beside her, and she realized her breaths matched with his in perfect rhythm. "No specific reason. My siblings have already gone to college and started their careers, and they know me better than I know myself. They think I'd be a good EMT and it'll help me become a nurse practitioner or a physical therapist or—"

"A doctor?" Zamzam filled in.

"Maybe," he said, but his frown seemed to disagree with the word. "I don't know if I'm worthy of the *do no harm* doctor's oath. Not after the Fourth."

Zamzam didn't think Abdullahi fully deserved his guilt, but nothing she had to say could alleviate him of it.

"That's what I want to be," she said to distract him. "A doctor."

"To help people?"

Zamzam hoped deep down somewhere that was her reason. She'd certainly lie and say that was her reason in every personal statement she wrote from here on out. But weirdly, she didn't feel good about lying to Abdullahi. "Just to be a doctor," she said bluntly.

For her, *doctor* was a synonym for *ambition, pride, success*.

"It's just a job," she explained. "You don't need some divine calling to a job. Your reasons can be selfish. Doctors don't have perfect morality. They're just people, and people make mistakes."

Abdullahi glanced at her and gave her the smallest of smiles, and he looked more like the boy on the badge again. She felt her cheeks grow hot.

She wasn't just getting a ride with a boy; she was getting a ride with a *cute* boy.

After a silence, Zamzam trying to cover up her blushing, Abdullahi asked, "What do you think about when you're driving down PCH?"

Zamzam looked out at the sloping cliffs of the curving highway, which opened to the perfect blue of the ocean. Usually her heart would feel light, the ocean removing her worries, but her heart was going through other things. She said, "I think, *How the hell did I get in this seat, and which of these things is the brake?*"

He chuckled, showing off his bright smile and dimples. Zamzam's stomach fluttered with butterflies. Butterflies weren't written anywhere in her plans. They had to stop.

"You don't know how to drive?" he surmised. "It's the left one, by the way. The one that sticks out."

"Noted," Zamzam said, then doubled back. "What do you think about when you're driving down PCH?"

Zamzam guessed he might say the ocean, stealing glimpses of the sweeping views of the ocean on the bends of the highway while keeping one eye on the road. That was the beauty of PCH to her, the way the ocean was the embodiment of promise and hope. Then again, she'd only ever been a passenger.

Slowing down, Abdullahi started, "When I drive down PCH, I think about how the street changes when you drive through the city. You ever notice that? That one second, we're driving by dumpsters and over potholes, and then there's a WELCOME sign and it's artistic downtown. There are opposite sections of the city that follow right after each other, blocked off by bridges or freeway ramps. And if you keep driving, you'll see it change from the good to the bad, then back to the good again. Over and over."

He slid his gaze off the road and caught her eye. Her cheeks flushed; she wasn't sure she followed.

"It's a cycle, Zamzam."

When Abdullahi said her name, electricity struck through her body. A feeling that made her want to scream, but in a good way.

She needed a distraction from his handsome side profile, his deep voice, his lips, the way he looked at her like she was the only person he could see. Boys were on her "Later" list, a distraction now and a treat to enjoy when she made a name for herself.

But what if later could be now? What if she could just live in the present for a short moment? What if she let herself look? Not just at Abdullahi's strong jawline and thick lashes, but at everything? What if the ocean wasn't just for looking at? What if one day she jumped in without her plans holding her back?

Abdullahi's profile contrasted with the beiges and whites outside, the occasional graffiti and the dumpsters and the squalid facades of foreign markets and immigrant-owned restaurants. What Zamzam thought of when she heard *Los Angeles*. Then, they passed by a ramp for the 110 south, and she saw the sign, decorated by a dolphin and a wave, fly by the window.

WELCOME TO MONARCH BEACH. A NICE PLACE TO SWIM.

Zamzam caught her breath. Memories of the Fourth flooded back, but she focused on the good: The crowded chain restaurants and art galleries with overflowing flower beds. Hyacinths, lavender, yarrow. Abdullahi slowed down in the light traffic by the Promenade.

"I was on this side when it happened," he murmured, his tone hollow and haunted. He waved toward the beach across the Promenade.

"And you saw Muzhda?" Zamzam asked carefully. "Before..."

She remembered the explosions, the fear that had ripped through her core, the warning to take flight. Grabbing Qays's wrist, sprinting toward the ocean. The ocean had called out to her, promised a path when she couldn't think of any. The unceasing waves like a comforting hope that that night would have turned out differently.

The light turned green, and Abdullahi inched closer to the intersection, where a crowd of people had gathered and were chanting loudly. Two sides, opposite each other, one with some signs with words Zamzam would rather not repeat. Zamzam's mom would tell her to wash out her mouth with soap if she'd said them. On the other side, Zamzam's face stared at her from dozens of posters. Abdullahi's too, and the other four.

FREE THE INDEPENDENCE DAY SIX.

The protesters chanted their names.

Zamzam. Abdullahi. Muzhda. Qays. Nasreen. Samia.

"No justice, no peace!" the chanters bellowed.

Protesters wore masks and shirts and held signs that read DON'T LEAVE ME and I DIDN'T DO ANYTHING.

Zamzam twisted in her seat to see how far down the Promenade the protest went. "Do you know these people?" she asked, not believing her eyes.

"Some of my friends are somewhere around here," Abdullahi said offhandedly. "But I think every Muslim in Southern California has dropped by for one of these."

The protesters exhibited shades of copper, ivory, and brown. Their appearances ranged from booty shorts to jalabiyas, kufis to kippahs, hijabs to cornrows. Little girls carried her digitized headshot, labeled ZAMZAM: FUTURE DOCTOR. They looked up to her, not because Zamzam held a diploma or wore a white coat, but because her face was on a banner as the falsely accused of an alleged terrorist attack. All those nights praying to be someone who mattered, to become a role model for younger girls, but not this way. They looked up at her picture with admiration for her bravery in the face of the upcoming trial.

An imagined bravery, a faulty admiration.

"They're all on the same side," Abdullahi told her as they passed the final protester. "We should all be on the same side too."

Zamzam wanted to agree with him, but…

"They're all on the same side," she began, eyes scanning the crowd. "But they're divided."

From above, it would be easy to draw lines and borders. The hijabis, the nonhijabis. White people and Black people and Brown people. The Arab community, the Desi community. The fair-skinned Arabs dressed like Americans and then those who wore long coats and tight scarves. Those who wore designer clothes and those who wore hand-me-downs. The Black Muslims who were first-generation Americans, and the Black Muslims who'd come to America centuries ago, been stripped of their religion, and then found it again. The white people, the non-Muslims, the Muslims. Everyone stood out in their group. Just like on the beach, they kept to their crowds. Monarch Beach, Valley, Huntington.

"Do you only see the differences?" Abdullahi asked.

"The differences stand out the most," she said. It was growing more difficult to harden her heart and make it sound like she believed her words.

"From where I'm sitting, they have a lot in common."

Zamzam looked between him and the protesters. For a moment, she saw what he saw. Their banners scattered evenly among the group. Their chants in one strong and steady voice.

And a young crowd that moved freely between the group borders, no visa or checkpoint required.

Though they came together for a common purpose, Zamzam still thought they lacked cohesion. "They have a long way to go," Zamzam said. "Maybe they want to see justice for us, but they don't care what happens to us after that. After this is over, we all go back to our communities and try to forget any of this happened. We always go back to what makes us different."

"Maybe we could change that," Abdullahi whispered. Zamzam let his words float in the air between them.

She studied his side profile with scrutiny. "Is it physically painful for you to be realistic?" she asked.

His mouth worked as he glanced her way. "Is it physically painful for you to be hopeful?"

Typically, yes, she thought. Even then, when she looked at the ocean from Monarch Beach again, the water was calm in the humid heat. Instead of an ocean full of movement and change, it looked more like a blue desert. Harsh and endless, the destination always too far out of reach. Her eyes showed her hardship rather than hope.

Still, there was something about being in this kind boy's car that made her think twice.

Abdullahi turned off PCH, and the water left Zamzam's view. He drove past the protesters, zooming away from Monarch Beach, inland toward Valley.

"Maybe I could do with some of your hope, and you could learn a thing or two from my grip on reality," she said finally.

"I could agree to that," he said. "But if I agree, you have to promise me one thing."

Zamzam hesitated. "I'm not gonna like this, am I?"

"Just humor me," he said. "If I agree to your realism, will you promise me you'll try again?"

She crossed her arms. "With Samia? She's literally the one dividing people."

"Trust me," he said, "she's acting weird because she's scared." Samia wore her emotions on her sleeve, and her escapes were social media concepts she inappropriately tied back to her life. "But she's reliable," he added, "and she'll do the right thing."

"You two have a thing going?"

He shook his head. "She's not my type."

"What is your type?"

He parked at the curb a block south from Valley High and a block north from her house. He looked at her, and even without saying a word, she felt like she knew.

Her cheeks blushed like wildfire. *Is this what it feels like to be a teenager with a crush?* she thought as her stomach somersaulted and didn't stick the landing. It was a surprisingly wretched feeling.

She'd never let herself have one before, a crush, so she didn't know how to respond or how to cover her feelings up. Was she supposed to cover them up? Or were they totally valid? Would suppressing them hurt more?

All questions that should be last on her mind. Zamzam had busied herself with school, extra tutoring, and volunteering in order to delay her life from catching up with her. Now that her busy schedules had come to a standstill, life was colliding into her head-on with one of the most delicate incidents. A crush.

She pushed open the door and flounced out the car. She flashed Abdullahi a civil smile that she hoped suggested nothing more than gratitude, and said the least flirtatious thing she could say to a crush:

"See you at the arraignment."

CHAPTER 25

MUZHDA

IN THE COURTROOM, QAYS LOOKED DASHING IN A SUIT AND tie for his first impression on the presiding judge. But all the ironing and starch couldn't make Qays look less wilted, despite his designer ensemble.

"Nice hair," Muzhda, dressed in her jail-issued clothes, teased. Qays raised his eyebrow at her and slicked back his gelled hair.

He cleared his throat. Muzhda must be out of her mind. There was nothing to giggle about here.

The others trickled in after them for what was basically just roll-call day. Today, they were showing up to prove they would; then they'd all go back to preparing their cases with their attorneys.

Nasreen was first, stone-faced and exhausted. The rumors had made their rounds up until the arraignment. Samia and Nasreen had some affiliation, but no one knew exactly what. Nasreen kept her eyes glued to the floor, blending into the background, her appearance purposely unremarkable. On the other side of the bench sat Samia, dressed in a pink silk-satin dress suit that reflected light like aluminum foil. Her outfit screamed for the eye's attention, and once she locked eyes with the others, they shot daggers.

Next were Zamzam and Abdullahi, arriving simultaneously. Zamzam stopped in front of Qays, as if to hold him in contempt of something.

The girls didn't so much as glance in Muzhda's direction. She might as well have been invisible in the courtroom.

Then Abdullahi reached the end of the public gallery and lifted his eyes to Qays's. He stopped midstep.

"You good?" Qays whispered across the tables at Abdullahi.

Abdullahi shook off a pained expression. "I'm good."

Qays turned to the others, his gaze lingering on Zamzam. But Zamzam turned away; neither of them had matured their apologies.

It was the first time since the Fourth that they had all been together, a bit less the strangers they had been when they were shepherded into police cars. Since then, they each had charges brought against them. Since then, each of them knew which way they'd plead, individually, with only their personal best interests in mind. They weren't strangers, but they weren't allies either.

After an eternity, Favreau walked in with Pennella and the DA, shooting a measured glare at each of them. The DA was a real owl in human form: hunched posture, deep-set eyes, and a frozen expression.

"It's the queen bitch," Samia muttered under her breath as Favreau passed her.

213

A door behind the judge's bench opened, and everyone in the courtroom stiffened. The judge settled in her chair, behind her nameplate. This was Judge Irene Min's domain.

Muzhda's first impression was that Judge Min appeared to be drowning in her official robes. The weight of her duty manifested itself quite literally.

Whispers erupted from the gallery. Irene Min was a kind judge; the Independence Day Six were lucky their case was appointed to her. Or so the optimists reported.

"Please rise," the bailiff ordered. He said a host of official words, like *the Honorable Irene Min* and *the People v.* all of their names. Zamzam's expression was pinched, and Samia scowled as he spoke. Nasreen sniffled, and Qays kept stealing glances at the other defendants. Abdullahi's expression was unreadable. Muzhda didn't feel any particular emotion; rather she felt a gaping hole where there should be anger and sadness and grief. All she felt was an absence of everything.

It was unreal to hear her name pinned up against the United States. There wasn't a thesaurus in the world that could describe how she felt. How they felt.

Judge Min went along the line, reading off the charges.

Domestic terrorism. Arson. Criminal attempt to commit murder in various degrees. Manslaughter. Most charges were shared. The six of them were coconspirators; they were one faceless entity. One that read *enemy* across its erased features. They'd arrived to fight the accusation separately, but they were in this together.

Except Abdullahi. The judge read extra charges for him. Two counts of assault and battery against Muzhda Ahmad.

The five of them turned their heads toward him. His lips pressed into a thin line.

Muzhda felt weightless. Thoughtless. All she remembered was hands trying to lift her. They were steadily helping her until they weren't, until Abdullahi was running, until Muzhda was screaming for him, until shots were fired.

The proceedings drew out the arraignment, and Muzhda felt like the dwindling wick of a nearly melted candle. The more the attorneys and judge nitpicked the language thrown about the courtroom, the more the defendants' faces deteriorated from scornful dignity to plaintive defeat.

Near the end, when Muzhda felt she was holding on to consciousness by a stretched layer of Saran Wrap, the DA and attorneys held council with the judge in a back room. Without the attorneys and Judge Min, who were the safeguards in place to protect them from a lifetime of prison, the bailiff and surrounding officers grew into giants.

All their lives in their many colors and flavors and variations were forced to fit into the confines of a courtroom that could fit fewer than a hundred or so people. The air tightened like a coil around their necks, knotting itself like a noose.

Upon returning, Judge Min addressed the room. "I have had a statue of Lady Justice on my desk for the last twenty years. It was given to me by my mentor, and it's a reminder to myself of what it means to reside as the judge in this courtroom. Throughout this trial, Lady Justice resides above me. As you can see, she's blindfolded because justice doesn't see color. It is served to everyone through evidence and an impartial jury that will exonerate or indict you of crimes beyond a reasonable doubt." She paused for an emphasis that was resoundingly off-key.

Judge Min continued, "Lady Justice holds balanced scales. Both the prosecution and defense will be given equal opportunity to reach a verdict that will keep her scales so. Just as Lady Justice wears her blindfold, I do not see color, race, or religion. Evidence shall not discriminate. I will answer to Lady Justice and the United States Constitution alone."

The Six appraised Lady Justice from her perch on the judge's bench. Had Lady Justice pulled the greatest prank on the US criminal-justice system by blindfolding herself? Surely there was more to every case than what people in suits laid out in front of her. Context was everything.

Maybe to balance the scales, Lady Justice should make her own judgments with her aptitude for justice. So why blindfold herself?

It seemed more likely that someone took Lady Justice with her perfectly balanced scales and blindfolded her.

The Six hoped that, at the very least, Lady Justice could hear color.

CHAPTER 26

SAMIA

THE ARRAIGNMENT WAS A PHOTO OP FOR SAMIA. SHE scrolled through the pictures online taken by all the major news outlets covering the case. Most of the shots of her were cut off by the press that swarmed them as they entered and exited the courthouse or by the protesters out front, but there was one worthy of a stand-alone Instagram post. The lighting hit just right, and the composition was spectacular. Even better, the angle made it seem that Qays was following close behind her. With a trick of the lens, they looked like a power couple, Samia in her pink dress suit and Miu Miu sunglasses and Qays in his all-black Hugo Boss suit. Sure, he was wearing actual handcuffs instead of cuff links, but Samia could do wonders with her Photoshop fingers.

But Samia didn't like Qays Sharif; that high school cliché bordered on criminal. She smirked and undid the Photoshop changes, with one click the security guards, his handcuffs, and her attorney shielding her from the cameras bouncing back into the scene.

There, she thought, *now we look like a real criminal cliché.*

Samia loved the power she had over photos; she could edit the ugly parts, all the parts of herself she didn't want others to see. She had all this extra time and energy and didn't know where to put it except into her social media page. It was either posting pics or facing reality.

Looking through the pictures, Samia came to a photo of Nasreen. While Samia imagined she looked editorial in her suit, Nasreen appeared small and young. Her clothes were shapeless and colorless. Even Zamzam wore her prints, and Abdullahi was dressed in a black-and-white houndstooth ensemble. Zooming in, she saw he wore a lapel pin of the Black Power fist. But unlike the others, Nasreen's face could be erased and replaced by anyone's. In some pictures it looked like Samia had photoshopped her face onto a googled image of *teenage girl.*

It bothered her more than she liked to admit.

Closing her laptop, she tried to get some sleep. She tossed and turned and scrolled through social media, but nothing gave her enough of a distraction. That night on the beach crawled in from the nape of her neck and ate away at all her other thoughts until it was all that was left in her mind.

She tried to think about the jury selection, about how the defense would be up all night picking out a vaguely sympathetic and liberal jury, and the prosecution would do the opposite.

But did all the details matter? There were rumors about Nasreen and her. Rumors about @mus_SM, about not-Faris, and her. If a jury was supposed to make a decision based on the facts, the rumors that either Samia or Nasreen would lie to secure their reputation were real threats to the freedom of the Six.

Except Samia didn't need to protect her reputation. She was a victim of injustice and the crime against her: catfishing. But Samia could get over that because as long as the case went her way, she could come out of this better than before. Her follower count had only increased since the Fourth. When she looked at everything with her social media lenses, it felt tolerable. But it was also fake.

Her attorney told her to just let it unfold. If Samia flew under the radar and Nasreen didn't act out, there was little that implicated Samia. Among the unlucky Six, Samia was one of the less unlucky ones. She could be hopeful.

Around midnight, a message came in on her phone from an anonymous number.

PetroMile, it read.

Samia would usually think nothing of it, but considering her circumstances, she sat up and looked it up online. Petro-Mile was that oil-and-gas company that had operated the rig. It owned most of the oil rigs in Southern California and was the main gas provider in the western United States. It'd been complicating evidence collection since the start, so the name only sparked irritation. She exited the tabs and threw herself against her mattress.

She thought about how it felt to let the others fend for themselves. She thought about what really might have happened that made the oil rig explode. The air in her room grew thicker until she couldn't breathe. She slid off her bed and began brainstorming the location of her next photo shoot to calm herself.

When the perfect location came to her, Samia dressed in loose overalls and a lazily draped scarf and donned her largest, most tinted pair of sunglasses. Her parents and siblings were in the seventh sleep, the deepest one, so Samia sneaked out the front door easily.

Samia drove to the botanical gardens expecting a quick drive-by, but the front gate was wedged open. In a lapse of rationality, she parked and waltzed right in. Trespassing was the least of her worries.

Following the signs of the gardens' labyrinth, Samia let her feet carry her where her heart wanted to go. Passing under a chipped archway, she tiptoed onto a greenhouse deck, where she was no longer alone.

In the center of the greenhouse, where the plants were quartered off, tiny bulbs of light swam upward before extinguishing like they'd never been. It was the most enchanting backdrop. The lights of dozens of fireflies pulled her closer; the deck creaked beneath her weight.

A figure dashed to her right. Going with a hunch as to who it was, Samia ran after it. Except the figure wasn't running away from her but toward the exit behind her. They collided, their heads crashing together. Samia grasped at the flailing arms tangled in her own. She wrestled with the other person, shoving them away, but when Samia pitched her weight forward, their two bodies toppled over each other off the deck and straight into the grass.

They groaned, and Samia flung herself off Nasreen's body. Neither of them moved. They lay there on the grass, their breathing hitched. Samia didn't get up to leave, for the same reason she had come there in the first place. Instead, she listened to their heavy breathing and stared up at the stars through the glass ceiling. She watched the fireflies fly upward in light, bright at the promise of the sky, only to go dark when they realized it was an illusion.

"What are you doing here?" Nasreen asked in a low voice once their breathing slowed. An unspoken rule established itself that they were safe to speak to each other here so long as neither of them looked at the other.

"Faris once told me that he came to the botanical gardens when he couldn't sleep," Samia murmured. "He said one day he'd bring me here and show me the fireflies because I'd never seen them."

They watched the fireflies in silence, little fires disintegrating into nothing.

Samia could hear her heart beating wildly. Other than in the interrogation room, she had never spoken of Faris out loud after she'd found out he wasn't real.

"Are they as beautiful as you expected?" Nasreen whispered.

Samia had never seen fireflies before. Science couldn't explain them, and watching them was an otherworldly experience. A fourth dimension.

"Even more than I expected," Samia replied.

It was the perfect backdrop for a shot. Under the fireflies' enchantment, Nasreen could have been Faris, and the lie wouldn't have ended the way it had on the beach the night of the Fourth. Samia let the moment stretch a while longer.

"Are you scared?" Nasreen asked.

"A little." Samia tilted her head toward Nasreen, who

deliberately looked away. They shouldn't break the rule. Samia turned her gaze back up to the glass ceiling. "Why didn't you come to meet with us?"

"My attorney said to keep to myself. She's building a case."

"Abdullahi says we should work together."

"My attorney doesn't think we can work together. Not if we want to have our best interests at heart."

Samia might have thought that earlier, but Nasreen saying it out loud made it obvious it was wrong. If the attorneys were scrambling to save their necks, who would try to find out the truth about the Fourth?

"If all of us are innocent," Samia began, "we could work together to prove it."

"My attorney—"

"Who cares about your attorney?" Samia snapped. She reined in her voice. "Your attorney didn't order you to ghost me. It's not every man for themselves. We aren't enemies who can speak to each other only through these fucked-up grown-ups. *God*, Nasreen, did our friendship mean nothing to you?"

Nasreen glanced at Samia. They stared at each other, and the admission of that word and of a past shared between them lingered in the air. Precious seconds passed without a reply from Nasreen. This was Samia's chance.

Samia reached out and held Nasreen's hand tight. "What would Faris do?"

Faris had been many things, but he was never replaceable or boring. He had a thoughtful opinion on everything, from mass incarceration to bee extinction to recycled clothes. If Nasreen was this small, timid girl she portrayed herself to be, then there was no way she had been Faris. But Nasreen was Faris, and Samia had made her feel like dirt for it.

Samia's entire online brand was Muslim-girl empowerment, but on the beach when Nasreen showed up instead of the imagined Faris, Samia had bullied her. She'd belittled her and dismissed her, and for what? Her own embarrassment? But why had she been embarrassed? Because Nasreen had fooled her? Because Samia couldn't believe she might have loved a girl?

No, that wasn't a big deal. Samia loved plenty of her girlfriends, but Nasreen had lied to her. She lied, and Samia was humiliated, so she'd attacked Nasreen for it.

That wasn't Samia's platform. Samia believed everyone deserved a voice and a chance. She spoke out against internet trolls that judged how Muslim Samia and the other influencers were based on how they wore their hijabs. Samia hated silencing girls, especially Muslim girls, first-generation American girls, and second-generation American girls like her, yet she'd silenced Nasreen on the beach.

Samia was another part of the toxic cycle. It was impossible to escape it.

A firefly crash-landed onto the hand that held Nasreen's. Its light flickered out. All that was left was a black-and-brown bug, wings fluttering closed, antennae and legs splayed against Samia's skin. All the draw that Samia had to the fireflies vanished. When she looked again to the lights, all she could see were dozens of brown-and-black bugs and their buzzing wings flapping against their bulbous bodies.

She pulled her hand away, disturbing the firefly, which flew away without so much as a glimmer.

Nasreen sat up, her face suddenly hard. "Faris was never real. He's a figment of your imagination."

"I have the receipts."

"Don't you have anything better to do?"

"Not really."

Nasreen scoffed softly. "You want to join Abdullahi and Zamzam in seeking out justice for yourselves? Is that why you're meeting against our attorneys' wishes? Then maybe you should be looking for leads instead of posting protest fashion online."

Samia's brows slid over her eyes. "At least I wouldn't sell them out." No matter how much she and Zamzam fought, she didn't have it in her.

Nasreen turned to her, exasperated. "Neither would I."

"Wouldn't you?" Samia shot back. This was the Nasreen she'd seen through the DMs. The one who got fired up about politics and had thought-out opinions on issues that mattered. Samia did her best to coax this Nasreen out, the Nasreen that was also Faris. She continued, "Then why are you acting shady? Why didn't you tell them about Faris? Why can't you just admit we were together on the beach that night?"

Nasreen blinked at her, a dozen answers in her eyes, yet no response.

Samia scoffed. With the fireflies' illusion over and her shallow curiosity satiated, there wasn't any reason for her to stay. She turned away, leaving Nasreen with one final question.

"What are you really afraid of?"

CHAPTER 27

NASREEN

IT HAD BEEN SEVENTEEN DAYS SINCE NASREEN HADN'T woken from her nightmare, and she didn't have an answer to Samia's question.

What was she really afraid of?

Her feelings for one, her desires even more. Her parents not at all, yet the idea of disappointing them made her want to hide in a brick tower that had no windows, no doors or escapes.

It was easier for Samia to admit to knowing Nasreen; she was the catfished, whereas Nasreen was the catfisher. Nasreen had known what she was doing yet returned to the screen every time, opening up to Samia as her unequivocal self despite the avi. Nasreen's parents wouldn't just be perplexed at Nasreen's catfishing; they'd ask her *why* she'd pretended to be Faris. Nasreen didn't have an answer to that question.

At least, not an answer that she felt comfortable sharing. Because Nasreen didn't understand her feelings yet, and her feelings were the reason she'd first clicked that Send button.

"Wait," Nasreen called. Samia stopped midstep.

Samia shook her head before whipping back around. "You know what I don't get? I'm your alibi. You're mine. We could easily get out of this mess. Why wouldn't you want that?"

Nasreen paced the deck above the glowing garden. She knew even with alibis there was no knowing what Favreau could imply. Or perhaps fabricate altogether. Ms. Carson had said so herself.

"Nasreen?" Samia pressed.

Nasreen stopped abruptly. "You don't understand. I did tell my lawyer I was with you. She said it doesn't matter."

Samia furrowed her brows. "How can it not matter? It's an *alibi.*"

"Not when we're both being charged," Nasreen explained. "This isn't a courtroom drama, Samia. We don't have alibis if we're coconspirators."

Even as she said it, it sounded wrong. Ms. Carson had virtually no papers on her desk—she was impeccably clean and had everything digitized—but on the off chance she had anything related to the case out, Nasreen zoned out and scoured the papers. Whatever work Ms. Carson was doing, it was clear that she wasn't giving the theory that Samia and Nasreen were coconspirators a second thought. There were other conspiracies to consider.

"When we prove we're not guilty, then it'll mean everything," Samia concluded hopefully. "Work with us. The attorneys are meeting tomorrow. Yours is the only one who refuses. Even Qays's stick-up-the-ass attorney is coming. I agreed to meet Abdullahi and Zamzam tomorrow night. We'll track down whoever framed us. We'll find the truth if they won't go out and find it."

Nasreen tried to hear the reason in Samia's statements, but it required more honesty than Nasreen was ready for. Generally, she wasn't the lonely type. She called it elected isolation. She liked it most times, but with Samia it had been different. When Samia responded to her first DM, Nasreen told herself Samia responded only because of the fake Faris avi. If she had made an honest account and messaged Samia as a fan of her work, Samia wouldn't have DMed her back. Or so Nasreen told herself. So she'd made the Faris persona, and she'd felt safe hiding behind it. Hiding her feelings behind Faris's.

"Why did you do it?" The question Nasreen had been expecting finally left Samia's lips.

Nasreen flushed with embarrassment. This was her battle with herself. There were no guidelines for Nasreen, no maps for navigating her emotions and her attraction. There were Muslims who thought her thoughts were a sin, Muslims who thought the only way to be this way was to leave the religion, but Nasreen wanted religion and she wanted to accept herself. Nasreen would walk a tightrope her whole life if she had to because ever since she could walk, she'd practiced walking on those two inches.

"I don't get it," Samia continued. "You didn't have to catfish me. We could have been friends, you know. We had a lot in common."

"Would we have been friends?" Nasreen whispered.

Samia paused, then said, "Well, we can try to be friends now."

Nasreen shook her head slowly but deliberately. Her parents didn't need to know about Samia and Faris, and Nasreen didn't have to confront her inner dissonance. She didn't know how to reexamine herself and her faith and make things right. She could push it aside and forget any of it ever happened. She could keep pretending Faris never existed. For now.

To buy herself time to keep figuring herself out before Samia ripped open that can of worms, she had to pass on joining hands with Samia. Nasreen decided. "I don't want to join you guys, and I'm not using you as my alibi. It's not worth it to me."

Samia crossed her arms and backed away from her. "I see how it is. You wouldn't blink twice if the rest of us were thrown in jail if it meant you could walk free."

Nasreen opened her mouth, but no words came out. How could she deny the truth?

Samia turned away, leaving her alone in the dark garden with the fading lights and her last few words.

"Faris would've worked with us."

CHAPTER 28

KANDI FAVREAU DID NOT SIT; SHE PERCHED. SHE DID NOT follow; she pursued.

Yet she was subjected to watching as Pennella ate and dropped half his BLT on her desk. He wiped his mouth with the back of his hand and smudged mayonnaise on his sleeve. He left used napkins strewn across his papers. Pennella did, but he did not think before doing. He was malleable, and she planned to mold him into whomever she wished. He disappointed her in all the right ways. He'd make an excellent chief of police one day.

"Any news on Mr. Talib?" she asked after she'd seen enough.

"I put the CCTV footage on your desk," Pennella said, mouth full to the brim.

She rolled her eyes. "And did you submit a summary? Am I supposed to watch hours of footage to find the clip?"

His ears turned scarlet, but he was otherwise unfazed. "It

shows Ahmad trip over the equipment, then how Talib trampled Ahmad. He groped her. It's clear they exchanged words, and then he left her there. Everything else is uncertain."

Favreau nodded, satisfied. Pennella was finally using the active language she coached him to use. *Trampled. Groped. Stolen.* His words painted a crime.

"Any news about the equipment?"

"Still with our trusted man in the IT department," he answered. "He confirmed that the hardware is property of Petro-Mile. We can posit that Ahmad and Talib accessed PetroMile's schematics and security systems to cause the oil rig explosion."

Favreau glanced at the door, which was closed. "And you confirmed this in person?" she asked. "I don't want any paper trail about PetroMile. We will go with the claim that the equipment was used to trigger the explosions, but no word about PetroMile. Got it?"

Pennella nodded.

"And PetroMile is locking their information up tight?"

"Navigating the company is a nightmare. I haven't been able to get ahold of anyone that gets paid more than minimum wage."

"Excellent. If you can't get through, no one else will be able to. We can make do with what we have since it's in our best interest that we keep PetroMile out of this trial as much as possible." She smiled. "Pull on the Abdullahi Talib thread. What do you come up with?"

Pennella rested his forearms on the table and dangled his greasy fingers. "Well, Abdullahi Talib is the only one who was missing that night. We have nothing to go off of other than his words and the footage. Muzhda was clearly partners with Qays, we could paint them as dealers. Muzhda could be his supplier—she's

230

from the Valley district and Qays is from Monarch Beach. Rich kid purchasing drugs from Valley to pass around to his friends? Everyone would buy it. Plus, he's our key player. The firework he fired was a clear distraction to spectators on the beach moments before the explosion. If we connect the three of them and keep the public suspicious of Qays by keeping him in custody, we have a case against him."

"Any trouble keeping Qays on remand?"

"Judge Min is allowing it because he's being tried as an adult since he's almost eighteen and therefore poses more of a danger to society." Pennella pulled at his necktie, discomfort coding into his body language. Nonetheless, Favreau was impressed. If he could sound convincing, then they stood a good chance in court.

"We lack evidence about Muzhda," he added, "but we won't see any backlash from her family, who have gone into hiding from ICE. Though they're doing their best to track them down."

"It's best we do *not* find her family, so be sure you let that department know to ease up on their search." Favreau clicked her tongue. "And I already told you evidence won't be a problem."

Pennella swallowed hard but kept following the thread. "Qays is then related to Zamzam since she was there when he fired the weapon on the beach. It won't be hard to prove a connection. Stringing the four of them to the other two can be done directly through Samia's relationship with Abdullahi over the years. They've known each other since childhood. And through Samia we get Nasreen."

Favreau's eyes glinted as she looked at the wall, where Nasreen's photo was pinned. "Nasreen Choudhry." She said her name as though letting it marinate in her mouth. "Has her attorney reached out?"

Pennella nodded once. "She's good. *And* willing to negotiate."

"They want a plea deal?"

"They want an acquittal in exchange for anything."

Favreau's lips spread into a hungry smile. "Nasreen Choudhry," she repeated. "You smart, smart girl."

She dismissed Pennella and perched on her chair, ankles crossed, hands folded. While Favreau had wanted all six, she figured she might have to let one go. She pursued only those who were too weak to play the game. Hand to God, Favreau would see this case through, and she would see to it that the weak were in chains and those who could contend with her begged for mercy.

CHAPTER 29

QAYS

QAYS PACED THE DAY ROOM.

He had not seen Muzhda since the arraignment. Before, he could get through the unending quiet by clinging to their time together, but now he had nothing.

On top of that, the guards had grown meaner and more hostile. The day after Muzhda stopped showing up, Qays paused in front of his cell for one moment too long. Next thing he knew, his body was pinned against the ground, his cheekbone and shoulder exploding in pain. The day after, he spent his entire time in the day room praying to calm his mind and find peace. His time was up while he sat midprayer, but he didn't break. Qays had never prayed regularly before, but in here it was one of the few activities that gave him a semblance of time, and so peace. When he didn't end the prayer early to go back in, the guards lifted him by his shirt and slammed him against the wall over and over until Qays saw stars.

The next day, when they took him out to the day room, the guard called Qays a slur. Qays had heard words like that only on his visits to Palestine from Israel Occupation Forces soldiers who took issue with the color of his shirt or the way he walked. The slur had made Qays see black. He kicked a chair across the room; he resisted their restraints. They kicked him in his torso and back so many times that he didn't see stars. He saw galaxies.

They holed him up in his cell indefinitely. He was in there for an eternity; visits or daily day room time didn't punctuate time. Eventually they let him back out, where he resumed his waiting for Muzhda.

He paced and paced and paced. He sat cross-legged in the center of the room. He wondered if they'd turned to violence because the arraignment was over and he wouldn't be in the press for some time. More likely, he guessed, he'd lost their favor because he practiced his faith when he openly prayed in the rec room. His prayers became his only act of defiance.

"What happened to you?"

Qays's eyes flew open. Muzhda stared back at him. She looked thinner than when he'd last seen her, so thin she was bordering on transparent.

Qays opened his mouth to speak, but only choked sounds came out. They dissolved into a dry sob. Qays bit the inside of his cheek and pulled himself together. He would not cry in front of Muzhda, no matter how he felt. He would be strong like his father; he had to be strong for them both, but the tears filled his eyes to the brim anyway.

Qays imagined what it would be like if she reached out her slender fingers and touched his cheekbone. How, beneath her touch, a thousand nerve endings would scream. Qays was a body of bruises, and Muzhda's touch could connect them like a constellation.

"Tell me a story," she requested, her fingers tracing a discolored mark on his cheek.

Qays hunched his shoulders. The world was shut out from him days ago. It wasn't just his future that he could no longer see—it was also the past and the present. "I don't have a story for you."

Muzhda waited. Qays's expression twisted with internal pain. His chest felt heavy; his heart hardened like iron.

"Then tell me what happened to make you this way," she murmured.

Qays breathed in a long and hot breath. There were more bruises on his body than he could count, but there was one bruise that hurt him most. He lifted his eyes to hers. "Here," he began, and touched his fingers to the center of his chest. "It's ...different."

Muzhda's hand drifted to his chest, where she flattened her palm against the fabric. His heart beat rapidly against her withered hand. "Different how?"

"Every day it gets heavier, and it *hurts*. At least I can escape it when I stop thinking. So I'm sorry that I don't have a story for you, and that I'd rather sit here and not think about one."

Qays closed his eyes again and pretended he could clear his mind with Muzhda's hand on his chest.

"Well, this is new," Muzhda said with a smile in her voice. "The last thing I expected from you was silence."

Qays half opened one eye. "I'm exhausted."

Muzhda laughed and took her hand off Qays to cover her wide grin. "That's nice, but I wonder how the rest of us have been holding up."

Qays shut his eyes harder this time. He wasn't sure what Muzhda's ploy was, but he wouldn't let his guard down because of her perfect gap-toothed smile. "I'm tired, you're tired. Let's just sit here exhausted together."

"No," Muzhda disagreed. "It's not the time for that. You don't get to be tired yet."

"Yes, I do," Qays countered, "because I'm angry at the world."

Muzhda made a dismissive sound. "You're angry at the security guards for roughing you up? Or at being stuck here when the others get to be out on bail? No, that doesn't sound like you to me. Where did all the *This is a mistake; we're getting out of here* talk go? What happened to your talk that this is temporary?"

Qays raised his brows high. "I'm still getting out of here, no matter how many times they beat me down." Qays came from a family of Palestinians, and Palestinians were famous for getting back up no matter how many times they were knocked down. It was in his blood.

"*I* know that," Muzhda said. "Which is why I said you're not angry at the world."

Qays's mouth sunk into a pout, uncertainty settling into his expression. "I'm allowed to be angry."

Muzhda snickered, and Qays couldn't pretend-meditate any longer. He gaped at her.

"You don't have it worse than the rest of us. What is it about you that makes you think you're special? That compared to the rest of us, you shouldn't be in here?" Her tone invited mockery.

"I'm Afghan, and no one looks twice that I'm in here. They probably think I belong here. And what about Zamzam and Abdullahi? They're Black, so don't tell me you have it worse than them."

Qays thought back to Abdullahi. How Abdullahi had seemed miserable, like something was eating him from the inside. He felt he was looking in a mirror. But over time, Qays had built defenses to protect his grief.

"What do you know?" Qays asked defiantly, his voice rising out of his control. "I won't deny I have some privileges, but don't act like you know me. Every room I enter I have to fight for my right to even say that I'm Palestinian. People erased my country from their histories and call me a political issue. I have privilege, yes, and I definitely take advantage of it when I can, but I'm not going to let you erase who I am too."

"We're not swapping sob stories," Muzhda said, a sharp edge in her voice.

"Then stop treating this like a game," Qays bit out.

"But it *is* a game. You and I are just pawns in something much bigger than us. You either play the game, or it plays you." She spoke clearly, her voice thick and magnetic. "When I say you don't have the luxury of feeling tired, I'm saying it because if you don't get it together, you lose."

"I can't," Qays muttered. "It's not going away. I prayed and prayed, and I still can't get rid of it. I don't know where it came from."

"Because you're searching for its source in the wrong place," she said. "You won't find it outside. Look for it here." She touched his temple, then let her hand fall to tap his chest.

That wholly disagreed with Qays. His mind raised its defenses, ordering him to shut out Muzhda's words and pray some more.

"Tell me the story of how you became angry," she requested again. "And don't lie to me. I can tell."

Qays's eyes darkened, and his heart felt like it was enveloped in so many layers of metal that Muzhda wouldn't be able to feel a heartbeat if she placed her palm on his chest again.

Muzhda. Muzhda, who reached out and held both his hands in hers. This solid and grounded Muzhda. Muzhda, who swayed their arms in the air between them. Muzhda, who waited patiently for Qays to drag down every last one of his defenses to find the source of his anger.

"I was an idiot," Qays whispered, his voice tortured. "I dragged you into this mess with me because of some weed. You shouldn't be here. You wouldn't be if it wasn't for me. I'm angry with myself all the time for doing that to you."

"And did you find a way not to feel angry?" Muzhda asked.

"Yes. I don't feel angry when I tell myself I shouldn't be here. That the world shouldn't have done this to me."

"Does that work?"

Qays shook his head emphatically. "I'm white passing. I'm Palestinian, but if I don't speak or tell people or hang out in public with my hijabi family, or if people don't hear my name, then I pass. If I use my Starbucks name, I pass."

"What's your Starbucks name?"

He grimaced. "Kyle."

Muzhda scrunched her nose. "That makes everything worse."

"Maybe." Qays couldn't wipe the grimace from his face. "But it's nice to pass. I don't need to also feel bad for passing. Other than the Feds who have it out for Arabs and Muslims, I fly under

238

the radar. If I'm honest I was so mad because that night on the beach, they almost let me go. But then they asked what my name was, and I told them my real name, and my life took a totally different turn. If it wasn't for that, I wouldn't be here."

"So it makes sense that I was. And Nasreen and Zamzam and Abdullahi and Samia?" Muzhda's grip on Qays's hands slackened, but his grip tightened. "Because we've got melanin or wear the hijab or go to Valley."

Qays wanted to disagree. A voice in his head said to fight back. Another said to cover up the humiliation of admitting that he also had prejudice. It told him to give up and let go of the feelings that made him so enamored with Muzhda, all that made him need her to feel sane. But instinctively, Qays couldn't let go of her hands, and frankly, he didn't ever want to.

Dejected, he agreed with her. "I'm so angry about it."

"Then imagine how we feel," Muzhda replied bitterly. "You don't get to be tired, Qays. You lose the fight if you give up because it makes you think too much and it's easier not to."

His eyes stung as he fought against the anger, not for himself, but at himself for how he casually wished Abdullahi was in his place and that he was out on bail. He was wrong for it, he was more than wrong, but it still made him feel better to think that. He was infuriated with himself.

The fury weighed so heavy, he wanted to buckle under the weight of his anger and give up. It was tempting to roll over and wait for things to play out in his favor, as he suspected they would. Qays wasn't scared he'd be locked up anymore; he was angry that the others who looked different from him were less likely to be released.

"I don't know what to do with all this anger," he muttered, suffocating. It felt like she was holding her hand at his neck.

"Let it go," she said. "Open your eyes, Qays. If you're angry, you're blindsided, and you lose."

"I already lost," he replied, giving up. Because if Qays let his anger melt, whatever was underneath would break him.

CHAPTER 30

ABDULLAHI

"FOR THE LOVE OF GOD, MY TEXT SAID BRING MASKS."

An object flew in Abdullahi's direction, and he caught it one-handed. He frowned at Samia's huge pair of silver reflective sunglasses before squeezing them on. Samia plunged back into her car and reemerged with a dusty pink bucket hat, which had an expletive stitched on it followed by a tiny yellow sun. She handed it to Zamzam.

Samia shut the door of her car. She wore a black face mask and red half-moon sunglasses that clung to the tip of her nose.

"I didn't wear one on purpose," Zamzam said nervously, glancing up and down the street. "I'm not trying to look suspicious. We're risking too much as it is."

"At least wear neutrals next time," Samia whined. "If anyone finds out we're meeting up like this, all hell will break loose.

Abdullahi would've agreed with her if hell hadn't already

broken loose and stuffing it back under wasn't the sole purpose for their meetup. For some reason, Zamzam thought it smart to wear her bright clothes an hour before midnight at Monarch Beach. They weren't supposed to come to the beach in general, because Monarch Beach was ground zero, and they *really* weren't supposed to come back together. Samia's genius resolution to that was to meet up at night, but that meant being out after curfew.

Inshallah we won't get caught, he prayed.

Zamzam glanced at Abdullahi. "You gotta be kidding me." She shot a dark look at Samia. "I'm *Black*. We're at Monarch Beach *at night* when we shouldn't even be here. There better be a good reason why we're here." Her inflections shut Samia up, but Zamzam wasn't done. "If anyone catches us out after curfew, they're gonna take us back into custody and use it against us. Is every Huntie this thoughtless?" she asked Abdullahi.

He knew what she meant because even though Samia was all right and she'd never backed away from squashing racist kids, she was like all his other friends at Huntington. They did their due diligence not to make him feel any different than them, but it always fell on him to adjust for them. He didn't wear hoods like his friends, and he wore medical masks only if he needed to. When they pulled pranks knowing the cops would show, he would peace out early without offering an excuse. He got his reputation as the friend group grandpa because he was always reminding them to be cautious or canceling plans to stay home. It wasn't that way with his Sudani friends, but most of his Sudani friends didn't go to Huntington.

This realization slowly dawned on Samia. They saw it in how her eyes darted around her, widened, and then relaxed.

Abdullahi would bet money that her face flushed under the mask. "I'm such a bitch. I'm sorry," she apologized. "I wasn't thinking. But I have good reason."

Abdullahi remembered when Samia would callously throw around her heritage and minimize it. She was second generation, so she knew so little Arabic. For a long time, she didn't even bring attention to it, until she decided to wear hijab. From then on, she was making a statement, but her disconnection with her parents' heritage remained the same. Samia could be an airhead sometimes, but she tried.

When Samia apologized, it meant she'd be pledging her loyalty to that person forever. Their own friendship had started when Samia apologized to Abdullahi for stealing his snack in kindergarten. Sure, they'd barely talked in recent months before the Fourth, but Samia had been there for him when he needed her in the past.

Not knowing that, Zamzam brushed it off, but Abdullahi knew they'd be turning a new page.

"Don't make me regret trusting you, Samia," Abdullahi said. He felt like he was being watched. At the supermarket, in his front yard, every time he left the house, his heart pounded as though he were running a marathon. But it was nothing like now. At Monarch Beach, he felt like the sky was so close, the world might rip open to judge him right there. It didn't feel right, or maybe Abdullahi just felt wrong.

"I just thought we should come back to the beach," Samia said. "To help us come clean to each other once and for all." After a moment, she added, more quietly, "And for me to check on a lead."

He cleared his throat and shoved his trembling hands into his pockets. "But is Nasreen coming?" When the lawyers met up today, Nasreen's attorney didn't show. At least that was what he'd heard, since the families were not included. Anytime their families got together, the party quickly escalated to yelling and accusations.

"I don't think she's coming," Samia murmured.

"In case it wasn't obvious," Zamzam started, voice level but unforgiving, "I'd choose you over her any day."

Abdullahi felt a smirk try to make its way to his lips but stopped it. Nasreen seemed awfully isolated. He had his own demons, but being around the others and going through the same trauma made his chest ever so slightly lighter.

"She's just lost," Samia defended, and Abdullahi was surprised to hear empathy color her words. She scanned the street. "If I'm honest, I had us come here because it feels like we're missing something. If we didn't cause the explosion, why isn't anyone trying to figure out what actually happened? They're too busy trying to make us look guilty, and we can only be guilty if the guilty party is hidden."

Samia sloped her body away from them, toward the beach and the source of the ocean's song. A ballad of crashing waves. Abdullahi stood beside her, and Zamzam beside him. Strings of lights crisscrossed above the Promenade's Main Street. They'd parked far from the shops, but their eyes could follow the lines of the street all the way to the caution tape that blocked off the blitzed pier.

"Then let's find out the truth," Abdullahi said into the wind as he took his first step against it. Following his lead, they began walking down Main Street.

Monarch Beach, always vibrant and bustling, had become a ghost town. They passed stores that were boarded up against daytime protesters, and save for some loiterers, including the three of them, most people respected the citywide curfew that the mayor imposed in light of the disaster and the protests that had become a daily occurrence.

As they approached the shore, the air grew saltier and the wind stronger. Copious tassels from the end of Samia's coat lifted in the breeze. Zamzam pulled the cap farther down over her forehead. Abdullahi breathed in, and no matter how many times his chest fell, it felt as if he could never breathe out.

It was a maze to reach the beach. Along the boardwalk, police barricades blocked pedestrian access, but no number of obstacles could separate Abdullahi from what he intended to tell them tonight. They risked meeting again to gain one another's trust, to help clear one another's names. He would lead by example.

"This way," Abdullahi told them, swerving their direction toward the stairs by the pier. Sticking to the shadows, he held up the caution tape to let them pass under. He peered behind them, but the boardwalk was empty. It was too late for anyone to be out, even at a beach that wasn't shrouded with as much tragedy as Monarch Beach. He led them under the pier toward the lockers.

"Why were you down this way?" Samia asked him, though Abdullahi knew they recognized the area from the video that had begun circulating. The one where Abdullahi was running. "I saw you when we arrived in the parking lot. When did you have time to come here?"

245

"I never went to the bonfire," he explained. "I walked down the beach this way to go to the bathroom. I have a small bladder."

"He does," Samia concurred.

Zamzam rolled her eyes. "You're telling me they got you on that video and they roped you in with us because you had to pee?"

Abdullahi felt bleak. "A comedy of errors."

"That's called tragedy," Zamzam said, tone flat.

"So you don't have an alibi? No one saw you except me?" Samia double-checked.

Abdullahi only nodded. He showed them around the lockers, then stopped. "Here," he stated.

Zamzam glanced at him. "There's nothing here."

Closing his eyes, Abdullahi tried to remember everything from that night, but it was painful. He wanted to help Zamzam and Samia. No, he *needed* to. Because he couldn't help her. No, he didn't help her. But maybe he was never meant to. He couldn't shake the feeling that everything that had happened until now was a trap. Starting with when he found her.

Once Abdullahi started talking, he couldn't stop. "I was walking when I heard a loud crash. I turned the corner, and I saw that she'd tripped and fallen over all this equipment. I swear I'd never met her before then. She could barely talk, but I could tell she was so afraid. Maybe I was being too nice, maybe it was a trap, maybe she had something to do with it, maybe that's why—"

"Wait," Samia interrupted, "are we talking about Muzhda?"

A silence descended.

"Did you know her?" Samia asked Zamzam, who pretended she hadn't heard the question.

Abdullahi continued, "I don't think she had anything to do with the explosions."

"Why not?" Zamzam's voice was small and...hopeful.

If they could blame Muzhda, if they rallied against her and built their case around her, they had a chance of winning.

But it didn't sit right with Abdullahi. There had been something in her eyes that night, a genuine terror, that wasn't a product of being caught in the act, but more caught in the same trap that had ensnared them all.

"She didn't know any of us. She was an outlier. And besides, she's..." Samia stopped midsentence as her eyes fell onto a word on the ground. "What does that say?" She knelt by the manhole that was just feet away from where Muzhda had fallen.

It read PETROMILE.

"There's that oil company again," Zamzam muttered bitterly.

Samia furrowed her brows. "They're everywhere. But maybe it's just a coincidence. Or maybe not." She squinted up at Abdullahi. "Why didn't you help her? You said you tried."

"I heard cars from here." Abdullahi pointed up the stairs to the parking lot just as a car engine cut out. "It was the police. I knew it would look suspicious. She was badly hurt, and I was right over her trying to lift her. But it was either dealing with the cops, who wouldn't have believed I had nothing to do with her injuries, or getting the hell away from there. I'm not proud of it, but I ran."

He was more than not proud; he was ashamed. Muzhda had deserved better than what he'd done. Zamzam reached out to his forearm. "It's not your fault," she murmured.

247

Samia stood again, her eyes lingering on the manhole. "You ran when you heard the explosions. We all did. We were spooked."

"No." Abdullahi shook his head. "I ran because I saw the police. Then the explosions happened."

Samia cocked her head in confusion. "Why would the cops be here before the explosions? That makes no sense."

"Maybe they were already there? Stationed in the vicinity in case of emergency?" Zamzam supplied without confidence.

Abdullahi just shook his head. He had distinctly heard them arrive, their tires screeching in the parking lot.

"So someone else called the cops. Someone who was already here," Samia mused, glancing back down at the manhole. "I don't know about you guys, but PetroMile being so quiet through all of this but then being everywhere I look is not sitting well with me."

Before Abdullahi could respond, more cars sounded above them in the parking lot. Too late, Abdullahi realized the beach's parking lots had closed over an hour ago. Even the other stragglers out after curfew shouldn't be able to enter the closed beach parking lots. This smelled like trouble.

The same dread from the Fourth seeped into his veins.

He locked eyes with Zamzam's before the uniformed officers exiting their vehicles in the distance confirmed his fears. Their eyes widened at each other. He knew what was coming; the world slowed down as he prepared for it. It pulled him back to the night with Muzhda, to all the things he didn't do, and he didn't want to make the same mistake again. "Go," he whispered to Zamzam. "Go with Samia, and I'll be right behind you."

His lie stabbed him in his chest. He memorized the worry on

Zamzam's face before she turned around with Samia and sped out of sight.

There was no time. He tried to imagine Maryam's anger. He tried to imagine Amin's and Fatima's disappointment. He'd never seen it, but he tried to imagine Muzhda's smile.

Once the officers spotted him, he was certain he couldn't follow the girls. Abdullahi thought of karma. He was sure he didn't believe in it anymore. It was just him against a world stringing him along a preplanned ride. He surrendered to it.

CHAPTER 31

ZAMZAM

ZAMZAM'S CHEST KNOTTED AS SHE HEARD THE OFFICERS shouting at Abdullahi, their voices distorted at an unnatural pitch. She could paint an image of what was happening around the corner without looking. Abdullahi's hands in his pockets, until they weren't anymore, until they were up in the air, until they were breaking his fall because the officer kicked out his knees, until they were twisted behind his back and cuffed.

The head start that Abdullahi had given them saved them. Samia and Zamzam had grabbed each other's arms in the heat of the moment. Samia fidgeted in Zamzam's grasp. Zamzam's internal struggle manifested physically for Samia.

She yanked Samia by her arm, forcing her to look forward. "We can't risk getting caught."

"But we're all out after curfew," Samia whined, glancing back every other step. Her eyes were rapidly filling with tears. "The judge won't let him out on bail for the second time. We have to go back."

Zamzam stopped abruptly. There was a delay before Samia lifted her eyes to meet hers.

"Go back, then," Zamzam told her, voice steely.

Samia looked like she was about to piss her pants. She hiccuped. "Let's go back."

"*No. You* go." Zamzam's voice was dangerously low. Her throat felt like fire as she fought the urge to go back herself. "But if you do, don't think you'll be changing anything. They've already got him. And he knows we can't be behind bars if we're gonna figure out who really did this. If you go back, you'll be wasting that chance he got you."

For the second time tonight, Zamzam saw understanding flash across Samia's open face. Abdullahi had seen the police, and he'd protected them. Zamzam wasn't going to let Samia throw his sacrifice away.

"That's *it*," Samia uttered through a clenched jaw. "We're going to find the people who did this." She wiped her tears, and Zamzam's anger subsided fractionally. She wouldn't soothe Samia's selfish tears, but she wouldn't let them touch her anymore.

"What the *hell*?" Samia marched past her and pointed down at another manhole. "Why are they everywhere?"

Zamzam walked over. Like the one before, it was labeled PETROMILE.

"I don't think it's a coincidence that they're all over the place," Samia said. "I think I got an anonymous tip yesterday. I looked them up again this morning. They operated the rig. They're always in the articles about the Fourth, so why have they been so quiet? Why aren't they being questioned like us?"

The two girls gazed out at the empty beach, and farther out at the black sea, where floodlights illuminated the wreckage of the oil rig. In Zamzam's peripheral vision, she could tell there were too many officers surrounding Abdullahi.

Samia gasped, eyes fixed behind her. "They're taking him."

Zamzam shut her eyes in seething anger. She led Samia back to the car; she couldn't lower her guard until they were safe at home. She didn't want to see Abdullahi, because she knew what could come next.

Abdullahi wouldn't resist—he'd pray silently that he'd be taken away with minimal force. He'd show up in court, and the judge wouldn't give him bail for the violation of the first. He'd be recorded in the system. They'd bring this as evidence against him. He'd be locked up for a crime he didn't commit. Some shadow of a crime that existed only to keep him from being free.

To Zamzam's ears, the sounds of the crashing waves turned from a soothing song to screeching wails, the howling winds of a desert. She hadn't set foot on the beach since the Fourth. And now that she had, it was feeling a lot less like the ocean and more like a dry desert filled with her worries.

There would be no swimming toward the light on the horizon, just an endless walk on the sand in a desert of hardship.

CHAPTER 32

THE TRIAL BEGAN THIS WEEK. FAVREAU WAS PLEASED WITH the case she'd built; it was messy, and she loved messy. Pennella, who had the imagination of a fish, could wrap his head around it, which meant it was strong. At a meeting with the prosecution, she let him take the stage. If he could explain the details of the crime in his laconic English, then a jury wouldn't have any trouble at all believing a man as eloquent as Renner.

Henry Renner, the DA less accustomed to the atmosphere in Favreau's office, listened quietly. She suspected he'd much rather be behind his computer reading about this in an email, but she'd summoned him.

Favreau leaned back in her chair. "Remember, Micky, we don't want your analysis. *Just* run through it for us."

Pennella cleared his throat and adjusted the map to face him. He pointed to the lockers. "This is the source of the signals that triggered the explosions of oil rig *Bonnie* and the pier, and the same location where Muzhda Ahmad was found. Her fingerprints on the lockers suggest she hadn't just stumbled by, because they're all over the scene and the equipment that triggered the explosions. The incomplete CCTV footage shows Abdullahi Talib meeting with Muzhda Ahmad—she was running, presumably from him. It suggests an argument took place in which Abdullahi assaults her, then runs at the sight of police. However, that interaction happened in the CCTV's blind spot."

"Must I ask again?" Favreau drawled, pinching the bridge of her nose. "Forget about the evidence. Just tell me what happened."

Pennella nodded dutifully. "No one had seen Abdullahi that night except for Samia, who is seen on parking-lot footage speaking with him. The two are friends, and we have a transcript of messages in which Samia writes, *The bonfire is gonna be* bomb*, you have to come*, to a group chat in which Abdullahi is a participant. Though it is a group message and not directly addressed to him."

Together they glanced at Renner, whose expression remained impassive. "I can work with it."

Three down, three to go, Favreau thought. "Continue," she requested.

Pennella pointed toward the pits. "Here we have Qays and Zamzam. We have eyewitnesses who can confirm that Qays and Muzhda spoke just minutes before the explosion, before Muzhda walked down the beach to the lockers. They can also affirm that he sent Muzhda to the lockers, where she could release the signal. Once he did, he set fire to an explosive, which set the attack in motion and acted as a signal to the other five of the imminent explosions. Zamzam was there with him, and they ran toward the ocean, where…actually, I'm not sure why they ran toward the ocean. They would have blended in if they'd followed the crowds."

Favreau didn't say anything; she merely pointed at the island off the coast.

Pennella snapped his finger like a fourth grader who had just cracked a long-division problem.

"They were going to the nearest island, where they would attempt to escape by boat with an unlicensed company operating off the island. Did you find evidence of that? I must have missed it." Pennella tried to search the papers.

Favreau nodded, bored. "We have evidence."

"Really?" Pennella sat up. "I'd love to take a look."

"That won't be necessary," she asserted with a pressed smile. Proof disinterested her.

Pennella glanced at Renner, who waved a hand dismissively. Pennella dropped it.

He continued, "Then there are these two. Samia and Nasreen. Samia, I can wrap my head around. She has a connection to Abdullahi, who is clearly guilty on the basis of his interaction with Muzhda, and it only helps matters that he was caught revisiting the scene, breaking curfew, and is being held in a juvenile detention center on remand. But Nasreen—she doesn't seem guilty. Besides being this Faris boy that Samia claims she is. However, the IP address for the account is a dead end. It could be a ploy to cover Samia's tracks and frame Nasreen as a part of this. That's the angle that Nasreen's lawyer, Penelope Carson, is taking, anyway."

Favreau did not like the sound of that.

255

"I agree," Renner said after a stretched silence. "Going after Nasreen could be construed as malicious by the defense. Carson is a talented attorney. She'll definitely throw us a curveball or two."

Favreau *hated* the sound of that. She didn't need them all, but it was the fault of her ambition that she wanted them all. Once she'd set her sights on six, it pained her to give up any of them. She'd take them all to prison; that way the nation could sleep feeling safe at night. She let her scowl fester in the silence.

"You need to entertain a concession," Renner told her. "There's no evidence here or elsewhere that could incriminate Nasreen beyond a reasonable doubt. If we press too hard, the media might go digging and find something we don't want them to see." He gave Favreau a long look, decidedly excluding Pennella from the information they were tasked with obscuring. Money was a strong motivator, even for the DA.

"I offered Carson a no contest plea deal, but she didn't bite," he said. "She wants to win."

No, she had to. If a suspect had to be spared in the process, Favreau would accept it.

"We'll keep working on Carson. She'll come around eventually, and we could use her," Favreau said.

"The others won't stand for it," Pennella countered.

"A pack of rabid dogs would chase each other's tails in a circle." Favreau placed her palms on the table and leaned closer to the two men. "I want each of these criminals locked up. If we give Nasreen a shorter sentence and the others scramble for scraps, so be it. Make an example of what happens when our liberties are threatened."

Renner leveled with her. "You were chosen because you could keep this case tight. Don't let your ambitions get in the way of our goal here."

Favreau chuckled and flicked her manicured fingers up into a fan. "You've looked over this case with your own eyes. It was handed to me for a reason. We don't need much to imagine the crime. Our other concerned parties can rest assured I've built a case with their best interests in mind." *And our savings*, she didn't add.

Pennella stared between Renner and Favreau, his ears turning a bright shade of pink. The time for recess had long since been over. No more talking circles around Pennella; this was the reality he better start facing.

After holding Renner's gaze in hers, Favreau leaned back, interlocking her fingers and placing her hands on her bony knee. "I want all six of them. Even if you need to make a deal with Carson."

Renner raised an eyebrow; remnants of his smirk tarried. "You are so sure they did this. Even with the information you got on PetroMile."

"Even without a lick of evidence," she maintained, hiding her irritation at the mention of the oil company. "These suspects weren't the only ones we took into custody on the Fourth. But when I saw the lines that connected them to one another, I knew it had to be them. The evidence is supplementary."

Pennella struggled with this in the back of his mind. Favreau could see it on his face, the way his brows pinched in the middle, the way the corners of his lips twitched, and the way the veins in his jaw protruded. But her seniority deemed her intuition

superior, her deduction matchless. Pennella would have to follow; he had no other paths to walk save for the ones she paved
for him. In this room, Pennella was as much her victim as the Six.

"It was obvious," Pennella finally agreed, though the words
sounded as salty as the ocean. "I should know, I was the first to
question them."

Favreau smiled, her face softening. "There you have it, Mr.
Renner."

Sighing, Renner didn't deny it. The two of them had achieved
what they had come for. If rule-following, simpleminded, and
painfully young Pennella could fall in line, then they were sure
to win.

CHAPTER 33

NASREEN

IT HAD BEEN TWENTY-ONE DAYS SINCE NASREEN HADN'T woken up from her nightmare, and the nightmare was growing teeth.

Abdullahi was in juvie. Or something. Nasreen didn't hear Ms. Carson when she spoke anymore. She just watched as her lipstick bled into the border of her lips and onto her skin. Occasionally, Nasreen's eyes drifted to a memo or file on Ms. Carson's desk, and she absorbed herself in deciphering it.

"...and the Mr. Talib development helps."

Nasreen wanted to bang her head on Ms. Carson's desk—maybe then she would listen to someone other than herself. Even Mama and Baba realized they should just let her talk and ask questions only before the end of their allotted time.

"Now I want to talk about the plea deal."

Baba sat up in his chair. Nasreen's stomach flipped.

"The DA, Henry Renner, approached us offering thirty years if we plead guilty, but I can talk them down," Ms. Carson said. "I think I could get fifteen years and parole."

"No," her mama began, her hands shaking. They trembled every time they met with Ms. Carson. "Fifteen years is her whole life."

Ms. Carson whisked her hand in the air. "Of course, it's not a deal we'd entertain. But the others might. The DA is going to go full-on offensive. They want to lock them up for life, if not fifty plus years. When the other attorneys cornered me, I gathered that they'd generously consider it. Which means..."

Ms. Carson spoke so enthusiastically about the deal that her red lipstick left a mark on her cleft chin. Nasreen crammed her left hand's nails under her right hand's, picking at the nonexistent dirt. She scanned the few documents laid out on Ms. Carson's desk.

"...isn't that right, Nasreen?"

Expensive seconds passed. "Yes," Nasreen managed, though she had no idea what she'd agreed to.

Ms. Carson gathered the papers on her desk into a pile and placed them in a drawer. That was how things went down with Ms. Carson. She told Nasreen how the trial would work, how they'd respond to this and how they'd react to that, and Nasreen continued her nodding.

At the end of their session, Nasreen stopped in the doorway. She glanced back at Ms. Carson. "I was thinking—don't we—" She stopped herself. "What really happened on the Fourth?"

Ms. Carson pinched her nose bridge. "What matters is how we can build a case against theirs. We're on defense, and our defense depends on how offense is playing. We can worry about that once we're not focused on defending you."

Nasreen didn't know sports, but the analogy was clear enough. "So the truth doesn't matter?"

Ms. Carson approached Nasreen and held the door. If only minutely, her sharp eyebrows relaxed with sympathy. "Dear, I want you to focus on what it'll take for you to go back to high school as soon as possible." August was fast approaching, and school would start. "You saw that calendar with court dates? They're all just speculation. The DA might press for a break for a few days, or we might need to take a break for our own reasons. I need you to do exactly what I tell you. Focus on what I tell you is relevant, and don't give anything else a second thought. From now on and until it's not, this trial is your life."

It had been twenty-three days since Nasreen hadn't woken from her nightmare, and her nightmare was shaped like a courtroom. Inside, she looked small in a plain blazer and old glasses beside Ms. Carson, who sat tall in her fancy suit. The other defendants sat with their own attorneys as they all stood for their joint trial. After all, they were being tried under the same facts, on the basis that the six of them had conspired against and attacked the United States.

Together, they listened to the DA's opening statements.

"Thank you, Your Honor." A long pause from Renner. "Ladies and gentlemen of the jury, the case we have here is not for the sensitive of soul. There was death and destruction. We have a well-loved beach community saddled with the grief and loss, an ocean ecosystem on the verge of collapse, and a population terrorized beyond consolation. I will put our case forth simply.

"On the Fourth of July, the day of American independence, the defendants staged an attack on Monarch Beach in which they bombed oil rig *Bonnie* and Monarch Beach Pier, subsequently destroying both and causing a devastating oil spill in state waters. Be wary that this case will not be straightforward. There was an assault resulting in murder, but we are dealing with something greater. Terrorism is defined as 'the unlawful use of violence and intimidation, especially against civilians, in the pursuit of political aims.' While the violence will be apparent, the intimidation and political aims require that you accept nothing at face value.

"The defense's job here will be to appeal to your better nature. These are, after all, minors, while there are some closer to adulthood than others. They could have been your children's or grandchildren's classmates. The defense will try to utilize your soft hearts and paint them as too young to be guilty. They might even appeal to your political correctness. It is imperative you remember this: It is not on account of their race or religion that they stand accused. I do not insinuate a relationship between the defendants and an international terrorist organization, though they will not be free of foreign influence. They stand here accused because of physical evidence and verbal testimony tying them to the crimes.

"Ladies and gentlemen of the jury, the defendants are not a reflection of our Muslim American friends. We do not attack their character and their backgrounds. Here in this courtroom, Lady Liberty presides over us, as does Judge Min. We use only hard evidence and the law as our guides. Only then can we do our part in restoring liberty and security for our nation."

Nasreen thought he deserved a round of applause. There was a great deal of courtroom drama in his performance, which glued her eyes to him like he was a character on television. He paced his speech so purposefully, stared deeply into the jurors' eyes, and crafted his words so deliberately that she expected everything he said from then on would be the truth, no questions asked.

Then Ms. Carson stood and walked her oiled legs to the jury's bench. Nasreen took a preparatory breath on behalf of Ms. Carson, a gasp for air that could be heard seats away. Samia glanced at her from the next table over. Zamzam's head was dipped down, her face obscured. The lawyers agreed Ms. Carson, with her big name and experience, could speak on their behalf. Alsace was the only other attorney with equal experience, but since Qays was to be tried as an adult, he conceded the crown to her.

As she spoke, Ms. Carson's words unraveled like yarn, too quickly to stop. She jumped from the night of the Fourth to Nasreen's grades and Qays's extracurriculars. If the jury knew nothing about them before, they now had a rough portrait.

"Why should we shy away from simple?" Ms. Carson asked rhetorically at some point in her remarks. "They're minors. They're kids, and we're talking terrorism. Like the prosecution said, these could be your children's classmates. And the allegations against them are heavy. They are far from simple.

"These children are strangers," she continued. "The prosecution will attempt to clump them together as a monolith. But they come from different backgrounds, cultures, homes. We need look no further than the schools they attended. My client Ms. Choudhry attended Saint Modesta, was educated at an excellent private Catholic school where she had little to do with the organizations the prosecution claim are associated with the Six." Nasreen's eyes remained carefully trained on her attorney, but she felt the others gape at her and shoot her dirty looks. Her singling out Nasreen in the opening statement wasn't what they'd agreed to. By emphasizing Nasreen's difference in the opening statement, she'd already set up Nasreen to be seen as different.

Ms. Carson had an agenda. When her remarks were over, she settled back beside Nasreen, ignoring the scowls from the entire defense bench.

"That was perfect," Ms. Carson whispered through a rigid jaw.

"That was unfair," Nasreen whispered back.

The smallest of smirks sprouted on Ms. Carson's painted lips. "Exactly."

CHAPTER 34

ZAMZAM

"WHAT THE HELL WAS THAT?!" SAMIA EXCLAIMED OVER THE roaring of wind on the 405 freeway. Her car top was down, and Zamzam slumped in the passenger seat, wrapping herself in her huge sweater to keep warm from the foggy morning air that whipped at her and Samia's hijabs. Samia huffed, "Carson is such a dumb bitch!"

Zamzam bit her lower lip. "I wouldn't call her dumb. She did everything as planned and then did a little extra for her client. She wants to win even if that means the rest of us lose."

Zamzam might've done the same weeks ago. But things had changed. When Abdullahi had been arrested again, she became even more sure she couldn't turn her back against the Six. Even Nasreen had looked miserable when her attorney went off script.

The trial was only part of the puzzle. Zamzam had agreed to investigate PetroMile with Samia, but they needed to be careful.

They couldn't afford to be caught this time, and she was glad Samia's plan didn't involve being out after curfew again.

Still, Samia drove like her driver's license should be revoked, well over the speed limit and swerving without blinkers. She didn't understand the meaning of lying low, so Zamzam kept her eye out for potential danger.

"She knew she'd played us and was going to move forward with whatever was going to be best for her and Nasreen." Samia made a face like she'd eaten something too sour. "And they tried to get us to take that plea deal? Ridiculous."

That plea deal meant Zamzam could never dream of becoming a doctor. She'd never be anything she had told herself she would be unless she was completely acquitted.

"You said you needed my help, so where are we going?" Zamzam circumvented the morbid plea-deal conversation.

"You'll see." Samia exited off the freeway. "I heard Abdullahi can have visitors. His other trial begins in a week, for the assault they're trying to pull over him. As if Abdullahi would ever."

"Have you gone to see him?" Zamzam asked, already knowing the answer.

Samia shook her head.

They couldn't go see him without it looking suspicious. She knew this, and she had lived her life like a statue, rigid as stone, but every day she became more flexible; the clay facade that kept her together was cracking, and all sorts of feelings were seeping through. She felt like an art piece from which paint bled through the margins of the frame. It became more difficult to keep it all from escaping. What was the use of all that time living for her mother, living to be the dependable older sister, living to be everything that Yazeed wasn't, if she was going to end up here anyway?

Slowing down, Samia put her car in park in the nearly empty lot of a tall glass building. PETROMILE CO. beamed in neon at the very top through the foggy marine layer. They could see into the illuminated lobby from the car. Employees trickled in, but it was still very early.

"Here." Samia handed Zamzam a neatly folded olive-green blazer and a pair of small heels. She began aggressively caking on powder and laying on thick bronzer. She aged herself fifteen years with a heavy hand of makeup.

"What's this?" Zamzam watched her blankly. It was like she was seeing another person.

"We're going inside."

"Oh, hell no."

Samia went through her bag and handed Zamzam a notepad. *Lori Cox* was scribbled onto the top note. "I found that in my bag yesterday after I got home from court. Someone must have slipped it in there, maybe when I was walking through the crowds outside or maybe when we were on lunch break?"

Zamzam narrowed her eyes. "Okay, who's Lori Cox?"

"Public relations and marketing manager of PetroMile's LA division." Samia smiled smugly like she'd cracked a centuries-old unsolved algorithm. "Someone's giving us another tip."

Zamzam felt a flare of irritation. "Or someone's setting us up. What if we go in there and the police are waiting for us? We can't just walk into this blindly."

Samia's smile fell. "I'm not dumb. I did my research. I have PR badges that I have for my social media sponsorships, so we'll look legit. And I forged some emails that we have job interviews with the hiring manager for marketing."

"And what if someone recognizes us?" Zamzam asked.

"You don't even recognize me right now." She smirked, and Zamzam noticed Samia was wearing colored contacts. Her eyes looked gray. "I'm a master of disguise. And I can talk myself in and out of almost anything. I'll distract the manager. She's a dinosaur, so I can dazzle her with my social media talk while you snoop wherever you can. If Carson is going to sabotage us in the courtroom, we need to find who did this ourselves."

"And how do you know there'll be anything useful to us in there?"

Samia shrugged. "I don't know. But this is the only lead we've got."

"And you trust this—this anon?" Zamzam asked. "I don't have a good feeling about this."

"Why not? Damned if we do, damned if we don't."

"I'd rather not be damned at all."

"Then don't sit on your ass and let things happen to you." She snapped her compact closed. "Let's go."

Zamzam squeezed her feet into Samia's heels, shouldered on her blazer, and accepted a pair of fake glasses from Samia's trunk of costumes. She wished she'd gotten a heads-up to do her own makeup tricks to better her disguise, but they looked like an odd enough pair that Zamzam hoped they wouldn't be recognized.

"Are they even open?" Zamzam asked hesitantly. It was only 7:00 AM.

Samia locked her car. "Capitalism never sleeps, sweetie."

"Shut the hell up." Zamzam shook her head but couldn't hide her laughter.

They entered the lobby, and the receptionist looked at them with droopy eyes. Samia took over as though she owned the place. She flashed her badge and talked up the receptionist. They were here for a job interview with the marketing department. Yes, it was very early for job interviews. Maybe there was a glitch in the system because here's the email thread confirming their interview appointment. No, they didn't need to be escorted up. Samia even knew the floor number. Zamzam's heart felt like it was beating out of her chest. The receptionist took a closer look at Samia's PR badges, which Zamzam saw had fake names. She mumbled something to the security guard, who used his badge to open the elevator for them. Samia nodded a thanks and clicked the button to the seventh floor.

"Like taking candy from a baby," Samia whispered with a grin, but her voice trembled. The elevator doors shut, and Zamzam sent a silent prayer up before they began their ascension.

Dear God, Zamzam thought, *please let us find something here that is not candy.*

CHAPTER 35

SAMIA

"I DIDN'T REALIZE WE WERE HIRING FOR THE SOCIAL MEDIA marketing department."

Lori Cox's assistant was a mess. His desk was a tornado of papers, and his hair might be a viable source of oil itself. He ran a hand down his face. He looked like he hadn't gone home all night. "Well, our hiring manager isn't in yet, and Lori hasn't been in all week."

Zamzam tensed beside Samia, so she had to do something to defuse the situation. "Did I read the email wrong?" Samia pulled out her phone and pretended to read the screen. "It definitely says today at seven AM. It's been set up for a couple weeks."

The assistant, who'd introduced himself as Mark, sighed. "Unfortunately, I wasn't cc'd on that email chain, *and* I didn't get an email from Lori, *and* she's not here right now." With every conjunction, the poor man slid closer and closer to the end of his rope. His eyebrows barely raised with an idea. "I'll check to see if she left a note on her desk."

"That would be great." Samia offered a sterile smile as he grabbed keys from his desk and turned to open Lori Cox's office door. Samia watched him carefully, and then her eyes swept the rest of the floor, a maze of cubicles with only one or two employees hunched over their desks in the early morning.

Mark unlocked the door. Zamzam and Samia craned their necks to peek inside. Lori Cox's office was as much of a mess as her assistant's desk. Piles of mail were stacked at the door, and her desk was covered in paper. Her assistant returned, keeping the door barely open. When he turned around, Samia reassumed her relaxed pose. "Anything?"

"Unfortunately, nothing."

"Perhaps one of your colleagues might have an idea?"

"Why would they know?" Mark sounded like he was on his last puff of patience.

"Maybe HR?" Samia insisted. She'd come this far, and she needed a way into Lori Cox's office.

"Listen, Sally, was it?" He scowled. "We're so very busy. I don't know if you know, but one of our operation sites fell victim to a terrorist attack, and the last thing we need is to hire more people for social media marketing." Zamzam fidgeted beside Samia. He added, "You must have mixed up the timing. You could reschedule for later, but you two should go."

"Of course," Samia said quickly. It didn't go over her head that this assistant had already passed judgment on the Fourth when the Six had not yet been found guilty in court. "We'll just get going, then. Oh, could I ask you for a quick favor? Could I get some water?"

He frowned. She saw him battle with himself, but he eventually gave in. "Follow me."

Before Samia stood up, she squeezed Zamzam's arm and glanced at the cracked-open door. She followed Mark across the nearly empty office, praying that Zamzam was on the same page as she was. They couldn't give up now.

The break room was across the floor, and Samia waited as the assistant filled a cup of water and handed it to her.

"Where's the other one?" he asked, his thick brows shooting up at the sight of just Samia behind him.

Samia shrugged. "I don't think she wanted water."

"You can't just be around here on your own," he said, frazzled. He hurried through the office, and Samia trailed behind. She arched her back to see over the cubicles, but she couldn't see Zamzam in the seat.

Oh no, oh no, oh no. If they were caught snooping, if security was called, if the police were notified, they were screwed.

Mark turned the corner to his desk and stopped. Samia nearly slammed into him. She gulped, bracing herself for the worst.

A woman who looked like an ancient, reincarnated crane leaned over Mark's desk, listening to Zamzam intently. Zamzam paused midsentence when Mark and Samia came to a halt.

"This is the other interviewee." Zamzam gestured to Samia. She looked surprisingly calm. "I was just explaining to Lori what influencers are."

Lori Cox narrowed her eyes at her assistant. "My door is unlocked, Mark. I never leave my door unlocked."

"Yes, sorry about that," Mark said. He was very much awake now and sweating.

Lori made a disapproving sound, then turned to her office. "Reschedule the interviews with these ladies. I don't have time this morning. Still dealing with this PR nightmare."

"Of course," Mark said. He rescheduled interviews that had never been scheduled to begin with for people who didn't exist, and the girls booked it.

Once outside and across the street, Zamzam leaned forward, and Samia feared she'd start heaving. "I can't believe we just did that."

Samia was still processing. "Did that woman call the Fourth a PR nightmare?"

Zamzam straightened up, but her hand remained at her mouth like she was keeping herself from expelling all her nerves. "It did sound like it."

"I would think that a company like that would make themselves out to be a victim pretty easily after what happened," Samia said. "Unless they're not a victim."

Zamzam's eyes widened. "Can we get out of here?"

They hopped into the car, and Samia closed the top. She felt defeated, like they'd done it all for nothing except more suspicion.

"Samia." Zamzam broke the silence. "Before Lori got there, I got into her office. I took pictures of the papers on her desk. If there's something there, we might be able to find it."

She heard it at the end there. And in the way that Zamzam said her name with such fullness—it was unmistakable. It wasn't hope just yet, but it was hope's distant cousin.

"Well, I'm never doubting you ever again." Samia grinned. "We might be able to find out the truth."

Zamzam made a face. "But it's not the truth they're looking for. It's the story that best fits their narrative. Nasreen's attorney knows that. It's why she went off script in court. And probably why no one else is looking into the truth except for us."

Samia pointed at Zamzam's phone. "Well, if they won't, then we will. PetroMile has to be a part of this. We're on the right track. I think we can win this case for ourselves."

Zamzam looked down into her lap. "I don't think it'll be that easy."

"So we figure out what the hell happened, and we expose everyone," Samia rebounded.

Opening the window, Zamzam rested her hand on the door, allowing the air to whip between her fingers. She sneaked a peek at Samia. "You're so sure we'll find a way out."

Samia pressed her lips into a thin line. "I'm actually not. But Abdullahi would be all over this. He'd be super optimistic and look up all the laws even though that's our attorneys' job, and he'd be searching for ways out. I owe it to him now that they've got him."

"You two are super close?" asked Zamzam, squinting at her.

Samia smiled despite the tugs of a frown at the corners of her mouth. "We were. Back in elementary school he used to fight off all the boys who liked me because they'd pick on me." She rolled her eyes. "In middle school he would read books with me in the library during lunch a couple times a week."

"You read?" Zamzam joked.

Samia gasped sarcastically. "Of course, I read. That library was like my sanctuary. Well, really my hiding place once I went from every boys' crush to the school outcast, once I put on my hijab. One week I was eating lunch with 'Ashley' and getting hit on by 'Drew,' and the next I didn't exist. It was hella humbling."

They exchanged an awkward look as Zamzam reappraised her.

"You have a question," Samia commented.

Zamzam pressed her lips together to hide a smile. "No, I don't."

"Yes, you do."

"I *don't.*"

"Mhm."

Zamzam sighed, resigned. "So then what the hell happened to you?"

Samia laughed. She became acutely aware that she had a pom-pom charm the size of a cat's head attached to her keys, her glove compartment was stuffed with workout clothes and lipstick, and her closet was a barrage of Met Gala outfits. "I stopped being so afraid. For three years, I let the Ashleys and Drews beat down on me. The library was the best hideout, but it became my cage. I finally let myself out."

The strength in her voice cut out, and she spread her fingers along either side of her steering wheel.

"You're happier now," Zamzam said, testing Samia's sudden unease.

Samia held her breath. "I'm happier now." She had the followers, the likes, and the satisfaction of turning Ashley and Drew away and not the other way around. She'd procured the tools she needed to cope with the ugliest realities.

"But..."

Samia narrowed her eyes at Zamzam, who blinked back at her, waiting patiently for Samia to finish her sentence. "But," Samia conceded, "I feel bad. I never thanked Abdullahi for how much he helped me by reading with me during our lunches. Honestly, other than a few times, I didn't even see him at all in the last school year. Yet he's still so kind to me, even when I'm acting all fake."

"Acting," Zamzam repeated without inflection.

"I'm not my social media profile," Samia defended.

"I'm sure Abdullahi knows that."

"I know he knows it. I just feel stupid for pretending all this time. I thought being @muslimsnatched made me less lonely because of the traffic on my page and because the Ashleys and Drews might even vote me homecoming queen, but I was playing myself," Samia murmured, mostly to herself. No wonder she had been so reckless with Faris, opening herself up to a stranger with a sparse online presence. She'd been lonely.

"At least you've been living," Zamzam mumbled. "I feel like I've been under a rock all this time."

Samia sucked air through her teeth. "The underside of a rock is a paradise compared to that courtroom."

"Ameen, sister."

The girls drove in silence save for Samia's pop music and the wind whooshing past their hijabs. Samia regretted little in her short life—not the online feuds or her plastic public image—but she wished she had said more than that handful of words to Abdullahi on the Fourth of July, the most she had said to him in two years.

Samia parked in front of Zamzam's house, and she turned toward Zamzam. "When this trial is over, the first thing I'm going to do is to make amends with Abdullahi. What will you do when you're free?"

Zamzam's hand froze on the car door. She locked eyes with Samia. "Even if we don't go to jail, how are you so sure that what we'll have is called freedom?"

The girls stared at each other, and every experience Samia ever had as a hijabi scrolled through her mind. Zamzam was a mirror to her, and when Samia looked at her, all the filters she'd put on her life faded away. The distractions she'd created fell away. No matter how much the world grew accustomed to the hijab, no matter how much Samia tried to make it mainstream through her social media pages, it still othered her. Samia loved being special. She told herself that she didn't mind being the *other*. But this time it was different. She wasn't othered within her curated bubble. This time, it was too real, and she couldn't answer Zamzam's question.

Samia didn't know what it was like to be truly free, and she might never know.

CHAPTER 36

QAYS

"DO YOU RECOGNIZE IT?"

Qays slowly raised his eyes, which were lined in shadows. His face was gaunt and yellowed from his summer tan paling under weeks of white light. He looked back at the photo evidence supplied by Henry Renner, which flashed on the screen in the courtroom for the jury and the judge to see. It was the firework, but it was all wrong. The photo was taken against the sand, the blown-off portion enlarged by the angle of the shot.

Alsace had briefed Qays on this in preparation for his testimony. The strategy was for Qays to present himself as the model student athlete. Since he was not guilty, he wouldn't shy away from testifying.

"Yes."

"Can you tell us what you see?"

"It's a firework after it's been fired."

"And you recognize this specific explosive from the night of the Fourth?"

Qays's lips pressed into a fine line. That word. *Explosive*. It was technically correct, but it carried weight that the word *firework* did not. To Qays on the Fourth, it had been a firework, a toy. In the courtroom today, it was a weapon. It was worse than it sounded to Qays's ears, but he had no choice. He'd sworn on the Qur'an.

Qays forced his jaw to relax. "I recognize the firework."

From her place on the bench, Muzhda didn't look up at him.

"How do you recognize it?" Renner continued.

"Because I fired it."

Renner nodded slowly. Stepping closer to the witness stand, he lowered his reading glasses over his eyes, then proceeded to read off his paper: "California Health and Safety Code Section 12677 states that it is illegal to possess dangerous fireworks without a valid permit. The legal limit of consumer fireworks can contain fifty milligrams of explosive material in a maximum of a three-inch-diameter shell." He lowered the paper. "That's half a tablet of aspirin in a tube the size of a baseball."

Renner pointed his laser to the second picture of the firework, substantially larger than the baseball placed beside it for comparison. "This firework that you fired on the night of the Fourth was double the size with triple the amount of flash powder than is the legal limit. It is altogether a crime to be in possession of such an explosive without a permit. Do you have a pyrotechnics permit, Mr. Sharif?"

"No."

He stepped closer to Qays. "Were you aware at the time of possessing and firing this explosive, Mr. Sharif, that you were committing a crime and putting the public in danger by violating California Health and Safety Code?"

Alsace stood at that. "Objection, compound, Your Honor."

"Sustained," Judge Min answered.

Renner didn't miss a beat. "In other words, were you aware that you were violating Health and Safety Code and therefore committing a crime?"

It was so quiet in the room, Qays could hear the stares. "Yes," he said.

"So, to be clear, you knew this violation might put the public in danger?"

Alsace objected again. "Asked and answered."

"Sustained. Move on, Mr. Renner."

Renner conceded. "Talk us through what happened when you fired the explosive."

Qays licked his lips. He'd practiced his story with Alsace. He had to project; he had to be the cool and confident, Stanford-bound Qays Sharif.

"I was with my friends," he started, his voice raw. "We had just finished a scrimmage. We all play soccer because a lot of us are on Monarch Beach's varsity soccer team. Then I went to my car and brought out the fireworks that I got from a guy who sells illegal fireworks to all the kids at Monarch Beach High. I wasn't the only one with them at the beach that night. White people buy them and fire them all the time."

"And this was after you asked Muzhda Ahmad to collect your stash of marijuana from the lockers? Where she was subsequently found at the source of the signal to blow up both the pier and the oil rig?"

"Objection, relevance to my client."

"Overruled."

Renner had posed the question to compound the fact that Qays was hardly innocent. He was a minor in possession of marijuana and illegal fireworks. But Qays had been invincible until then. Some laws were more guidelines than anything else for boys like Qays.

"Yes, that was after."

Renner nodded. "Please continue."

"Then I returned to the bonfire pits and…and then…" Qays's face grew hot. He glanced between Muzhda and Alsace. *What will you say about me?* Muzhda's question was loud in his ears.

He looked down at his hands, which were cuffed, and he remembered Muzhda's bracelet and a much simpler time than now.

"Mr. Sharif?"

Qays's head snapped up. Alsace wanted him to blame her. But Qays refused to speak badly of Muzhda, so Alsace tried to use Zamzam.

"Yes," Qays murmured. "Then—then I bumped into Zamzam Thompson."

"This Zamzam Thompson?" Renner clarified.

"Yes, but at the time I didn't know her. I still don't know her. We crashed into each other by accident, and I didn't apologize. She tried to warn me that I didn't set the firework steady enough—no, it was because the sand wasn't sturdy enough."

Renner was pleased with this admission. Qays was ad-libbing, and Alsace would be furious. "Then?"

"Then it shot up and snaked down into the crowd."

"Would you say this caused a frenzy?"

"For barely a second," Qays held. "Then the oil rig and pier exploded, and everyone ran."

"Where did they run?"

"Every direction," he answered vaguely. There was a brief silence, then he added, "Toward the parking lots."

"And you? Where did you run?"

Qays lowered his head. He was not the Stanford-bound Qays Sharif. He was completely despondent, his eyes were rimmed in shadows, and he had effectively ejected himself from the case. He tried his best to carry on. He raised his head and looked at Zamzam, whose face seemed to say it was going to be okay if he told the truth. "Zamzam grabbed my arm. She pulled me with her toward the ocean."

"Now, Zamzam Thompson, a complete stranger and substantially smaller than you, managed to drag you through the sand and the crowds toward the ocean, and you couldn't stop her?"

"I was panicking—"

"Answer the question," Renner warned. "You didn't stop her?"

Qays clenched his jaw. "I guess..." He wondered back to that night and why he hadn't stopped her from dragging him when he easily could have. *Fate?* "No, I didn't."

"In other words, you'd like us to believe that you ran toward the present danger in the ocean with Zamzam Thompson, who is a complete stranger to you? And you couldn't stop her despite being ten inches taller and quite stronger?"

"Objection. Asked and answered, Your Honor."

"Sustained."

Renner crossed his arms. "The defense has maintained that the six of you are strangers and therefore could not have worked together in committing these crimes. You would lead us to believe that you and Zamzam Thompson are strangers despite what your story suggests. What would you say, then, of your relationship with Muzhda Ahmad?"

Qays's heart skipped a beat. "I didn't have one. I barely knew her."

There was a show of courtroom jargon before Renner exhibited evidence for the jury.

"May I approach the stand, Your Honor?" he asked.

"You may."

"Do you recognize it?"

Renner's voice barely registered. The air had been knocked out of Qays's lungs. Muzhda's bracelet was within arm's reach.

"Yes," Qays managed breathlessly.

"Could you describe the bracelet to us?"

Qays could because he'd already memorized everything about it. Twenty-seven beads. Ten red, ten black, six letters, one heart. Muzhda's name.

"Why did you have this bracelet on you when you were arrested?" Renner asked smugly.

Qays couldn't see anything; his vision was a mixture of brown and beige. "Because Muzhda gave it to me right before I asked her to fetch the weed from the lockers." He couldn't look at his father. He hated the sickly yellow of disappointment that descended on him with his admission.

"So when you say you have no relationship to Muzhda or

Zamzam, do you mean you had never seen them *in person* before the Fourth, or that you had no relationship with either of them?"

"Objection, leading question."

"Overruled."

Alsace was wrong, Qays thought. *I never should have testified.*

"Mr. Sharif?" Renner stepped closer.

Everything was jumbled. The Fourth and the before and the after, they weren't on a linear timeline; they existed simultaneously. Qays's words jammed in the back of his throat. "I didn't know Zamzam. I—I don't know her," he stammered.

"But you knew Muzhda?"

Qays's cheeks reddened. He knew her through stories and writing, and it felt like there was never a time when he didn't know Muzhda. He'd always known her. "I—I knew her."

Alsace sighed.

Renner barely masked his smirk. "How did you know Muzhda Ahmad?"

The words dribbled out his mouth. "I used to tutor her at Valley High School last year, but it was just an assignment for English. I had to tutor kids at Valley for a few months, and then it was over. I never got her number. I hadn't seen her after that until the Fourth."

Renner didn't let up. "So you did have ties with Ms. Ahmad. On the night of the Fourth you were seen committing illegal acts and colluding with Zamzam Thompson, who ran from the scene. You sent Muzhda Ahmad to the exact position where she was found, and where her fingerprints are all over the equipment that signaled the explosions. Are we to believe that you are innocent of the premeditated acts of terror by Muzhda Ahmad and the attempted escape with Zamzam Thompson?"

Alsace leaped up with another objection.

"Sustained. Mr. Renner, be warned."

Renner smirked as he turned his back to the jury. He reserved it only for Qays and the defense. Qays's anger flared. "No further questions, Your Honor."

There would be no further need for Qays. No matter how good Alsace made him look, he had done the damage. His eyes slid to his father, who sat up straighter, puffing out his chest. Arab dads did that when they were disappointed. He must've known about the weed all this time and not said anything. It was becoming abundantly clear how far down Qays had fallen off his pedestal.

"It looked stressful."

Qays ignored Muzhda. *It should be a capital offense to sound so happy.* Happy despite Qays's royally screwing up his testimony, abandoning himself to the mercy of whatever evidence they were twisting to frame him.

"Zamzam must be pleased. I don't think she expected that honesty from you." She giggled, and Qays could have snapped right through a pair of handcuffs if he had been wearing them. He was fuming. And he wasn't even angry with her. He was angry with himself. "Is Abdullahi testifying next? That should be interesting to watch."

"How are you enjoying this?" Qays snapped at her.

"What's not to enjoy?" Muzhda shot back.

"We're fucked," he seethed. "They're acting like if they can connect us to each other then they can imagine a crime none of us committed. Our lives are over."

Muzhda snorted. "Did you expect anything else? I haven't lost my mind. This isn't fun to me, but I've passed more stages of grief than you have. I already went through the denial and the anger. I already mourned my life, and now there's nothing left but acceptance. Better catch up, homecoming king."

And Qays couldn't help it, couldn't hold it in any longer. He broke. It came not in the soft tears he'd shed when he had watched *Coco* with his little cousins. Silent tears he didn't want anyone else to see.

These felt deserved because they came from the bowels of grief.

Qays wept. His body shook with sobs he didn't know he had in him. He felt each one in his bones and his gut; his time locked up had atrophied his muscles, and he was hollow. So much of who he was lay in who he planned to be. He was always respected on the potential of his projected success alone. But he finally came face-to-face with the casket that held the man that Qays Sharif was supposed to become. After his performance today, he had none of that, and he had no one to blame but himself. So he mourned the future he had lost.

Through the sobs, Qays felt arms fall around him, and Muzhda held him against her as he crumbled.

"You told the truth. That was the right thing to do," she whispered to him.

"I shouldn't have," he choked out.

Her embrace tightened. "But you did."

Qays sobbed until he had no more tears left. He broke away

from Muzhda, and while he wiped at his eyes, she straightened up and scooted away from him. She adjusted her scarf, and he watched her careful movements. Only later in the deep hours of the night did he realize what had struck him as different. He swore he had seen it on her wrist.

The twenty-seven beads of Muzhda's bracelet.

Ten red, ten black, six letters, one heart.

CHAPTER 37

ZAMZAM

ZAMZAM ZOOMED IN AND OUT ON THE PHOTOS SHE'D taken of Lori Cox's desk. The photos were puzzle pieces of letters and memos.

"Zamzam!" her mom called through the house. "Jamal's not home again!"

Her little brother was acting up. For the third time this week, it was past his curfew, and he still wasn't home. Zamzam's mother had already called every auntie she knew who had a son aged five to thirty. It was useless, of course, but it gave her mom a chance to publicly shame Jamal's reckless behavior. And, she supposed, some comfort.

As for Zamzam, she had to stay home and hold down the fort, metaphorically speaking. She was there for in between phone calls when her mom needed someone to listen to her both insult her sons and profess her unwavering love for them. Sending out prayers for them with *Oh, Allah, keep my good-for-nothing sons safe and in your protection. Do not let any evil touch their ungrateful asses.*

When the doorbell rang, Zamzam leaped up to answer it. "You are so dead, Jamal," she muttered as she opened the door, and her mom called out a prayer.

"Who is Jamal?" came Samia's sardonic voice through the doorway. "And is he okay?"

"Oh shit, I totally forgot," Zamzam said. The two of them were supposed to continue investigating the photos she'd taken at PetroMile together. But between all the testimonies, which got worse by the day, and Jamal's fickle attitude, Zamzam had pushed it to the bottom of her worries list.

"Jamal!" Zamzam's mom called, distress leaching into her voice.

"It's not him, Momma," Zamzam shouted over her shoulder. She turned back to Samia. "It's my brother. He was supposed to be back home hours ago. We're not sure where he went."

"I can go." Samia gestured back to her car.

Sweat lined Zamzam's brow. "That's probably best."

As the door almost shut, Samia reached out to stop it. "Or we could go search for him. I can drive."

"There's no way we're gonna find him."

"It beats you sitting at home waiting," Samia offered. "We'll come back before our curfew. I promise."

Throwing on a scarf and sweatshirt, Zamzam was out the door in minutes. Samia drove at the speed limit through the residential area, their eyes peeled for anyone walking in the empty streets.

"Is he little?"

"What?"

"Is he very young?" Samia revised. "You and your mom seem really scared for him."

"He's young enough," Zamzam muttered, leaning her head against the window.

They drove around for an hour before Samia parked in front of Valley High. Zamzam's knee bounced as she sat in silence with Samia aggressively scouring every online outlet.

"Is he here?" Samia offered her phone. The video playing showed loads of kids mingling on someone's patio and pouring out the front door.

Zamzam squinted at the screen. "I don't see him, but he might be. Do you know where that is?"

"I can find it." Samia tapped away. Obtaining the address, she sped down the street. "Don't forget to breathe," she joked as they climbed out of the car.

"Is it that obvious?" Zamzam muttered, voice dry from nerves. She had taken so much care being the good daughter that she'd never been all that comfortable around kids her own age if she wasn't mandated to be around them at school.

Samia offered a smile. "They're mostly freshmen and sopho-mores."

"All the more reason to be terrified," Zamzam replied with a shudder. "Plus we don't want to be recognized." She pulled her hoodie on.

"Maybe we'll blend in more if we split up," Samia suggested, and they did.

Dodging elbows and hips, Zamzam combed through the crowd outside on the lawn and all through the house. It was a house in the Huntington district, but the demographic was surprisingly mixed. It was a deliberately Muslim crowd, and the boys-to-girls ratio was a strong four to one. As the crowd thickened toward the back of the house, her breathing shallowed. Running in from the backyard patio door, a boy slammed into her shoulder as he raced past her.

Fragments of her memory rushed through her mind. The smell of salt in the air. Her body hitting the damp sand. Qays's eyes wide with horror. Waves obscuring her vision.

Her feet pounding packed sand as she tried to run.

Pressurized water striking her skin like a million needles.

Someone was shaking her.

"Zamzam. Zamzam!"

"Did you find him?" she asked, feeling her focus squirm out of that daze.

"Someone said they saw him out here earlier," Samia told her, looking worried herself. "I overheard some people saying that everyone's here for some protest."

At some point Zamzam had walked into the backyard, but she couldn't remember when. "Then we shouldn't be here," she said, glancing around her. Others were taking notice of them.

"Hey! They're from the Six!"

Zamzam hung her head, and even Samia tried to shield her face.

"Yeah, that's two of them!"

"Justice for the Six!"

"Free the Six!"

The hoots and hollers came from both every direction and no one in particular. Samia and Zamzam became the subject of every gaze. Zamzam felt big and small all at once, and it made her woozy. Then the backyard shifted as an influx of bodies pouring out of the house surrounded them.

"It wasn't me!" someone shouted.

Zamzam whipped her head at the phrase.

"It wasn't me!" The crowd returned it, a choir of long-indignant voices. Her gut pinched at the chorus; she hadn't heard the phrase being used except for in videos.

The crowd started chanting the words Abdullahi had yelled back at the police the night of the Fourth before they sent the officers after him.

At first, it was only half the crowd shouting his words, but then their energy multiplied, filling her whole body until she felt like she was bursting. Her silence was a cap that barely held on.

They began another chant. "Don't leave her!" It was in the video well circulated by the prosecution. Though Renner was using it to imply guilt, the people had watched it in horror as Abdullahi failed to help Muzhda off the ground, as the police sent officers to apprehend him and fired shots at a girl who had already fallen.

Muzhda had screamed on the video, "Don't leave me!"

Tonight, the underclassmen echoed her. Zamzam's heart and muscles felt weak, like it was taking all her effort to keep silent. Her hesitation felt like a crime.

"Don't leave her!"

But Abdullahi had. He hadn't had a choice. She wondered if the lines in Abdullahi's face were all sadness and guilt for leaving her. She considered what could've been different if she'd tried to understand his struggle instead of prioritizing her own. She wondered what it took to leave.

She thought, briefly, about Yazeed.

Before they knew it, Zamzam and Samia were ushered to the front of the horde of teenagers.

"It wasn't me!" The chant made another round.

"Justice for the Six!"

The cap on Zamzam's silence nearly popped. They weren't in the backyard anymore. They were walking down the street, patio lights turning on as the chants woke up residents. Random kids were patting Zamzam on the back, telling her to "be strong" because "you're innocent and God will grant you justice." She accepted their words without a reply. She didn't have words for the wave of emotions that were slamming into her.

"Zamzam!"

She whirled around at her brother's voice. Relief rushed over her as his lanky arms flapped as he ran toward her, his mouth spread into a goofy grin. Her body felt a bit more whole with her brother in her sights. She found the strength to be irritated that he'd made her worry.

"What are you doing here?" he asked, nudging her playfully. "You never come to these things!"

These protests had been sprouting across the nation, some organized and sanctioned with permits, others naturally occurring, others turning violent. Some news outlets called them riots, but that was far from the truth.

"I came to find you." Zamzam resisted the urge to flick his forehead. "And now that I have, we're going home."

They reached the end of the street, and Zamzam's senses were on high alert as the residents observed the kids from their front doors.

"We can't go home." Jamal crossed his arms. "They're just getting started. We've been planning this all week. That's why I've been out so late."

"We're not a part of this, Jamal," she hissed. Even as she said it, she knew it was a lie.

Jamal draped his arm over his sister's shoulders, brought her close to him, and gestured around them. "You're the reason for this."

She wondered at her brother in amazement. Jamal could so easily forget that Zamzam was fighting for the right to the life *they* threatened to take from her. Did he not worry that if she was taken from him, he'd be alone? Yazeed had left her, and the abandonment had pummeled her into this soldier of a girl. She found solace in living within the boundaries. She didn't want Jamal to have the burden of filling the places left by his older siblings.

As they approached the clearing at the end of the street, through a thin curtain of willow branches, a boy about Zamzam's age jumped up to a picnic table. Cars passed behind her, and a vise gripped Zamzam's chest. But then the cars would pass without so much as an echo of a siren.

If the police came here, Zamzam and Jamal might be arrested. But she didn't worry about herself. She wouldn't let that happen to Jamal. She shoved his arm off her shoulders. "We're going home *now*."

"Let's just stay for the speech." He held his hands together in pleading prayer.

Zamzam's heart tugged in too many directions. Eventually, her cautious side won. "You're not safe here."

Jamal raised a brow at her. "Don't pretend it's safer for me anywhere else."

Zamzam's cheeks burned, and her eyes stung. Her immature little brother had aged years. She might eventually forgive Yazeed for leaving her mom and her, but she would never forgive him for leaving Jamal. For making his life just a fraction less bright. And now Zamzam's conflict with herself was hurting him. She didn't know if she could forgive herself.

Because Jamal didn't seem upset. No, he seemed empowered by the protests for the Six, and she couldn't take that away from him. He didn't have a cap on his life yet, and who was she to create one for him.

The boy on the picnic table hushed the crowd with a finger to his lips. "We're *angry*. We're *tired*. We're sick of being treated like we need to be patrolled. No privacy, no freedom. We don't even have the right to walk down the street without a target on our chests, and no decency to aim for our backs. And still our parents tell us to stay quiet and stay safe."

Zamzam shot glances in all directions as her face grew hot. There was danger in the air, and she wanted to grab Jamal and flee. But her little brother's face was so hopeful, absorbing the boy's words like they were water from a well that had been cut off from him for years.

"There is no safe place for us. Not at school, not the mall, not the beach, not even our fucking homes. We're guilty until proven innocent. They would convince us of our guilt for a crime we didn't commit." The boy's unwieldy gaze landed on Zamzam and

Samia, and the frustration in his voice mounted. "The Six are innocent. Do you need the proof? Why does the security footage they released to the media cut out before shots were fired? Why does it conveniently suggest Abdullahi's guilt in attacking Muzhda? Why do you think the leaks from a closed courtroom only further incriminate the Six? A weapon or a firework? Some of us were there, we know Qays is innocent, but no one takes us seriously when we approach them with our testimony unless our story is vague enough to fit their narrative. Why is it that the media already blamed Islamic organizations the day after the Fourth without a shred of evidence? We want the real answers!"

Zamzam and Samia exchanged a look. They had begun to search for the answers, but their search only supplied them with more questions.

The boy continued, his voice steady and strong. "Our parents might be happy with the status quo, and they may even be thanking God it wasn't any of their own kids that were roped in with the Six. But it could've been any of us. If their generation is going to take this lying down, we won't! We want a better life for us!

"It wasn't me!" He rallied the chants again. Jamal's voice shook as he repeated after him. As the chants augmented, Zamzam grew light-headed. She swayed in her spot until a hand clasped around her own.

"Sorry," Samia murmured breathlessly, her grip on Zamzam's hand tightening. "I just can't feel my body anymore."

Zamzam felt it, too—a feeling of weightlessness, of the energy overflowing, of knowing that for the first time since the Fourth, these kids felt what she felt, hurt because she hurt.

"Come up here."

Before she could refuse, the boy on the picnic table was tugging her and Samia toward the table. Every pair of eyes watching them was hungry with anticipation, and Zamzam's eyes swept the sea of kids and their cell phones held high. She let herself think, for just one second, about Yazeed watching her on his television screen. About him persisting with not contacting her, even after seeing her on the news and all that she'd had to shoulder without him. She'd eventually find the resolution within herself to give up on him, because she'd clung to the last shred of hope for him for too long.

The willow trees behind them billowed in the breeze, and Zamzam swayed. This was some kind of cruel dream.

"Say something," the boy urged her.

Her attorney's counseling echoed in her mind. *Lie low. Distance yourself from the protesters. Do not let anyone antagonize you with them. Do not make a public statement without me present. Do not express your innocence or guilt unless under my careful instruction.*

So many rules. Zamzam loved rules; they blanketed her with warm and toasty security.

Her gaze locked on her brother's in the crowd. He grinned at her.

This is definitely a dream, she thought. Because there was nothing for Jamal to grin about, not when Zamzam's hopes and dreams were in tatters. She was sacrificing everything. Her life was on the line. Did these kids not understand that? Zamzam could imagine herself being dragged to this protest by Jamal, chanting without a second thought if, by some miracle, he managed to get her away from her studying. But never did Zamzam imagine herself standing as the face of a movement.

She didn't want this. She wanted a way out, and the only way out was becoming clearer.

Through.

Jamal joined in with the others asking her to speak up, his eyes bright, his face open, proud. What did he have to be proud of?

Samia's hand felt heavy in hers. This was too much responsibility for the pair of them.

Jamal had never looked at her with such earnest pride. Not when she'd explained or implemented her grand plan to make it to medical school and beyond. Not when she'd helped Momma pick herself back up after her parents' divorce or after Yazeed left. Yet here on this weightless night at the edge of summer, Jamal was looking at his sister like she was the missing piece of a puzzle that he'd been waiting for. That even if she did go to prison with her innocence holding her chin up high, he'd be proud of her for giving the voices of their generation a vessel through which to speak.

She needed to be for Jamal the person Yazeed would never be for her. She had to fill the hole in her chest herself.

"It wasn't me," she murmured, chest bubbling.

Samia did a double take at her.

Zamzam's hands were fists. "It wasn't me." The sounds of the end of summer, crickets chirping and frogs croaking, filled the silence after.

That was all she was. A vessel. She had no speech to make. But she could affirm their beliefs. She raised the hand that was entangled with Samia's.

"It wasn't us!"

Her voice rang strong through the clearing. Her words echoed from every mouth ahead of her. The ground trembled from their conviction.

They didn't stop.

They would never stop. Not when police cars arrived, nor when tear gas was thrust at them. Not when rubber bullets turned their skin red, black, and blue. Not until the earth broke under the soles of their stamping feet, resettling into a new history.

THE LOS ANGELES JOURNAL

PROTESTS OVER THE INDEPENDENCE DAY SIX TAKE A DANGEROUS TURN

Violent protests erupt as two of the accused Six spur discontent among the public

LOS ANGELES—Over fifty protesters rampaged in a Los Angeles neighborhood in the early hours of Friday evening. Adolescents were galvanized by the appearance of Zamzam Thompson and Samia Al-Samra, two of the Independence Day Six who stand accused.

Despite their ongoing trial, Thompson and Al-Samra took to the streets, fueling anger and resentment among the public in an effort to gather support for their case. "It wasn't me!" chants were heard blocks away from the LA neighborhood.

Following police response to resident calls,

the increasing number of protesters reportedly resorted to violence. As the situation escalated, police were pressed to fire tear gas and rubber bullets into the crowd. While the exact reason for the escalation is unclear, an unnamed officer claims one protester's suspicious loitering caused a skirmish, which prompted police retaliation. The protest dispersed, and no protesters were taken into police custody. Thompson and Al-Samra, in addition to Nasreen Choudhry of the Six, remain free on bail for the duration of the trial.

LA County cautions residents that protests may be held only with written permission from the city. The confrontational response by the police was deemed necessary because of the unlawful nature of the protests, which took place just before the mayor's citywide imposed curfew.

◆

CHAPTER 38

ABDULLAHI

IF ABDULLAHI'S LIFE WERE AN '80S MOVIE, HE WISHED IT could be like *The Breakfast Club*. He'd watched the movie with his siblings, and it gave him nostalgia for a time when he didn't exist yet.

If Abdullahi's life were a scene from a '70s movie, he could picture it perfectly, could feel his heart beating erratically as he watched the OG Willy Wonka sing a horrifying poem as the boat of kids careened down the chocolate river. His parents—his siblings—should never have let him watch that movie at five years old. He learned then that all his favorite wholesome things that brought him security also had a dark side to them.

Just like that scene, the Fourth had unfolded faster and faster, and when he closed his eyes, he could see it all: the trampled beach, the crying kids, the police-car lights, the sounds of ambulances, Muzhda on the ground. Muzhda—

He was on a ride that was moving too quickly, everything coming from all directions, all at once. It was dark, and then it wasn't, and then it was dark again. He braced himself for the inevitable crash.

"Mr. Talib?"

Abdullahi looked up. The DA was speaking to him. He had taken the stand, but he only vaguely recalled agreeing to testify. He barely remembered what he was supposed to say. His body felt heavy, but his heart and his mind felt light. They were racing, unfolding, hurtling toward an understanding he'd so far struggled to come to.

Abdullahi couldn't remember a time when he wasn't all remorse. He wished to feel only regret because at least that meant he would be one step closer to resolving his guilt. But no, he still felt like the bad guy.

"Would you please identify the people in the frame?" Renner asked.

The paused frame of the video was visible to everyone in the courtroom. Abdullahi glanced at it, but he didn't need a video. He remembered the night perfectly. As the video played, he looked at his fellow defendants. His eyes glossed over Samia and Zamzam and Nasreen. They landed on Qays, whose face was all pain.

The video kept playing. Abdullahi forced his eyes to the screen. He'd spent his nights in juvie replaying the scene in his head. All alone with no one but himself and his guilt. Muzhda lay on the ground in a tangle of wires as Abdullahi approached. Abdullahi was crouched over her body. They exchanged words.

Renner paused it. "Can you tell us what was said here?"

Abdullahi wrung his hands; his throat felt almost entirely

closed. "She couldn't move. I don't know why—maybe her body was still in shock. She was in so much pain when I tried to lift her."

"But you could lift her," Renner said. He pressed Play. Past Abdullahi managed to lift Muzhda off the ground. Then, all at once, he let her go. Her body slumped over. He knew what would come next.

He should've done more. He never should have left her there. *Don't leave me. Don't leave me. Don't leave me.*

The Abdullahi on the screen looked up. His face was so clear in the footage as fear painted across it. He turned and he ran. The video cut out, the most important part of the video omitted.

Renner held up a file that he introduced into evidence as Muzhda Ahmad's autopsy report. The crash was coming. "No indication of paralysis," Renner listed, "not so much as a fracture. Just some bruises from the fall. Muzhda could have easily run."

"No," Abdullahi murmured to himself. It didn't matter what an autopsy report said. If Muzhda were here, she'd be able to tell them the pain she'd been in. That she couldn't have run.

"Mr. Talib, what was your relationship with Ms. Ahmad?"

"I'd never met her before then. I'd never seen her in my life," Abdullahi heard himself say.

"You say you had no relationship with her, so what was your motive for helping a stranger?"

"I just wanted to help." Abdullahi sounded miserable. He felt sorry for himself, and that might have been the worst feeling he'd ever felt in his whole life.

"Yet when she was examined, there was no indication of serious injuries from the fall."

Abdullahi's expression hardened. He looked between the others. Qays's face was paler than ever. Zamzam's chin quivered, and Samia's glare at Renner was icy cold. Nasreen wore her blank mask to cover up her true emotions.

What happened next was what had haunted Abdullahi from the beginning. The reason why he'd pestered Zamzam into trusting him. The reason why he'd had to convince Samia there was strength in numbers. The reason why he'd accepted his fate in juvie rather than fighting back harder.

"If she were here, she could tell you." Abdullahi tried to have strength in his voice. "If the cops hadn't shot her—"

"Muzhda Ahmad was found at the location that triggered the explosions that led to the chaos and destruction of July fourth," Renner interrupted. Using the remote, Renner zoomed in on Abdullahi's digital face. The fear. The selfishness. The desire to survive.

It looked all too much like guilt.

"The video ends." Abdullahi's voice trembled. "It ends before you see what happens next. Why does it end?"

Renner stepped forward. Clicked Play on his remote. Past Abdullahi ran off the screen. From the leaked body-cam footage of one of the officers, the world heard rounds of shots fire and then Abdullahi scream, "It wasn't me!" But Renner's video simply cut out.

"The camera broke from the impact of the explosion. Observe the time stamp," Renner noted, indicating carefully at the paused screen. Everyone knew that hour, minute, and second. They'd mulled over it every day on the news, online, in person. But it was leaked footage, which the prosecution too happily provided, that the police would usually try to keep from the courtroom.

It was the exact second the first explosion set off and the glass of the beach houses shattered. The exact moment after Qays's firework shot into the sky. The precise moment each of their lives ended and Muzhda's heartbeat dwindled until it finally stopped.

Renner drove it home. "The police who were called to the scene were aware of the dangers. They acted to protect themselves from the threat Muzhda Ahmad posed. I am not here to dispute whether the police acted hastily, or whether or not they fired shots too eagerly, the public has enough discourse on that. But Muzhda Ahmad didn't run, and now she is dead. Though the crimes she is suspected of still have lasting consequences. You ran that night so you can speak today. The threat you pose still exists."

Renner's words were like knives pushing into Abdullahi's ears. The truth that haunted him spoken openly. It had become impossible to exonerate himself of the guilt. As Qays's face crumpled, Abdullahi claimed responsibility for his torment. When Abdullahi caught Fatima staring at him from her seat, she mouthed something to him.

It's not your fault.

Abdullahi's guilt shattered. Regret seeped in, filling all the cracks.

"Why did you run, Mr. Talib?" Renner asked.

The entire courtroom shifted left. He knew this question was coming. He knew how the truth could sound. The transformation of his guilt gave way to some clarity. "I saw the police, and

I was confused because nothing happened yet. No explosions, nothing. I was worried they'd think I had something to do with Muzhda being hurt. I was trying to avoid a confrontation that could've ended with my arrest."

Renner's lips curled ever so slightly. "You ran from police to avoid looking guilty and getting arrested, which then only made you look more guilty and got you arrested?"

"It's not my fault that police look at people like me and automatically think the worst. They shouldn't have been there anyway." Abdullahi paused. "Unless they knew what was going to happen. They were in full gear."

Renner barely bristled, but Abdullahi instantly regretted provoking him. "The police responded to a civilian call. They were notified via IT of the signal from Muzhda's location. Muzhda is the one who set it up, who was the premeditated portion of your operation. So when you saw the police approach the source of your operation and your plan with Muzhda went south, you panicked and ran. Isn't that right?"

Objections rebounded across the courtroom. It didn't matter that Abdullahi no longer had to respond to that; Renner had already planted the idea in the jurors' minds.

Renner turned his back to him, and Abdullahi knew he wanted to end it there. But he couldn't, wouldn't let that be what he left the stand at.

"The questions remain," Renner said methodically, more to the jurors than to him. "How much of this crime did you know of, and how much did Muzhda Ahmad keep to herself?"

Abdullahi knew he could retain some innocence if he blamed Muzhda and claimed ignorance. Instead, he was all the more positive that Muzhda was as innocent as he was, except she didn't have what Abdullahi did: the ability to defend herself.

As Renner took a seat, Abdullahi's brain raced with the poem that kept him up at night. The final stanza of Willy Wonka's poem echoed in his mind. Because the danger was growing. And he was speeding straight into it. Faster and faster and faster.

It ended in a crash.

CHAPTER 39

QAYS

HAD IT BEEN TWENTY-EIGHT OR TWENTY-SEVEN BEADS ON her bracelet?

When had Muzhda gotten it back? How was she here?

The fuses in Qays's brain were popping and sparking in short circuits. He watched Muzhda pace in front of him in the common area, her arms swaying exaggeratedly, the bracelet resting on her wrist for everyone to see. Earlier that day, Abdullahi's testimony had tilted his reality. Renner referenced an autopsy.

Autopsies were for dead people, and Muzhda was right in front of him. All of her. Skin and bones but solid, tired but bright, and so very restless. She was describing the way Favreau had looked at Samia and Zamzam in court and spun tall tales about the connection she imagined between them. Her voice was as true as every breath he took. Muzhda breathed like he breathed, lived like he lived.

Muzhda turned to him then. Her lips curled, revealing the slight gap between her teeth, and her long lashes framed her eyes, which sparkled like stars. She took a step toward him, and he flinched. Her smile smudged, and Qays's chest pulsed with fear.

She recoiled, her hands moving unnaturally slowly, as though she were reaching from another place. "You're scared of me."

Qays's mind was a flurry of the events of the Fourth. He'd sent Muzhda down the beach; that much he knew was true. But the videos of what followed that night, the videos he'd seen today in court, those were real in a way that Muzhda wasn't. And if what they said was true, then Muzhda wasn't here. She was a figment of his imagination, a hallucination manifested from his guilt. He dreaded the guilt more than the apparition in front of him.

In the courtroom, Abdullahi was a mirror of him.

"Y-you're not real," he stuttered. But wasn't she?

She laughed. It was a wonderful laugh; he remembered it from the long afternoons reading her stories. Its memory was the only thing keeping Qays from giving up and resigning to life in a cell. "Of course I'm real," she said, but her voice was strained. She didn't sound like herself.

Qays felt his composure breaking; he needed answers quickly, before his mind came to a conclusion it wasn't ready for. He needed her to tell him the videos weren't real, that she was. "Then why don't you testify? If you'd speak up, you could poke holes in their case. They use you in every way they can to make us look guilty. You're their key piece."

Muzhda shrugged and spun in a circle. The borders that made her whole were blurring. He felt his thoughts fray along with her. It took every ounce of his strength to not fall to his knees.

Her eyes fixed on him, and he desperately searched for her in their fierce gaze. "But you know I didn't do it," she whispered.

"They don't care what I think," he snapped.

She hummed to herself, ignoring him as she swayed in a half dance about the room. It was so out of character that he tried to call on a story or a memory of her to make sense of this version of her. Nothing he could recall could remedy her. It was like looking at a ghost.

"Give me your bracelet," he demanded.

She closed the distance between them cautiously. Picking her bracelet off, she handed it to him. He counted twenty-eight beads.

It was all wrong. He hadn't forgotten. He'd counted them over and over and over again until he'd committed it to memory.

Twenty-seven beads on Muzhda's bracelet. Ten red, ten black, six letters, one heart.

But this one had twenty-eight beads. Eleven red, ten black, six letters, one heart. It was all wrong because it wasn't real. It faded into nothing.

Qays's heartbeat drummed loud in his ears. It was as if the lights had been off all this time, and now that they'd turned on, he had no clue where he was. Along the way his shiny life had rusted in an unlit corner void of color, and he'd become accustomed to the dark.

He had to say it louder. He had to taste the words and give Muzhda the chance to deny it.

"You aren't real."

This time Muzhda didn't laugh. Her lips pressed into a thin line, and her artful brows knit. Anger flashed across her face, coloring her eyes with betrayal. When he looked at her, his eyes couldn't focus. She was losing definition. She was leaking color.

She was turning gray. Qays wished he could scream—*anything but the gray, don't let it take her too*—but he was empty.

She clutched Qays's wrist, but he didn't feel her touch. She pressed his palm firmly against her chest over her heart. Still nothing. He pressed, desperately trying to anchor himself in something solid, but all he felt was air. His skin prickled, like a million ants numbing him from all sensation.

"Say that again," she challenged. "Tell me I'm not real."

He wished so badly to feel her against his palm that tears shot up into his eyes. He'd tricked himself so long he nearly duped himself again, imagining a heartbeat where there wasn't. But she was so real to him. The stories she'd written lived in his mind and had filled in all the gaps. They made her real. He cupped her hazy cheek in his hand. Nothing, nothing, nothing.

Yet her apparition fluttered her eyes closed and tilted her head into his palm.

"Tell me you don't feel this," she whispered.

A strangled sob escaped Qays's throat. He didn't feel anything. It was all a lie. His memories righted themselves and surged through his head at a cruel frequency.

She hadn't been in the cop car when they were arrested and he was placed in custody. Hadn't been there as he lay in tatters in his police cell wondering if he'd achieve all he wanted. Hadn't been transported to this jail with him. Hadn't been telling him her fictional fantasies or her sincerest secrets every day to pass the time. Hadn't been there to hold him as he mourned his future.

312

Every part of him felt fractured, impossible to be made whole again. It ached to erase her.

But she wasn't erased. She had never been. Qays had projected her, called on the memories of her stories to help him bind her to the world of the living instead of letting her go. Even now, he grasped at her when she wasn't there.

"It's my fault," he cried.

Her eyes opened in slits. The anger had dissipated into bitter acceptance. "Why did you make me go down the beach that night?" she murmured, tears leaking and streaming down her cheeks. "I would still be here if you never told me to go."

"I was so selfish," Qays croaked. "I didn't think—I—I just didn't think."

He remembered it then, the stretcher that had carried her on the Fourth. While he was ushered into the police car, he watched them wheel her into an ambulance, her body unmoving. Her smooth brown skin lacking its glow, without its color.

Muzhda pulled away from him and wiped at her tears, feigning resolve. "You did think. You knew you were using me, and you thought I'd be happy to do whatever you wanted as long as it pleased you."

"No." Qays shook his head furiously. "I would never think that. I was just being stupid."

"Look at where that brought me!" she yelled. Her silhouette splintered into a million sparks that shot back into one dark figure, but she wasn't going back to the Muzhda from before. "I'm *dead*. They shot me four times in my back because they thought I was trying to blow up the beach. Trying to blow up my *home*. And for what? To get high with your friends?"

Qays's body rejected the truth in her words. He felt bile push up his throat, and he dropped his head between his arms to stop it from coming up.

"And I can't even defend myself." Her voice softened. "This case will end, and you and the others will go to prison because I can't testify that I can't type with all my fingers on a keyboard, let alone work that equipment. But it doesn't matter, because I am the image of anti-American."

He lifted his head. She stood with her chin up, hijab swathed across her chest. An immigrant. Brown. Undocumented. Muslim. Her words were so obviously faulty. None of that delegitimized her, but that didn't matter in a system where the four bullets in her chest were never questioned.

"I'll get justice for you." Qays didn't know where this promise came from.

Then she was kneeling in front of him, smoothing away the tears on his cheeks with her thumb. "I'm already gone," she said. Her voice was gentle and almost forgiving. Qays didn't deserve it. She continued, as tender as she'd ever been. "You sent me down the beach that night, but I'm the fool that went. I *wanted* to go. It was my excuse to see you again. If you want to honor me, then never, *never* stop believing in your future, no matter what happens. You're my Stanford-bound homecoming king."

He looked deep into her eyes; she was so real, so present, he felt he could kiss her. She wasn't an illusion, she was Muzhda, *his* Muzhda, and she'd stay with him for as long as he didn't let her move on.

She nodded, just barely. Qays leaned forward into her embrace. He might have cried into her shoulder for hours, but time held no meaning with Muzhda. When he couldn't stay awake anymore, and his eyes began to twitch and his eyelids grew heavy, he had no other choice. His weak muscles screamed in protest as he relinquished his grasp on her, and she faded until finally, Qays was truly alone.

CHAPTER 40

SAMIA

SAMIA SPENT HOURS PINCHING HER PHONE SCREEN, EYES scanning the pixelated papers for clues. She searched every name she came across until she started to think that she'd been given a false lead. Maybe she'd banked too hard on the anonymous tips she'd received. Maybe Lori Cox was nothing but a dead end.

Samia made sure her parents and siblings weren't home before texting Zamzam to come over, so they could pore over the final photos together. Her parents wouldn't be happy that she was hanging out so casually with another defendant, but Zamzam was her friend now. Besides, the less people knew about their private investigation, the easier it would be for her to swallow her disappointment if nothing came of it and the less attention they'd call to themselves and the investigation.

Zamzam opened up her laptop on Samia's bed while Samia blew up the pictures on her desktop computer. They perused the photos, picking out names or departments, chasing dead ends.

"Wait, I didn't see this one yet," Zamzam said. "It says Alexander Nguyen." She showed Samia her screen. A file on Cox's desk had a copy of a nondisclosure agreement addressed to Alexander Nguyen, filed by PetroMile's human resources department.

"But I can't read what the NDA says," Zamzam said. The words were impossible to make out zoomed in on her laptop.

"I can fix that." She spun away from the bed to her desk. Meanwhile, Zamzam propped herself on her stomach as Samia clicked away at her big desktop. She opened an editing app, cropped the photo, and sharpened the quality in seconds. She read it off for Zamzam.

"The Nondisclosure Agreement, hereinafter referred to as the 'Agreement,' is entered between PetroMile & Co., hereinafter referred to as the 'Disclosing Party,' and Alexander Nguyen, hereinafter referred to as the 'Receiving Party,' as of July fifth. Whereas this Agreement is created for the purpose of preventing unauthorized disclosure regarding the events that took place the evening of July fourth..."

The air left Samia's lungs.

"Keep reading," Zamzam urged, hands waving frantically.

"The rest is covered with other papers. I can't see it."

Zamzam crossed the room to get a look. "There's an address."

Samia widened her eyes at her. "You want to go see this person?"

"Maybe we can get some answers."

"He signed an NDA. He isn't going to give any answers," Samia said, though she hoped it wasn't true.

Zamzam's lids were heavy with impatience. "Aren't you the one who sneaked us into PetroMile? Why so reserved?"

Samia pushed her hexagon-shaped lenses up the bridge of her nose. Ever since Abdullahi's testimony, she was worried that the more they chased the truth, the more disappointed they might become. "And how are we doing that?"

"We'll learn something," Zamzam insisted. "You know, with each of our half a detective's brain."

Samia reached for her hijab and wrapped it with practiced efficiency, no mirror required. "Are you being an optimist?"

Zamzam side-eyed her. "Never."

Samia laced her arm through Zamzam's. "You can't lie to me."

Once they reached the car with the GPS locked on their location, Samia peeled out of her driveway and sped onto the freeway. She cut the estimated time by seven minutes, and the girls were one beige town house door away from an answer or more questions.

Zamzam rang the doorbell. Twice. Samia counted the seconds until the door opened. Just a crack. A man peered at them, sparse stubble across his chin.

"Can I help you?" His voice cracked.

Samia seized up, her eyes falling on the dozens of moving boxes stacked behind him.

"Are you Alexander Nguyen?" Zamzam asked.

"Who's asking?"

Samia threw a furtive glance Zamzam's way. "Um..."

"We just have some questions." Zamzam took over. "We aren't reporters or anything."

Alexander's eyes widened. "I know you two. I've seen your faces on the news."

Caught. Samia reached out for Zamzam's wrist to get ready to leave.

"How did you find me?" His eyes darted behind them, as if Zamzam and Samia brought backup or cameras. Maybe they should have.

"We just want to ask you a few questions," Zamzam promised.

"I don't have anything to say to you," he said, already shutting the door.

But Zamzam was faster. She reached out to stop it from closing. "We both know that's not true. You were at Monarch Beach on the Fourth. Maybe you can help us."

He slinked back from the door. "I wasn't anywhere on the Fourth."

"Please," Zamzam pleaded. "We know you signed an NDA with PetroMile. We know you know the truth about what happened."

"I can't," he bit out, immune to Zamzam's desperation. "I can't help you. Don't try to find me again." He began to close his door.

Zamzam pressed against it. "Did they pay you?" she asked. Her question gave Alexander pause. *"Please."* She sounded so small and hopeless that Alexander's eyes softened.

"You can't be here," he whispered, peering outside to look

behind them. Samia pulled her sweatshirt closer to herself, remembering there could be people watching. He spoke in a hushed voice. "I don't work at PetroMile anymore. I'm moving away from here, and I'm not going to have anything to do with any of this anymore. If they knew you were here, they'd come after me thinking I breached the agreement. I can't help you."

"So that's it?" Zamzam asked. "You're going to let them send us to jail even though you know it wasn't us?"

"Only if they find you guilty," he replied. Impossibly, Samia heard sympathy.

"PetroMile is a billion-dollar company," Samia interceded, heart pounding. "You think we have a chance against that?"

The tiles were falling into place for them. They weren't only up against a system that already believed them guilty; they were up against more money than they could imagine, money that crushed everything in its path to protect its own.

Alexander shook his head. He shut his door and locked it with a decisive click. The girls blinked at the beige paint.

Alexander Nguyen was a dead end.

"What now?" Zamzam's voice was tinged with desperation.

Samia shut off the recording on her phone. Though she'd had the foresight to record their exchange, she doubted there was anything in it the prosecution couldn't pick apart. They'd show the NDA to their attorneys. Samia would share her recording of Alexander saying fuck all. Zamzam, Samia, and Nasreen would testify soon. The prosecution would tear them apart as they had Abdullahi and Qays, and nothing could change that because they had run out of time. Muzhda couldn't come back from the dead.

Her life was already taken from her. The rest of theirs were to follow.

Even with what little information they'd gathered from Alexander Nguyen and PetroMile, it was too late. Their attorneys could do nothing but stare at these extra pieces of a puzzle that was already complete.

CHAPTER 41

NASREEN

IT HAD BEEN TWO MONTHS SINCE NASREEN HADN'T WOKEN up from her nightmare.

Ms. Carson prepared Nasreen with stunning accuracy for her moment on the stand. She answered every one of Renner's questions just as they rehearsed. Short and vaguely truthful.

Nasreen was last in the line of questioning. Zamzam's and Samia's testimonies were fraught with anger and objections; the two girls had brought it on themselves to be defensive. They seemed obsessed with what really happened.

From Nasreen's time with Ms. Carson, she knew that digging deeper into the truth was useless. Ms. Carson had done her fair share of digging, except she hadn't gone poking where she wasn't supposed to. Instead, she focused on making Nasreen's testimony faultless.

In the face of Renner's gargantuan insinuations, Nasreen acted small.

"Why were you at an event when you have no affiliation with the participating schools?"

"These events are open to the public. A lot of nonstudents attend," Nasreen answered him. It was a half-truth, and she avoided Samia's gaze as she said it.

Nasreen coasted as well as she could, reading off a script in her mind, her voice disassociating from her body. Next, Ms. Carson approached the stand to tie up loose threads.

"Could you tell us about your experience at the bonfire?"

Nasreen delivered the scripted words effortlessly. "I go to Saint Modesta. It's a Catholic private school, so there aren't that many Muslims at my school. I'm the only one in my class. Even though I went to the bonfire, I didn't feel like I belonged. I didn't belong."

Even as she said the words, she knew them to be false. Her parents had assured her that they were white lies. A version of the truth that distanced her from the others. So that the jury might see them as the *Other* and not her. She'd agreed to this in Ms. Carson's office, so why was she so ashamed? Why couldn't she bear to look at Samia?

Samia had given a white lie too. She had testified under oath that she didn't know Nasreen before the Fourth. For Samia, that was technically true.

Ms. Carson posed her next question. "You have no affiliation with any clubs or organizations linked to practicing the Islamic faith? At school or otherwise?"

Nasreen's shoulders tensed as untruths bubbled in her chest. "Not really. I go to the mosque for prayers in Ramadan sometimes, but that's all."

"Ms. Choudhry." Ms. Carson shifted so that she wasn't facing Nasreen and the jury, but Nasreen alone. Her tone turned sympathetic. "Is there a reason why you distance yourself from other Muslim boys and girls?"

Nasreen froze. This wasn't in their rehearsed exchange. Ms. Carson inclined her head toward her. There was an answer she wanted. Nasreen had been around Ms. Carson long enough to know what it was, and Ms. Carson had all Nasreen's secrets.

The question threw her off guard. "I'm not sure I understand your question," she said.

"Let me rephrase," Ms. Carson amended. "Do you have any reason to feel unsafe among your Muslim peers?"

Nasreen's eyes swept the bench. Samia was red with anger, but she was always angry when the subject was Nasreen. Even though there should be only one defense, the four remaining Six were on one side, and Nasreen was on another. This was her chance to save herself from everyone else's fate, should fate swing the wrong way for them.

She hadn't been thoughtless. She had cloaked her IP address when she corresponded with Samia as Faris using the skills she'd learned from her coding class at SM. It gave her a chance at innocence. How could she let go of that?

"Not really," Nasreen murmured.

"Not really?" Ms. Carson repeated louder. "In other words, you feel unsafe in front of some of the defendants to some degree. Could you tell me why?"

Her parents sat in the gallery, watching her with stricken faces. Nasreen was shocked by her answer herself. Was this a white lie anymore, or were they very real lies? "Not—not unsafe," she stammered. "Uncomfortable."

"But if these are your peers, why would you feel uncomfortable?" Ms. Carson pressed.

Nasreen's eyes darted to Samia. Ms. Carson was cornering her into an answer. "I feel different." She materialized the words. "It's uncomfortable when you feel different."

"How would you say you're not like the others?"

Renner objected, perhaps out of confusion. Ms. Carson assured the judge of the validity of her question.

Stifling discomfort cloyed at Nasreen's vocal cords. Her eyes swept the bench, to a despondent Qays, an exhausted Abdullahi, an exasperated Zamzam, an irate Samia. She didn't feel so different from them then. The opposite was true; she was all the things they were, with some additional emotions unique to her. Like her, they were victims of their own selves in other ways.

But Ms. Carson wanted an answer. A white lie would do. Ms. Carson's job was to exonerate her. The truth didn't matter.

Nasreen's nails dug into her palms. "We're not the same. We come from different places. We go to different schools. We don't all adhere to the same rules."

"And what rules do you not adhere to, Ms. Choudhry?"

Nasreen didn't want to go further. She didn't care for the final push that would set her apart from others, because it wasn't Ms. Carson's decision to out her. The truth was, Nasreen didn't know who she was or what she liked. She had lived her whole life hiding behind different faces: the daughter to make her parents happy, the ideal boy to keep messaging Samia, the confident girl to cover up her feelings of not belonging anywhere.

Ms. Carson was still waiting for Nasreen's answer. Nasreen gulped, feeling miserable. They couldn't have rehearsed how pitiable Nasreen looked. She wasn't that good of an actor.

The jury would buy it.

"I just don't," Nasreen murmured into her lap. She couldn't look anyone in the eyes. She hadn't come outright with the truth, but Ms. Carson had set her up, and Nasreen was the perfect victim. She knew what she had to say. Ms. Carson may have been mean, but she had her best interest at heart. "I'm just not like them," she said emotionlessly.

Ms. Carson nodded, satisfied. She went on, spinning a narrative that saved not only Nasreen but Samia as well. She wondered why Ms. Carson was lumping them together—was it just for the convenience of them being found so far away from the others? Was she lessening the blow to Nasreen's conscience by not turning all of them against her?

Ms. Carson was the professional, and Nasreen had entrusted her with her life. But that didn't make her actions feel any less dirty. Perhaps she could take back her words before she left the stand, and she could make things right. And by *right* she meant *true*.

"That'll be all," Ms. Carson concluded.

As Nasreen stood, she glanced at Samia. Her freedom for the mortifying disappointment spreading across the other girl's face.

Maybe one day, after Nasreen figured out who she was going to be, she could reconcile with Samia and rekindle a friendship that wasn't prefaced with a fake profile picture. Maybe Samia would be kind enough to forget this day.

326

But that didn't seem likely, not anymore. Nasreen had thrown the remaining Six to the wolves for her chance at getting her life back.

She walked back to the bench. Once she was no longer under oath, she told herself a lie that would keep her awake for years to come.

For their freedom, they would have done the same as me.

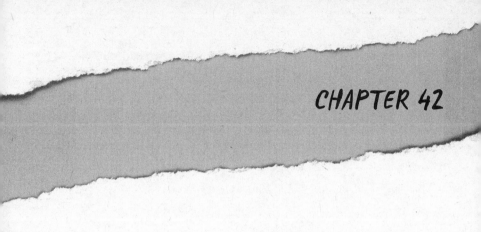

CHAPTER 42

THE FOLLOWING WERE THE EVENTS OF JULY 4 AS BELIEVED
by the jury in the case of the Independence Day Six.

1. Witness testimony and video footage support that
   Muzhda Ahmad, Qays Sharif, Zamzam Thompson,
   Samia Al-Samra, and Abdullahi Talib were in
   communication and/or correspondence the night of
   and/or prior to the date of attack.
2. There is reasonable doubt that Nasreen Choudhry
   and Samia Al-Samra were connected to the other
   suspects and in the following events.
3. In a premeditated attack, as evidenced by Exhibits
   121–134, Ahmad triggered the explosion on oil rig
   Bonnie using stolen PetroMile technology. Substantial

evidence in the form of a civilian call and video footage incriminates Ahmad.

4. Talib and Sharif abetted Ahmad on the night of attack, as evidenced by video footage and eyewitness accounts. Additionally, Sharif and Thompson acted as a distraction to aid Ahmad and Talib in carrying out the attack. Implies conspiracy to the terror attack.

5. Prior relationships between Talib and Al-Samra suggested Al-Samra's involvement; however, a sentence recommendation was rescinded. Al-Samra and Choudhry were apprehended on the north side of the beach, wherein they had been arrested owing to the suspicion of foul play; however, any damage sustained was from residual vibrations of the explosion site.

These facts led to verdicts to be declared the following day in court.

Favreau did everything in her power for American democracy and freedom. A few months of grueling work, and the country was safer for it. After the trial, along with millions of other Americans, she'd rest her head on her pillow and sleep without worries. Her morning coffee would wake her up, not with a jolt, but with a calm, flowery awakening. She'd happily drive up to the drive-through window and collect her breakfast before her work schedule returned to its routine. That was the American comfort she vowed to protect. The comfort she had restored.

CHAPTER 43

ZAMZAM

IMAGINE A BEACH, BUT THE WAVES STOP CRASHING.

Imagine looking out at an expanse of sea, watching the water break at the crest of the wave, slamming against the sand, except no sound ever reaches you.

Imagine if the ocean were a desert.

Zamzam's world went silent in her ears after the words left from the presiding juror's mouth.

"We, the jury, find the defendants Zamzam Thompson and Abdullahi Talib, guilty—"

All sound cut out. Like a vacuum, the courtroom stilled about her and then began to swallow her life. Slowly from the periphery, then sharp and fast at the center. The presiding juror took his seat, heads dropped into hands, red faces screamed empty air, the bailiff sprung into the gallery, and the gavel struck wood.

Then Zamzam's eyes shut, and there was a cluster of hands

touching her, her body hitting the seat of her chair, her tears wetting her cheeks. The rest of the juror's words came through later, muffled under thousands of layers of soundless space.

Qays Sharif, guilty.

Muzhda Ahmad, even in her grave, *guilty.*

Nasreen Choudhry and Samia Al-Samra, not *guilty.*

Zamzam's eyes shot open, but the courtroom had already emptied, the thick air swimming with remnants of rage. As she was escorted out, her eyes locked onto Favreau's, her mouth twisted into a smug expression. Pennella tweaked his tie beside her.

Her attorney spoke rapidly to her, saying the word *appeal* to her in various sentence structures and sometimes the words *retrial, more evidence,* and *PetroMile.* But Zamzam had eyes and ears only for her mother, in a puddle of her tears, Jamal's lanky arm swooping her into a side embrace. His chin quivered as he hid his tears, his gaze averted behind their mother.

When her world went quiet, a heavy weight pressed against her eardrums instead of sound. The lines under her eyes were after-products of weary time, like the irreversible cracks in centuries-old stone.

She blinked, and she was back on the beach on the Fourth, hand clasped around Qays's wrist, panting breaths and thudding pulse. But instead of the sirens and the roaring waves, the quiet consumed everything. Nothing before or after the word *guilty* had audio.

The ocean had become a desert.

She would never hear *MD* after her name. She would never hope to see Yazeed sitting at the very back of the auditorium at her graduation as she gave her valedictorian speech. *What was the point?* Zamzam thought. *That girl will never be me.*

Zamzam's everything diminished with one word. She'd never be able to see London or Seoul. She'd never be able to make hajj. No matter how much she tried, she'd never be able to work in the one field that had defined her existence until then.

Her voice cracked, and she released a tortured sob. Sound rushed back all at once. Like a tsunami it crashed into her, pounded against her, drowned her. It rushed and flooded her ears, filling them like a cup overflowing with water. There was sound now, but it reached her through a thick panel of liquid, so dull it meant nothing.

The word *guilty* meant nothing. Not when Zamzam was innocent. Not when she and Samia knew there was a paper trail and their attorneys floundered around, failing to touch the giant that was PetroMile.

Zamzam stood, bracing her feet against the floor. If they went after PetroMile, the tsunamis would keep coming, crashing into her, filling her mind and ears with static, but for her mother and Jamal, she couldn't let the waves topple her.

She turned, her eyes falling on Abdullahi, who remained on the bench, an unreadable expression frozen on his face as he waited to be transferred to another juvenile-detention hall, where his sentence would mature. Because they were kids who'd been sentenced for crimes only adults could do. Unless the kids looked like them.

They lived in Schrödinger's box. In the experiment, a cat was locked in a box with a radioactive atom. The cat went in alive, and so long as the box was locked, the cat was dead and alive until the box was opened and revealed its fate.

They lived in that box like free people, but as life unfolded, the illusion fell away. In Schrödinger's box with that radioactive atom, they would always be free and not free, equal and unequal, alive and dead.

Zamzam was acquainted with the box. She had planned to become a doctor despite its limits. But the events on the Fourth shook up the box, and the paradox she'd become accustomed to was no longer a theory. It was life.

She ripped her eyes away from Abdullahi's and was escorted out of the courtroom, profoundly and strangely calm. Because for Zamzam, she finally had an answer to her Schrödinger's paradox.

CHAPTER 44

NASREEN

It had been ninety-three days since Nasreen hadn't woken up from her nightmare and thirteen days since her name had been cleared. While school had been in session for over a month, Nasreen had yet to attend classes. But as she entered the second week post-trial, she couldn't put it off much longer.

Her mama and baba were adamant: Nasreen was to continue her life as if this summer had never happened. They thought resuming normal life would bring their daughter back to them. The one who didn't lie in bed waiting patiently for her alarm clock to ring, blinking up at the ceiling fan as the sun gradually brightened her bedroom. The one who got more than two hours of light sleep a night that she sometimes fell into after Fajr. The one who greeted her parents with a smile and a hug. The one who wasn't haunted by the words she'd said in the courtroom.

Not like them.

Her alarm went off, and she lifted her duvet, which seemed to weigh tons. She dressed in her long navy stockings, despite the hellish October wind and scorching sun. Lethargically, she slipped on her burgundy-and-white pleated skirt that hung low on her shrunken waist, her undershirt, and her blazer. She smoothed the Modesta the Moth badge, the unremarkable Saint Modesta mascot, over her breast pocket. She tied her hair back in a low ponytail and adjusted her glasses. She turned away from the mirror before she could see her reflection.

She was sure she looked exactly as she had on the last day of the previous school year, if a couple centimeters taller and pounds lighter, but now she barely glanced at Carrots and never cleaned his cage, leaving that to her parents. She skipped breakfast most days, today included. Mama gave her a ride to school, Nasreen's eyes trained on the polished flats Mama had bought her for the new school year. They were too tight around her toes, and the stiff insole applied pressure up her legs. She hyperfocused on the feeling in her cramped feet.

Mama craned her neck down to peek at Nasreen's face. Her eyes turned down, the crinkles in her face communicating sorrow, telling a sad story. "Allah hafiz."

Nasreen snapped out of her daze and shot a look out the window, where she glimpsed the stone SAINT MODESTA HIGH SCHOOL sign down the street. She opened her door and returned her mother's farewell. She was sure to shut the door without glancing at Mama's affected gaze.

As Mama drove away, Nasreen bowed her head, making her way through Saint Modesta's tall iron gates, to first period, into an empty seat—all without raising her eyes off the floor. Pairs of shoes turned away from her wherever she walked, and in her class, forearms and desks shifted away from her. She heard the screeching of table legs as they jerked away.

The whispers followed. The rumors were more zealous than the news stories. They were too untrue and vicious to repeat, and they echoed in her mind.

"Ms. Choudhry."

Nasreen flinched and looked up, but it wasn't her AP English teacher who had called her name. The head of Supervision, Joan, filled the doorway, staring straight at her, her signature scorn plastered on her face, but with a shade more enmity than usual. "Come with me, please."

Nasreen gathered her belongings with shaking hands. She'd never been called up by Supervision before. She'd thought she'd gone through enough this summer that it would've made her immune to any authority. Rather, it made her more anxious.

She followed Joan down the English hall as the girls in the classroom erupted in a volcano of gossip as soon as she was out the door. They left the air-conditioned halls and walked across the quad. Joan held open the door to the science hall.

"Watch your step," Joan warned as they approached a janitor's cart beside a row of lockers. "Your locker is here," she told her. "Some girls made a bit of a mess."

Nasreen wanted to stop and take in the vandalism of her locker, but Joan quickly whisked her away. But Nasreen had seen enough. Awful words were graffitied across her locker, and a person's silhouette was drawn on it, black Xs scribbled for eyes.

Nasreen's heartbeat clawed at the base of her throat. The trial was over. She was found *not guilty*, so she should be free of their hate. But it made no difference; she would always be lumped together with them. Ms. Carson's expert games and tactics didn't change that. The only place she was innocent was in the law. In the real world, she fit the image of their enemy.

Joan knocked on the principal's door, said, "Wait here," and then left in a cloud of acrimony aimed at her. When the principal finally opened the door, Nasreen's panicky friend Gustavo tugged at her fears.

"Good morning, Ms. Choudhry." He greeted her with a curt smile. "Come in, come in."

Nasreen managed to take a seat.

"It's so nice to have you back," he lied, but Nasreen saw right through it. In his eyes, Nasreen was surely a public relations nightmare for a school that gleaned profit from prestige. "As Joan might have told you, we have concerns about your safety on campus. There are some who are very passionate about our country and are understandably angry. We've spoken to the students and prepared them for your return, but it seems there are those who are still upset about the events of this summer and are lashing out."

Nasreen didn't lift her eyes away from his chin. Gustavo radiated anxiety through her head.

"I want you to know that you'll be completely safe here and that our Supervision will be vigilant to make sure no one steps out of line," he said. "Does that sound good?"

She nodded minutely, but she'd already heard all of this. Before her decision to return, she had had a meeting with her parents and the principal over video to discuss it. Her parents had never been as content to wire the thousands of dollars for her tuition as after that meeting.

"Now," he began hesitantly, "I will have to ask you to be extra cautious. I've discussed with the school board, and they agreed that we impose a couple of rules. These are simply guidelines to keep you out of harm's way."

"Guidelines?" Nasreen repeated, her voice hoarse. Her skin prickled with gooseflesh, but it was the principal who licked his lips and crossed his shaky hands over his desk.

He's nervous, she realized.

"They're quite simple," he said, his words spilling out of him too fast. "You may not sign up for any clubs nor participate as a board member nor be a part of a sports team or any school committee or organization such as Yearbook or ASB. Nonacademic classes such as art, band, theater, and the like will also be restricted to minimize unnecessary extracurricular activity. It will also be helpful if you indicate the locations in which you will eat lunch or study on campus so we can provide proper protection. We'll only be able to do that if we know where you are at all times."

Nasreen lifted her eyes to his. A slick sheen of sweat gleamed off his forehead. He waited patiently, observing her reaction carefully while maintaining a mask of innocence. He wanted Nasreen to believe that he only wanted what was best for her, but she knew this wasn't for her. This was for the school's reputation. This was because he saw her as a threat and he wanted to protect the other students from her.

"If it's so unsafe for me here, why didn't you just revoke my admission?" she asked, regaining control of her voice and kicking

Gustavo out of her head. Her parents had spent thousands of dollars for her to be a fish in a fishbowl where she couldn't learn to play instruments or be on the debate team with any of the other fish. Sure, Ms. Carson said they'd press charges for the damage the trial had done to her life, but this couldn't be fixed by any amount of money.

The damage was already in people's heads, and it had been there so long that no one knew it was there or that it needed a name. It had been there so long that it was a part of their minds' framework.

He pulled at his tie. "You're a Modesta Moth. Once a Moth, always a Moth."

Something in Nasreen broke. Her mouth split into a wicked smile, and before she knew it, she was guffawing. He wanted to monitor her, segregate her from the rest of the school under the guise of protection. He'd probably taken her parents' money knowing this was the plan. Maybe to some degree the school's plan would keep her safe, but they were juggling her like she was radioactive, careful not to disturb the environment around her that could combust at any moment.

She was familiar with this controlled environment. Sometimes it felt like Nasreen's whole life was a big, controlled experiment. She didn't step on anyone's toes, and she did her best to make it to the next day without causing trouble. Not so much as a ripple in the events. Even when her life had come to the brink of destruction, she'd stepped aside and let Ms. Carson find a way to bring her back to this screwed-up normal.

Nasreen could take the principal's guidelines at face value, just like she'd done with everything else in her life. She could attend school quietly, live within the security of her diving bell. Or she could take his guidelines and shove them up his ass.

She'd had the same feeling when she was on the stand—that flicker of anger at Ms. Carson. The knowing that she was wrong even before saying the words.

Not like them.

Her life was a cage called freedom. *Freedom. Free. Dom. Freed. Om.* If she said the word enough times, it was just disjointed sounds. It had no meaning.

She looked up through the little window in her diving bell. It wasn't too bad, the diving bell. Maybe she'd stay in there for a while longer. Days, months, years. It was safe and deceivingly comforting. But to stay in her diving bell, she had to do it on her terms.

She rose to her feet, ignoring the pain in her soles, and clasped her hand over the badge on her blazer. She pulled it off quickly, ripping the fabric in places. She tossed it onto his desk.

"Fuck your Moths."

Before he could reply, she was out the door, running through the front office and out the front doors, her chest heaving as she gulped air. Stomping toward the gates, she looked up at the length of the school's parking lot. She expected to feel laden with humiliation; instead she felt like she was taking the first breaths of fresh air she'd had in months.

Her stomping softened to a light stroll as she reached the gates. She stood in the center of them, facing the school grounds. Spreading her arms and tilting her head back, she screamed curses at the school, the Moths, Ms. Carson, Favreau, all of them.

"And fuck you, too, Nasreen!" she yelled at herself in the third person. That one made her feel the lightest of all.

A slow clap sounded behind her. She spun around, flinching. Samia stood there, leaning against her car, lollipop in her mouth, legs crossed. She was dressed in pristine white coveralls, a patterned hijab like Neapolitan ice cream swirling over her hair and tasseled fuchsia earrings floating above her shoulders. She wore no makeup, her face scrubbed so raw it was also a shade of pink.

She looked exhausted from sleepless nights, just like Nasreen.

Samia pressed her rose-colored sunglasses back up her nose after she'd given Nasreen sufficient side-eye. "Love the outfit," Samia commented out the side of her mouth. "I personally couldn't pull off the prep-school style."

It was a lie—Samia could pull off anything. "What are you doing here?" Nasreen asked, an edge of worry inching into her voice.

Samia tilted her head toward the gates. "I came to see the campus. I'm thinking of transferring."

"Then we'll just miss each other. I doubt they'll have me back now that I blew up in front of the principal."

Samia shushed her. "Don't say 'blow up' or the FBI will come after us again."

"Right, right," Nasreen replied. Samia hadn't intended it as a joke nor as a true comment—it didn't render anything more than a passing acknowledgment.

Over time, hurtful words started to lose their original meaning. Years ago, the word *terrorist* could cause injury; the word bothered Nasreen's parents much more than it bothered her. *Blow up* and *bomb* used to be words that Nasreen was careful not to say in front of them. Careful, careful, careful. Nasreen was sick of it.

Those words were only words, and said enough times they were just sounds. They carried their malicious intent only when weaponized by those with hate in their hearts. To Nasreen and Samia and others like them, they were words that they repurposed for themselves to prove they no longer had power over them.

Samia lifted her chin at the intricate landscaping beside the gate, where flower beds were arranged to spell out the school name. "How's it being the Muslim *it girl* at chapel?

"I'm excused from services."

"Well, that's a pro."

"What are you doing here?" Nasreen snapped. "Don't you have school?"

"I cut class," she said. "Kinda like you."

"And what do you want from me?"

Samia took the lollipop in her hand and pushed off her car. She pointed the lollipop at Nasreen. "I came to make nice."

"How's that?"

"We're the lucky ones," Samia explained. "But we're still a part of the Six. Did you know Muzhda's family was deported after the police officers shot and killed her? She had siblings who were born here and some on DACA, and they all got split up because their parents' pending residency application was scrubbed."

"I didn't know Muzhda," Nasreen murmured, but without conviction. Her thoughts rankled in the leftover adrenaline of storming out of the principal's office.

"And Zamzam and Abdullahi and Qays? They're innocent,

and you know it," Samia gushed, her cool demeanor fraying. "I have a few leads on PetroMile—but they haven't gotten nearly enough attention in the press. I know they had something to do with this. Zamzam and I were starting to find things out. We need to be ready if the appeal request is approved."

"Appeal?" Nasreen faced her, genuine fear gripping her. "Why would we appeal?"

Samia cocked her head in confusion. "Three innocent kids are in jail for a crime they didn't commit. They're going to appeal, and I'm going to help them. I can't just forget about them."

"Why not?"

Samia blinked at her. "They're our *friends*."

Nasreen tried to clear her head. Ms. Carson would be doing her best to avoid an appeal, and her baba's money would be pouring into her bank account to secure that. Besides, Qays, Abdullahi, and Zamzam weren't her friends. Not really.

"When did you get so close to them?" Nasreen asked.

Samia scoffed. "This really isn't the time to be jealous, Nasreen."

Nasreen's heart skipped a beat. "I'm not jealous."

Samia approached her. "I got these anonymous tips that Petro-Mile might be behind the explosions. If you help me keep going after them and if you get Ms. Carson to look into it, we might be able to prove that all of us are innocent. Not just me and you."

Nasreen's heart raced. "That's not going to happen."

"Why not?" Samia's tone was accusatory.

Nasreen faced her. "Where do you think you got the tips from?"

Samia searched her face, and her eyes widened as she detected

Nasreen's insinuation. "You sent me that text message. You dropped the note into my bag."

Nasreen's heart leaped. She'd done something, or at least she'd tried. She hadn't sat around, and someone was finally acknowledging it. "But nothing came of it," she muttered. "I found those names and those clues on Ms. Carson's desk. She already knows, and she probably knows more than you." She began to walk away.

Samia slid in her path. "Why didn't you say anything? To us or to Ms. Carson? Did she say you could get off scot-free if you kept things hush-hush? Is that why all you did was give me clues that led to dead ends?"

Miserably, Nasreen wished she had an explanation for why she hadn't done more. She'd known PetroMile was involved, she'd seen papers on Ms. Carson's desk and gathered as much, but beyond the casual perusal and secret hints to Samia, she'd kept quiet. She hadn't even questioned why Ms. Carson knew more but wasn't doing more.

Samia scowled at her. "You let them fend for themselves, and no one would ever know any better if I didn't miraculously manage to get away without a conviction."

"That's not true."

"Then what is it?!"

"I didn't know what else to do!" Nasreen shouted. She stopped abruptly, then advanced toward Samia. "I only knew they were keeping things secret, and I only had the clues from what I read off Ms. Carson's desk. When she spoke with Renner and Favreau, she didn't tell me everything. She wanted to win, and she won. We are the lucky ones. Can't we be content with that?"

"You're gonna tell me you're content?" Samia shot back. "Do you sleep anymore? Because I sure as hell don't."

"The trial is over."

"And the real shit show begins." Samia gestured around her. "Tell me you were welcomed with open arms today at school. That must be why you're out here instead of picking lab partners in chemistry."

Nasreen opened her mouth to respond, but no words came out.

"You screwed up," Samia seethed, "and I'm literally begging you to help me fix it."

"You don't understand." Nasreen's voice trembled. "My parents sacrificed everything to get me that attorney, who did everything she could for this result. I can't screw things up because I have trouble falling asleep."

"It's just going to get worse."

The tension mounting in Nasreen's chest threatened to break skin. When it finally released, would she cry? Would she scream? Would she be able to stop herself like she did in the principal's office, or would she start throwing things at the walls and the ground, shattering apart her life just to feel some control?

"You don't have to go through this alone," Samia said, placing her hands on Nasreen's shoulders. "Faris and I would've made great partners. You and I aren't any different."

Samia gave her a little shake as Nasreen bit the bottom of her lip. Nasreen was used to being an acquaintance but never a friend. She kept people at an arm's length at all times. It was hard for her to set her nerves aside and wholly open up to a person. Behind Faris's mask, she had opened up to Samia, but she was tired of hiding under different guises. She'd convinced herself it was for the sake of safety and privacy and reputation, but mostly, it was lonely.

She peered at Samia. "Do you have a plan?"

Samia whipped out her phone. "I always have a plan."

CHAPTER 45

ABDULLAHI

EVERY OTHER WEEKEND, ABDULLAHI'S SIBLINGS CAME TO see him on visiting days. They made the two-hour drive, bringing their parents when they felt strong enough. To his heartbreak, they were only getting older, and every time they came to visit, they aged even more.

He wasn't sure when or if he'd ever be permitted contact visits. Maybe it was because he had recently entered the system or because he was a special category of inmate that he would be forbidden to hug his mother and older sisters or get his father's shoulder slap for years to come.

One week, on a day that blurred with all the rest, Maryam brought him a letter. It was lightly perfumed and glittered even in the dim light of his cell. Folded in three, it was sealed in the center with an ellipsis sticker. He ran his fingers along the sparkling parchment. It made the throbbing in his broken lower lip, courtesy of the inmate Abdullahi had accidentally bumped into, ebb. The fear of the next day and the next and the next dissipated for a moment.

My friend Abdullahi,

I feel silly writing you a letter like we're living in the 1900s, but I guess it's very old-fashioned and you like old-fashioned things, right? You introduced me to James Brown and James Dean, and Aretha Franklin and Whitney Houston. I saw you reading Angela Davis once, and you told me that writers build links with letters so strong they last centuries.

That was profound as fuck, Abdullahi. It makes me sad to think Angela Davis's letters were stronger than our friendship. I was so stupid, and I feel so phony for reaching out now.

I wasn't approved for an in-person visit. I get why not, but I'm also angry with the decision. I'm innocent, right? I should enjoy all my freedoms, right? But I can't, and it's not even because of how everyone treats me like I'm the one who got away. It's because how can I be free when you aren't?

We didn't always agree, and I wasn't always kind, but your friendship meant a lot *to me before, and I'm mad at myself for not realizing it sooner. I know I can be such a habla sometimes, but I'll make it up to you. An appeal approval is the first step. Once you and Zamzam and Qays are free, then we can start looking outward. There are too many like you, too many like the Six. Too many not as lucky as me. I know that too.*

Don't give up, Abdullahi. I'm working on it. We'll find a way out, I promise.

Xoxo,
Samia

Pressing his thumbs into the letter, Abdullahi fought back the tears. Samia was a patchwork of colors, a disorienting flurry any-time she walked past. As a friend, she was loud and fearless. Even when she'd gone through her timid phase, when she read book after book at the library, she was strong. When their classmates snickered at her behind bookcases or left her mean notes on her notebooks, she kept her chin up and didn't hide her face in her books. She was proud, in the best sense of that word. He couldn't not join her at her library table. Not for pity, but for her admi-rable persistence.

He couldn't blame her for reinventing herself when she got to high school. For leaving Abdullahi to read books alone at the high school library table that became his. Eventually, he also grew out of lunches in the library, but the libraries they shared would always be a safe space for him.

Samia had to survive, and Abdullahi would have to find a way to. Still, it comforted him knowing she was out there, sleepless like him. In a place where everyone was a stranger, Samia's letter reminded him he wasn't alone.

He daydreamed about a future in a different world in a different life, in which he'd ask Samia out on a date. They'd eat tacos from the food trucks, and they'd go to the beach and not have awful flashbacks of that night. Maybe a spark might light up between him and Zamzam in a different version of his future, and he'd meet her mom and her brother, and they'd apply to universities together and do all the things you see in those '80s movies. He wished he had made a move when they were out on bail instead of being so reserved, but maybe being locked up just made him all that much more of a romantic.

These were nice dreams, but they almost always took a bad turn.

Because while he was wishing, Abdullahi started to wish that he hadn't gone to the bathroom on the beach that night. He wished Muzhda hadn't been there when he was, wished that, since he'd ended up in prison anyway, he could have helped her. He was an EMT in training. Maybe he could have reduced the bleeding. Maybe he could have saved her and himself.

That was the natural progression of his wishes. And the only thing that stopped him from spiraling was going to the prison library, taking a pencil and paper, and writing a letter. He wrote letters in response to Samia. Sometimes he wrote letters to Zamzam, asking about herself. They were dumb letters, telling her about his long days or his interests. Little tidbits like how he'd tracked down every rare Pokémon card for his vintage Pokémon card collection. Or how he located his new ideal car, a 1961 Jaguar E-type, which he'd purchase as soon as he had enough money.

He addressed all these letters to Samia. He trusted she would find a way to get Zamzam's letters to her. And if she didn't, she could save them, and one day Zamzam would read them.

He used the letters and the wishes to distract himself from the grief of his choices. Because even though his attorney was able to disprove the assault charges against Muzhda and get them dropped from his case, he would always feel guilty for his part in what had happened to Muzhda. His struggle was self-inflicted because he couldn't have changed the events that led to her death. It was her time, and it had been his fate to be tangled in its cause.

Abdullahi believed in fate. He only hoped his belief would be strong enough to allow him to reconcile with it.

CHAPTER 46

QAYS

WHEN QAYS CLOSED HIS EYES, HE SAW YEARS. THEY PASSED beneath his lids like the flipping pages of a book.

Qays arriving at his dorm room in the fall, gym-bag strap across his chest, slicing through the Stanford emblem.

Muzhda's bracelet on his wrist, their fingers interlocked, a sunset ahead of them.

The roar of the crowd, Qays's head down with the national anthem playing, his knee resting on the turf.

Her eyes fluttering open, their noses grazing each other's.

A graduation cap and tassel. No ceiling, only sky.

Qays in a tux, Muzhda in an emerald firaq partug, their families posing around them for a group picture on the wedding settee. Mansaf and shir berenj and dabkeh and attan. A marriage of their cultures and a nikkah both.

Their first night together.

A newborn's tiny fingers wrapping around his pinkie. Tears welling up in their eyes.

Stubby legs toddling about him as he teaches their child how to kick the ball.

Years and years and years. Muzhda's eyes flutter open again and again and again.

Her eyes, her eyes, her eyes.

One leathery hand resting upon another, creased and feathery from time, a beaded bracelet, the thinned thread barely holding it together. The sun rising another day.

He knew it couldn't be. They had spoken for so little time, but his guilt over the end of her life made the memory of her hold him in its prison.

Qays kept his eyes closed to watch their unwritten future unfold. The images were like a novel some days; others it was a reel that skipped scenes so fast he never got the chance to revel in the moments. But every time, when he had to open his eyes again, they peeled back like they were weighted by the sixty years he'd spent with Muzhda while his lids were closed. And every time, it broke him more than the last.

It was his only break from the routine of his physical prison. Months passed, more than he cared to count because each day felt like the length of the lifetimes he lived with Muzhda under his lids. When the others pushed him around the facility, he let them. When the others beat him in the hall, he didn't fight back. He took the brunt of their aggression until they grew bored of badgering him. He withered away until he was nothing more than a skeleton, his muscle thinned out, his skin a pallid shade of gray. His curls were sheared off so that there was nothing to distract from his dull eyes and hollow cheeks.

Another long day passed, and Qays stretched onto his cot, rubbed his hand over his buzzed hair, and sighed. He stared at the ceiling for as long as he could before the pain became too much. He could manage only a minute. His heavy lids began to shut.

"Qays."

His eyes shot wide open; his body lurched up. "You aren't real," he said. She was a figment of his imagination, shrouded in the dark shadows of his cell, as ethereal as ever.

Muzhda moved toward him. "I'm not. You know that, I know that, yet here we are."

"No, you aren't real, so leave," Qays muttered. "I see enough of you in my dreams."

"Why?"

"Stay where you are," he warned.

She stopped. A yearning look transformed into pain. Her eyes flashed with rage. "What happened to you?"

"They framed me and locked me away for the rest of my life. That's what happened to me."

"No," she said, "what did you do to yourself? You're not the boy I loved."

Qays scoffed, a sick smile twisting his expression. "The boy you loved wouldn't be talking to a figment of his imagination."

"You don't think I'm a ghost?" she asked, arched eyebrow raised.

"Ghosts aren't real. I've just lost my mind."

He tossed his body against his cot and shut his eyes tight. The pages didn't flip. He opened his lids and shut them again. Still nothing. When he opened them again, Muzhda leaned over him, her hand resting on his head.

"You lost your curls," she murmured, stroking the rough ends of his hair.

"Get away from me," Qays replied, unnerved that she was touching him, because she wasn't real.

"Don't talk to me like that," Muzhda snapped. "I'm trying to help you."

"Help me? I can't sleep at night because of you."

"So it's like that?" she teased.

He made a face. "You keep me up like a nightmare."

Her face softened, eyes the warmest shade of amber. "Do you lose sleep because I'm your nightmare or because I became your dream?"

Tears sprung into Qays's eyes. With every passing day, the reel of pages showed less and less of Stanford and his jersey number and his goal sheet as the story centered itself around Muzhda. *She* was the dream.

"It's okay to mourn me," she whispered, her face looming closer to his. "But I don't want this for you, Qays."

"I don't have a choice." His voice cracked. The appeal was pending, and even then, none of the official stuff mattered. His life was on hold, Stanford was no more, but worst of all, Muzhda was gone.

"Your life isn't over," she said. "Don't waste what I wasn't given. You have a chance at this life, in whatever way it may be. Live it for the both of us."

A mountain range of regret spread across Qays's lungs. Peaks of betrayal and a summit of sorrow clawed up his throat. Words reached his tongue, banging behind his teeth, begging to be let out.

"I love you." The words were tortured, his voice cracking.

Muzhda smiled a pained smile. "No, *I* loved you. *You* barely knew me. Don't let my memory hold you back like this."

Qays's heart shattered. "I can't forget you."

"And I don't want you to."

She placed a kiss on his forehead, a kiss that he could never feel, and when his lids grew heavy over his eyes and they finally closed, the pages didn't come. Time passed, and they still didn't return. When he sat up for Fajr, in the darkest moments before dawn, the shadow of Muzhda had gone. He waited to see if she'd come back, but when she didn't, he stood up tall, prayed two ruk'aahs, and took back what little he had left. All the while thinking: *For the both of us.*

CHAPTER 47

NASREEN

IT HAD BEEN ONE HUNDRED AND FIVE DAYS SINCE NASREEN didn't wake from her nightmare. The courts approved the appeal that came from Zamzam's, Abdullahi's, and Qays's attorneys. It meant a headache for Nasreen's parents, and it put them back in Ms. Carson's office.

Nasreen's mama was profoundly upset with her, since her stunt in the principal's office gave her a suspension and put her on probation. Also, Nasreen started cutting class, as in her mama dropped her off in the morning at school and Samia picked her right back up.

Samia's plans took precedence over her schooling. And so focusing on the plans and exhausting her mind gave Nasreen an extra half hour of sleep at night.

"We'll have to be more offensive this time around," Ms. Carson was saying. "The appeal was filed on the grounds that not all the kids were sentenced, assuming there was some type of misinterpretation in the case. The courts won't be satisfied unless all the kids are indicted or acquitted." She sighed. "I might as well be everyone's legal counsel. I'll be carrying all this extra weight."

Nasreen's gaze was fixed on a spot in the distance, Samia's words still echoing in her mind. "Shouldn't you have just taken the high road the first time around, instead of just securing my acquittal?"

"If you're looking for a guilty conscience, Ms. Choudhry, look elsewhere," Ms. Carson muttered. "There are no saints in the real world. Which brings me to my next point. I need to reconsider my fees if I'm going to be taking this on."

Nasreen's mama and baba exchanged a worried glance. Their savings were dwindling, and they were already using up their retirement funds. Nasreen huffed loudly and received an equally troubled look all around.

Don't rock the boat, Nasreen. Don't so much as ripple the water.

But that was the old Nasreen, the one who used to get a good night's sleep, the one who hadn't agreed to Samia's plan for justice. It was time to give this boat a shakedown or throw herself overboard trying.

"May I speak with Ms. Carson alone, please?" Nasreen requested, the polite tone stripped from her voice.

Ms. Carson checked her watch. "I suppose we're still on your time."

Nasreen scoffed to herself as her parents made a begrudging exit. Ms. Carson and Nasreen began a staring contest, each of their expressions alternately growing more pinched than the other.

"You're upset with me."

"You can tell?" Nasreen responded, deadpan. "I thought you didn't have a conscience."

Ms. Carson folded her red-manicured fingers. "I don't. I can't. Not in my line of work. But I'm not a sociopath. I care about my clients."

"The law is your business. You keep your emotions out of it."

Ms. Carson shrugged, and her tight blazer rode up. "True. But this isn't a normal case. There's a lot going on behind the scenes that you don't understand."

"Help me understand, then," Nasreen pleaded. "What was with the PetroMile documents? What does Alexander Nguyen have to do with any of this?"

Ms. Carson pressed her glossed lips into a fine line, perhaps irritated that Nasreen had pieced together so little, yet so much, information. "The information that I had and that Samia and Zamzam so inconveniently found and provided their attorneys will make a mess of the appeal. They'll likely require us to go to a retrial to bring new evidence. And we don't want a retrial because it's best that we don't return to court."

"And why's that?"

"Because you were already acquitted, Ms. Choudhry. We'll press charges if you'd like compensation, and I would support that, but what more do you want?"

Something burned in Nasreen's chest. She couldn't stop herself. "What if something came out and they were forced to drop the charges? What if we could uncover evidence that proved everyone's innocence?"

"Some answers are hidden behind millions and billions of dollars. Old money that runs deeper than the law."

"I already know that," Nasreen pressed. "I'm just asking for another lead. You don't have to worry about what I'll do with it."

"A lead?" Ms. Carson's brow furrowed.

"I haven't been sitting thoughtlessly during our sessions." Nasreen's expression was flat, but deadly. "I know you have more information about what really happened on the Fourth that you're not telling me. I've been looking into PetroMile, or at least I have been in my own way." She felt a pang of guilt at the white lie. She resisted the urge to give in to her feelings of inadequacy and shut up. "I'm just asking for *one more lead*. One more that'll get me one step closer to understanding the truth that you seem to already know."

Ms. Carson's eyes glinted with warning. "That's enough, Ms. Choudhry. You forget this is a professional relationship." She lifted the phone in her room and instructed her secretary to let Nasreen's parents back in. They shuffled through the door, looking between the two of them, searching for clues.

As they discussed Ms. Carson's unbelievable fees for the next stage of counsel, Nasreen seethed in her seat. She felt that at any moment the armchair would combust from her sizzling temperature. The meeting ended as the room became unbearably stifling.

She followed her parents out of the room, but cold fingers grasped her wrist. She turned back to Ms. Carson tentatively, who clasped her scorching hand in an icy grip.

"I'm the best in this business, dear," Ms. Carson murmured to her, her words spilling so fast that they were unmasked, revealing a disparately benign timbre. "Professionalism over everything, and the professional world can be quite cruel. But if I may speak as just Penelope for a moment..." She paused. "There's a reason

I won the way that I did. Some secrets you think will give you peace will only distress you more. Not all monsters should be pulled out from under the bed."

Nasreen blinked at her. "I'm too old for monsters under the bed."

Ms. Carson smirked. "You're never too old. The beds only grow bigger, and the monsters too."

Then Ms. Carson released her grip and ushered her out. Only when Ms. Carson's office door shut did Nasreen notice the crinkled paper Ms. Carson had left in her hand.

A business card for notary services conducted by Adam Trill. On the back, abbreviations scrawled in Ms. Carson's script: *PM's NDA.*

Nasreen glanced back at the closed door and closed her fist around the paper. Ms. Carson had given her a lead, but she also had given her a warning. But Nasreen wasn't scared anymore.

I live in a nightmare, she thought. *Monsters under the bed only exist in the real world.*

CHAPTER 48

SAMIA

SAMIA SET OUT ON THE 10 EAST DURING RUSH HOUR ON A Friday. She'd left the beach behind hours ago, crawled her way out of the city mile by excruciating mile. Gradually, red mountains and scattered wind turbines emerged across the terrain.

Nasreen tapped her fingers on the passenger seat to the beat of Halsey's songs humming from the stereo. She was unlike Zamzam in a lot of ways—where Zamzam never passed up the opportunity at a jab, Nasreen simmered in silence. The silence was worse for Samia.

When the traffic let up, Nasreen mercifully sighed.

"Finally." Samia breathed along with her.

"It's the next exit," Nasreen instructed her, the location locked into the GPS on her cell phone.

After hours of driving in the dry desert sun, they arrived at a shabby square office space beside a cracked cement parking lot. "A-plus for landscaping," Samia commented snidely, as they passed the dilapidated cacti along the pathway to the entrance. A slanted OPEN sign hung in the window beside the door.

Nasreen grabbed Samia's wrist before she twisted the doorknob. "Maybe I should do the talking."

Samia rolled her eyes. Sure, she was far from calm; she'd raged half the drive about the traffic and swore she'd get answers out of the mysterious Adam Trill no matter what, but those were just words. "I can handle this," she told Nasreen.

"I'm sure you can," Nasreen said, "but I just don't want him to suspect anything. I'll go in alone."

Finally, Samia saw the benefit of Nasreen's conventional demeanor, the practiced way that she leaned into what made her look and seem common.

Samia relinquished the doorknob. "Fine." She turned back as the bell above the door dinged to announce Nasreen's entrance.

Samia paced, almost as much as when she was rereading the first letter she'd written for Abdullahi. As the minutes passed into the next hour and the sun dropped low, the chill of the desert night seeped into the air. The kind of cold that nestled into bones like a parasite. She dug through the mess of her trunk until she found an old patchwork sweatshirt, two sizes too big, and slipped it on. Restless, she lay down in the back seat of her car without bothering to lift the convertible top, despite the dry cold. She stared at the swaths of purples and pinks coloring the sky.

The bell above the door announced someone in the vicinity. Samia propped herself on her elbows. Nasreen walked over to her, folding her leather jacket over itself to shield herself from the chill. The shadows on her face were deep from the setting sun and the harsh street lighting.

Without a word, Nasreen opened the back seat door and slid in as Samia folded her legs to her chest to give her room. She tilted her head back and blinked at the sky. "Adam Trill is the man who notarized Alexander Nguyen's NDA. Do you know what that means?"

"A notary is someone that certifies a legal document, right?" Samia had looked it up as soon as she saw the business card.

"Right." Nasreen nodded. "But doesn't PetroMile have plenty of people who can do that in their company? Why outsource such a routine step to Adam Trill, who has more papers stashed in his office than dust mites?"

Samia tilted her head back, mirroring Nasreen. Stars started to pop out of the velvet navy sky. "Because no one would think to come here?"

"Because Adam Trill is only half as clever as he is professional, so much so that he'd let a fake attorney's intern without a lick of proof look through his messy log of notarizations. PetroMile's rep from the NDA is on there, Samia. July fifth."

Samia sat up, her heartbeat gaining speed. "Did you get a copy from him?"

Nasreen ran a hand down her face, desperation tugging at her brows. "There is no copy. Adam Trill is clueless. He wouldn't recognize me from the news and the protests, and he probably wouldn't have recognized you even if we told him. He barely looked up when he spoke to me. In Adam Trill's world, Adam Trill is the only person that exists. He signs papers for a living with barely a first glance."

364

"But it's a lead," Samia started, her words reaching, reaching. "They could subpoena his records. He has to have records. If we force it out of him, we could bring it back to him, and he could prove that PetroMile is hiding something—"

"Samia."

"You can't deny it's hella suspicious—"

"Samia."

"We'll show them reasonable doubt—"

"Samia, stop!"

A frigid breeze swirled around them. The girls exchanged glares. When Samia spoke, her voice was tiny. "Why would Petro-Mile let this happen to us?"

Nasreen listened to the rustling of wind. "Maybe because they caused the explosion of their own oil rig."

"On purpose?!"

"Most likely by accident," Nasreen said, speculating. "It would be a nightmare for them if they caused an oil spill in the Pacific Ocean that threatened ecosystems and endangered hundreds of thousands of residents along the LA coast. They'd have to pay millions of dollars in damages. They probably did pay millions, but at least they didn't have to do it to save their reputation. With scapegoats to take the fall, they become the victims.

"We don't think about all the other consequences of the Fourth, because we're so worried about ourselves. But if they were behind it and they were so quick to cover their tracks, if Alexander Nguyen was shut up tight like he was, if we found out this much and Ms. Carson has names, then the FBI likely knows too. And yet Qays, Zamzam, and Abdullahi are the ones in prison. If all of this was planned, then I can't see us ever being free of this."

"Don't be so pessimistic," Samia said, her words childlike.

"Wake up, Samia." Nasreen's chin quivered. "Maybe we have to accept that we're the villains and the victims. It just depends on who's judging."

Samia bit her lower lip. Victims were too often relegated to the footnotes, and villains too often reduced to their role. All the important stuff that made them real was overlooked. Samia had never planned to be in history books; she wanted only the temporary fame of social media. But if the world was set on writing her into the books, she would not be an asterisk or a fleeting reference.

"We're only victims if we give up," Samia muttered. "I won't, for as long as I live. Will you?"

Samia reached out her hand, opening it palm up to Nasreen on the seat. Tentatively, Nasreen held it in a limp grasp.

"Do you ever think how different our lives would be if I didn't send that stupid DM? If you never agreed to meet Faris at the beach that night?" Nasreen murmured.

"I try not to regret. You shouldn't either." Samia jumped out of the car and stormed into Adam Trill's office, leaving Nasreen alone to choose if she would follow.

CHAPTER 49

NASREEN

NASREEN BURST THROUGH THE FRONT DOOR WITHOUT A second thought to her nightmare.

Adam Trill barely lifted his eyes from his pile of papers to look at her. He spoke to Samia. "Sure, I can draft and sign an NDA for you." He handed her a clipboard. "Those are the services and the fees."

Samia slid it back onto Trill's cluttered desk and took a seat across from him. Nasreen's head spun. *What was she doing?*

"I don't know if you know," Samia started, "but I'm a pretty famous influencer. I was referred to you by a client of yours. They say you're real neat and tidy with your work. If you know what I mean."

Nasreen's heart clawed up her throat. Trill glanced at her, then lowered his glasses onto his nose and stuck it into his papers once again. "I'm not sure what you mean," he said flatly.

Samia rolled her eyes at Nasreen and leaned into it. "Oh, don't worry about her. She's just my business partner. I sent her in earlier to make sure you were the right guy."

Trill was unruffled. Or perhaps extremely ruffled. Nasreen couldn't tell which. He grunted. "She asked about a pretty specific case."

Samia gave a short laugh. "My business partner was referencing our source. A friend of mine at PetroMile said you take care of some of their NDAs. NDAs that they want to kind of *poof*"— Samia made a floating gesture with her hand—"disappear."

He wiped the sweat from his forehead with a used napkin. Nasreen was sure then. Trill was ruffled, but he was too flustered within himself to deal with it outwardly.

Samia continued full throttle. "You may not know this, but influencers like myself have enemies, enemies spread rumors, rumors become scandals, and scandals lead to the social media career dumpster. I want a simple NDA, I promise. I pay well."

Trill didn't say anything for a long moment. Nasreen felt like she'd been caught, but she didn't want to run away or act small. She wanted to see it through. Trill gave Samia a form. He told her the process.

"Then I burn my copy, and I don't keep a record of it in my journal," he told them.

"A journal?" Nasreen repeated.

Trill looked at Nasreen like she was the one who was thick. He pointed to a safe behind him. "I have to keep a record of all notarized acts performed by me in a journal that I keep locked and safe. But from time to time, I get someone with a document that shouldn't leave a trace."

"So I'm the only one with proof of its existence?" Samia asked, the chair barely containing her energy.

"Yes. The parties involved have copies if they want, but I won't record it."

"And no computer trails?" Nasreen asked.

Trill gestured to his office. "I don't have a computer in here on purpose."

Samia and Nasreen exchanged a horrified glance. If PetroMile was the only one who had proof of the NDA, how would they be able to get it?

"What did you say your name was, Miss?" Trill's voice was skeptical.

"I didn't," Samia replied quickly. "But I'm sure it doesn't matter to you anyway. It is your job to forget clients, right?"

"Yes, yes, I suppose you're right." He talked Samia through the form. At the end, he provided her with the copy containing his signature and shredded the other in front of them. He didn't so much as glance at the safe containing his journal.

Once they made it outside, Nasreen gasped for air, but it wasn't until they were enough miles west that her chest felt lighter.

"Holy shit," Samia murmured.

"No one is going to believe us," Nasreen said.

Samia threw her phone at her. "That's why you have everything on record."

Sure enough, there it was. The scene in Trill's office on video. Samia had her camera on and angled in the chair.

"What do we do with this?"

"We release it," Samia muttered. "This and the Alexander Nguyen information. We force the appeal. We fight to the end."

Nasreen's stomach flipped upside down, inside out. She clutched the edge of the passenger seat. The air whipping around her face felt slick with moisture. It made her feel sick. "Can you pull over?"

Samia did. Before the car came to a complete stop, Nasreen stumbled out onto the desert dirt and threw up. She doubled over, gagging. Again and again, Nasreen couldn't escape the confrontation. She couldn't even confront herself; confronting the world was even worse.

Samia approached her from behind. She didn't say anything, but she passed her the filled form, completed and signed by Adam Trill.

Nasreen read. *The Nondisclosure Agreement, hereinafter referred to as the "Agreement," is entered between Faris Khan, hereinafter referred to as the "Disclosing Party," and Samia Al-Samra, hereinafter referred to as the "Receiving Party," as of July 5. Upon entering this Agreement, these parties are hereby agreeing that:*

The Agreement shall be Mutual: Both parties shall not disclose the nature of their relationship and shall be prohibited from sharing learned confidential information shared between the two parties.

This Agreement shall be taken into effect until the Disclosing Party terminates the Agreement.

Nasreen exhaled. Light shined in from the little window in her diving bell. It looked like hope. Her eyes stung with tears. "Don't you want to know why I did it?" she asked.

"Meh." Samia shrugged. She kicked the sand, and dust blew across them. "Do you even know your reasons?"

Nasreen blinked, hoping the tears would go away, but instead they silently spilled over. In truth, she didn't understand her reasons. Not fully. She didn't know when she would.

And that realization frightened her, the unknown being unknown for her foreseeable future. But she was safe, so long as she was allowed to stay in her diving bell.

"Carson used me," Nasreen said, her voice hitched. "She used the fact that I don't wear a hijab, that I go to Catholic school, that I'm different, against you guys."

"Well, it worked," Samia said.

"I hate that it worked."

Nasreen looked up at the sky. This far inland, the stars were bright and many. It was easier to breathe outside the city.

"I wish I didn't trick you."

The words were out before Nasreen could trap them inside.

"Same." Samia sighed. "Not because it brought us here, but because I would've liked to be your friend even if you hadn't."

Nasreen kicked the dirt this time. Her boots were dusty, and her stomach was empty. She didn't know why she'd done it, not fully. And she wondered how many years she'd lose to figuring it out. Perhaps those years wouldn't be lost. Perhaps they would be lived.

"Hey."

Nasreen snapped her head forward. Samia flashed her cell phone at her.

"Ready to set fire to this thing?"

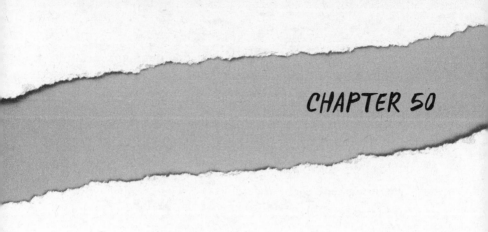

CHAPTER 50

FAVREAU TURNED THE SHOWER OFF WITH A TAP OF HER elbow. The water shooting from her shower walls and waterfall faucet shut off. She slipped into a plush bathrobe, threw her hair up into a towel turban, and stepped out into her sunlit living room.

She opened the sliding doors all the way and reclined on her leather couch, one leg over the other, peering out to her pool and garden outside.

She turned on the national news with a smile. It was a glorious Saturday for her prerecorded interview about the Independence Day Six to air.

An email notification pinged, but she turned her phone on silent and raised the TV volume. Back from commercial break, the camera panned across a newsroom. Favreau cocked her head. This was not the special.

It unfolded before her like a bad sitcom.

The video of Abdullahi running from the dead girl at the beach. *Muzhda*, Favreau remembered belatedly. It was old news, but they were calling it breaking.

The names *Alexander Nguyen* and *PetroMile* flashed across the screen. Favreau stood up, slowly, slowly. Those weren't names for the public. She'd made sure of that. As she swiped at her phone to try to get someone to end the broadcast, Adam Trill, a man whose name she'd given to important people who needed a cover-up, said too much.

And now everyone knew too much.

Her blood boiled from a point at the top of her head down to her extremities.

Footage of protests played across the screen. The people were in uproar, even more than before. Then the screen switched to a frame of her face.

This was not the planned program. The program was supposed to be Favreau on the screen describing the legal processes that had been followed to get justice for the American people. She was a national hero; she'd put the bad kids away. This wasn't the headshot she had sent in. This was a picture of her in court, sneering at the defense.

The anchors were saying words like *granted appeal* and *subpoenaing Kandi Favreau*, all words that were not supposed to come after the sentencing of the Six. Favreau had so beautifully crafted a lie that was meant to crush the six truths that were placed before her. And it almost had.

Favreau couldn't contain her anger anymore. When the remote wouldn't disintegrate in her tight grip, she hurled it at the wall, and it shattered across her marble tile.

Favreau fumbled with her phone. The Face ID didn't recognize her for all her rage. She nearly chucked her phone at the wall, but it finally opened. Her inbox, which had been at seventy-eight before, hit four hundred and counting.

She called Renner. They had worked together, after all, to ensure the Six were the public enemy. They'd got their pockets full of PetroMile's money so the company could get away with the oversights that had caused a national and environmental disaster. If PetroMile was going to go down, she and Renner would be placed to break their fall, and she couldn't have that.

"Where did this come from?" she barked into the phone as soon as it stopped ringing. "Didn't I tell you to cover up the tracks with PetroMile? How did they get Trill to talk? He doesn't leave traces. Did Pennella snitch? He wasn't supposed to know anything about our work with PetroMile! I assured them those kids would take the fall for their mistakes, and I should've gotten the job done!"

The receiver was silent for a long moment.

"Kandi Favreau."

This voice was not Renner's.

Pennella—ignorant, left-in-the-dark Pennella—said through the receiver, "Kandi Favreau, bring yourself down to the station."

This time, her phone went flying.

CHAPTER 51

A RED HERRING.

Not the food fished from the sea, dried or smoked. An element that misleads. Like the hijab on one's head or the color of one's skin, elements introduced in a courtroom to misinform a verdict. Some red herrings are sowed into minds over centuries; they stop being seen for what they are.

Like the word *unbelievable*.

Like everything else we call unbelievable, the events of the Fourth were quite believable. For some, a part of life to be avoided yet expected.

The following were the very believable events of July 4 as they happened that night on Monarch Beach.

1. Alexander Nguyen arrived at Promenade Parking Structure 2 at 8:30 PM. He proceeded down the

Promenade with his case of equipment. His boat ride to oil rig *Bonnie* for his annual two-week maintenance shift was scheduled for the next hour.

2. Nguyen opened the manhole beside the lockers and set up his equipment. Wires and gadgets, all sorts of bits and bobs, all for a simple reading. He would record the numbers and cross-reference them with the diagnostics on board *Bonnie*.

3. The formation pressure reading was abnormally high. Nguyen reset the equipment, but the number kept climbing. Again, he tried, and again the number rose.

4. Nguyen phoned it in. His supervisor brushed it off, said the blowout preventers would safeguard them against any danger. Nguyen told him that he was going on the rig to perform maintenance on blowout preventers that hadn't received funding for years. He was told the onshore equipment was wrong. Nguyen panicked. He was a man of numbers, and numbers didn't lie.

5. He called the cops. Left a tip that there would be danger on the beach. His phone fell from his hand as he ran past a girl in a black dress and headscarf. He had to get as far away from the pier as he could because if *Bonnie* blew, the pressurized pipes beneath the pier would too.

6. Muzhda tripped over the equipment Nguyen left beside the locker. Abdullahi found her, tried to help her up, but the cops had traced Nguyen's call straight to that spot. Abdullahi fled the scene.

7. Qays lit up his firework, flashing a stupid grin at Zamzam as he did.

8. Miles away in the dark of the ocean, the formation pressure from the oil rig reached its limits. It blew, and the rusted blowout preventers didn't stand a chance of stopping it.

9. The pier went up next, a chain reaction in the pressurized tanks beneath it.

10. The explosions bathed the beach in an auburn glow. People, like ants, scattered from the fire.

11. Cops with cocked guns pulled their triggers. Not one but four bullets shot into a teenage girl's thin frame. Blood seeped into Muzhda's clothes. The lights in her eyes went out.

12. Five Muslim teenagers were cuffed and taken into custody, each with an expression more ashen than the last. Qays watched as EMTs stretchered Muzhda's lifeless body into an ambulance, his eyes not registering the scene in front of him.

13. Around midnight, a PetroMile representative knocked on Alexander Nguyen's front door. He laid out an NDA and pressured Nguyen to sign.

14. Adam Trill, glassy-eyed and overworked, notarized the NDA and eliminated any record of it from his files.

Those were the facts of July 4. If Lady Justice could see, that was what her eyes would have shown her.

TWO YEARS LATER

CHAPTER 52

ON HIS HIGH SCHOOL SOCCER TEAM, QAYS PLAYED START-
ing center mid. As a midfielder, he had a bird's-eye view of the
pitch despite being on the ground. He saw pathways that had
yet to be stalked, saw three or four passes ahead of the play, envi-
sioned a goal before the striker ever knew he'd have a chance at
the ball. Qays was so certain of the future because he was the one
that made it happen on the field. That translated to his life. It was
what made Qays who he was.

After his last night with Muzhda, he stopped resting. He spent
every waking moment in the prison gym, planning and plotting,
meeting with the lawyer, but never leaving his fate up to the limits of what his legal counsel could do. He would get out of prison
one day, whether sooner or later, and when he did, he had to live
enough for two lives.

The day eventually came. After two years of daily muscle

cramps; of drawing up imaginary soccer plays; of correspondences with Samia and Nasreen, who exposed PetroMile and Favreau with Zamzam and Abdullahi fighting alongside them. The appeal went by in a blur. The supercompany PetroMile took a blow, but it would survive. Kandi Favreau and Henry Renner would not.

The day arrived.

A guard opened the gate of the high-security prison. Beneath the Death Valley sun on the second anniversary of Muzhda's death, a sea of people, press, friends, and family stood to welcome him back to their world.

The only cage he felt around him was the one he'd carry forever, the love he had for Muzhda, a love that had never been allowed to be a love at all.

Abdullahi approached him first, having been released a few days prior. He extended a hand, and they shook hands as two strangers who shared too much not to be friends. Samia and Nasreen followed behind him, Nasreen's chiseled face and Samia's coal character both refined into diamonds from pressure.

Zamzam followed behind them next, and the memory of his immature stunts on Monarch Beach flashed between them. Then she smiled, a smile that looked like it took strength to form, reached for his wrist, and unfurled his fist.

"I think this belongs to you."

Zamzam released his hand, and in his palm lay Muzhda's bracelet. Twenty-seven beads. Ten red, ten black, six letters, one heart.

Zamzam's thinned face lifted. "It got mixed up with my things, but I distinctly remember that it was yours."

Qays slipped it on.

The five of them turned to face the press. Cameras flashed, questions shot out at them, but no one said a word. There were five of them left, but there were six lives to live, since Qays had the duty of living two. Arms directed Qays away from the crowd and into an area shaded from the summer sun. Sweat began to line his palms, not from the heat or the media attention but because of the teenage boy who was ushered over to Qays.

The boy's amber eyes were lined with thick lashes. He had a willowy frame that made him look younger, though he must have been the same age Qays had been when he was arrested two years prior.

"Salaam," the boy said.

"Salaam," Qays replied, then extended his hand for a shake. The other hand followed it, accustomed to the way his arms moved in handcuffs outside of prison. When he let his left hand fall away, it did.

"I thought you'd be shorter," Qays commented, attempting and failing to break the ice. He was tall like her, and when her brother shyly smiled just like she had, Qays couldn't stop the tears from escaping.

He cleared his throat, but not from embarrassment. He could cry an ocean for Muzhda, and it wouldn't be enough.

"I come from a tall family," Ehsan said with a shrug, breaking the ice in Qays's stead. Qays chuckled softly to himself. Of course, an Ahmad sibling would have Muzhda's delivery, Ehsan's words easing the air between them.

While he was holed up in his cell, Qays agonized over how he could remember Muzhda. Not just by himself, in his head, but in a real way. He reached out everywhere, searching high and low, asking far and wide for Muzhda's family. They had returned to Afghanistan, but her siblings were still US citizens. The US was their home, the only one they knew. Though her parents never wanted to return to the US after their daughter's death, Ehsan had wanted to. Ehsan had answered his letters.

He kept Muzhda alive for Qays. Together, they could keep Muzhda alive for the rest of the world. Her story, her home, her pain. There was power in it, and they would be the vessels that would allow her to help others.

Alone in the gray, Muzhda's stories colored his world. They'd gotten him through those few months after the Fourth, and the years after.

"Thank you for coming," Qays said with a hoarse voice as he raked a hand through his curls.

Ehsan sighed. His eyes, the same as Muzhda's, tugged at the edges with an unexplainable sorrow. "I did it for Muzhda."

CHAPTER 53

ZAMZAM PUT HER HAND OUT OF THE CAR WINDOW. THE wind whipped fast around it, allowing it to glide without effort. The sun beat down on her face, and she closed her eyes. She sat in the passenger seat, only feeling. Responsibility and expectations didn't weigh on her. Those things existed in her still, but they weren't all that she was anymore.

Samia drove her car up, twisting upward endlessly until finally they stopped, and the engine cut out.

"We're here," said Samia, jostling her car keys between hands.

Zamzam opened her eyes. The three girls, Nasreen, Samia, and Zamzam, walked to the edge of the cliff where the blue-and-gray ocean stretched as far as their eyes could see. The sun hid behind a thin layer of clouds, so its rays didn't reflect like a staircase to the sky ascending from the ocean.

Hope. The promise of the ever-changing ocean. The promise

that one day there would be an ascension to somewhere greater. But now Zamzam didn't feel that place could be so rigid as to be defined by a jumble of letters that came after a name. She felt it might be a place where none of that mattered. A place where there was compensation for the years she'd lost in a cell. A place without toiling over a hardship or dreading an unending desert.

The blue and gray ahead of her was both an ocean and a desert; it just depended on how the sun shined on it.

"You made it up before us."

Zamzam broke off her hard stare with the blue and gray to look behind her, to see Abdullahi. Qays followed not far behind.

A weight lifted off her chest. Nasreen and Samia had lost sleep to secure their release, but they didn't understand how it had felt over the last few years. In front of Momma and Jamal, Zamzam remained a pillar of strength. When Zamzam heard Yazeed finally reached out to Momma with a measly text to check on her, she'd felt nothing. She didn't feel the absence of the role her older brother never filled. She accepted she'd have to love and care for herself that much more. Maybe one day, she'd find someone who'd love her enough, someone who didn't make life feel quite as hard. Until then, this was okay.

Because when Abdullahi and Qays were around, Zamzam could walk with less effort in her step. She could show how tired she was because they'd gone through what she had. Abdullahi stood beside her, and Qays stood on the other side, completing their line facing away from the cliff. Qays looked down at her, his eyes soft and understanding. She felt her fingers burn as they remembered the feeling of grabbing his wrist that night and pulling them toward this future. He gave her the smallest of smiles.

Zamzam would eventually see *MD* after her name. Though she'd received her GED in an electronic certificate in prison, she would get to see Jamal walk across a stage with a diploma in his hand.

Qays would claw his way back to Stanford. He was still a soccer star, still Muzhda's homecoming king.

Abdullahi would live the romanticized life of the lead role he'd always wanted. He would hear Muzhda's stories and know she would have forgiven him. He would be able to live. He was a dreamer, and reality could be dealt with along the way.

Nasreen and Samia would open a law firm many years down the line, and maybe along the way Nasreen would learn the secrets of her heart, and Samia would learn the beauty in subtlety.

And they promised that every year, on the day their lives intertwined forever, they would return to the cliffside cemetery that overlooked Monarch Beach. They would place flowers beside Muzhda's grave, recite Surat-Al-Fatihah, and sit together around it. Most times Qays would do nothing but count the white stones over her grave. Sometimes he would tell the others how many undocumented immigrants or refugees the Muzhda Foundation helped that year. Samia would tell her outlandish stories, Nasreen would roll her eyes, and Abdullahi and Zamzam would blush at each other. They would dance around one another's nerves until finally, they could find the courage to speak about the scars that were left by the years they lost, by being vilified everywhere they went. Until then, they relished in the release of the cliffside breeze, and in the second chance not all of them were given.

AUTHOR'S NOTE

Six Truths and a Lie is about many things—surveillance of Muslim communities, systemic racism, Islamophobia—but most of all it's the story of a Muslim ummah divided. As unrest rattles home-lands, Muslim communities highlight their differences and compare their oppressions. The newspaper entries in this novel serve to show how language in the media shapes the general public's image of Muslims. That language filters how Muslims are viewed but also how we Muslims view one another. I hope this book can be a demonstration of what might happen if we reflect on our prejudices and come together.

Like my characters, my life has been shaped by marginalized identities. I grew up in a visibly Muslim family, and I've always lived in an America that views me as different. I've navigated a world that doesn't accept Muslims as we are. I've had to learn how to exist as myself every day without prejudice dictating what I do and how I do it.

My characters are Muslim, but they come from a plethora of backgrounds, all with their own unique experiences. If you are looking for books that further delve into the diversity of Muslim identities and stories, there are so many amazing authors who write them. Deeba Zargarpur, Sahar Mustafah, Ayaan Mohamud, and Adiba Jaigirdar are just a few. I hope you can find these and other authors, and feel represented in more ways than I was able to show in this book. There is so much more to all our stories.

ACKNOWLEDGMENTS

"And whatever you have of blessings—they are from Allah."
—Qur'an 16:53

I am so grateful for God's timing and the swing of fate that allowed me to bring this book to you.

A million thank-yous to my agent, Serene Hakim, for always believing in my writing and my stories, and for providing me support and reassurance every time I spiral. I'm so thankful to have you in my corner.

Thank you to my editor, Ruqayyah Daud, who is a rock star in the publishing industry, bringing fresh new Muslim stories to bookstores. Thank you to my publicist, Cassie Malmo, for being so passionate about my work. Many thanks to Jenny Kimura, who designs the most amazing covers, and to Kingsley Nebechi for the incredible cover art. Thank you to the rest of the team at Little, Brown Books for Young Readers who helped bring this book to readers: Sasha Illingworth, Savannah Kennelly, Stefanie Hoffman, Amber Mercado, Virginia Lawther, Jake Regier, Victoria Stapleton, Shawn Foster, Danielle Cantarella, and Nina Montoya.

To my friends in the industry: Maeeda Khan and Sara Hashem, I'm so lucky I can share my writing, my wins, and my worries with such incredible Muslim authors. Emily Charlotte, thank you always for your friendship and for being my cheerleader. Shannon C. F. Rogers and Tina Ehsanipour, thank you for supporting this story and celebrating the small wins with me. Thank you to Aiya and all the sensitivity and early readers.

To the people who kept me sane while writing this novel: Sundos, thank you for having the same hometown as me and being my oldest friend. Safa, thank you for validating me when I'm struggling most. My cousins, thank you for supporting me; I am so grateful to all of you. Wendy, I'm so thankful for your friendship and for helping me survive grad school.

Most of all, thank you to my family. My most beautiful parents, Abier and Monier, I appreciate every moment of support and help you've given me over these few hard years. I wouldn't be who I am or where I am without you. I dedicate everything I do to both of you.

Omar, thank you for being my point of reference for Qays— he's almost as cool as you. Thank you, Noor and Jessica, and thank you for bringing Muneer, Ayden, Audrey, and so much joy into my life.

Bushra and Tessniem, you are my dedication because our sisterhood means the most to me. Thank you, Tessniem, for keeping me company in Boston and always. Thank you, Bushra, for showing me what hope can look like. And, Amal, all of this is for you.

Finally, thank you, reader, for picking up this book and allowing my words to be part of your life. I hope to reach you again.

Above all, I praise Allah for everything.